Finding Serenity

OTHER TITLES IN THE SMART POP SERIES

Taking the Red Pill
Science, Philosophy and Religion in The Matrix

Seven Seasons of Buffy
Science Fiction and Fantasy Writers
Discuss Their Favorite Television Show

Five Seasons of Angel
Science Fiction and Fantasy Writers
Discuss Their Favorite Vampire

What Would Sipowicz Do?
Race, Rights and Redemption in NYPD Blue

The Anthology at the End of the Universe
Leading Science Fiction Authors
on Douglas Adams' The Hitchhiker's Guide to the Galaxy

Anti-Heroes, Lost Shepherds
and Space Hookers
in Joss Whedon's *Firefly*

Finding Serenity

EDITED BY
JANE ESPENSON
WITH
GLENN YEFFETH

BenBella Books
Dallas, Texas

"The Reward, the Details, the Devils, the Due" © 2004 by Larry Dixon

"The Heirs of Sawney Beane" © 2004 by Lawrence Watt-Evans

"Asian Objects in Space" © 2004 by Leah Wilson

"The Rise and Fall (and Rise) of *Firefly*" © 2004 by Glenn Yeffeth

"Who Killed *Firefly*?" © 2004 by Ginjer Buchanan

"'The Train Job' Didn't Do the Job" © 2004 by Albé-Shiloh, Inc.

"*Serenity* and Bobby McGee" © 2004 by Mercedes Lackey

"*Firefly* vs. *The Tick*" © 2004 by Don DeBrandt

"We're All Just Floating in Space" © 2004 by Lyle Zynda

"More Than a Marriage of Convenience" © 2004 by Michelle Sagara West

"Zoe: Updating the Woman Warrior" © 2004 by Tanya Huff

"Whores and Goddesses" © 2004 by Joy Davidson

"The Captain May Wear the Tight Pants" © 2004 by Robert B. Taylor

"I Want Your Sex" © 2004 by Nancy Holder

"Just Shove Him in the Engine" © 2004 by John C. Wright

"Mirror/Mirror" © 2004 by Roxanne Longstreet Conrad

"Star Truck" © 2004 by David Gerrold

"Chinese Words in the *Firefly*verse" © 2004 by Kevin M. Sullivan

"Listening to *Firefly*" © 2004 by Jennifer Goltz

"Kaylee Speaks" © 2004 by Jewel Staite

"Unofficial Glossary of *Firefly* Chinese" © 2004 by Kevin M. Sullivan

Additional materials © 2004 Jane Espenson

BenBella Books, 6440 N. Central Expressway, Suite 617, Dallas, TX 75206
www.benbellabooks.com
Send feedback to feedback@benbellabooks.com

PUBLISHER: Glenn Yeffeth
EDITOR: Shanna Caughey
ASSOCIATE EDITOR: Leah Wilson
DIRECTOR OF MARKETING/PR: Laura Watkins

Printed in the United States of America

10 9 8 7 6 5 4 3 2

Library of Congress Cataloging-in-Publication Data

Finding Serenity : anti-heroes, lost shepherds and space hookers in Joss Whedon's Firefly / edited by Jane Espenson with Glenn Yeffeth.
    p. cm.
  ISBN 1-932100-43-1
  1. Firefly (Television program) 2. Serenity (Motion picture) I. Espenson, Jane. II. Yeffeth, Glenn, 1961–

PN1992.77.F54F56 2005
791.45'72—dc22

                                                            2005001006

Cover design by Todd Michael Bushman
Text design and composition by John Reinhardt Book Design

Distributed by Independent Publishers Group. To order call (800) 888-4741 www.ipgbook.com
For special sales contact Laura Watkins at laura@benbellabooks.com

Dedicated to the
many fans of *Firefly*

Contents

"You take people, you put them on a journey,
you give them peril, you find out who they really are.
If there's any kind of fiction better than that,
I don't know what it is."

—JOSS WHEDON, *on Zap2it.com*

Introduction

ONCE UPON A LUNCHTIME, Joss Whedon took me with him as he ran an errand. We ended up at a jewelry store in Santa Monica where he picked out a gift for one of our young actresses on *Buffy the Vampire Slayer*, who was about to celebrate her sixteenth birthday. As he looked at various configurations of pearls, he told me about his idea for a new show to be called *Firefly*.

I listened as he laid out the world and its characters. I tried hard to understand the show as he described it, slowly realizing basic points such as that the main characters comprised the ship's only crew, and that the ship wasn't actually named "Firefly." It was already an impressively complete world, and I wanted to know what it meant, what he was saying with this show. Because Joss is never about the stuff, but about the stuff behind the stuff. I saw the connections between his fictional world and our current world. That was easy. And I also saw parallels with the workplace we all shared. The Joss-as-Mal, co-executive producer Marti Noxon-as-Zoe parallel struck all of us in those days. I got all that. But I didn't "get it" yet.

I asked a lot of questions about why there weren't any aliens in this conception. In fact, for a long time, I simply refused to understand that there really weren't any. To me, a space show without aliens felt like *Buffy* without vampires. I have always liked the way an outsider's sensibility allows us to see ourselves more clearly, and I didn't yet understand that Joss wanted to say something clear and honest about *human* nature without bringing different hard-wired psychologies and physiologies into it.

I also kept asking him about an underlying metaphor. The post-Civil-

1

War American West had never held much allure for me. Stories set there were invariably dusty, very male and rarely whimsical, in my estimation. The notion that the only metaphor was seeing the future as another *then*, or as another *now*, seemed limiting. Where was the "High School is Hell" concept that had guided *Buffy*? Again, I had missed the point. Joss was going for something real and direct with this show, something that didn't require a metaphorical lens to focus it. His most clearly "sci-fi" television project to date was also going to be his most literal. And it was the stronger for it.

After difficult birth pains that included Joss' writing and filming a two-hour pilot, recutting it as a one-hour pilot, and finally writing an entirely new pilot in a Herculean last-gasp weekend shared effort between Joss and the amazing Tim Minear, the show finally became a show, and not just a hope. As it entered regular production, and as more episodes were written, it became clear that this really was, in its important respects, the show he had described to me in the jewelry store. It was smart, and deep, and emotional, and it was about what it means to be human in a world where no obvious rewards await the virtuous.

Early on, members of the *Buffy* staff, including myself, were brought in to help construct and write some of the episodes. I wrote the one called "Shindig." In doing so, I got to invent a card game, write Jane Austen-like dialogue, and witness a sword fight on a hot early morning, framed so viewers wouldn't see the "Country Bear Jamboree" barn just out of view at a Disney-owned production facility. I also had the wonderfully surreal experience of trying to exit a women's rest room as a half-dozen female extras in hoop skirts tried to enter. Every day was a blast.

There was a real and palpable sense that we were creating a new television universe. Imagine being on the set for the first few episodes of the original *Star Trek* and getting a tingly sense of what it would become. I wanted to pocket props just to preserve the evidence that I was there. A metal playing card, a gift from the prop guy, served that purpose well.

We didn't know that our universe would be tragically short-lived, although I suppose the difficult early days had given us fair warning.

The surprise is not that *Firefly* was cancelled. After all, the vast majority of new shows are. The surprise, really, is that the show lives on in DVD sales, in a new feature film and in books like this collection of essays.

As I write this, I have recently been fortunate to see an early version of the Universal movie *Serenity*. The music is not final, the effects are unfinished and even some scene choices are still flexible, but the movie is a movie, and a brilliant one. It is the show that we loved, and it is more, because a big screen and big bucks put us more squarely in the middle of Joss' vision, which is a very good place to be. The political parallels between their world and ours are especially strong in the movie. And so are the emotions, the characters, the entire rich world of a very real future.

The authors of the essays in this book haven't seen the film. As I write this, its release is still some time in the future, but they remind us that the vision was already there, on the small screen, accessible to anyone who took the time to go along for the ride.

These essays range from a humorous exploration of a hypothetical *Serenity-Enterprise* mix-up to an examination of Existentialism as it relates to the show. They are by writers, actors, scholars and fans. Each of them directs a light onto another facet of the show that left us too soon.

It's shiny.

ENJOY,

Jane Espenson

Build a character from the floor up and little character details come incredibly easily. But if the character exists to fill a dotted line, the details flow like stone. Dixon points this out beautifully and extends the argument to aspects of set design, set dressing and cinematography.

He's right. Everyone whom I met from the Firefly *production seemed genuinely excited by the challenge, and driven to find the perfect details. I once spent a good part of a production day discussing metal playing cards with the prop guy. The conversation really brought home the degree to which the smallest thing was given its due.* Firefly, *more than most television shows, was, briefly, a way of life for those involved with it.*

The Reward, the Details, the Devils, the Due

LARRY DIXON

FIREFLY IS A SHOW THAT I FEEL COMFORTABLE WITH. It kind of caught me by surprise that way. It isn't that I've worked on it, though it's on the short list of ones I'd like to, and it's not that I've vacationed at Persephone or deadheaded on a space freighter. It's not just that it engaged me like few other shows ever have, and blindsided me with its heartful portrayals.

Nope. . . .

Damndest thing about *Firefly* is that sometimes it made me feel like I was coming home.

Now, first off, I've gotta tell you, I'm an Okie. The western-movie way of speaking you find on the show isn't a far sight different from how we talk down here every day. The easy manner and drawl persist in the present day because they function well. It's a sort of talk that suits the time and place, same now as in Browncoat time, I reckon. Slang gets picked for its sharpness, and long words get clipped, while a twang or "ah" draws speech out to reflect the thought being given to a subject. Language can be just as much about misdirection and bluff as it is about straight talk, and it's masterfully used in *Firefly*. There are nuances in how words were used in the show that just tickle me to death because they work—often so well that I didn't even realize I'd been played until a third or fourth viewing. I delight in the show's details, and not only in how language is used. Design, pacing, scene-building and timing all weigh in, and bear up well. To me, the wonder of *Firefly* is that world-class creative talents worked together on it so skillfully that the significance of the details can be mined as deeply as I might feel like going.

Firefly reassured me that going that extra mile to do your very best really *can* matter. One of the toughest struggles that a creator has comes when he's pushed himself to the physical and emotional edge and has to come to grips with the dreadful realization that, yes, this might just be as good as it gets. It is a form of facing mortality, but in a creative sense: you might have gone as far as you're going to be able to, and no one's going to care. The only way out, as in so many things in life, is to go through: the creative personality has to accept that even if that's true, the effort is worth it. You have to live with yourself, and know you gave it your best even if it matters to no one else but you. The clouds part and miraculously, while the work is being done, it becomes something infused with the spark of genius; a life is given to it that could never have been there if the artist had settled for doing something merely adequate. Something beautiful can be made, and it counts. But it comes with a price. *Firefly* was a labor of love in the most sobering sense—a gathering of superb professionals, each giving his and her very best, but in the employ of people who didn't appreciate or understand what they were getting. An artist's greatest external foes may be ignorance and incomprehension, but the fiercest nemeses inside an artist are doubt and despair. *Firefly*'s partnership of creators faced all four and pushed on through to make something inspiringly beautiful.

As an artist, I've been fortunate enough to attend master classes under true greats and study in some of the world's finest museums. As a writer, I've been privileged to be mentored by some of the best. When you've had a lot of training in creative fields, you become a fundamentally different person—you see the world differently, and it can't be shut off. It isn't just a matter of having a repertoire and a library of techniques. It is like having extra sensory organs implanted; you literally now perceive every room in terms of ambient light, shadow and juxtaposition of edge to field of color. Stories aren't just linear anymore; the masterwork tricks of foreshadowing, beats and characterization are appreciated in exactly the same way that a fellow stage magician appreciates a well-done sleight-of-hand trick. When you know how it's done, sometimes it becomes even more impressive.

Half the fun of *Firefly*, for me, is catching how these brilliant people did their thing.

I think Joss, Carey, Loni and compadres are right on the money when they call *Serenity* the tenth character. It isn't the first time we've seen this happen; from the *Bebop* to the *Millennium Falcon*, to sentient starships like the *Carrier* from Grant Morrison's *The Authority*, *Moya* from *Farscape*, or the beautiful *Sol Bianca* from the eponymous anime (try saying that three times fast), we've found ourselves concerned for the fate of a vessel as much as any of the leads. Someone—and I wish I could recall who—wisely observed that even on the original *Star Trek*, the *Enterprise* herself became a character we knew as well as any of the human ones.

What is even trickier than getting an audience attached to a vessel as a character or even a setting, though, is getting the vessel to be a part of the storytelling toolbox. The views of the *Nostromo* told so much about the characters in the opening minutes of *Alien*, before you ever laid eyes on a human character. If someone is known by who—or what—he or she associates with, those slow pans around the corridors and cockpit gave the viewers a look at what kind of company the ship kept. When you saw the interiors in the original *Star Trek*, you knew these were professional people working in a naval setting, as Spartan as the berths of a destroyer. *Star Trek: The Next Generation*, well, these were Highly Dignified professional people in a flying office building. And *Deep Space Nine*? Eh, the space station's a rental. They never even repainted the thing.

For my money, there's been no other spacecraft interior that has helped in the subtle art of describing characters more masterfully than the *Serenity*.

Many advanced techniques for scene composition depend upon human anatomy and psychology of perception. For example, there is a compositional concept called "visual arrows" that the interior of *Serenity* lends itself to, and the creators of the show used it very effectively. Simply put, visual arrows work like this: when a viewer looks at a scene, his or her eyes naturally flick across the entirety of the image like a pinball, lighting on a point then zooming away a fraction of a second later as the mind processes the image and evaluates the importance of its elements. Viewers instinctively tend to follow edges, and pass over wide fields, to concentrate on junctions of intersecting lines, contrast or colors—for example, the vee shape in a bent elbow, creases in clothes or the edge where a shoulder is seen against a background color. Visual arrows are how an artist keeps your attention where he wants it; the artist can use objects in the background that "bump" your eye along their edge and back to what the artist wants you to pay attention to. Corners can be made dark, tricking your gaze into staying inside the border of the artwork. Items held by the figure can be set against a contrasting color, or made to seem connected to another figure by the lines of a background shadow. Tension can be created by *almost* having one visual element touch another; similarly, unity can be implied by making edges blurred or incomplete.

A ship interior contributes to storytelling through several major factors: lighting, color, depth and composition. The forward cargo bay, just as one example, is a design of astounding artistic versatility. The paneled grid of the cargo bay walls is reminiscent of interlaced, overlapping oriental designs, cleverly reminding us of the American-Chinese Alliance setting while artistically forming a patterned plane for background scale reference. The catwalk and stairs provide strong diagonals and patterned shadows. In composition, diagonals tend to imply action—unless they are used to frame a figure symmetrically, which implies stability. Horizontals and dark panels toward the lower half of a scene imply strength, and patterns add visual interest. The horizontal lines of the catwalks can often be noticed intersecting the eyes or mouths of characters, drawing the eye to focus there.

So now, when you watch the show again, check out how the connections between the characters are expressed in how the backgrounds are composed. When Wash and Zoe were being shown as a loving couple you often saw them framed through a doorway, with the rails of the stairs leading toward them, directing your eye to the vignette. Early shots of Simon were off-center, and usually against a flat background, giving him a slightly unsettling demeanor, but as the episodes progressed he was lit with more and more of the ship's colors, and the visual arrows formed connecting lines between him and other characters. When it was Inara and Kaylee together, you'd notice strong horizontals, almost like equals signs, accenting the stability and the connection between the two. Zoe and Wash generally mirrored each other, with heavy horizontals linking them. Mal and Inara's arguments frequently showed them in mirrored positions, and the frame was sometimes unbalanced by a few degrees of tilt when one of them felt uneasy. When Mal was to be taken seriously in a scene, you'd very often see him positioned such that diagonals guided your attention directly to his eyes and mouth.

Every bit as much as visual arrows, color affects how we perceive a character's grounding in a scene. At the beginning of the show, Simon's wardrobe was made up of starched white and cold metallics, very orderly and in uneasy contrast to the earth colors of the core crew and *Serenity's* interior. Simon tended to be the only character who wore white, and, especially at the beginning, it made a connection between his closed, almost-reptilian manner and the literally antiseptic style of the infirmary. Stiff white upright collars and perfect creases echoed the white enamel cabinets and brushed steel surfaces—he seemed at home in the infirmary because it matched him in scheme. As he grew more fond of the crew, his clothes shifted to resemble their outfits...a little looser, more unbuttoned, sometimes just a vest and shirt rather than a whole suit.

In "Out of Gas," texture as well as color palettes were used as storytelling tools: color sets and film grains were different according to the time period being shown. Anything around five years in the past was saturated, very grainy and overburned, subconsciously evoking "old film" in the viewer. Warm tints were used for the recent-past timeline, and a cooler palette was used for the wounded-Mal "current" timeline. Some well-executed digital color modding was done to further enhance the story points, making the red of Mal's dripping blood very bright against the blue and black of the floor grid.

Mal and Zoe were instantly understood as being connected to *Serenity* because the color palette used for their clothes matched *Serenity's* interior. Inara and Kaylee both had environments of rich reds, with mixed foreground and background objects creating a sense of depth. A nice film-noir touch: some scenes with Inara had background elements in silhouette (such as ferns, sculptures, etc.) but the entire scene lighting was so dark that her hair blended in with the background shapes. It firmly grounded her in the scene but still made for a shadowy mystique. In Kaylee's case, the reds came mostly from rust, contrasting with the splashes of color and decoration that showed Kaylee's cheerful nature.

Now here's an interesting train of thought about that rust. The Firefly-class vessel, I noticed, appeared to be made by shipbuilders in much the same way present-day seagoing cargo ships are: not built like a yacht, with composites and flat decks, but built like a cargo vessel, and not a particularly well-designed one. In fact, there are design flaws everywhere, from exposed sharp corners to inadequate railings, forehead-level pipes and trip hazards (very reminiscent of World War II bomber and destroyer interiors). Welded steel, bolts, rivets, paint and grates suggested that a Firefly was a lowest-bidder, low-rent utilitarian workhorse,

probably originating from privatized surplus tooling once the government contract ran out. It's the rust that's the telling part to me. Aircraft
today are built of aluminum and spacecraft are built of titanium—both
materials are strong, light, expensive and difficult to fabricate, but the
mass of the craft is a major factor in the weight-to-power equation.

Apparently, the technology for lifting extremely heavy mass became
cheap enough in the *Firefly* universe that privately owned spaceflight
became common. So, if heavy-lift engines became as widespread as, say,
big-block internal combustion motors are today, you could find starship
builders whose origins were simply retooled naval shipyards. Like how
Spartan in Tulsa shifted from making aircraft to travel trailers when war
demand ended in the 1940s, industries can adapt in surprising ways.
Street rod bodywork today can trace its roots back through coachwork
builders to medieval armorers. The English Wheel, a simple machine
used for curving and compressing sheet metal, is fundamentally the
same as when it was used to create compound curves in 1500s armor.
Like a claw hammer, a shovel or a piston pump, some things persist in
human history for the basic reason that there just isn't a better design
for the job—and others because there just isn't a cost-effective reason to
change. I think that's why you see revolvers in *Firefly*; even in the future
they are still literally the best bang for the buck—easy to manufacture,
cheap to maintain, reliable and effective. I think that's also why you see
starships made of good old rusty steel.

The Firefly-class' original designers, the shipwrights who built her,
understood that this was not just a space truck used for a day; it was
designed to be a home to people. It was made for carrying passengers
and cargo as well as the crew that called it home. The "guest quarters"
are characteristically different from crew quarters because of their level
of finish. The rooms, at the time Malcolm Reynolds owns the ship, are
of fairly miserable quality. The general decrepitude of *Serenity* is made
even more plain by the fact that, while maybe when the ship was new
these weren't bad berths to have, now the wall panels have grime in the
seams and the paint has chipped or faded. Ladders are omnipresent,
even used as hall and room dividers.

The captain's rack: well, I'd say there's a direct response to the age-
old *Trek* question of "Where are the bathrooms?" because you catch Mal
taking a leak in your first glimpse of his quarters. And it's obvious that
he doesn't really care about décor…the walls are miserably streaked
and dirty, and everything personal about it is just hung on plain brackets or stuffed on shelves. The walls curve into the floor, accenting the

fact that he's in a berth on a ship, not in a flying hotel room. The toilet and sink are surplus-airliner-lavatory quality. The toilet paper (same as today's—why change a design that works, eh?) hangs on a loop of rope. The hand towel is plain Kmart style, nothing exotic at all. Woven oriental mats are on the floor (the same make of mat as on the floor in the dining room, under the big wooden table), and paper items taped or tacked to the wall appear to be mostly old maps of planetside locations. Brilliant characterization, teaching us in moments about a man's history just from the details. I dig story, and history, greeblies.

"Greeblie" is a model maker's term for details that create believability. Those vents, antennae, conduits, hatches and other funky cool stuff that you see on model starships that give them visual interest, a sense of scale and a realistic look are greeblies. Some mighty smart storytellers build in literary versions of greeblies to enrich, well, everything. Throwaway tertiary characters can stick in your memory because they had a limp, a scar, a speech peculiarity or a bit of jewelry. They've got a story behind those details. I'm a greeblies guy. I love the details, because the details make me think and explore. *Firefly* has juicy details everywhere: it's a greeblie-rich environment.

Sometimes, as a writer, you come into a project that has its own greeblies, and you get to retrofit the story behind them—such as working on an anthology in someone else's universe and riffing off of a minor character's unusual habit or a bit of scenery. I'd have a blast doing that with *Firefly*—heck, I've already got notes on backstories for everything from Kaylee's ideal machine shop to Wash's family, humor and education and the significance of the plastic dinosaurs. When we watch a show, we see characters who are the way they are because they've lived the twenty, thirty, forty years it took to get them to that moment when we peek in on their lives.

I bring this up because it's an important factor in why I feel so attached to this darn show. Let's see if I can explain. Believability breaks down when you have a person doing what a plot requires rather than acting from motive or reacting to the circumstances around him or her. Most stories around suffer from plot-push syndrome—characters are introduced to give a single bit of information and are defined only enough to serve the story line. When the flow-chart plot isn't served by them, they aren't around. If they're seen again, there are no lasting effects upon them. Such characters aren't thought of as people by either the audience or the creator; they are merely tools used for a limited purpose.

For better or worse, that isn't the approach I take, with even my most

minor walk-on characters. The reasoning's simple: to us, they're characters, but in the character's world, he's a complete person, and every
person is the star of his own life. From his point of view, he's the hero
of his own story. Even if we only see someone for an hour in a story, the
other twenty-three hours of the day he's still living, breathing, feeling
and dreaming. If you respect your characters—whether they're walk-
ons or divas—and give them their due, then they'll be memorable. In
their lives, they aren't there to walk into someone else's story, drone off
dialogue and walk out—they're living the only life they've got.

That's where you find genius in *Firefly*. These people came from
somewhere and there's no doubt of it. They have adventures not because
they have nothing better to do, but because adventure is practically a
by-product of the ongoing process of their lives.

Life isn't a spectator sport for the *Serenity* family. They take dangers
seriously, and sometimes they run from them. They don't have the flim-
sy "Let's go defeat the Evil Empire today!" enthusiasm of generic space
opera; these are folk with the odds stacked against them, trying to make
something of the one life they're entitled to without becoming monsters, or worse, numb bystanders. They have to be for real, dangerous
and smart. Posturing gets a body killed in the post-Unification outer
worlds. These folk can get ten kinds of crippled or dead from a rash
decision, and they know it. Because these characters take their lives
seriously, *we* can take them seriously.

I've had a fairly interesting life. Might be called adventurous. I'm the
son of a commando (sergeant major, Delta Force), who was son of a
pilot (Air Force major), and on back through generations of soldiers,
racers, inventors, explorers and risk-takers. I grew up immersed in the
lore and travel of the military, but my own talents were in different
areas, to the delight of the family. I became an artist and writer in sub-
stantial part because I was what they were fighting for: they were the
warriors who used the skills and aptitudes they had to help create a safe
cradle for "the gentler arts" of exploration of the human condition. Like
them, I couldn't stay passive about my tasks. Now, you have to understand, I'm no bronze-skinned, square-jawed archetype of manly-man-
ness. In fact, I'm kind of frail, depressive, hydrophobic, nearsighted,
color-blind, a little deaf and prone to making incredibly brave (stupid)
moves for honor, friendship, love or whatever else won't make me feel
like a lump on the planet. I want to go to Antarctica—I hate cold, and
water, but hey, it's as close as I'm going to get to walking on the surface
of Mars. Sure I'm scared. Sometimes, that's the point. I'm not an adrena-

line junkie—it's just that I know that awesome experiences don't come from staying in the simulators. Even as I'm writing this I'm recovering from an aikido injury that deep-sixed another New Zealand trip for cave rafting and jumping from the Auckland Sky Tower and plain old "I wonder where this road goes?" exploring. Fire, floods, tornadoes, stalkers, crashes, chases, firefighting, rescues, exploring ruins, walking volcanoes, injuries, standoffs, going in harm's way for love, hell, even being at sea between two colliding hurricanes—I've had enough hard knocks and close scrapes that writing danger-filled adventure's sometimes just a case of carving off a slab of the past, basting it with tasty adjectives and grilling it to taste.

When I kick on back, with only three or four other things happening, to enjoy a movie or TV show, I wince and frown and twitch as I see characters get banged up. Hey, that stuff hurts—believe me, I know. A movie or TV show loses me a little bit more every time the hero shrugs off something that ought to have put tears in his eyes. That's something that caught me about *Firefly* right away. These people get hurt, and it's brilliantly acted. My wife, bless her heart, has too many times listened to me murmur, "Yep, that's about how that feels," when one of the crew gets thumped.

I have a warmth for Mal and Zoe because they show very well what, alas, all too few screenwriters grasp—that very often, soldiers are there in the thick of danger because they care very deeply, and that care deepens the more they have to personally risk and sacrifice. A smart soldier isn't ready to die for his cause; he's ready to risk death, which is a much different thing. "The Military" or "the Government" are usually quick and easy generic bad guys for an unskilled storyteller to plug in when his Fiercely Independent Protagonists need someone to blow up. As a fellow sci-fi writer, Ben Ohlander, puts it, a faceless military or monolithic government is a "large, slow-moving target"—in other words, a cheap and easy shot. The thing is, a military is made up of individuals, each with his own ethics, dreams and quirks—and not only the military on the protagonists' side. Even in the pilot, I was delighted to see that the big mean Alliance cruiser was diverted by a commander who wanted to help out civilians in distress; even though he was going to cause trouble for *our* protagonists, when he fell for the Crybaby his motive was to help innocent people. I once dealt with a sheriff in real life whose advice about a stalker was, "It's going to take me twenty minutes to get anyone to you—just make sure the body's on your porch by the time I get there." The outland sheriff in "The Train Job" made me smile because he had the same sort of weather-beaten practicality—extra work went into writing him, when he could have been portrayed as a two-dimensional face-and-a-badge.

Even the most "shallow" of characters received deep thought. Niska wasn't a terrifying sadist just because a story line called for one. He was a businessman, who understood that his most valued commodity was reputation. Jayne cracks me up because I've spent time around GIs who were pretty much just like him: about as classy as a jockstrap in a punch bowl and half as charming. And, oh Lord, have I ever been in role-playing games with folks who had characters just like him: gunbunnies with every stat maxed for lethality, and so two-dimensional you could put a stamp on 'em and mail 'em. Still, Jayne isn't dismissed by the writers (or Adam Baldwin) as an iconic merc with a flickering forty-watt bulb in his forebrain. Big attaboys go to Adam for the tough task of playing Jayne; to paraphrase Bette Midler's wardrobe comment, "It takes a lot of smarts to act this dumb." Jayne isn't gifted upstairs, but he does the best he can with what he's got.

That brings me around to one of the reasons why this show feels so much like coming home. Doing the best you can with what you've got is a theme in my life. I didn't grow up as a child of wealth and privilege. My youth was an interesting mix of scavenging, making do, doing without and having appreciation for what was there. On payday we'd splurge and go to McDonald's, but there were times when we had to go fishing just to have something to eat. Part of my play was finding useful bits of junk to repair, clambering around the family dirt-track race car and figuring out how to make some money. I spent many an hour playing with bartered Hot Wheels and cardboard-box buildings between the family print shop's machines as they went kerthacka-kerthacka, falling asleep against the rusty girders. It didn't demean us that we weren't wealthy, and we did our best to stay honest and generous. We might not have had much, but our home was open to those in need. That's part of the Okie way, going back to when it was an unexplored territory and if you got in trouble, your neighbor was your only hope. We'd find a way to make each day a little bit better than the one before if we could manage it. Sure, the roof might leak and the pipes might be rusty, but that could always be fixed with a little salvaged tar paper and a slap of that paint you found behind the hardware store. Every once in a while, you might even have an adventure.

I think the whole *Serenity* crew would have fit right in with us. You don't have to own a lot to have a lot.

The last, most deeply personal reason that the show gets to me is that there've been a few times when the ghosts came out to say hello. There were moments where Mal and Zoe's style of humor was so much like that of departed comrades that I'd experience a fleeting suspension of time, a sensation that the seconds were stretching out so far that the past and the present were touching each other. Wash's one-liners cracked me up because I knew folks like him. The crinkles in the edges of Nathan Fillion's eyes when he grinned recalled a couple of old friends who won't be sitting at the table anymore. Even though I'm mostly toasting with antacids these days, I give the ghosts their due, and I smile when I think of them—and I give thanks for this show, lovingly created, for reminding us that pride in workmanship does count, and for taking us along on its adventure. Here's to the Big Damn Heroes who gave it to us.

Larry Dixon is an acclaimed artist and interior illustrator with work ranging from Harvard Press to Marvel. Son of an extraordinary Okie farmgirl and a Delta Force commando, Larry has been a race car driver, volunteer firefighter, stormspotter and all-around adventurer. His passions are falconry, technology, music history, special effects, custom cars, comedy, games, fashion and model making. Larry was also the Great Eagles reference advisor for the Lord of the Rings films. With Mercedes Lackey, he's credited for popularizing gryphons and has been Guest of Honor at more than 200 conventions worldwide.

He lives in Oklahoma, where he collects comics, odd cars and injuries.

You will not soon forget the story of the heirs of Sawney Beane. Here the story is chillingly well-told—even the name fills me with delight. Oh, to have created a character named Sawney Beane.

Watt-Evans uses old Sawney as a tool for indulging in some insightful analysis and speculation about the origin and nature of the Reavers. And of those who are unfortunate enough to meet up with them. He discusses the forces that we like to call "evil," and the various way humans react to those forces. It's a good read that raises many questions.

I'm tempted to tell him, and you, gentle readers, that I know the answers to all these questions about the Reavers. That the answers dwell in the Serenity movie. But that isn't strictly true. In going from television show to feature film, the rules change. Parts of the board are wiped clean. The mythology of the Reavers on Firefly *is not quite the mythology of the Reavers in* Serenity.

This means, of course, that Watt-Evans is soon going to have a whole raft of new questions about which to speculate. It's the circle of life.

The Heirs of Sawney Beane

LAWRENCE WATT-EVANS

ONE OF THE ANNOYANCES IN FOX'S INSISTENCE on showing the episodes of *Firefly* out of order was that it messed up the introduction of various elements of the Alliance universe. We first encountered the Reavers in "Bushwhacked," rather than in "Serenity," which left some of us—me, at any rate—wondering whether Reavers were *real*.

After all, in "Bushwhacked" they're never seen, merely described, and the circumstances are such that one is left wondering whether the stories are even remotely accurate. Couldn't it be that the Reavers are actually aliens, whose space humanity is intruding upon? Might there be no Reavers at all, but only some form of space madness that causes people to turn on one another?

But then when the two-hour pilot finally aired we got to see that, yes, the Reavers *are* real, and they *are* nominally human, or at least fly human-built spacecraft—though they do so in suicidal fashion, with the shielding removed. It wasn't meant to be a question; we should have known by the time we saw "Bushwhacked" that the Reavers are real.

But can you blame anyone for wondering? After all, how likely is it that there would be communities of degenerate cannibals cruising the frontiers, preying on whoever came their way? Not savage natives of the hinterlands, but the descendants of civilized humanity, still able to fly spaceships. And why would one of their victims, as seen in "Bushwhacked," try to become a Reaver himself?

At first glance it seems absurd.

Well...perhaps it's not as absurd as all that. The historical record apparently shows at least one case of civilized people reverting to cannibalistic savagery for an extended period: the story of Sawney Beane and his family.

According to the most common version of the story, Sawney Beane was born late in the sixteenth century and raised in a perfectly ordinary Scottish family; accounts differ on exactly where. As a young man, though, he decided he did not care to spend his life at the backbreaking toil he had seen his father do, and instead he and his similarly inclined girlfriend fled the town one night and took up residence in a cave, whence they proceeded to rob and murder unwary travelers. The entrance to the cave was underwater except at low tide, so they were safely hidden by the sea much of the time, and able to carry on their criminal career largely undetected. Fearful of being recognized as thieves when they ventured into town to buy the supplies they needed, they did not dare attempt to barter or sell any of the jewelry or other valuables they collected, but used only the coins.

Most travelers of the day did not carry much cash, and there weren't that many people who dared travel alone in the first place, so the take was meager, not enough to fill the young couple's bellies reliably—especially not once their children started to arrive. There was also the matter of disposing of the bodies of their victims.

You can see where this is going, I'm sure; they solved both problems with a single solution by butchering and eating their victims.

For twenty-five years, they lived hidden in their seaside cave, feasting on human flesh. In that quarter-century they produced fourteen children and thirty-two grandchildren, the grandchildren all being the result of incest, since none of the children were ever allowed any contact with anyone outside the family.

And *all* of this clan, it seems, subsisted largely on human flesh; the reports estimate something over a thousand victims.

Finally, the accounts say, a large group of travelers interrupted the Beanes in the process of attacking a couple; they rounded a bend in the road to see a horde of savages swarming around a husband and wife. The woman had already been dragged from her horse and slaughtered, but the man had drawn his sword and had been fighting for his life when the larger party arrived.

Seeing themselves badly outnumbered by the new arrivals, the cannibals fled. The travelers, unprepared as they were, did not pursue them immediately, but noted the route of their departure, then attended to the survivor, listening to his tale of horror, tending his wounds, and seeing that his wife's mutilated corpse was properly covered.

This was the break in the case that the authorities had needed; they used bloodhounds to track the Beanes back to their lair, although even then, it was not until the search happened by the right spot at low tide that they were able to locate the cave's well-concealed mouth.

Moving swiftly, so that their prey would not escape them, the king's men gathered on the shore and pursued the criminals into the cave. A large party of soldiers entered the Beanes' home, lighting their way with torches, and after making their way up a long passage, reached the family's quarters.

They were horrified at what they found—the carcasses of men and women strung up like sides of beef, severed limbs scattered about, while countless human bones and a fortune in clothing and valuables were piled together to one side, testifying to two and a half decades of terror.

With the cave's entrance blocked by the troops, the entire family was easily rounded up, and at the direction of King James I of England they were taken immediately to the city of Leith, where they were summarily executed—the men by having their limbs chopped off and being left to bleed to death, while the women and children were burned alive in three great fires. Most protested vigorously the entire time, insisting they had done nothing wrong, but only what they needed to do to survive.

This is the basic tale, as reported fairly consistently from 1719 on.

And if it could happen in seventeenth-century Scotland, why not on the frontiers of space in the far future? The very basis of *Firefly* is that even centuries from now and light-years from Earth, human beings will still behave like human beings, and will create the same familiar problems for ourselves that we always have. The Reavers are the heirs of Sawney Beane, living in the cave of space, preying on unwary travelers, sunk into cannibalistic barbarism. They produce nothing, they have no contact with the rest of humanity—they're subhuman parasites.

Terrifying subhuman parasites.

One interesting aspect of the story of Sawney Beane is that after a quarter-century of slaughter, the Beanes got very good at it; the accounts of that final attack say that they pulled the woman from her horse so quickly she had no time to react, and they had disemboweled her almost before she reached the ground. Practice can make one an expert at almost anything, even murder.

And on *Firefly*, nobody ever even *suggests* actually fighting the Reavers—if the Reavers catch you it's just a question of how you die, because this is *what they do*, kill people, and they're experts. You can die fighting, die cowering, or kill yourself before they reach you, but the idea of *surviving* a Reaver attack—well, that doesn't happen. Not really.

And in "Bushwhacked," we see exactly that. Mal Reynolds knows it, and lays it out for us—after seeing the kind of horror the Reavers perpetrate, any "survivors" try to become Reavers themselves, because you can't live with that kind of memory and still be a rational human being. It's a sort of extreme version of the Stockholm syndrome, where hostages come to identify with their captors.

But there's nothing like that in the Sawney Beane story; they never left anyone alive until that final failed attack, never recruited anyone from outside the family. I do not mean to say that there's any particular reason that Reavers *should* be modeled exclusively on Sawney Beane, but it's interesting how similar the stories otherwise are—and that this part of the story doesn't follow the Beane pattern.

That doesn't mean that it doesn't fit *any* pattern, though. Human literature is *full* of stories of people driven by encounters with monsters to become monsters themselves: in European legend those bitten by a werewolf become werewolves; in some American Indian tales a wendigo's victims become wendigos; and more relevantly, there are many stories about people forced into cannibalism in an emergency who then develop a taste for human flesh and find ways to keep consuming it long after the emergency is past.

But does it really happen?

In 1846 a group of settlers known as the Donner Party was trapped by early snow in the mountains of eastern California and resorted to cannibalism to survive—those who died were eaten by the rest. Out of eighty-three in the group, forty-five survived and eventually returned to civilization; it's believed at least half of those forty-five, perhaps far more, had tasted human flesh. Most of them were young and healthy, and lived long lives afterward.

There's no evidence at all that any of them had any interest in repeating the experience. Of the forty-five, just one is reported to have been later mocked by his neighbors as a crazy old cannibal, and even in his case there's no sign he ever did anything to harm anyone after that horrible winter; the experience seemed to have damaged him with what we would now call "post-traumatic stress disorder," or PTSD, but it hardly turned him into a monster.

In 1972 the survivors of a plane crash in the Andes ate the bodies of their dead companions; again, this doesn't seem to have given any of them a craving for long pig.

Or simply look at any of the tribes known to have practiced cannibalism; most of them had no great difficulty in giving it up.

Getting away from the specific issue of cannibalism, people who have survived horrific experiences—anything from abusive childhoods to the death camps of Nazi Germany or the killing fields of Cambodia—almost never show any interest in reliving any part of the experience; on the contrary, they tend to be hypervigilant in avoiding anything of the sort.

It's those who survived the camps who swore "Never again." Surely we've all heard tales of Holocaust survivors who still keep an escape kit ready, who are constantly wary of police or other authorities, who respond to, "It can't happen here," with, "That's what we thought in 1933."

But on the other hand, consider the Stockholm syndrome, where hostages make common cause with their captors. This is a very real phenomenon, the most famous example being heiress Patty Hearst's kidnapping by the Symbionese Liberation Army, which resulted in her joining up as a revolutionary—but does it have any long-term effects? Does it last after the victims are freed?

Amazingly, yes. In the case that gave the pattern its name, a hostage-taking in Stockholm in 1973, the victims considered their captors to be friends.

Stockholm syndrome is now recognized as a survival mechanism—by bonding with their captors, victims force those captors to see them as human beings like themselves, rather than as a threat or an annoyance that can be readily disposed of.

Psychologists have recognized four factors that are needed to bring about Stockholm syndrome:

A perceived threat to one's survival and a belief that the captor would carry out the threat.

Some small kindness from the captor to the captive—such as allowing him to live.

Isolation from perspectives other than those of the captor.

Seeing no chance of escape.

Those all obviously apply in "Bushwhacked." The lone surviving settler saw the rest of his company slaughtered, so there was obviously a threat to his survival; he was allowed to live; he was left alone aboard an abandoned wreck, where the chances that the ship would ever be found were slim.

So here, perhaps, is an explanation for that would-be Reaver. No, he didn't develop a craving for human flesh, nor was he possessed by the evils he had seen—but he identified with the Reavers in an extreme case of Stockholm syndrome, in an attempt to survive. He saw them ruthlessly slaughter anyone and anything aboard the settlers' ship—*except each other*. The only way to be sure of surviving the Reavers was to *be* a Reaver.

And once he's rescued, he does his best to become one—not because it's the only way to deal with the horrors he's seen, but *in case they come back*.

No, that's not rational—but neither are Reavers, and neither are our survival instincts. The odds are excellent that he'll never see the Reavers again; after all, most of the billions of citizens of the Alliance never encounter them—but he's had that long shot come in once, and he had a *second* long shot come in when he *survived* the attack. . . .

So he's not taking chances. To him, in his damaged, unthinking state, the fact that it's far more likely he'll get killed (as in fact he does) by acting like a Reaver than that he'll ever encounter Reavers again just isn't going to register. He knows what he saw, he knows how to survive it, and he does what he must.

To Mal Reynolds, it's a matter of a mind being broken, a soul destroyed, by what it's experienced—the survivor can't cope with the horror except by becoming a monster. He's been bitten by the werewolf, clawed by the wendigo, and must become one.

That certainly fits with the myth, but the reality, surely, is simply the Stockholm syndrome writ large: our survivor has moved Reavers to an uncontested first place on his personal threat list, and knows, to the bottom of his heart, that the only thing the Reavers won't kill is another Reaver. He has presumably seen what Zoe described in "Serenity"—seen the Reavers rape people to death, seen them eat their victims' flesh, and seen them sew their victims' skin into their clothing—and he wants, more than anything else, to be sure that doesn't happen to him.

That this will make him a monster himself—well, he probably doesn't care.

Had he lived, he might have defended himself by saying that he was just trying to survive, that he was only pretending to be a Reaver—but as Kurt Vonnegut says in *Mother Night*, "We are what we pretend to be, so we must be careful what we pretend to be."

This sort of effect is quite likely something the Reavers want. It makes their jobs easier if their victims are so utterly terrified that they don't dare fight back; in fact, I suspect that they leave these occasional survivors deliberately, just to promote their own legend and weaken resistance.

And it might help their own mental health, if you can call it that—they can tell themselves that the way their victims imitate them shows that they're *right*, that their lifestyle is natural and reasonable for human beings, as demonstrated by the way other people adopt it once they've seen it in action.

Which brings us back to Sawney Beane. While there are no detailed transcripts, he and his clan are alleged to have gone to their deaths protesting vigorously, saying they had just done what they needed to do to survive; the children and grandchildren in particular had no reason to think they were doing anything wrong, or even unusual, since they had never known any other life.

Do the Reavers know they're human? Do they remember where they came from?

Jayne says, "They ain't men." Mal says they are, albeit pretty poor ones. What do they think, themselves?

How did they *get* there? Did they start out as ordinary pirates, and degenerate?

And it's clear from one single observed fact that they really *are* degenerate, that it's not an act put on to enhance their terrifying reputation—they fly ships with unshielded reactors.

That's suicidal. It's insane.

But do the Reavers know that? They know how to operate their ships, and presumably how to repair them, but do they understand how they work?

Are they civilized men gone bad, like Sawney Beane, or are they the grandchildren, unaware they could ever be anything better than they are? Can it be that the Reavers, monsters though they are, do have families and raise children, whom they bring up in the family trade, as the Beanes did, and these children are unaware that they're monsters? Those unshielded reactors would seem to imply that they don't know what they're doing, that they're innocents, in their monstrous way. It

may be that these people have lost their humanity over several generations, rather than in a single lifetime—we're never told how long the
Reaver menace has existed. Long enough for tales to be widespread, but
not universal—how long is that, in the *Firefly*verse?

Or perhaps the reactors are unshielded because the Reavers really
are suicidal—they *do* know who and what they are and are deliberately
courting death out of some lingering remnant of guilt or shame.

But there are so many faster, easier ways to die in space! Perhaps it's
not an actual death wish, but merely fatalism. They don't *care* whether
they live or die. Whatever might once have motivated them has presumably been lost, and nothing has filled that void; they have no morality
we would recognize, make no effort to improve themselves—but they
don't simply suicide, either. Perhaps whatever destroyed their humanity has left them so empty they cannot even bring themselves to care
enough to do *that!*

But in that case, why prey on others? No, there must still be some
motivation there, even if it's only hatred or despair.

And yes, I recognize that my description of people who have lost everything but refuse to die also fits Mal Reynolds. That may or may not
be significant; we don't know. It's all guesswork with *Firefly* gone.

There are so many unanswered questions about the Reavers. They
really are rather hard to believe in, that there could be such a culture
surviving out there, interstellar heirs of Sawney Beane—especially since
Sawney Beane probably never existed.

I imagine you protesting at that, given what I said earlier in this essay, and I don't blame you; I did write as if Beane's history were fact.
And for more than a century and a half, the tale was indeed accepted
as fact—from 1719 until the 1890s no one seriously questioned the
story. There were all those lovely corroborating details—the name of
king who had the Beanes executed, the place the execution took place
and all the rest of it.

But then some spoilsport historians began taking a closer look and
began noticing things like the fact that the name Sawney Beane doesn't
seem to appear anywhere prior to 1719, even though he was allegedly
executed about a century earlier. They noticed that the stories say that
James I took 400 men to Scotland to hunt down the Beanes, but that
records of King James' reign make no mention of any such expedition;
one would expect some documentation any time a company of 400 soldiers went traipsing off after a gang of cannibals with the king himself
in command.

They checked the court records at Leith and found no mention of the execution of forty-eight murderers at the king's express order. The stories say that the niceties of trial and sentencing were dispensed with, and that Sawney and his sons had their limbs lopped off and were left to bleed to death, while the women and children were burned alive; while that's certainly not any more barbaric than some very real killings, it *is* the sort of thing that would be recorded as an event of some moment— exsanguination and burning were not common methods of execution, even in the seventeenth century.

And there's the whole question of how a thousand travelers could be murdered in a thinly populated area like seventeenth-century eastern Scotland without creating an immense panic that would have been mentioned in any number of contemporary accounts.

It seems likely, then, that the whole story was made up, and its publication in 1719 in a book of stories about famous criminals was intended not so much to accurately record history as to help sell lurid books.

Yet readers believed it implicitly for well over a century; no one seriously questioned it. Even now, many people believe it—I've heard it told as fact and only learned just how unlikely to be true it is when I began researching this essay.

Why are people so eager to believe in stories like this, stories telling us that civilization is only a thin veneer, easily sloughed off when it becomes inconvenient? In fact, ordinary people are capable of appalling atrocities, of ferocity and cruelty as bad as anything found in the animal kingdom. We need only look at the historical record to find innumerable instances—from soldiers collecting ears to conquerors building pyramids of skulls, from abusive parents torturing their own children to religious persecutions in every century, from pogroms to death camps— of how hideous human behavior can be. But in almost every case, the participants in these abominations returned to human civilization and went about their lives afterward. The survivors of the Donner Party did not become slavering monsters living in caves like Sawney Beane. Soldiers who committed ghastly atrocities returned home to marry and raise children. Civilization is *not* a veneer we can easily lose forever at all—instead, it's something we can close away temporarily and restore when the crisis is over.

But that's not how the stories tell it, because that's not how we *want* it. We tell each other that our humanity is delicate and precious, that if we go too far it will be irretrievably lost, because if we admit that we can be monsters and then become human again and go on as if nothing had happened, then it's that much more tempting to be monsters. It's like a mother telling her child, "If you keep making faces like that, your face will freeze that way!" It's not true, the mother know it's not true, often even the *child* knows it's not true, but it reduces the temptation to make faces, because, hey, what if your face *did* freeze like that?

What if committing an atrocity *did* mean you could never be human again?

So we tell ourselves stories of people who became monsters and could never again be human.

I started out by saying that the Reavers might seem absurd, were it not for known cases like Sawney Beane. Now, we see that Sawney Beane probably never existed—that in fact, I haven't been able to find *any* reliably reported cases of small groups reverting to that sort of extreme barbarism for an extended period. Does that mean that the Reavers *are* absurd, an impossible element in the otherwise believable backdrop of *Firefly*, merely another cautionary tale with no basis in reality?

Well, sort of; if we take them at face value, as the heirs of Sawney Beane, then, yes, they do start to look a bit ridiculous, like the monsters in old campfire tales that may scare you when you're out in the dark woods but just seem silly by daylight. After all, how could such a vicious culture survive out there? What do they do for food? Yes, they're cannibals, but in order to sustain a viable fighting population they would need to eat a *lot* of people; they wouldn't be a mere legend to the inner worlds, but a menace the Alliance would be determined to wipe out. Not to mention just how unhealthy a diet of nothing but human flesh is. Historically, cannibals have eaten people for ritual reasons or in emergencies, not as a regular diet; it's just not *practical* to live entirely on humans.

Where do they get fuel for their ships? We know that *Serenity* needs lots of expensive fuel; presumably all ships do. Where are the Reavers getting theirs?

And why do they leave the ships they attack as intact as they do? Why haven't they stripped the wrecks of every salvageable spare part, every trace of food, every bit of fuel? The drifting wreck in "Bushwhacked" still had all its air—and they left uneaten corpses aboard! How can they afford to leave that food supply behind?

Clearly, these are not true scavengers. They *do* look impossible, and it's easy to see why the people of the core planets consider them a myth.

But we know the Reavers *are* out there! How can this be?

One possibility is that Joss Whedon and company didn't think this thing through and just came up with scary monsters without working out the details, but I think we can dismiss *that* theory for a very simple, obvious reason: it's no fun. So what other choices do we have?

We know at least one large shipful of these terrifying raiders exists, and probably more than one, going by the reactions of *Serenity*'s crew to the events of "Serenity" and "Bushwhacked." We know they need food, fuel and resources to keep their ships flying and their crews healthy—or as healthy as they can be, flying with unshielded reactors and eating human flesh—and that their depredations can't really be supplying all their needs, or they would be much more thorough in their scavenging.

So they must have some *other* source of supply.

Which means *someone* is deliberately funding and supplying the Reavers.

It's the only possibility. As I've said, despite how common it is in fiction, we have no real historical examples of small groups reverting to barbarism for extended periods of time—but we *do* have examples of entire civilizations going blood-mad, from the Aztecs to Pol Pot's Cambodia, and we *do* have countless examples of civilized soldiers using terror and deliberate atrocities to scare their enemies into staying clear: from Tiglath-Pileser to Attila the Hun, from the Norse berserkers to the Mormon Danites, from the shrunken heads of the Amazon jungle to the headhunters of Borneo, human beings have always used terror to say, "Don't mess with us."

Someone out there is trying to send the expanding Alliance that familiar message.

But whoever it is doesn't want an open fight; presumably, they know they'd lose a real war. They're just trying to discourage the Alliance from expanding into "Reaver territory," trying to make it too expensive, too risky, to go in that particular direction, all without letting the Alliance know there's a real enemy out there. They're playing the role of boogeymen, of the monsters from the id, of Sawney Beane, to scare intruders away, trying to maintain a careful balance between being too small to have an effect and too big to ignore. They've deliberately modeled themselves on the most horrific legends they can find, and relied on their victims being too frightened, too demoralized, to realize that a genuine Reaver society, with nothing backing it up, is impossible. After all, people believed in Sawney Beane for more than a hundred years before anyone even began to question the story—why would anyone doubt the reality of the Reavers, when there's solid evidence of their depredations?

It all fits.

And just who are the Reavers, then, if they aren't the actual society that sent the ships out? Are they volunteers, or draftees?

Well, wait a minute—who would volunteer to go out on an unshielded ship to murder and *eat* men, women and children? What sort of society would expect draftees to do that?

Maybe they really *aren't* men. Maybe Jayne was right all along.

Androids, perhaps? Madmen? Criminals offered amnesty if they survive?

And just who did send them? Who's out there? Aliens? Bitter remnants of the rebel Independents, seeking revenge on the Alliance? Some bizarre corporate offshoot within the Alliance, for reasons we can only guess at?

We don't know—and with *Firefly* cancelled, damn it, we probably never will!

Lawrence Watt-Evans is the author of some three dozen novels and over a hundred short stories, mostly in the fields of fantasy, science fiction and horror. He won the Hugo Award for short story in 1988 for "Why I Left Harry's All-Night Hamburgers," served as president of the Horror Writers Association from 1994 to 1996 and treasurer of SFWA from 2003 to 2004, and lives in Maryland. He has two kids in college, a pet snake named Billy-Bob, and the obligatory writer's cat.

I am not enough of a political animal to comment intelligently on issues of the Dangers of Globalism versus the Benefits of Multiculturalism, which seem to me to be raised by this essay. But I do understand the well-reasoned point that Wright is making. Certainly, nonwhite actors are underrepresented on television. Asian and Latino actors ludicrously so. And features of Eastern cultures are sometimes used as shorthand for "exotic." Wright is sure we can do better. Wright is right. (Hee!)

Joss himself would be needed to craft a really informed rebuttal, should he think one necessary, and I hesitate to do anything that could be seen as putting words in his mouth. So this comes from me. Despite the valid arguments that Wright makes, I still see Firefly as having made a step in the right direction. Nonwhite actors were featured in leading roles, an ethnically mixed universe was not just shown, but presupposed, and even white characters reflected the influence of other cultures.

The real shame, it seems to me, is that the disappearance of the show offers little encouragement to others who want to take the next step. The elastic nature of the network television business snaps the norms back into place. I guess the only answer is to keep plucking at them.

Asian Objects in Space

LEIGH ADAMS WRIGHT

THE ALLIANCE.

Futuristic cultural conglomerate, and space cowboy Malcolm Reynolds' worst nightmare. The end result of the twenty-first century's globalization obsession, in a far future marked by a postmodern pastiche of Earth-that-was, a multicultural and multitemporal collage proliferating on a hundred terraformed worlds. Its symbol: a modified Chinese flag superimposed over American stripes.

The sets, the costumes, the sprinklings of Chinese would all have you believe this is a future that, if not precisely perfect, has solved at least one problem we've yet to overcome: the peaceful (possibly corporate-sponsored) merger of all cultures, with meaningful representation for all peoples.

Look at Zoe and Wash. They've been lauded as an anomaly: a happily married, sexually active couple whose relationship is not the focus of the show but rather an unobtrusively integral part of the ship dynamics. What's even more amazing is that no one even bothers to comment on the fact that they're an interracial pairing. The predominant inequality in their relationship is that she's a gorgeous, stacked, battle-hardened warrior and he's an only semimuscular man with an overactive mouth and humorously poor sense of timing—not that he's white and she's black[1]. And no one's ever mentioned it on ship. Clearly this oversight is symptomatic of a society so far beyond our present-day equality struggles that making the couple's difference explicit in the narrative just wouldn't make any sense.

So there are people of color in the 'verse, living in what looks very much like equality. But where are the Asians? The Indians, the Vietnamese, the Filipinos? Most importantly, where are the Chinese, the other half of the great Earth-that-was merger, the *other*, whose vibrant, multifaceted culture Joss and Mutant Enemy have tried their darnedest to integrate into *Firefly*'s kaleidoscopic future world? Where are they?

More present than you'd think, actually. Upon close examination, every crowd scene seems to include a healthy number of nonwhites (though sometimes it's hard to tell, thanks to the layer of rustic western dust that reduces everything to muted earth tones and dim light; poverty and its attendant grime, it should be said, is a great equalizer), and a respectable number of Alliance henchmen and other bad guys look to have at least a couple of ancestors on the Chinese side of the merge.

But of course, despite River and Simon Tam's last name, none of our heroes are Asian. None of the speaking parts in the first and only season went to Asian actors either.

You could blame the world we live in—a world sadly lacking in meaningful parts for Asian actors, resulting in a small pool of potential candidates for speaking roles. But while this argument might go a ways toward explaining the absence of Asian characters on TV *in general*, it falls flat in excusing a show where the premise is a material merger of the Chinese and the American. Surely if Joss really wanted a Chinese actor—or for that matter a Filipino or an Indonesian—he could have

---

[1] Gina Torres happens to be Cuban, but that doesn't preclude her—or Zoe's—blackness.

found a great one, particularly if it was central to the story he wanted to tell.

But how much does the presence of Asian actors matter, really? You can still see the obviously Asian influences on the culture, right? Chinese lanterns, Kaylee's pagoda t-shirt (too bad about that nasty gunshot wound), a belly dancer here and there. I mean, they use chopsticks at dinner. What more evidence do you want that this future has succeeded in creating an ethnically harmonious interplanetary society, a global melting pot with a distinctly Asian flavor?

Well, let's start there—at *a distinctly Asian flavor*.

There's a concept that cultural studies theorist bell hooks[2] terms "eating the other," in which "the other"—the mysterious, the unknown, the exotic—is employed to add "spice" to everyday life. The goal is not a true understanding or appreciation of the Other, but an enhancement of one's own situation, an experiential vacation yielding the conceptual equivalent of a piece of mass-produced Indian pottery and slideshow to impress the neighbors. It's bits of authentic culture recontextualized for a bored white mainstream's use.

Think of Africa used as a backdrop for a British clothing catalog—and the history of colonialism it covers up. Think of hip-hop clothing styles being sold, overpriced, in boutiques where the lower class and minority originators of the trend would be followed under suspicion of shoplifting—and the inequalities this co-opting blithely ignores. Or, more innocuously, the recent trend in screen-printed tees with Japanese characters, divorced from their original linguistic meaning and exploited solely for their decorative aesthetics. Nor is the concept a distinctly Western one—the use of English in Japanese pop culture (songs, commercials, cleaning product labels) signifies not a true engagement with American culture but a simulation of it, borrowed currency in a solely Japanese exchange, a conversation that doesn't extend outside the country's borders.

What's happening here is that cultural artifacts—organic expressions of a particular people, situated in a particular time and place—are being divorced of their meaning in order to be used as a metaphor for something else.

This is what the world of *Firefly* does: it takes Asian culture (Asian cultures), takes each artifact, and strips it of its original meaning until it's just an object ("it doesn't mean what you think"), which can be

---

[2] No, the copyeditor wasn't falling down on the job. hooks' name is lowercased.

used to signify something else entirely—in this case a future in which our world's superpowers have come together into something, we are to believe, entirely new. Like America's recent obsession with yoga (*without* the Buddhist spirituality), the result is entertaining but curiously empty.

The clearest indicator here is the blurring of the line between Chinese and other Asian cultures. Belly dancing is Turkish (among its many other Middle Eastern origins); geisha (Companion precursors) are Japanese. I've taken up the term "Asian" to refer to the whole range of Chinese, Japanese, Indian, etc., signifiers for simplicity's sake—the show didn't distinguish between them, making it difficult for me to. The merge, thus, seems to be less between American and Chinese than it is between west and east in the broadest possible sense. And as in many situations in which you lose the particulars, the result is a vague approximation of nothing at all. Again: pretty, but ultimately without meaning.

Of all the Asian-influenced trimmings of Joss Whedon's newest universe, Inara's geisha-inspired Companion comes the closest to a true engagement with its original's purpose and intent. The Companion's high social status demonstrates a fundamental change in the world as we know it—that not just purchased sex, but purchased company should be not only acceptable, but *respected* as a profession is a marked departure from Western modes of interaction, where selling one's emotional time has always been viewed with suspicion if not downright scorned, from prostitutes to actors. While the geisha model being used here is obviously a romanticized ideal (especially with the show's premature end cutting off future exploration of the role and the role player's experience in it), it does make a sincere effort at understanding the original's place in a mature, civilized society.

So the question to be asked is: what is the metaphor here? What do the chopsticks, the saris, the occasional (untranslated) Chinese curses mean? What are Joss and Mutant Enemy trying to accomplish?

I don't know: I don't have a direct line to the powers that be. But what it does *end up* accomplishing—and very well, I might add—is a sense of *difference. Firefly* looks like no other space show you've ever seen.[3] This is not the future world we usually imagine, not a sterilized *Star Trek* (though the Alliance ships parallel its image strongly enough to make us start thinking about what Gene Roddenberry *wasn't* showing us), not the bleak wasteland of *The Road Warrior*'s environmental collapse; it's

---

[3] Although, like much modern science fiction, it owes a visual debt to *Blade Runner*.

neither utopia nor dystopia. It does not depend on the gut familiarity of a solely white (and male) rule—though plenty of white men still appear to be in charge—for its believability. It asks for more from the viewer, and given the chance, likely would have delivered more as well. The opening scenes of "The Train Job" (intended introduction or no) are particularly adept at communicating to viewers that they're not in Kansas anymore—or at least, not the Kansas they remember. They can't call it a space opera; it's too dirty for that. They can't classify it as a western, really, because—forget spaceships!—who ever heard of a belly dancer in the Wild West?

This use of Asian culture without context may be empty, but it works. It's an immediate cue to viewers, all the more effective for its relative—but not entire—obscurity. It tells us that this world is different, but it is not the kind of difference we are used to: not laser beams or bumpy foreheads, jumpsuits or cyborgs. It's new. And that takes it a step above the average show about spaceships.

So why isn't that good enough?

Using what is Other as a metaphor for difference, as a storytelling aid, is not, in itself, wrong. Metaphor is an essential part of living, whether you're tired as a dog, happy as a clam or as honest as the day is long. It's healthy, vibrant, creative; it lets us make new connections and discover new insights. Would *love* mean the same thing if it had never been compared to a red, red rose, the way it blooms and fades in a season? (Never mind the impact on the flower industry.) In this case the metaphor sets the stage for a richly imagined social order, the difference it implies making it easier for us to see our own situation more clearly.

The problem with this use of Asian culture is that Asians are not inanimate objects, or even far away, abstracted, unknowable Others; they're a strong American minority (not to mention a global majority) struggling to dispel stereotypes and achieve a social equality that's more than just in name. "Asianness" is not something separate, outside, that we can use to understand our own culture better or to picture an exotically future version of ourselves; it *is* us, or part of us. Using it in this manner, as exotic, as a future fantasy and not as a contemporary reality, is damaging to attempts at multiculturalism *now*.

I'm not saying that *Firefly*'s treatment of Asians is a major cultural crime; it's just that I expected more.

And maybe this is just my occasionally slavish devotion to Joss talking, but I can't help thinking that this isn't all there is to it—that, if we'd been given a couple more seasons, there would have been some brilliant, entirely logical, infinitely sensible reason for the lack of Asian representation. It's such a glaring absence as it stands that the writers would have had to say something about it sometime, right?[4]

Maybe all the Chinese people with tongues are hanging out on Sinhon living the high life with the amusingly snooty descendants of those who crossed the wide expanse of space in the USS *Mayflower* starship. Maybe our ragtag bunch of crooked freedom fighters are galactic mutts, so mixed-breed that their original ethnicities have receded into jumbles of facial features the individual origins of which are entirely indistinguishable. Or....

There's a line that was cut from the "Serenity" shooting script. In the scene in which we first met Shepherd Book, fresh out of the Southdown Abbey and walking through the Eavesdown Docks on Persephone looking for passage, in between the interaction he had with the first ship barker and his conversation with Kaylee, we were supposed to see a man, described in the shooting script as "fancy . . . his ship is clearly high class," conducting a bidding for his remaining passenger berths. Part of his spiel: "we are not interested in Asian or Catholic passengers."

It's possible that Joss changed his mind about this part of *Firefly*'s universe, but more likely it just had to be cut for time and he figured, hey, there's plenty of time to get it in someplace else. It's also possible to view this as the isolated prejudice of a single man—a man who was perhaps picked on by a Chinese classmate in the futuristic equivalent of middle school, or mistreated at some past moment by a Chinese-run bureaucracy. But that doesn't seem likely. If he weren't so clearly marked, even in the script, as someone so unmistakebly well-off, his words could be dismissed as the small-minded bigotry of a backwoods (backgalaxy?) space hick resentful of Chinese political power, but he is obviously one of the Alliance's success stories. So what's happening behind the scenes here?

A lot of time has elapsed since humanity left Earth-that-was for greener, less ravaged pastures. Plenty of time for one-half of the great merger to have ascended and the other to have fallen out of favor. Plenty of time for genocidal wars or more insidious (but equally effective) methods of wiping out whole groups of people.

The question is which way the wheel has turned, and why. Are the non-Asians the ones on the governmental outs, forced to eke out liv-

---

[4] What follows could, in any other context, be considered a "fan wank." I prefer to think of it as rigorous critical extrapolation.

ings on the rough-living, imperfectly terraformed planets we see most episodes? Or, as the ship barker's line suggests, are there even worse places to be, somewhere in the universe, where the scattered remnants of our world's most populous ethnicity aren't faring nearly as well as our heroes, even while their cultural trappings are all the fashionable rage, colonized by high society, successfully severed from the peoples who created them? Is this a universe where Asian culture has been eaten, in an almost literal sense, with its own chopsticks?

If so, it's an old story. Our history is full of genocides and ethnic cleansings, of the exploitation if not destruction of one neighbor by another. Maybe, in *Firefly*, our world hasn't been altered all that much at all. Maybe it's just another example of that old adage: the more we change, the more we stay the same.

After all, isn't that what Joss & Co. were really trying to say? Humanity is what it is, wherever it goes. No matter how far out we travel, we can't ever escape ourselves.

Leigh Adams Wright is an intellectual dilettante, and a fan of anything that pushes boundaries, dares to confound and includes chickens.

I'm nowhere near this particular offering. I'm way over in the corner. In fact, I think I saw me leave an hour ago.

The Rise and Fall
(and Rise) of *Firefly*
(the Behind-the-Scenes Story)

GLENN YEFFETH

THIS IS A JOKE. FOX executives, to the best of my knowledge, take only legal pharmaceuticals, make love (gently) to only their spouses and make all their programming decisions based on thoughtful analysis and intelligent consideration. Okay?

FOX Programming Department
"Fair and balanced programming"
EARLY "NUTCRUSHER" JUBAL, VICE PRESIDENT, FOX PROGRAMMING

July 17, 2001

Dear Josh,

Great seeing you at the party last week. My God, does Marty know how to throw a party, or what? My sinuses still hurt! And the idea of bringing in a film crew, inviting a horde of D-list bimbos and pretending we were shooting *Who Wants to Be a FOX Television Star*? Brilliant, just brilliant. Normally we have to pay those girls!

Listen, I've heard good things about you and that *Bunny the Vampire* show and I'm starting to think you might be ready for the big time, you lucky SOB! Honestly, I can't remember much of what you were talking about except it had something to do with space and rocket ships and stuff, and you know how big that *Star Wars* is.

Anyway, I'm mostly a conceptual guy, and I think this is very promising. Write up a proposal for me and I'll take a look. Do it fast, before I forget about it. I'm a busy guy, as you can imagine.

This just might be your lucky day. Don't blow it.

Yours in quality programming,

Early

.   .   .

FOX Programming Department
"Celebrity Midget Wrestling…it's the next big thing"
EARLY "NUTCRUSHER" JUBAL, VICE PRESIDENT, FOX PROGRAMMING

October 3, 2001

Dear "Joss,"

Sorry it's taken me this long to get back to you...I've just been swamped. I've been trying to get my celebrity sumo wrestling show going but I've only been able to sign up Rush Limbaugh and Hilary Duff, and our lawyers are all worried about liability. And I had this idea for a date rape reality show that our lawyers squashed in the first go-around. We have too many laws in this country!

Anyway, read the script and proposal you sent. Well, actually, I read the two-page synopsis my secretary prepared. Specifically, she read it to me, while sitting on my lap. But that's not the point.

The point is...brilliant! Just brilliant! I knew you had it in you and I loved what you did. LOVED IT!

I want you to do another round on this, but I can tell you I'm very, very positive. Now I have some editorial "suggestions" I want you to incorporate into the next draft:

1. It's pretty clear from your script that the Alliance represents the Democratic Party, in its ongoing efforts to crush state rights and tax us into oblivion. And obviously, Malcolm Reynolds is intended to be George W. Bush. Very nice. But Americans aren't exactly quick on the uptake (at least FOX viewers aren't, according

to our studies) so it wouldn't hurt to make it a bit more explicit. Let's work in an evil Alliance leader named "Heinz Kerry" who speaks with a French accent.

2. Let's make the Reavers evil Muslims. Also, can you put a big "W" on the ship?

3. I can see you are going for a Sam and Diane thing with Reynolds and the whore. That's fine, but can't they still have sex? Remember the rules from the FOX Programming Guide (I did send you this, didn't I)? Let me remind you of the first five rules:

Rule #1: Tits
Rule #2: Gratuitous sex
Rule #3: Breasts
Rule #4: Explosions
Rule #5: Washed-up celebrities and/or midgets

As you can see, you can easily comply with rules #1, #2 and #3 just with the whore. See that you do.

4. Can one of your crew be a midget? Or Anna Nicole Smith? Or maybe JJ from *Good Times*?

5. Did my secretary screw up or are you making Malcolm an atheist? That might have flown pre-9/11, but we are at war with the Godless now, and the Muslims too I think. So change this. If you really feel the need to be exotic you can make him Catholic, but that's the limit. I don't need Ashcroft on my ass.

6. You can have Wash and Zoe married, or you can let them have sex, but not both. No one wants to see married couples having sex! Sheesh! And they say I'm sick.

7. Can we make Badger French or German? The English are on our side.

8. This is my secretary's stupidity, I'm sure—she's a bit of a dimwit, but hot—but she doesn't seem to think any of the crew are aliens. How ignorant can you get—thinking anyone would make a space show without aliens! Anyway, which one of the crew is the alien? If it's the whore you might want to consider giving her three breasts.

Yours in quality programming,

Early

* * *

FOX Programming Department
"Our attention span is as short as yours"
EARLY "NUTCRUSHER" JUBAL, VICE PRESIDENT, FOX PROGRAMMING

October 10, 2001

Dear Joss,

Your response to my note of October 3 was way out of line; don't be so sensitive. We are partners here and, I like to think, friends.

Also, I don't think that it's an exaggeration of the facts to say that your career, your financial well-being and the lives of you and your family are dependent on the vagaries of my whim, so I'd watch my step if I were you.

You are lucky that I'm in a great mood. My new reality project "Sexiest Relationship" is rocking! The concept is that we pair up three single men and three single women who have never met before. We form them into three couples, and they compete before our celebrity judges to see which couple is sexiest. Now here's the twist—each couple consists of twins, separated at birth! The episode where they find out they are twins is absolutely hysterical! My sides hurt from laughing!

So I'm going to forgive you this time. I'm greenlighting you for thirteen episodes. It had better be good.

Yours in quality programming,

Early

* * *

FOX Programming Department
"Hilary Duff has regained the use of most of her limbs…she's fine, really"
EARLY "NUTCRUSHER" JUBAL, VICE PRESIDENT, FOX PROGRAMMING

May 3, 2002

Dear Joss,

Your pilot sucked. One word. BORING.

I'm a busy man, and to have to take time out to watch a piece of crap like this pilot pains me. Obviously, I didn't watch the whole thing. I had my secretary edit it down to the most interesting seventeen minutes—nevertheless I fell asleep twice.

The only part that caught my eye was the naked girl in the box...and then it turns out she's his sister! Boring! Have you considered making all the girls whores? Sort of a Mustang Ranch in space? Now that would bring ratings!

Things continue to go well for me. Our administration contacts are paying off, and it looks like our Guantanamo Bay reality show is going to happen. As it turns out, enemy combatants don't have to sign releases. In fact, according to my administration sources, *they have no rights at all.* Not even Geneva Convention! This is a reality show producer's wet dream, as you can well imagine. We've promised John A. that we'll keep the death toll down, but otherwise we have free rein. This will be huge. This will be bigger than *Littlest Groom* and *Celebrity Boxing* combined!

So life is good, and I'm feeling generous. I'm giving you another chance. I'm going to make my instructions clear, because I sense you aren't real good with instructions.

One, dump the pilot. It's not remotely savable.

Two, make a new pilot. It needs to have the following elements: torture (ideally by someone with an Old Europe accent), a big shootout, a whore (with a heart of gold), trains (everyone likes trains), and the gratuitous but justified murder of a captured prisoner (special request from John A.). Can you manage this? Let me rephrase. Manage this!

We need a script in two days. So stop loafing around!

Did I make it clear that your *job* is at stake?

Yours in quality programming,

Early

* * *

FOX Programming Department
"See The Littlest Honeymoon on FOX Pay Per View"
EARLY "NUTCRUSHER" JUBAL, VICE PRESIDENT, FOX PROGRAMMING

July 25, 2002

Dear Joss,

I watched seven minutes of your new pilot and I guess it was OK. We're going to go forward with *Firefly* Friday nights (except for nights when there's baseball, or a new reality show's second showing, or when we just forget).

Frankly, my main reason is to screw James Cameron, who is worse at taking direction than you are. If he took my advice (hint: her special power is nymphomania) *Dark Angel* would have been bigger than *The Anna Nicole Smith Show*. Sorry, Jimmy, go back to making third-rate movies, you loser!

So you finally made the big time, after wasting away at the wannabe networks (FOX is the third-largest network, you know, by certain obscure measures). Good for you!

Don't blow it.

Yours in quality programming,

Early

• • •

FOX Programming Department
"Morons need television, too (actually, they need it more)"
EARLY "NUTCRUSHER" JUBAL, VICE PRESIDENT, FOX PROGRAMMING

September 22, 2002

Dear Joss,

I just looked at the ratings for "The Train Job." Maybe you should have called it "The Blow Job," because it SUCKED.

A couple of points that you shouldn't need me to tell you:

One, the whore has way too many clothes. Maybe she always dresses in a bikini, or a genie suit like in *I Dream of Jeannie*?

Two, they shouldn't be stealing; that's practically against the law! You should make them catch thieves using high-tech investigative techniques, like in *CSI*, but in the future. That show does great, you know. I wish it was on FOX.

Three, you need a new sound man. I couldn't make out half the dialogue...it could have been Chinese for all I could tell. That isn't the kind of quality FOX viewers have come to expect.

Do I need to remind you that I turned down *Amputee Bachelorette* to make room for *Firefly*?

Yours in quality programming,

Early

* * *

FOX Programming Department

"Coming soon, Morbidly Obese, where the biggest gainers are the biggest winners"

EARLY "NUTCRUSHER" JUBAL, VICE PRESIDENT, FOX PROGRAMMING

September 29, 2002

Dear Joss,

"Bushwhacked" ratings are down, and are terrible. You need to think out of the box, shift your paradigm, move your cheese, whatever! You need to do something quick.

The ending in particular was so so weak. Instead of skulking away, you should have had them blowing up the Alliance ship. Everyone knows that the really big ships always have one sensitive spot that if you shoot it, or even hit it with a rock, it blows up. Why couldn't they attack that spot?

I'm looking into whether we can get Paris Hilton to do a guest spot...maybe she can be some kind of sex alien.

Yours in quality programming,

Early

P.S. "Bushwhacked" isn't some sort of political reference is it? It had better not be. Trust me, these guys have NO sense of humor.

• • •

FOX Programming Department
"Are you watching TV right now? You should be!"
EARLY "NUTCRUSHER" JUBAL, VICE PRESIDENT, FOX PROGRAMMING

November 17, 2002

Dear Joss,

As you know, *Firefly* ratings continue to be terrible. I heard you in an interview where you described *Firefly* as an "intelligent" show. I hope you were not serious about this. "Intelligent" is the kiss of death; this explains a lot.

Anyway, your show is killing us, and I'm thinking we will soon return the favor.

Yours in quality programming,

Early

• • •

FOX Programming Department
"Get Venom, the new fragrance available at fox.com. Each bottle of Venom guaranteed to have genuine O'Reilly spittle."
EARLY "NUTCRUSHER" JUBAL, VICE PRESIDENT, FOX PROGRAMMING

December 8, 2002

Dear Joss,

Saw "War Stories" (three and a half minutes' worth, which was plenty). What's with the lesbian stuff...this isn't *Bunny*, you know.

By the way, you missed the chance to have a great mano a mano fight at the end of the show between Mal and that torturer guy, like in *Lethal Weapon*. What were you thinking?

Yours in quality programming,

Early

P.S. Hilary Duff is suing FOX, the wimp, and my bosses are pissed. I blame you for this (my reasons are obscure but heartfelt).

*   *   *

FOX Programming Department

"Proud to be cancelling rubbish such as Firefly, Wonderfalls, The Tick, Futurama *and* Andy Richter Controls the Universe*"*

EARLY "NUTCRUSHER" JUBAL, VICE PRESIDENT, FOX PROGRAMMING

December 20, 2002

Dear: Joss

We at FOX are delighted to have featured your excellent show, Firebug, as part of our programming lineup. The many excellent reviews and critical acclaim that your show, Firebug has received is a source of pride for our network.

Nevertheless, after reviewing the ratings of the first fifteen minutes of the pilot episode, we are very sorry to have to tell you that we've decided to:

cancel

put into indefinite hiatus

sell to al jazeera

your excellent show, Firebug . The remaining episodes will be:

aired at the usual time

aired sometime after midnight

aired on FX

ritually burned at our weekly orgy

Obviously, this is difficult for all of us. In order to smooth your transition to AM radio, we will be keeping you, and your team, on the payroll until the end of the day. Thanks are not necessary.

It's been my pleasure to be associated with your groundbreaking show.

Yours in quality programming,

Early Jubal

*   *   *

Early "Nice Guy" Jubal
"Will Work for Food"
INDEPENDENT CONSULTANT

September 6, 2003

Dear Mr. Whedon,

I couldn't help but notice that your wonderful series *Firefly* is being made into a major motion picture
by Universal Pictures. I couldn't be happier for you;
I've always been a big fan of *Firefly* and of all of your
work.

　As it happens, I may be available to work with you
on *Serenity*; I'm very flexible regarding specific positions.

　I look forward to your call.

　Your friend,

Early

---

*Glenn Yeffeth is a publisher, editor and writer (in that order) and has
edited* Taking the Red Pill, Seven Seasons of *Buffy* and Five Seasons
of *Angel. As with many explorations of the occult, Glenn's attempts to
channel a FOX executive quickly went from fun and silly to grotesque
and deeply scary. Fully recovered now, Glenn has resumed his normal
life (except for the compulsive need to shower seven times a day).*

Ginjer Buchanan is a very smart woman. I think she gets this exactly right. Perversely, she makes me want to go out and combine unpopular genres, just to prove it can be done. Because sometimes it's the very combination of two unlikely ingredients, neither of which can stand on its own, that creates magic. I offer as proof those little pre-packaged treats of peanut butter sandwiched between cheese-flavored crackers. A darn fine snack. Someone, clearly, decided to take cheese-flavored crackers, which have a loyal but small group of followers, and peanut butter, which hasn't been successful in vending machines in decades, and combine them. And it worked.

Never give up.

Who Killed *Firefly?*

GINJER BUCHANAN

THE ANSWER TO THE QUESTION POSED ABOVE, most would say, is "FOX Executives in the Boardroom with Bad Decisions." Clearly, they didn't understand the show, and further aggravated the situation by some amazingly dumb scheduling choices. I've been to or on enough *Firefly* panels at conventions and read enough online to know that is the general consensus among the fans, both those who watched from the beginning and those who discovered the series on DVD.

Certainly, there is some truth to that opinion. FOX, in its desperate search for another Friday at eight P.M. hit, a la *The X-Files*, has failed to understand a long list of series, ranging from Chris Carter's very own *Harsh Realm* through *Brimstone* through *John Doe*. They obviously have no clue what made *X-Files* a success, but they have figured out that it was at least partially because it wasn't easily categorized. It wasn't a cop show, or a doctor show, or a lawyer show. So they keep programming that time slot with things that are also not cop/lawyer/doctor shows, in hopes that ratings lightning will strike once again. And then giving up on the chosen projects when the magic doesn't happen quickly enough. So, in a sense, *Firefly* was just the next cow out of the chute.

But my premise is that there are those, other than the usual suspects, who share culpability in *Firefly's* demise. And I intend to name names and point fingers. But first, let me present the evidence, in the form of a brief guided tour through the history of genre television, westerns and science fiction specifically.

In the beginning was *Captain Video*. And *The Lone Ranger*. The year was 1949. Back when the number of households owning television sets was barely triple digit. *Captain Video* ran daily on DuMont. *The Lone Ranger*, originally a radio serial, was on ABC once a week. *Captain Video*, done on a budget of $2.27 an episode, was a huge hit—or as huge of a hit as a series could be on a network that was soon to be driven out of existence. *The Lone Ranger*, on until 1957, was in the Top Ten in 1950—the first year that ratings existed.

Now, even back then, programmers existed, too. And, seeing the success of these two shows, they applied to the rapidly growing media the newly articulated First Rule of Scheduling: if it works, do more of it.

Thus were born *Tom Corbett, Space Cadet* (which during its run appeared on ABC, CBS *and* NBC), *Space Patrol* and *Buck Rogers* (based on the comic strip), half-hour shows rooted firmly in the pulp sci-fi (and I use that term purposefully) of their day. Action. Adventure. Heroic pilots and their young sidekicks. Phallic rocket ships. Mad scientists. Killer robots. Nubile blondes threatened by killer robots and mad scientists. Plots that Robert Heinlein could have written. Pure unadulterated space opera—but then sophistication was *not* the watchword in the very early days of television, across the board.

And thus was also born the horse opera. Shows featuring square-jawed, straight-shooting heroes abounded. Hopalong Cassidy. (I mean, really—*Hopalong*??) Roy Rogers. Gene Autry (star of perhaps the earliest sf/western crossover known to man—*Gene Autry and the Phantom Empire*).

Some sang. Some had faithful gal pals and/or faithful comic sidekicks. All had faithful horses that had names and distinct personalities. (Gene Autry's horse Champion even had his own series in 1955!)

Some were period pieces; some were modern day. (Roy's comic sidekick had a faithful jeep named Nellybelle.) They grew out of movie serials, where the heroes and villains (who indeed often wore black hats) were clearly defined. And they proved to be very popular.

The ripped-from-the-pages-of-*Astounding*-magazine shows, on the other hand, didn't do all that well. And the programmers took note.

Flash forward a bit, to 1955, when the first western for grown-ups debuted in what we would now call prime time—*Gunsmoke*, whose parentage traced not to the movie serial but (as with *The Lone Ranger*) to a radio drama. It was complex, character-driven—and it became the first "longest-running series on television."

(It was followed the same year by another redone radio show, *The Life and Legend of Wyatt Earp*, a similarly complex show, which during its six-year run told a highly arced, continuing story.)

Gunsmoke was more of the same, yet different, in that Marshal Dillon, while square-jawed and straight-shooting, was rather world-weary. He did have a comic sidekick *and* a gal pal, but his horse was nameless and he never, ever sang. Exemplary of the "a man's gotta do what a man's gotta do" school of drama, Marshal Dillon, every week, went stolidly about his job—keeping the streets of Dodge safe for decent folks—but sometimes his white hat got a bit soiled and often the color of the other guy's hat wasn't all that clear.

The early westerns had been popular, but *Gunsmoke* reached an entirely new level of success. It was most definitely working—so everyone decided to do more of it. In 1955, there were seven westerns on the three networks. By 1958, there were twenty-four.

Some of them—particularly those that came from the Warner Brothers "stable" (or to be specific the Warner back lot western set, which to anyone who has been watching TV since the fifties, would be as familiar as his or her own backyard)—did away with the supporting cast and focused on a single protagonist (my guess is that was because hiring one Clint Walker was cheaper than hiring one James Arness, plus one Milburn Stone, plus one Dennis Weaver, plus one Amanda Blake). *Cheyenne. Bronco. Sugarfoot. Maverick.* No one sang, although each series had a theme song that ran over the credits. Horses were nameless. Gal pals were picked up along the way—a different pal every week, usually. A man still had to do what he had to do—but it wasn't necessarily his *job* to do it. (And in the case of Bret Maverick, he tried to avoid doing it if at all possible.)

Later series, not filmed at WB, reached for variants upon ensemble. They were chock full of manly men driving cattle (*Rawhide*), running ranches with their motherless sons (*Bonanza*), or leading wagon trains across the prairie (*Wagon Train*). No singing—except for the occasional guest star and once or twice when an excuse was found to have Flint McCullough, the wagon train scout (played by musical stage actor Robert Horton) burst into song. There were no clever horses, although, since we are talking ensemble here, comic relief sidekicks were present.

For a decade or more, westerns, in one form or another, ruled the airwaves. Only two science fiction series—one based on a successful movie (*Voyage to the Bottom of the Sea*) and one based on Robert Louis Stevenson (*Lost in Space*)—appeared, and were moderately successful. Though not quite as pulpish as the offerings of the fifties, neither could be said to be a masterpiece of nuance.

Thus was the state of network television (and of course there wasn't anything except network television then) in 1965–66 when a man named Gene Roddenberry sold a sci-fi series to NBC, using as his pitch "*Wagon Train* to the Stars" (*Wagon Train* had gone off the air the previous year).

Well, the show wasn't that really—but I assume Gene knew that "Horatio Hornblower to the Stars" wasn't going to cut it with the executives, so he did what every smart producer does when pitching a new idea—he lied.

So Gene, the Great Bird of the Galaxy, brought forth *Star Trek*—a science fiction series most definitely not in the pulp tradition. A little Horatio H., a little male action-adventure (Roddenberry was ex-military and an ex-cop). And a *lot* of the producer's own decidedly liberal vision of what the future could be/should be like.

That future would be one in which all the nations of the Earth (while still producing native sons with marked accents and ethnic identities) were nonetheless at peace. A future where we were color-blind. Where women were equal to men. (Kinda.) Where war was no more. A future where we wanted only to come in peace all over the galaxy—a galaxy *teeming* with intelligent alien life. (Keep that in mind—it's important.)

But *Trek*, alas, was only a qualified success, although it generated a lot of buzz and got serious critical attention for the issues it tackled. Premiering in 1966, it was off by 1969. Following its failure, it looked for a while as though science fiction on television was as dead as—the western.

Because, by this time in the history of the tube, boots and saddles were right out of fashion, too. Sure there were a few *Bonanza* offspring, like *Big Valley* and *High Chaparral*. But they were more soap-oaters than classic westerns. By 1975, when *Gunsmoke* finally ended its twenty-year run, it was the *only* western on the prime-time schedule. Except for a failed attempt to resurrect Bret Maverick in 1981, no new western series debuted on network in the eighties. At all.

For the next decade, other genres dominated television. Sitcoms and heartwarming family dramas had come into their own. (I didn't watch a lot of TV in the eighties. . . .) Even the phenomenal success of a little movie called *Star Wars* couldn't revitalize the science fiction genre on the small screen, although the producer of *Battlestar Galactica* (which really *was Wagon Train* to the stars—starring Pa from *Bonanza!*) tried.

But help was on the way, in the person of none other than Gene Roddenberry. Corporately exhilarated by the continuing success of the original *Star Trek* in syndication, and presented with a television landscape that allowed it to sell its product to broadcast outlets other than the networks (there were four by this time, FOX having just grown from netlet to network), Paramount got Gene back on the Bridge. In 1987, *Star Trek: The Next Generation* premiered. Followed over the next couple of decades by *Star Trek: Deep Space Nine* and *Star Trek: Voyager*. They were successful enough to trigger the "let's do more" response in programmers, which led to *Babylon 5*. And to a certain extent, to *Stargate* and *Alien Nation*. (Although the underlying intellectual properties for both were films.) The audiences for these shows, none of which were on the major networks, weren't huge—but they were loyal enough to allow these series to have some success, even before the existence of the specialized umbrella that is the Sci-Fi Channel. Not that it was easy—I'm sure that *Bab 5* and *SG-1* fans could quote chapter and verse on the vicissitudes of these series—but they did get made (and *SG-1* has gone on to great success on Sci-Fi).

It goes without saying that all of the *Trek* iterations are set in the same future that Gene Roddenberry imagined. But more than that, though he is no longer with us, his notion of a galaxy populated with an almost infinite number of alien species (yes, I know they all look a lot like us with various facial blemishes, but they are alien, dammit! Gene said so.) has prevailed. Certainly, *Bab 5* takes place in the Roddenberry-verse. And *Farscape*. And *Andromeda*. And *SG-1*, which long ago diverted from its source material. In fact, I can't think of any successful space-set science fiction series that hasn't featured a universe teeming with intelligent alien life. Television viewers think science fiction and then just automatically think "Vulcan" or "Cardassian." *Trek* is iconic—and it's hard to ignore icons.

So, we are now well into the nineties, and science fiction has reestablished itself as a moderately successful niche genre, thanks largely to the late Mr. Roddenberry. But where has the western been during this time? Well, pretty much nowhere. The proliferation of channels has allowed a few attempts to revitalize the genre. *The Young Riders*, a network show, in 1989. *Lonesome Dove* in 1994. (All right, if you want to count *Dr. Quinn*, you can. But I'm not going to talk about it. . . .)

And, of course, in 1993 that other glorious attempt to meld the two genres of western and sf—the late, lamented *The Adventures of Brisco County, Jr.* (a series with a square-jawed, straight-shooting hero, a faithful clever horse named Comet, a faithful companion, a faithful comic sidekick, a somewhat-faithful gal pal—and a time-traveling villain who wore a black hat and carried an Orb of Power). Boy-howdy, did it fail!

It was pretty clear that the western was kaput. Completely. (And remains so. To date, it seems that *Deadwood* stands pretty much alone.)

Which brings us into the new millennium. The television landscape is western-free. There's some science fiction, but it's very niche-y—and most of it has Mr. Roddenberry's fingerprints all over it.

FOX TV is looking to program Friday night at eight—the death slot. They go to Joss Whedon, the successful television producer of two genre series. Joss, as he said at great length in all of the preshow hype interviews for *Firefly*, *loves* westerns. He also, being Joss, has his own definite notion of the future. It's rigorously worked out, very believable (probably the most believable sf future that has ever been done on the small screen)—and not at all a happy place. Plus, we *are* alone. No aliens, human or muppet-oid, share the cosmos with us. Humanity is it. We got problems, they are of our making, and we gotta solve them on our own. (There isn't even a furry alien pet on *Serenity*...and you know if furry alien pets existed, Kaylee would have one.)

Bleak much?

At any rate, the show gets made, and it premieres (after it is made somewhat less bleak, at least in theory), and it dies, an early, untimely and unnatural death.

Killed. But by whom?

Well, primarily by the FOX executives who cancelled it.

But I say that they are not the only culprits.

J'accuse two others of being complicit in the crime.

First—Gene Roddenberry, for creating a science fictional future that has so much emotional power and longevity that for many genre television viewers, it (or some variant of it) *is* the future. I deduced his culpability after the ninth or tenth person that I know who *should* have been a *Firefly* fan said, in so many words, "Where are the aliens? It can't be science fiction—there are no aliens. It's just a western with spaceships and I don't like westerns." Thank you, Gene. If we ever do get Out There, I hope we aren't too disappointed not to find Worf waiting to greet us, even though we will be prepared to converse with him in his own language.

And second—Joss Whedon. Brilliant man, great writer. A creative genius, possibly. And a definite follower of pop culture. So he *must* have noticed that the western was, like, totally moribund....

How did his thought process go, I wonder? "Let's take two marginal genres, one of which tends to have loyal though small audiences and one of which hasn't been successful on television in decades, *and combine them!*"

Creatively bold—and enormously risky. Particularly when *Firefly* was headed into the black hole of eight P.M. Friday night on FOX, a network that—while claiming to want it—hadn't shown much patience with bold and risky in the past. I stand in awe of his chutzpah—while I mourn the fact that it produced a show that, in my humble opinion, was doomed from the start. Even given a different time slot on a different night, it would have been difficult for the series to find a viewership beyond those (myself among them) who will watch anything that Joss has a hand in. (This does not include all *Buffy/Angel* fans, by the way. Many of them didn't even sample *Firefly.*) *Firefly* had to reach beyond them, but Joss' vision was simply not going to resonate with the core television science fiction audience, raised from the cradle to think of the future in *Trek* terms. And, realistically speaking, there wasn't any television western audience around to reach! (Those of us who are old enough to remember—fondly—the days of twenty-four westerns a week are not the Coveted Demographic, so FOX wouldn't have much cared if we were tuning in anyway!)

So, in conclusion, I hold that multiple perps killed *Firefly.* The impatient and clueless folks at FOX. The spirit of Gene Roddenberry. And Joss hisownself, whose brave attempt to create an intelligent, adult sf/western hybrid television series was ill-timed and ill-placed.

Case closed!

Ginjer Buchanan, born in Pittsburgh, Pennsylvania, long enough ago to remember the invention of television, moved to New York City to work in social services. She also freelanced for Pocket Books as consulting editor for the Star Trek *novel program. In 1984, she was offered a full-time job as an editor at Ace Books. Her current title is Senior Executive Editor and Marketing Director, Ace/Roc books. Her first novel, a* Highlander *tie-in titled* White Silence, *was published in February of 1999, and she had an essay in the third* Buffy the Vampire Slayer *episode guide.*

Laws and sausages, the saying goes, are the two things you are better off not watching as they are created. I would add to the list nuclear fireballs, bleu cheese and television pilots.

The process of creating a show, selling a show and getting that show to the air is complex. The writer and the studio and the network have, in fact, the same goal: a popular and creative product that everyone can be proud of. It's tempting to imagine that network executives don't care about the "pride" part, but they do. They just have to balance it against issues of the checkbook that writers can pretend to be above.

The process of "development," in which studio and network executives help shape a show through their decisions and suggestions, can either clarify a writer's voice or obscure it. I know of several examples of executive's notes that allowed a word-weary writer to find a clearer focus, to allow their vision to reach their viewers. I myself have received notes like that, for which I am very grateful.

But sometimes adding other brains to a creative process is like adding more dogs to a sled. If they pull in a different direction, even if they are just off by a few degrees, the sled goes nowhere, or even overturns, leaving everyone with snow down their pants.

Did that happen with Firefly? This thoughtful essay analyzes a number of choices made early in the show's run. If different choices had been made, he makes a case, maybe we'd've all had a good sight less frost on our nethers.

"The Train Job" Didn't Do the Job: Poor Opening Contributed to *Firefly's* Doom

KEITH R.A. DeCANDIDO

THE FIRST EPISODE OF A TELEVISION SHOW makes or breaks it. That is when people give it its first shot and decide whether or not to keep watching. If they're bored half an hour in, if the characters don't engage them, if the plot is dull, they switch the channel and never watch again. If they're engrossed, if they care about the characters, if the setting intrigues them, if the dialogue sparkles, if the acting shines, then they'll be back next week. And for many weeks after that.

But the onus is on that first episode to create the right first impression. Just as broccoli in your teeth can ruin a blind date, a poor first episode will kill any chance of a relationship between viewer and series.

Science fiction and fantasy shows have it much harder, as the one thing a genre show has to do that others don't is establish the setting. sf and fantasy are the only fictional genres in which the setting isn't real—or is changed in some significant way from what we know to be real (vampires exist, aliens have landed on the planet, etc.).

In Joss Whedon's two previous shows, *Buffy the Vampire Slayer* and *Angel*, he was fortunate in that the world-building was already done—for *Buffy* in the feature film the show spun off of, for *Angel* in *Buffy*—and both shows took place in contemporary America. However, with *Firefly*, Whedon had to create a universe from scratch while still telling a good two hours of television.

And therein lies the first problem: two hours. Very few two-hour pilots can really justify their length. After viewing "Serenity," the two-hour *Firefly* pilot, FOX rejected it and asked for a new one-hour leadoff for the show—which unfortunately had to be written over a weekend, as Whedon and Tim Minear revealed in the DVD commentary for that hastily written new first episode, "The Train Job." This would be viewers' introduction to Whedon's new universe.

There are many things that killed *Firefly*. Its schedule was sometimes erratic in the beginning, thanks to FOX also showing the baseball postseason (though a big chunk of the advertising for the show was also done during those games). FOX also showed the episodes out of order, which caused problems; though not as "arc-based" as such genre shows as *Babylon 5* or *Star Trek: Deep Space Nine*, or even Whedon's other two shows, *Firefly* did have a proper running order, and FOX's episode shuffling messed with that.

But to my mind, the thing that really killed *Firefly* was "The Train Job." By showing this episode instead of "Serenity" first—indeed, by not airing "Serenity" until late December, after the show had been cancelled—FOX did not give the show an opportunity to make that good first impression, nor did it give viewers sufficient reason to tune in the following week.

FOX's standards for success are considerably higher than they are for the WB or UPN—which are, in turn, higher than they are for cable or syndication. Shows like *Stargate SG-1* and *The Dead Zone*—not to mention *Deadwood* and *The Shield*—can afford to attract a smaller viewership because a show needs considerably fewer viewers to be successful on Showtime, Sci-Fi, USA, HBO or FX. Those shows can thus afford to appeal to a more limited audience because that'll be enough to sustain them.

On the big four networks, however, the appeal has to be *much* broader. *Buffy* and *Angel* were always at the top of the WB's ratings charts, and the former occupied a similar spot atop UPN's in its last two seasons, but *Firefly* needed to attract considerably more viewers than either show enjoyed in order to be viable on FOX. This meant it needed to go beyond the realm of genre fans and into that oh-so-nebulous group, the mass audience.

"The Train Job" wasn't the way to start.

Leaving aside the fact that, as one of the fourteen episodes of *Firefly*, I would rank "The Train Job" in the bottom three, it pretty much struck all the wrong notes for the necessary introductory world-building.

In "The Train Job," the conflict between the Alliance and the Independence movement—on which both Mal and Zoe fought for the losing independent side—was not shown to the viewer, but told in a standard bar fight scene. (Fill in obligatory "show-don't-tell" rule of writing here.) Book, River and Simon's reasons for being onboard *Serenity* weren't shown, but rather told in some awful expository dialogue between Mal and Book. Later on, the crew's usual work was discussed by Book and Inara in a similarly clumsy scene unworthy of the talents of either fine scriptwriter.

Jayne is a much more complex character than he came off as in "The Train Job," where he was simply obnoxious and tried to take over the ship when Mal and Zoe were captured. The new viewer was left to wonder what possible reason Mal had for keeping him around. At least in "Serenity" (and in other episodes), his usefulness was made clear. All he did in "The Train Job" was ride on a hook. Beyond that, Jayne ascribed less-than-noble motives to Mal for taking Simon and River in, when in fact the only one with less-than-noble motives was Jayne himself (as was later seen in "Ariel").

However, the worst aspects of "The Train Job" were the villain and the plot. Niska was a ridiculously simplistic villain. Most of the bad guys on *Firefly* were arrogant rich people who exploited the poorer folk for their own benefit (Magistrate Higgins in "Jaynestown," Atherton Wing in "Shindig," Rance Burgess in "Heart of Gold," Durran in "Trash," not to mention the Alliance in general). Indeed, one of the main themes of *Firefly* was that of exploitation, and the separation between haves and have-nots; the majority of the villains on the show reflected that. But Niska was just a brutal, sadistic gangster, complete with Eastern European accent to make it clear that he's *really* nasty. In case that wasn't enough, we saw him torturing a man who stole from him. Tellingly, the DVD commentary on "The Train Job" reveals that FOX requested a larger-than-life villain for the first episode, which goes contrary to the whole point of *Firefly*. What made Higgins, Wing, Burgess, Durran, et al., effective was that they *weren't* larger than life; they were recognizable people who happened to have a certain amount of power. Niska was larger than life, yes, but he was also distressingly over-the-top.

Niska's one-dimensional villainy also presented another problem: Mal and the gang's willingness to do business with him—worse, their choosing to not ask what they were being contracted to steal—gave the viewer absolutely no reason to like our alleged heroes. The episode did nothing to show us the severity of *Serenity*'s plight. Instead, the crew came across as petty thieves who were only in it for venal purposes. The motives behind their need for independence, the hatred Mal carries for the Alliance and for being beholden to anyone else and the economic desperation that is part and parcel of their daily lives wasn't at all clear, and the casual viewer wasn't going to tune in the week after to find out. Mal's change of heart when he found out they were medical supplies, needed to help sick colonists, was too little, too late. He had the opportunity to find out what he was stealing back at Niska's, and for him to suddenly get self-righteous came across as disingenuous, a feeble attempt to make him look more heroic than the plot allowed him to be.

Although the sheriff, when he recovered the medical supplies from Mal, said that he could understand why, in these times, someone would take a job without looking too close, it was yet another case of telling rather than showing, and the audience had been presented with insufficient evidence to support the sheriff's statement.

On top of all that, the eponymous heist was very unconvincing—especially the part where the very large spaceship hovered over the train for a long time while stealing the goods, and nobody seemed to notice. (The sheriff's inquiries after the heist never mentioned the huge Firefly-class ship that hovered over the car with the medical supplies for five minutes, which is difficult to believe.)

The episode was not all bad; it was full of the good characterization and crackling dialogue that is the hallmark of shows with Whedon's executive producer credit after the final fade. Those viewers who knew the track record of both Whedon and Minear (not to mention Ben Edlund, creator of *The Tick*, whose presence on the writing staff was a huge plus) would be willing to give it a shot after this weak opening. But most viewers—the larger audience that the show needed—would not.

When "Serenity" finally did air, the dedicated viewers who remained (or who got to watch it first on the DVD set) were gnashing their teeth, because everything that "The Train Job" did wrong "Serenity" did right.

We *saw* Mal and Zoe in the war; we saw their hopeless final battle in Serenity Valley, and saw Mal do everything possible to keep his troops' morale and hopes alive, only to find them dashed by Command's orders to lay down their weapons. The slow-motion shot of the devastated look on Mal's face as the Alliance ships descended with no retaliation from Independent air support was a visual that seared itself on the viewer's consciousness.

We *saw* the contrast between the Alliance's high-tech shininess (via the *Dortmunder*) and the horrible life led by those on the outskirts on Persephone. (That contrast was present in "The Train Job" to some extent, admittedly.)

We *saw* Book's arrival on *Serenity*.

We *saw* River and Simon's arrival, and the story behind their fugitive status.

We *saw* the desperation of *Serenity*'s situation when Badger refused to pay them for their hot goods—which were getting hotter by the minute. Mal and the gang came across as people trying to survive by living on their own terms, not thugs out for money no matter what its source.

We *saw* how hard the crew's lives were, with the simple visual of Kaylee eating a strawberry, a piece of real fruit that is a true luxury when you spend your life flying through the black.

We *saw* the complexities of Jayne, who was brutal and forthright, but also incredibly useful in a lot of ways that make putting up with him worth the trouble.

This is not to say that "Serenity" is flawless, either. FOX's concerns were not wholly unwarranted. If FOX's primary issue was the two-hour length, this story could very easily have been cut down to an hour, and it would have made a much stronger opening that the deeply flawed "The Train Job"—indeed, a much stronger opening than the two-hour version would have been.

Some of that cutting could have been simple edits. A lot of scenes in "Serenity" went on too long and could easily have been trimmed. In the aforementioned strawberry scene, we saw Kaylee enter the dining area, walk over to the table, set the box down, open the box, pull out the strawberry, stare at the strawberry, then eat the strawberry with an orgasmic expression on her face. That entire bit could have been cut in half, in part by eliminating the first three steps. In addition, both the battle sequence and the heist in the pre-credits teaser could have been tightened.

Perhaps the biggest edit that should have been made was the setup for the confrontation with Patience on Whitefall. The scene started with their landing, then had Mal, Zoe and Jayne setting up their ambush and talking out what they planned to do. This is the equivalent of David Copperfield opening one of his shows by explaining how he does all his magic tricks. Not only was all the setup unnecessary, it took the wind out of the sails of the subsequent confrontation—which also took way too long.

The remaining running time to be excised would be the bits with the Reavers. They were wholly irrelevant to the plot of "Serenity," had no bearing on anything else that happens in the episode and served only to provide a lengthy action/FX piece that looked very pretty (and showed off Wash's piloting skills). The Reavers were a concept that really needed their own episode, rather than being consigned to an add-on to an overcrowded plot. In fact, folding together this aspect of "Serenity" and "Bushwhacked," the only subsequent episode to deal with the Reavers, would have greatly improved both episodes.

Ironically, the episode that set up the milieu of *Firefly* best was "Out of Gas," which, through flashbacks, established Mal's purchase of *Serenity* and recruitment of Zoe, Wash, Kaylee and Jayne. Unfortunately, that episode relied too much on knowledge of the characters from previous episodes to really work as an introductory piece.

It's ironic that FOX hired Whedon to create *Firefly* because it wanted Whedon's pedigree on one of its shows, but then did not allow his considerable skills to be put to good use. "Serenity" introduced the world; FOX rejected that, and instead asked two great writers to come up with a script from scratch, over a weekend, that would do the same job. If FOX wanted a Joss Whedon show, it should have trusted him to do it right, as he had already done twice before.

It is common for a genre show to take several weeks—sometimes as much as a full season or more—to get its legs. *Star Trek: Deep Space*

Nine didn't start to hit its stride until the middle of its first season, and didn't click until that season's last two episodes. *Babylon 5's* first season was a muddle; it didn't become the great show it is remembered as until the second season commenced. The same can be said for *Star Trek: The Next Generation* (though some don't credit that happening until the third year). *Gene Roddenberry's Andromeda*, *Farscape* and *The X-Files* didn't settle in until the middle of their respective first seasons. *Firefly* followed suit; the best episodes were in the latter portion of the show's fourteen episodes, and in fact the three episodes that didn't air ("Trash," "The Message" and "Heart of Gold") were among the strongest.

However, aside from *X-Files*, none of these shows were on networks. Syndication and cable stations are much more forgiving, willing to give a show a full season (or more) to iron out the kinks. Networks, however, are much quicker to wield the cancellation ax, a sad reality that dashed the hopes of *Firefly* fans.

Tellingly, the one refrain that has been heard consistently from Whedon, the actors and the production staff of *Serenity* is that Universal has left Whedon & Co. completely alone. Had FOX done the same, there might not have been a need for the September 2005 feature film at all; that month would have been the start of *Firefly's* fourth season.

Keith R.A. DeCandido is the author of the novelization of Serenity *for Pocket Books. He's no stranger to genre-mixing: his novel* Dragon Precinct *is a high-fantasy police procedural. He has also written dozens of novels, novelizations, short stories, comic books, e-books and non-fiction books in various media universes, such as* Buffy the Vampire Slayer, Star Trek *(in all its various incarnations, as well as a few new ones),* Gene Roddenberry's Andromeda, Farscape, Marvel Comics, Resident Evil *and lots more. He has also edited many anthologies, most recently the award-nominated* Imaginings, *and the Star Trek anthologies* Tales of the Dominion War *and* Tales from the Captain's Table. *Find out too much about Keith at his official Web site DeCandido.net.*

Wonderful. Firefly *as seen through the lens of politics, politics as seen through the lens of* Firefly. *There is truth here, and there is nothing more to say.*

Serenity and Bobby McGee: Freedom and the Illusion of Freedom in Joss Whedon's *Firefly*

MERCEDES LACKEY

"I don' care, I'm still free. You can't take the sky from me."

—JOSS WHEDON, "Theme from *Firefly*"

I'M A CHILD OF THE POSTWAR GENERATION, a Boomer, a holdover hippie. I grew up during the fifties and sixties. When I was a kid, you could be thrown in prison for having a relationship with a person of the "wrong" color, much less the "wrong" sex. The governments of the countries of the "Free World" routinely wiretapped their own citizens, used them as nuclear and chemical experimental guinea pigs and kept us in line by scaring us with tales of how evil the enemy was. Everything old is new again, and having not studied the past sufficiently, not only is the current generation of this world doomed to repeat it, but apparently the generation of the world of *Firefly* is, as well.

The dystopian society in which the crew of *Serenity* operates feels *real*. It resonates with us, and not just because so many of the trappings—the settlers, the horses and cattle and slug-throwing weaponry of the mythic Old West, as well as the crowded alleys and station corridors that call to mind the alleys and backstreets of India, Hong Kong and the Middle East—seem so familiar. It resonates because the rules by which this dystopia operates are familiar.

The Alliance uses a lot of the same psychological weapons on its own people that all the major governments of the world used back when I was growing up and are still using today. Demonization of the enemy, even the construction of enemies that don't exist, create the fear of nebulous threats and the willingness to sacrifice freedoms for security. By using smoke screens, misdirection and distraction, those who wield power keep the attention of those who are controlled off what is actually happening.

And yet more misdirection and the building of elaborate façades hide just how much juggling those in power are having to do to keep things going.

The further into the series one goes, the more one realizes that the Alliance is built on the shaky ground of compromise, make-do and Orwellian contradictions, just as the real world of the here-and-now was, and in fact, still is. How each member of *Serenity*'s crew views that world and what illusions he or she holds about his or her place in it has a very familiar flavor.

The Alliance is a behemoth, a juggernaut: insensate and ultimately faceless. During the course of the series, we're never given any idea of exactly who, or what, is in charge. I suspect this is deliberate. For most of us in the real world, the actual power that is exercised over us is in the hands of faceless bureaucrats and corporate-hive minds—the directors of boards that we will never see; in the *Firefly*verse, the same holds true. It doesn't matter if the person (or persons) nominally in charge is called president, chairman, or dictator-for-life; the decisions are carried out, if not made, by those who have no faces or names, and they prefer it that way. Real power in the Alliance, as in the real world, is exercised from the shadows, behind closed doors, by people no one will ever recognize in the street. That is always the way real power is wielded—not by the man on the poster, but by the man who tells him what to say and coaches him in how to say it. "Trust me," says the man on the poster, and he is such a *nice* man, and seems so likeable, so honest, so just-like-us that most people are lulled into a dream of acceptance of the unacceptable because such a *nice* man would never do such a thing. . . .

And in the Alliance, that means the Blue-handed Men and their labs, their "schools," their monstrosities that are only hinted at.

In the larger sense, the Alliance is run by, and on, money. Money dictates power, and as in the real world, how much of either one has determines to a precise degree how much real (as opposed to illusory) freedom one has. And yet money does not equate to power; up to a point, especially in the fringes, one can have money without having anything other than purely local power.

In several episodes, we get a glimpse of what life is like for those who possess either or both in abundance, and it is, as Mal would say, "shiny"—just as money is shiny, as jewels are shiny, as the polished and carefully crafted world of the inner planets is shined up to a fair-thee-well. This is a lovely façade, as glittering as a movie set and just as false. Another distraction in the game of smoke and mirrors: those who aspire to this world gaze into the mirrors and are mesmerized by it.

And yet, by the same token, having money does not by any means equal having freedom. In fact, in many ways, it is the opposite.

There are constraints even (or especially) in those high strata of society; don't rock the boat, don't question authority, and above all, when someone in a stratum above you exerts his or her power, either you must make the decision to ignore the fact that you are being forced into something you would rather not do, or you must *pretend it was all your idea.*

That was certainly the case in the fifties, when Senator Joseph McCarthy was systematically hauling up anyone who dared to speak out for freedom of speech in front of the House Un-American Activities Committee. The examples then were clear: support Tailgunner Joe's agenda, or you never worked again, whether you were a famous scriptwriter or a white-collar clerk in a business. The signs and symptoms are all too clear to someone who has seen them before, and is seeing them again.

In the case of those in the Alliance version of high society, freedom is as much part of the smoke and mirrors as the gracious façade. Because those living in that rarified atmosphere have so very much to lose, though they will never publicly acknowledge the constraints by which they live, they are, for the most part, acutely aware of them. Unless they are terribly sheltered (as Dr. Simon Tam once was) or terribly stupid (as some minor characters quite clearly are), the knowledge of those constraints and the high cost of trying to get beyond them is ever present in the backs of their minds.

One would think that it would be the rich who harbor illusions about how little freedom they actually have. You have only to look at the subtle signals (and sometimes not-so-subtle signals) that they give off, to know that the opposite is true.

It is the underclasses, perversely, who tend to harbor the most illusions about their freedom. Ask any settler who isn't laboring as a bound servant or operating as a slave-like laborer (like the Canton mudders) and he will tell you he is the freest of the free. This is in part because they are *told* that they are, and the more often that is repeated, the more likely they are to believe it.

Query Capt. Mal Reynolds about how much freedom *he* has, and he would tell you immediately that he is absolutely free, that he is slyly flying under the Alliance radar, pulling the wool over its eyes and getting away with whatever he wants to.

This is an illusion; in fact, his "freedom" exists only because he and his crew, on the one hand, are too small to bother with, and on the other, provide the Alliance with a service that it would otherwise have to pay for.

For all the trappings of totalitarianism, the resources of the Alliance are clearly, from the very first episode, shown as being stretched thin enough that there are holes appearing in the fabric. When the Independents lost and the Alliance won, it was a decidedly Pyrrhic victory. The Alliance literally bit off far more than it could chew. Now it holds more territory than it can possibly administer; it is sitting on the back of a crocodile with the dilemma of knowing that it can neither stay there nor jump off. This is not the first time in history such a situation has occurred; every empire faces it sooner or later. The Egyptians, the Romans, the Byzantines, the Holy Roman Empire, the British Empire—every time a power takes on more people and territory than it can effectively police, it faces the choice of losing what it has seized or losing everything. The Alliance has reached this point by the first episode of *Firefly*.

The Alliance does not dare permit rebellion, but the cost of maintaining its hold over the worlds and people it conquered is so high that it risks losing it every moment. It can't provide basic services, it can't police the frontier, it can't even get accurate intelligence about what is going on in the fringes. It has to allow crime bosses and petty warlords to govern pretty much as they please; the Alliance has to ignore them, because it hasn't got the ability to stop them.

If the Alliance's reach were as sure as it portrays itself, there would be no Reavers, no petty warlords running the fringe worlds—in fact, its reach would extend so far that the *Serenity* would never have been allowed to launch. But then, there are also the signs that before the war, the Alliance's hold over its own people was not nearly so draconian. Now it maintains control by a combination of internal and external fear—the internal fear of rocking the boat and losing everything, and the external (and largely manufactured) fear of the Enemy. No matter how bad things may be inside the Alliance, the Enemy is much worse . . . the Enemy is capable of every terrible thing.

The Alliance has much bigger troubles to worry about than the crew of a tramp freighter whose own resources are so thin that whatever crime it is going to engage in is going to be by any definition petty. Should the *Serenity* happen to fall into the lap of law enforcement—well, that would be one thing. If they get caught then, they'll manage to provide another Alliance commander with an opportunity to put another gold star on his record. But there's not a single reason in the galaxy to spend one man or a drop of fuel chasing them. A demi-Robin Hood like Mal, someone with a conscience (as demonstrated in "The Train Job"), sees to it that things don't degenerate to the level of the intolerable for the rest of the underclasses on the fringe—for that *would* trigger rebellion.

An exaggerated version of this shows up in the episode "Jaynestown," in which Jayne has been elevated to the status of mythic folk hero. The "hero of Canton" is nothing like the real Jayne, of course, but that hero is something that the people of Canton need—and though it might seem to be the very opposite, it is actually something that the Alliance needs. Hope provides a safety valve. Having hope and heroes means that the underclass does *not* get to the point of being backed into a wall and feeling that it has nothing left to lose. The Alliance can never let things get that bad, because someone who thinks he has nothing left to lose is a very, very dangerous person indeed. The wise tyrant knows that to keep control, he must keep the fear of everything except himself to a maximum. Most especially, he must keep the fear of losing however much or little one has torqued up as high as it can go, because that fear will keep rebellion to a minimum.

> "Freedom's just another word for nothin' left to lose."
> —KRIS KRISTOFFERSON, "Me and Bobby McGee"

In the big picture, the Alliance doesn't particularly care *how* goods and services move in the fringe, so long as what is desperately needed gets where it needs to go with no or minimal cost to the bureaucracy of the Alliance itself. If those goods get moved clandestinely, if in fact they are stolen, gray-market, or even black-market, it pays the Alliance to ignore how they got where they ended up, below a certain level of activity, of course. Mal doesn't see this; in fact, he is almost completely unaware of how integral a role he and those like him play in holding the Alliance together.

He also does not realize that by taking on Simon and River Tam, he crosses that invisible boundary—the point past which the Alliance has to notice him and do something about him. By the end of the series, he is beginning—but only just beginning—to realize that the longer they remain with him, the more likely it becomes that the Alliance will actually put some effort into going after *Serenity* and her crew.

Scratch the surface of Captain Reynolds and you find Sgt. Malcolm Reynolds, who takes personal responsibility for the well-being of everyone in his command. It began with Zoe; it has not ended at River and Simon. Every time someone in "his crew" is threatened, even when it is someone as untrustworthy as Jayne, to the best of his ability he steps between him or her and the threat. He wears his accountability like the uniform he thinks he left behind. Make an appeal to his instinct to *protect* and a set of Pavlovian responses snaps into place that will make him act entirely counter to his own best interests. He can never escape that particular prison and still remain the man that he is now. He still has a lot left to lose, and that blinds him to his true estate.

He's not by any means alone in his illusions. Jayne demonstrates Mal's blindness taken to the furthest extreme as someone who concentrates entirely on himself and the here-and-now and as a consequence has absolutely no idea how completely he has been manipulated by circumstance and authority his entire life. Like most in the fringes, he refuses to see past the moment, and in the moment, there is always a chance for one big score. He, too, has too much to lose to be willing to take the blinders off.

Simon Tam is only now beginning to realize how much of his life was built on illusion. Another of his self-deceptions is stripped away nearly every moment. But he is very far from realizing that it is largely accident and chance that allow him to keep his illusion of being able to escape the blue hands of Interpol. He still thinks he will actually survive a confrontation with the upper-level agents if they ever get their hands on him. And he still thinks that if he can take River far enough away, somewhere they will find a place where the Alliance can't find them. Like Lancelot, he hunts for the Grail; like Lancelot, he likely will never find it.

Inara not only deceives herself as to her measure of personal freedom, she succeeds in deceiving most of the viewers. After all, she is a member of an apparently powerful and respected profession and is clearly someone who is near the top rank of that profession. She can go where she chooses and select her clients herself. She is only with *Serenity* because she wishes to be. Surely of all of the crew, she is the one with the most real freedom, is she not?

Yet, like all those others with a great deal to lose, she is restricted by all the things that give her apparent freedom. Beneath that gossamer gown, she is as tightly corseted by those restrictions as any Edwardian debutante. She may look serene and graceful and utterly composed, but if she has to step outside of those strictures, as she does in the final episode, "Heart of Gold," she cannot breathe, cannot think, and turns mindlessly back into the apparent safety of the only world she knows. If for some reason she was grounded again, her choices would be severely limited. If she loses her license she loses the respect, the clients, and the protection of the Guild. If she dares to become emotionally attached to anyone before formal retirement, much less to become emotionally attached to a renegade like Mal, she *will* lose her license.

Her freedom is as thin as the piece of paper her license is printed on. Without it, she's no longer respected or respectable; she goes from being a sought-after professional to nothing but a lovely and exquisitely trained whore.

She is also nowhere near as free to operate with relative safety and impunity as she thinks she is; the episode "Shindig" showed, if the viewer was paying close attention, how nearly Inara could have gone from Companion to sex slave. A single error of judgment, and she could all too easily find herself the prisoner of a former client—or his victim. She thinks she is immune from that danger. In reality, she is no more immune than the whores of the Heart of Gold. Her freedom is just as illusory as Mal's, and yet she clings just as tightly to that illusion as he does.

We haven't seen a great deal of Shepherd Book; he is one of the more enigmatic members of the crew. Fan speculation runs along the line that he had been some highly placed member of the Alliance military or paramilitary and had been involved in some atrocity that caused him to retire to the religious life; my personal feeling is that this cannot possibly be the case, because he is constantly being blindsided by the state of things within the current Alliance. That he once held *some* position of importance within the Alliance is certain; the ID card he holds commands instant respect, deference and aid from Alliance facilities, and we haven't seen anything to indicate that a shepherd is held in that level of esteem by anyone within the Alliance. Further, he shows far more facility with martial arts and weaponry than an ordinary citizen should. However, he has, by his own admission, been in a cloistered situation for a very long time, a period of time which I believe predates the Alliance-Independent War. I believe that his particular illusions of freedom date from that time; the Alliance has changed out of all recognition from when *he* was last "out in the world." He seems to still be in a partial state of culture shock. Whether he will come to accept that he has been living in a state of illusion is a question we can't answer. Whether he has given up enough to be in the position to actually see clearly what is going on is another.

Kaylee and Wash both operate from a similar mindset; like so many of the parents of my contemporaries, they're forever focused on what's near at hand. It's not as if they refuse to see the cage that holds them. It's as if, like Jayne, they literally can't; they never actually think about anything other than their passions. For Kaylee, this is "her" ship and "her" engines; for Wash, it is Zoe, and to a lesser extent (as demonstrated in "Out of Gas"), piloting. For them, whether or not they are "free" is incidental to those passions. Nevertheless, they, too, labor under the same delusions as Mal; they think they are cleverly eluding the constraints of the Alliance, when all the time they are only able to remain "free" as long as the Alliance can afford to ignore them.

"Freedom is a cage in which the bars are farther away than you care to fly."
—POUL ANDERSON, *The People of the Wind*

And now, here is the apparent contradiction embedded in this situation; for all that Jayne is physically threatening and dangerous, he will never be as dangerous as the one person aboard *Serenity* who has no illusions about freedom whatsoever—River.

It might seem odd to say that River has no illusions when she seems to exist in a fog of hallucination. But that fog is nothing more than the deflections of damaged synapses, an information flood she has to try and think through every waking moment, compounded by treatment at the hands of Interpol that fits every reasonable definition of torture. Down in her core personality, River has been stripped of every illusion she ever had. She *knows*, with absolute certainty, that there is no safety for her anywhere, that no one can protect her, that she cannot protect herself. She *knows* that when the blue-handed Interpol agents of the Alliance really choose to come after her, there is no escape from them—and that this time there will be no rescue. She *knows* that the freedom she is experiencing now is temporary and illusory, and for that reason, while she has it, she lives absolutely and completely in the *now*.

This leaves us with Zoe.

If there is a single person in the crew who has a real grasp on the situation, I suspect it is Zoe. I do not believe she harbors any illusions with respect to freedom or anything else in her life. She seems to have come to a Zen-like state of acceptance of whatever enters her world; it is not good, it is not bad, it merely is, and she will deal with it. She plays whatever hand she is dealt, and waits and watches for the single opportunity to make her move. I think she sees the *really* big picture; she lived through the defeat of the Independents, but she knows that this current situation can't last. She might not live to see the Alliance fall, but she knows it will, eventually, and she's hoping that a little push here, and another one there, on her part, might bring that day a little closer. This may be why she maintains an outwardly unruffled composure; she knows what will happen in the end, whether or not she is there to see it. For her, freedom or lack of it is just another situation to deal with. Or not. There are only two constants in her life—her loyalty to Mal and her love for Wash—and as long as she has those, she can work with what's thrown at her. Everything else is subject to change, and change is what she handles best. I believe she knows exactly what the situation is with regard to the Alliance, and she is doing her best to help Mal maintain his illusion of freedom, while she herself is perfectly well aware of how much of an illusion it is.

However dark and pessimistic all of this seems, nevertheless, it's like the real world in another way. Even those who understand the entirety of the situation can still choose. There is a freedom that no government, however despotic, can take—the freedom to use your mind and make the most of every unlikely opportunity. And the less illusion you have, just as with Zoe and River, conversely, the more real power you attain, until, in the end, like the aikido master, you wait for the great force to exert itself on you, slip aside and assist it into a wall.

River may have that power.

If she gets beyond her fear, into the state where she knows that she is in the worst possible place she can ever be, she could be the most dangerous person on the crew. We've seen some glimpses of what she can do when she isn't afraid, and they are formidable.

Zoe probably has more of that power than she realizes at the moment. Because she has clarity of vision, she can not only see the bars of the cage, she might be able, like River, to see and exploit the weaknesses in those bars.

If Mal's eyes are ever completely opened—which will mean that he will have to give up a lot of cherished illusions about himself—he certainly will attain that power.

Shepherd Book may already know those weaknesses; he simply has to lose another set of illusions—that the door to the cage has been left unlocked and the bars are there to protect, rather than confine. So he may be another factor in the equation. But first, he has to accept that the world has changed, and the people he once trusted have been corrupted by the power that he, and those like him, once gave them.

> "We are the little folk, we,
> Too little to love or to hate
> But leave us alone and you'll see
> How we can tear down the great."
> —RUDYARD KIPLING, "The Pict Song"

Kipling knew; he saw it happening in his time, in India and China, as resistance built when conditions became intolerable. Once illusions are gone, and the bars of the cage are revealed, so are the weaknesses in the bars. As the military-industrial behemoth of the United States discovered in my generation—and has forgotten—there is a lot of damage that small, "insignificant" groups and individuals can do. A push here, a weakening there, and the whole façade comes crumbling down. Spread out the police far enough, use up money and resources, and eventually it all falls to pieces.

Beyond the state of "nothing left to lose," there is, perversely, hope. Perhaps not hope for oneself, but hope for a broader future. This is the real hope, knowing that while you may go down, you will be taking the oppressor with you, as opposed to the illusory "Robin Hood will save us" sort of hope that helps keep the masters in control.

So there they are, the lowest and least likely, and yet the ones most likely to succeed where armies fail. Who, after all, would have believed that a major nuclear power could have been brought to defeat by a lot of barefoot peasants in black pajamas? Yet it happened; and in the world of *Firefly*, at least, it can happen again. The crew of the *Serenity* have everything they need to free themselves—and far more than themselves. The keys to their cage are there, if they can take off the blinders they wear and see the cage for what it is.

Mal has to face the fact that he has been controlled by his own virtues, and aikido-like, turn those virtues against the controllers. Inara must come to the understanding that her cage is not worth the cost to her and others of maintaining, and be willing to give up a great deal—in short, she will have to learn something she has never yet been forced to learn—self-sacrifice. River must give up fear. Simon must give up his illusions and turn his own powerful intellect against the Alliance, as he did so well in planning his foray into the hospital. Shepherd Book must accept that the Alliance he knew no longer exists. Wash and Kaylee must raise their eyes past the moment and look unflinchingly into the future, and accept that they, too, will have to give up much—perhaps everything—in order to bring that future to pass. And Jayne—well, Jayne is a junkyard dog. He is all flaws; but he just might have some redeeming qualities, and if anyone can ever get real loyalty out of him, there is no telling what he might be willing to do.

If they can all muster the courage to face the fact that they *are* controlled, they will have the tool they need to break that control. If they can dispel all their illusions of freedom and discover that they really do have nothing left to lose, they will realize that they are in a position of power that makes them a terrible enemy.

If they can learn the difference between false hope and the real thing, they will understand what they need to do to bring the Alliance down. Because when hope is not being used to control us, when it is paired with courage and self-sacrifice, it is what lights the way to true and non-illusory freedom.

Mercedes Lackey is an internationally famous supermodel, who spends her free time climbing Mount Everest, diving in the Antarctic and acting as a consultant for International Rescue, and she thinks that if you believe any of that, you need to get out of the house more.

She lives in Oklahoma with her husband, artist and author Larry Dixon, and their flock of parrots in a house that is never very quiet. She has written, alone or in collaboration, over sixty books, including the Valdemar and Joust series for DAW, the Diana Tregarde and Elvenbane series for Tor and the Five Hundred Kingdoms series for Luna. She has never been a psychic medium, a spy or a contortionist, nor played one on TV.

Some of the higher math in the second half of this essay eluded me, and the Russian novel excerpts would perhaps have been better presented in translation, but I think valid conclusions are reached—Wait! Come back! I'm only kidding! It's funny. Sweeet sweeet humor. Mmm.

Firefly vs. The Tick

DON DEBRANDT

DESPITE WHAT THE TITLE IMPLIES, this essay is not about a squabble between entomologists. It concerns two very entertaining but vastly different TV shows: *Firefly*, created by the talented Joss Whedon, and *The Tick*, created by the equally talented Ben Edlund.

Whedon is best known for his two previous shows, *Buffy the Vampire Slayer* and *Angel*. But *Firefly* didn't have supernatural menaces, teen angst or pop culture; instead, Whedon gave us interplanetary outlaws, a frontier of hard vacuum and a kind of *patois* that's half laconic cowboy and half Chinese profanity. In short, a western in space.

The Tick was a cartoon (there was a live-action show too, but let's ignore that for now) about a big, blue and extremely dense superhero who lived in an apartment with his sidekick, Arthur. Arthur used to be an accountant, but eventually succumbed to the call of an alternate lifestyle that involved being pummeled while wearing tights. Arthur's battle cry was, "Not in the face! Not in the face!"

Ah, the parallels almost *jump* out at you, don't they?

Yes. Well.

Perhaps a side-by-side comparison will clear things up....

Firefly—though set in outer space and on various planets—had no actual aliens.

Neither did *The Tick*. Well...okay, maybe it had a few, but it was hard to tell because of communication difficulties:

(supposed) ALIEN: Listen, buddy—for the last time, it's—

TICK: Four acts in a bog?
ALIEN: *Thrakkerzog*—
TICK: Ahh...laxative log.
ALIEN: No, no—
TICK: Laplander Zog?
ALIEN: Thrakk—
TICK: Four yaks and a dog.
ALIEN: No, no, no—
TICK: Sapsucker frog!
ALIEN: NO!
(beat)
TICK: Suuuuusan?

Firefly may not have had aliens per se, but it did have savages. In a classic Hollywood western this niche is occupied by Indians, but the *Firefly*verse takes a less stereotyped approach—its savages are the Reavers, ordinary men driven mad by the eternal, empty night of space itself. They have stared into the abyss, and the abyss has stared back; its awful, all-encompassing darkness has crept into their very souls, eating their humanity the way a singularity eats light. The Reavers are raping, murdering cannibals, human in form only, capable of any atrocity.

And here is where we find the first parallel between the two series. *The Tick* also featured a race that embraced the abyss, that worshiped Ultimate Entropy and the End of All That Is; they possessed a black hole-powered device they simply called the Big Nothing. When activated, it would devour the entire universe.

Which they would have done some time ago, but seeing as how this was a big deal, the point of their entire civilization, etc., etc., their leader had to make a speech first. And then he had to thank his parents and his first-grade teacher and the decorations committee, and you know, the ceremony dragged on a bit.

Thirteen years or so.

Which would be mind-numbingly horrifying all by itself—but there's also the fact that their language consisted of one word:

LEADER: Hey? Hey *hey* hey. Hey! Hey hey hey hey—hey hey—hey hey hey: *Hey*.

Of course, that quote is taken slightly out of context.

Fortunately, the Heys were opposed by a race called the Whats, who by a quirk of intergalactic linguistics also had a language consisting of only one word. Unfortunately, this led to some confusion when the Whats mistook Arthur for a Hey and tried to interrogate him:

INTERROGATOR: Hey!
ARTHUR: What?
INTERROGATOR: *Hey!*
ARTHUR: *What?*
INTERROGATOR: Hey hey *hey!*
ARTHUR: What? *What?*

Well, you get the gist—much like when the crew of *Serenity* swears in Chinese. We don't need a literal translation, because our imagination fills in the gaps.

That's also why the Reavers were so scary; we saw their ships, we saw horrors they committed, but we never actually met one in the flesh. The monsters we imagine are far worse than any reality could be.

The Heys, on the other hand, we saw many of—all dressed in white bunny suits. Which proves, I suppose, that either Ultimate Evil is truly incomprehensible, or just has bad fashion sense.

Either way, language figured prominently in both series, and both had their own very distinctive style of dialogue. Here's the captain of *Serenity* talking to a group of desperadoes at gunpoint (he's also disguised as a woman, but that's sort of incidental):

MAL: Now think real hard. You been bird-dogging this township a while now. They wouldn't mind a corpse of you. Now you can luxuriate in a nice jail cell, but if your hand touches metal, I swear by my pretty flowered bonnet, I *will* end you.

Kinda flows off the tongue real natural-like, don't it? Now, some might have a problem with that kinda palaver bein' delivered by folk who fly around in spaceships and such, but I'd have to disagree. There's somethin' about a frontier that calls for plain speaking, and it don't matter one whit whether that frontier's at the edge of a country or a solar system. A frontier means settlers, and that means those as don't got it so good back home lookin' to put down stakes somewhere better. Those people tend to be a lot closer to the bottom of the barrel than the cream floating on top, and they hardly ever hold with highfalutin speech.

And then we have Tick-speak, a language all its own:

TICK: Not so fast, naughty-spawn! I say to you, *stop your evil ways!*

Or, on landing on the Moon:

TICK: This is one small step for the Tick, and one giant step for…say…a little bug! Or some guy who's been shrunk to the size of a *penny!*

And perhaps most significantly, on facial hair:

TICK: Rugged, self-assured, adult—these are the words that describe the man who wears a *mustache.* "Yes," it says to the world, "I'm a man of action!" Ah, but action tempered with *maturity*…like a, a fireman! Or somebody's *dad!*

You wouldn't think hair would play that big a role in superheroics— *or* in outer space—but you'd be wrong. Witness the following exchange from the *Firefly* episode "Trash":

MAL: —the beard! You shaved off the soup-catcher!
MONTY: Yup.
MAL: I thought you were going to take that ugly chin-wig to the grave.
MONTY: (chuckles) So did I. But she didn't much like my whiskers.

"She" turned out to be Bridget, a con artist who preferred clean-shaven marks. Mal exposed her scam and Monty left in a huff (apparently a model of spaceship):

MONTY: Damn you, Bridget! Damn you ta Hades! You broke my heart in a million pieces! You made me love you, and then y—I SHAVED MY BEARD FOR YOU, DEVIL WOMAN!

Clearly, mouth-bordering follical enhancement is an important theme in both series…but to what end? Roguish symbol of masculine power, or something more sinister?
I'm gonna go with the second one.

BOOK: Yes, I'd forgotten you're moonlighting as a criminal mastermind now. Got your next heist planned?

SIMON: No, but I'm thinking of growing a big black mustache. I'm a traditionalist.

In fact, the western archetype represented by Simon's mysterious sister, River, *is* the mustache. Both bristle with dark, unknown power, and both contain things they shouldn't—in River's case, information, and in the other, bits of food.

River's powers let her know things she shouldn't—and apparently have also alerted her to the evil potential of hair, facial and otherwise. When she saw Shepherd Book's hair—normally kept tied back, but in this case white, frizzy and standing up about a foot in every direction—she screamed, ran away and hid.

RIVER: They say the snow on the roof is too heavy. They say the ceiling will cave in. His brains are in terrible danger.

BOOK: River? Please, why don't you come on out?

RIVER: No! I can't. *Too much hair.*

BOOK: Is—is that it?

ZOE: Hell, yes, Preacher. If I didn't have stuff to get done, I'd be in there with her.

BOOK: It's the rules of my order. Like the book, it symbolizes—

ZOE: Uh-huh. River, honey, he's putting the hair away now.

RIVER: Doesn't matter. It'll still be there. Waiting.

Just like the mustache that appeared overnight on the Tick's upper lip—it was *also* waiting and eventually revealed it had a mind and agenda of its own. Much like River, it was a government-created superweapon, on the run from the people who made it. When the Tick discovered his new adornment was a lot more mobile and feisty than he had suspected, he went somewhat…berserk. The mustache attempted to shut him up. When that didn't work, it wriggled up his nose.

TICK: Arthur! *My mustache is touching my brain!*

Yuck.

Somebody's also been touching River's brain, which is why she talks in non-sequiturs and sometimes rubs soup into people's hair. Either that, or soup possesses anti-evil follicular properties.

The Tick even featured a rampaging dinosaur with a mustache, which Arthur got tangled in:

ARTHUR: Tick! I'm trapped!
TICK: The mustache of a *titan!*

I should mention that I'm extremely grateful for the appearance of Dinosaur Neil. He allows me to segue from facial hair to giant prehistoric lizards, a leap that would cause most works of prose to derail in the sort of horrifying spectacle that actually causes injuries in adjoining essays.

The scene that introduced Wash, *Serenity's* pilot, placed him at the ship's controls. He was not paying attention to them, and he did not have a mustache. He was, however, playing with two small plastic dinosaurs, which he pitted against each other in a scene fraught with betrayal, horror and lots of evil laughter. He is obviously a very bad man, and we will talk of him no further.

It is worth mentioning, though, that when the captain and Zoe first met him, he *did* have a mustache, and Zoe didn't trust him. Six years went by, they got married, and the mustache disappeared.

Coincidence?

I think not.

Firefly's preacher, Book, has a past as murky as his denomination. His name implies that he's someone you shouldn't judge by his cover—because a cover is exactly what it might be.

The Tick had its own enigmatic religion-based (or at least religious holiday-based) character, one whose saintly demeanour hid a dark secret. I speak, of course, of Multiple Santa.

TICK: Lowly wretch! This is the last time *you* make epic naughty in Santa threads!

A thief in a stolen Santa suit who generated clones of himself every time he got a charge of electricity, Multiple Santa proved one of the Tick's biggest challenges. I mean, who can hit St. Nick?

Oddly enough, one of the nastiest bad guys in *Firefly* also referenced Santa. A bounty hunter named Early snuck aboard *Serenity* and surprised Kaylee in the engine room:

KAYLEE: H-how did you...get on?
EARLY: Strains the mind a bit, don't it? You think you're all alone. Maybe I come down the chimney, Kaylee. Bring presents to the good girls and boys. Maybe not, though. Maybe I've always been here.

He then threatened to rape her. It was a very creepy, menacing scene, made more so by the mention of something presumably as innocent as Christmas.

When Jayne betrayed Simon and River to the authorities in return for a big reward, the cops double-crossed him and arrested all three—prompting River to tell him that "They took Christmas away." And when the con artist Bridget (a.k.a. Saffron, a.k.a. Yolanda) dosed Mal with a narcotic-laced kiss, the first thing he said when he woke up was, "Is it Christmas?"

Ah, yes. Nothing invokes the holidays like betrayal, drugs, thievery and sexual assault. . . .

Must be that big white beard.

Malcolm Reynolds is a smuggler and a thief, but one with ethics and a strong sense of decency. Hatred of the Alliance is what really drives Mal, what makes him an anti-hero instead of just a criminal. He isn't just smuggling and stealing; he's defying a corrupt authority he refuses to bow down to.

His mirror image in *The Tick* is also a rebel, the walking sunflower known as El Seed. A spoof of the revolutionary El Cid, El Seed dresses like a mariachi player and talks in a bad Spanish accent:

> EL SEED: When I was taking night courses at agricultural college—a fine school—I learned three things: one, never stand behind a cow; two, people and plants can never learn in harmony; and three, if you want something, take it—and I want the world!

Mal doesn't want the world, of course—just the freedom to travel from one to another—but his hatred of the Alliance and El Seed's loathing for all things animal converge on two specific points: defiance of the status quo, and monkeys.

> EL SEED: Eat my revolution, blue monkey!
>
> MAL: Were there monkeys? Did some terrifying space monkeys maybe get loose?

To which the answer is: yes. Or at least they did in *The Tick*, where monkeys abound. There's Yank, a bad-tempered chimp who acquired a supergenius IQ when the U.S. sent him into orbit (tragically, his new IQ faded away by the end of the episode, sort of a *Bananas for Algernon*—but on the bright side, he was appointed the new head of NASA), and

then there was the monkey that suddenly just popped into existence in
Arthur's apartment:

TICK: Arthur! *Monkey out of nowhere!*

Even crankier was the orangutan Arthur encountered in the Sidekick's
Lounge. The Lounge was just a wooden shack with a pop machine behind the glitzy superhero nightspot the Comet Club, but at least he got
to meet a few fellow 'kickers, including a talking dog in a cape:

DOG: Been all across this crazy, mixed-up country, 'kickin' for a hero
   with a brain the size of a walnut...and what I got to show for it?
   High blood pressure, an artificial hip and a case of the worms. But
   man, I love it.
ORANGUTAN: Not me, pal. I just want to get back to the jungle. Oh Borneo, sweet Borneo...if you wanted a snack, you just reached up
   into a tree and plucked it! Not like here, oh, no sir, no! Some hairless jerk had to go and invent *money!* Some hairless jerk like *you!*

He grabs Arthur and hoists him over his head, wrestler-style.

ORANGUTAN: Sixty-five cents for a candy bar? What are you, *nuts?*
ARTHUR: You frighten me terribly. I'd like to go now.

An orangutan, unfortunately, who could be described as *a monkey
with a beard.*
And then there's the ship herself, *Serenity*. She's not just a means of
transport; she's what lets them make their living, what keeps them one
step ahead of the authorities. She's their refuge and home. Her name is
important, too; the Battle of Serenity Valley is what opened the series,
and it was the battle that ended the war between the Independents and
the Alliance. Malcolm and Zoe were on the losing side—but six years
later, Mal is still fighting.
The visual design of the ship is somewhat unusual. The long neck
and triangular head are reminiscent of a horse—appropriate for a western set in space. But its creators describe it in an interview as a cross
between a bug—a firefly, natch—and a bird.
Hmmm. What *kind* of bird isn't mentioned. Well, it's got a long neck,
a wedge-shaped bill, and a roundish, squat body. . . .
It's a duck.

ARTHUR: Tick, you can't fight evil with a macaroni duck!

Truer words were never spoken.

Okay, so maybe it's not a *macaroni* duck...but definitely some species of aquatic waterfowl. A Crested Grebe, maybe. And while its actual physical composition remains unknown, I'm guessing some sort of linguini polymer, or perhaps a ravioli/rigatoni alloy.

The logical conclusion, then, is that pasta with a high quack potential—while unsuitable for crime fighting—is in fact space-worthy while in a mallardous state. Which is undoubtedly why the crew of *Serenity* indulges in crime; if they did otherwise, their ship would fall apart. Of course, they could always grow beards, making them more evil and reinforcing the noodlosity of their craft, but too much hair *might* attract the attention of space monkeys.

Or even worse, Santa.

TICK: Isn't sanity really a one-trick pony, anyway? I mean, all you get is one trick, rational thinking! But when you're good and crazy...ooh hoo hoo hoo...the sky's the limit!

So, to sum up: the links between *Firefly* and *The Tick* are obvious. There's the hair data, the dinosaurs and the monkeys, stuff about Christmas and weird language and, uh, they're both funny as hell, and there's all this material about the color blue and cows and high school French I didn't have room for, and it adds up in a perfectly logical, *not at all insane* way. . . .

Ah, *gao yang jong duh goo yang.*

They're both *bugs*, okay? Fireflies and ticks and El Seed's henchmen the Bee Twins and Betty, Queen of the Ants, and Kaylee mentions space bugs this one time, and bugs are used by *spies*, and, and, spies are often morally conflicted, just like the crew of *Serenity*, and James Bond is a spy *and* a superhero, so. . . .

JOSS WHEDON: Ben Edlund is like a James Bond that can draw, write, play guitar, sing and do everything.

Uh, yeah. Thanks, Joss. And he's also *what? A producer* on *Firefly?* Really. And he wrote the episode "Jaynestown" and cowrote the episode "Trash"?

Huh. How about that.

TICK: You know, Arthur, it's really been quite a day. From the outside, on the surface, oh, sure, we were pursued by Swiss industrial
spies, trapped in the belly of a whale—but what *really* pursued us?
Where were we *really* trapped? Come on, Arthur—*get meta with
me!* What pursued us were our own obsessions! I'm *good*, you're
evil! I'm a *superhero*, you're a *sidekick!* I'm a *woman*, you're a *man!*
What does it all mean? Nothing! And where were we all trapped?
I'll tell you where, Arthur—in the *belly of love*.

There. I hope that makes everything perfectly clear. . . .

---

*Don DeBrandt is not the secret identity of the caped crusader known
as Captain Fun—they've never even been seen together. He is, however,
the author of* The Quicksilver Screen, Steeldriver, Timberjak, V.I.
and the Angel *novel* Shakedown. *He has written two books under the
pseudonym Donn Cortez:* The Closer, *a thriller, and* The Man Burns
Tonight, *a mystery set at Burning Man (to be published in August
2005). He is currently working on two* CSI: Miami *novels.*

*He does not have a mustache, does not consort with space monkeys
and rarely dresses up as Santa—once, twice a year, tops.*

Joss Whedon doesn't believe in "moves." Moves are plot developments within a story that are there because they are cool, amusing or convenient for the writer. Instead, Joss likes events in a story to occur because those and exactly those events get at the emotional truth he is demonstrating. This essay is about a particular emotional truth of Joss' experience of the world.

It is another demonstration of the power of television (when the system is working), as a medium well-suited for the expression of a single author's voice. Firefly *allowed Joss to say things he wanted or needed to say, about the world, the human mind and the relationship between the two.*

We're All Just Floating in Space

LYLE ZYNDA

"Happiness and the absurd are two sons of the same earth."
—ALBERT CAMUS, *The Myth of Sisyphus*

"OBJECTS IN SPACE"—the last episode of *Firefly* broadcast during its all-too-brief run—is notable both in terms of character development, as River, until then a mysterious figure, moves to a fuller relationship with the rest of the *Serenity's* crew, and in terms of the broader themes that it evokes. In particular, series creator Joss Whedon, inspired by classic existentialist literary works, aims to dramatize themes about the contingency and meaninglessness inherent in existing things—and about the only possible source of value, in our free choices. To this end, Whedon creates the character of Early, a bounty hunter who, like River, seems to relate to his surroundings in an unusual way. Together, they form a contrasting pair, reflecting two distinct ways of responding to the contingency of existing things. For Early, it is a source of pain; for River, it is a source of joy.

The episode begins when River awakes suddenly, hearing in her head the voices of the other crew members, along with that of a stranger. The stranger's voice (which says, "We're all just floating,") belongs to Early, who is closely trailing *Serenity* in a small one-person spacecraft, unbeknownst to its crew. He is after River, for whose capture a huge reward has been set by the Alliance. Throughout most of the series, River has been a mysterious figure; she has seemed passive, childlike, dysfunctional, somewhat erratic and unpredictable. However, there have been hints that the unknown, experimental alterations made to her brain have resulted in heightened sensitivities. In "Objects in Space," these sensitivities are more fully revealed than before; most centrally, River appears to be able to sense the thoughts and feelings of others. After being awoken by Early's voice, she walks, somewhat disoriented and confused, around *Serenity*, and hears the crew members' private thoughts. What she hears the others say is disturbing to her, even hostile. Her own brother, Simon, appears from her point of view to say, "I would be there right now." It seems accusatory. Though he does not actually say those words then, later he does say exactly those words to Kaylee, expressing the fact that he would never have left the hospital where he worked and felt at home and become a fugitive if not for his sister.[1] In a surreal scene, River happens upon a branch lying on the deck, which is scattered with leaves in bright fall colors. Again, she is seeing what is not there; the "branch" is actually Jayne's gun, fully loaded and unlocked. Examining the branch (gun), she murmurs, strangely, "It's just an object. It doesn't mean what you think." After the alarmed crew gets the gun away from her, they meet to hold an impassioned discussion about River, who now seems to them not just dysfunctional, but dangerous. The possibility is mentioned that River is "psychic," a "reader"—a possibility (ironically) dismissed by Wash, the ship's jocular pilot, as "science fiction." All the while, she listens to them through the deck below them, by apparently extraordinary means, since the deck appears quite solid and impervious to eavesdropping by ear alone. Early eavesdrops, too, from above, using quite ordinary means (a contact microphone).

After the crew has retired for the evening, Early somehow sneaks onto the *Serenity*. Early seems both highly capable and somewhat damaged—not all is "right" with him. He is a man of action (swiftly knocking out the captain and locking most of the others in their quarters as they sleep)

---

[1] Other examples: River hears Jayne say, "I got stupid; the money was too good." (Perhaps, we later wonder, he was responsible for the tip that helped the bounty hunter find them?) Book, a "shepherd" (clergyman), says (rather uncharacteristically), "I don't give half a hump if you're innocent or not. So where does that put you?"

and cunning (he deals with each crew member in a way most likely to achieve his aims). He also can be terrifying: in a disturbing scene, he coolly threatens to rape Kaylee, the ship's able and ever-positive engineer, if she gets in his way—and we believe him capable of it. Yet he also seems distracted by seemingly small and irrelevant features of his surroundings and digresses repeatedly into what appear to be meandering "philosophical" questions. Perhaps, we surmise, his solitary life as a bounty hunter—as well as the violence that job requires—has taken its toll on him. We sense there is deep pain in him. The episode climaxes when River, who has disappeared from the ship, speaks over the ship's intercoms and claims to have *become* the ship. No longer the passive and dysfunctional character she seemed before, she speaks confidently and authoritatively to each crew member, instructing each of them based on an apparently fully developed plan to defeat Early. Disoriented by the strangeness of these developments, the others (and we, the viewers) begin to consider seriously River's claim that she has indeed somehow "become the ship." She also confronts Early with his own demons; while he maintains he only hurts others when the job requires it of him, River accuses him of sadism, of *enjoying* the violence his job requires. She brings up details only he would know, e.g., that he tortured animals as a child and that even his mother thought him damaged. Early begins to lose his composure. However, River has not "become" the ship;[2] in a development unexpected in its own way, she—a seemingly dysfunctional adolescent—has donned a space suit, disembarked from *Serenity* and boarded Early's ship. After deceiving Early into thinking she will go back voluntarily with him, Early is pushed into deep space by Mal, who (as River has instructed) is waiting for him on the ship's hull. A single Steadicam shot moving through the ship shows all the crew members in turn, who after this experience seem more united than ever before. Kaylee and River (who we now see in a new light) play jacks with a ball strikingly similar to the planet the *Serenity* passed in the episode's opening shot. The episode (and the series, as broadcast) ends as Early is seen calmly awaiting his own asphyxiation in deep space, when the air supply in his space suit runs out; he says, resigned, "Well, here I am." As his voice said to River in the episode's first audible line, he is literally "floating"—now, alone in empty space, doomed.

---

[2] In his DVD commentary, Joss Whedon says making River "psychic" was as much "fiction" as he was prepared to put into his science fiction; he did not consider actually making River the ship. However, leading us to half-believe that she did makes us, the viewers, look at the ship in a different way.

In the DVD commentary to "Objects in Space," Joss Whedon relates the unusual personal genesis of the episode. When he was just sixteen years old, Whedon discovered that he lacked religious faith. Soon thereafter, as he began to think for the first time as an adult about life and reality, Whedon reports having an experience in which reality as a whole ("the totality of things") presented itself to him especially vividly, "but with no coherent pattern." A friend, after hearing the young Whedon tell him about this experience, gave him what Whedon refers to as "the most important book I have ever read": Jean-Paul Sartre's novel *Nausea*. Sartre's novel is in the form of a diary, ostensibly written by one Antoine Roquentin, who is working on a historical work in the French town of Bouville, where the library holding letters and documents related to his subject (de Rollebon, a fictional marquis) is located. Roquentin has an odd and heightened sense of his surroundings. Periodically he enters states in which things seem strange and alien. He acutely feels their existence, which gives him a feeling he describes as "nausea." These experiences culminate when the root of a chestnut tree appears to him as a bare object, that is, simply as something that exists, with its qualities devoid of any meaning or connection with other things. Roquentin feels that he has gained an important insight into the nature of existence. Concrete, particular objects are what truly exist, not abstractions. Generalizations about objects or particular conceptualizations of them (e.g., as regards their use, value or function) are secondary, removed from their true existence. For example, about the root, Roquentin writes, "The function [e.g., transporting nourishment from the soil to the tree] explained nothing; it allowed you to understand generally that it was a root, but not [what made it] *that one* at all. This root, with its color, shape, its congealed movement, was...below all explanation" (126). In this scene, Sartre dramatizes several themes that he would develop in detail in later philosophical writings and literary works. First, there is the idea that everything is *contingent*.[3] Anything that exists might not have. For example, the tree whose root Roquentin contemplated would never have existed if the seed that became the tree was eaten by a bird before it could sprout. Moreover, if this is true of every individual object, it is true of the universe as a whole. The universe might have been completely empty, from eternity past to eternity future. In addition, everything that exists

---

[3] Concerning this, Roquentin writes in his diary, "The essential thing is contingency. I mean that one cannot define existence as necessity. To exist is simply to be there; those who exist let themselves be encountered, but you can never deduce anything from them" (131).

could have been other than the way it is. There is thus no necessity in things. The second point follows from the first—namely, that things have no *essence* that necessarily makes them the way they are. They exist first as, you might say, bare facts; later it is determined "what they are." In particular, whatever *meaning* (in the sense of significance, value or function) something has is not intrinsic to it, but is *conferred* on it[4] freely by beings, like us, capable of valuing. Sartre was to sum this up later in the slogan "Existence precedes essence." When one experiences an object without its conferred essence, as it is in itself (as a bare fact, unconceptualized and unrelated to other objects), its qualities, now meaningless, make it appear *absurd*. Without value, meaning or function, there is no *reason* for it to be the way it is. However, that is how everything in fact is, in and of itself. Roquentin writes, "Every existing thing is born without reason, prolongs itself out of weakness and dies by chance" (133).

"Objects in Space" is in part Whedon's attempt to create his own version of Roquentin—namely, Early. However, Whedon also aims to provide us with further insight into the character of River by making her appear like Early in some respects—they both relate to their surroundings in similarly "odd" ways—yet we find that River's response to absurdity (bare objects in space) is not the same as his. She would seem to agree with Camus (another existentialist writer whose influence Whedon cites): "Happiness and the absurd are two sons of the same earth."[5]

Let us now look more carefully at these themes and think about how they apply to the characters of Early and River. If nothing has any intrinsic essence, function or meaning, if these are freely conferred on things, then at first glance it would seem that there are *no limits* to what things can mean. (Indeed, Sartre often says that our freedom is "absolute.") Second, if the choice of what value or function to confer on something is completely free and undetermined, then it would seem to be *arbitrary*. For if I choose something *for a reason*, doesn't that just mean that my consideration of that reason is what determines my choice? Hence, if my choice is *undetermined*, then it must be based on no reason at all; that is, it must be arbitrary. Is this how the slogan "Existence precedes essence" is to be understood?

---

[4] Whedon likes the word "imbue." It appears in the episode when Early, finding River not in her room, asks, seemingly irrelevantly, "Is it still her room when it's empty? Does the room, the thing, have a purpose, or do we...?" He is unable to think of the proper word at first, but suddenly the word "imbue" occurs to him. However, he does not complete the thought—i.e., that the room itself has no purpose unless we "imbue" it with one.

[5] *The Myth of Sisyphus*, p. 122.

Let us begin by considering a simple example—a gun. A gun can be used as an instrument to kill, as an artifact made with skill and possessing beauty to be displayed on a wall, as a club or as a paperweight. If used to kill, a gun can be used to commit murder or it can be used in self-defense, to stop oneself (or another) from being murdered. So, you might ask: What is a gun *really* for? Are guns *intrinsically* good or bad? It is obvious that these questions have no answer: a gun can be used for a variety of things, and guns are good or bad depending on how they're used. You might reply, "Yes, but what were the *intentions* of those who made them? Doesn't that determine what they're for?" No. To think so is confused for two reasons: (1) those who made them might have intended a variety of things; but, more fundamentally, (2) things can always be treated, used or viewed in ways their makers did not intend. Thus, a gun has no *fixed* meaning or purpose. Even the intentions of the gun's makers do not determine its meaning or purpose.

On the other hand, the physical constitution and form of the gun do limit what it can do. A gun is definitely better for some things than others. A gun is good (if functioning properly and loaded and operated by a skilled user) for killing, or knocking a can off a fence. Guns can also make good (if unusual) doorstops or paperweights. On the other hand, they are not very good as spatulas or screwdrivers. The features of a gun that limit its uses Sartre refers to as its *facticity*.[6] Sartre's point, then, is not that there are *no* limits—just that there is always a *free choice* about how to operate within the limits that exist. Within those limits, one's freedom *is* "absolute."

We will return to the question of arbitrariness shortly. As you might have guessed, I started with the example of a gun because it is relevant to "Objects in Space." Recall that River sees the gun she is holding as a harmless object, a branch. This scene obviously functions figuratively. River appears through much of *Firefly* as innocent, childlike. In this episode in particular, she sometimes seems to relate to objects around her in a way that is divorced from the functions and meanings others give them, most notably in the case of the gun. One might view this as simply a sign of pathology or dysfunction, but there is another way of looking at it. She has a childlike sense of wonder when she examines things as "bare" objects, existing as such. The gun, then, appears to her as a harmless object of beauty (specifically, as a branch), because that is how she experiences it. "It's just an object," she says. "It doesn't mean

---

[6] More precisely, those features of the gun of which I am conscious as limits are part of *my* facticity.

what you think."[7] In a sense, a gun is just a configuration of parts with a certain physical constitution, arrangement and appearance. Thus, when River views things in a way that is divorced from the functions and meanings others give them, they appear benign; moreover, this is a source of joy for her. She experiences things (as a child does) that others miss, because they take things for granted. For another example, when she moves through the ship, she seems acutely aware of the associated tactile sensations (e.g., on her feet), and of the ship as environment, as it is constituted (its orientation in space, how it is arranged). There is a sensual joy for her in doing so.[8]

Early considers the functions and meanings others give objects reflectively, too. At several points in "Objects in Space" he considers what makes things what they are. For example, he considers his own gun as an object of beauty. He notes that his gun is "pretty" and that he likes "the weight of it"—features not particularly connected with its intended function. Yet he also admires the way its design serves its function. For him, however, there appears to be no sense of innocent wonder; instead, there is pain, and despair. Like Roquentin in *Nausea*, he sees the object as alien. The same is true of his musings about whether River's room is "hers" when she's not there. He feels the environment of the ship and appreciates it (admiring the way the walls of the ship turn outward). He also is aware of the fragility of their existence: the ship's engine ("such a slender thread") can fail if one of its many parts does, killing them all; they are separated from deadly empty space by only the ship's hull; and they are far, far from any help, if things go wrong. Finally, as is the case with River, Early has a sensual appreciation for the ship as a physical object. He says, "People don't appreciate the substance of things. Objects in space. People miss out on what's solid." He has sensibilities that others do not; yet none of this seems to add up to much for him.

Early also seems acutely aware of arbitrariness and incongruities (as he sees it) in human life. (He notes that we require psychoanalysts to undergo their own treatment, but not surgeons; women are weaker than men but only they can "create life"; and so on.) Thus, both his physical and social surroundings seem to him absurd, alien. Yet he exists; he has a job to do.

---

[7] In saying this, she obviously must at some level be aware of what others think—namely, that the gun is *just* a weapon, it is *essentially* an instrument of death.

[8] Whedon intends River's experience to reflect his own. As he says in the "Objects in Space" commentary: "For me, [the realization of objects' absurdity] has a kind of rapture to it, and I find meaning in objects to be a beautiful thing *because* I have no plan to put them in." (Here he apparently refers to the meaning with which we imbue the objects, not any inherent meaning.)

There is a reason why the existentialists were so "negative"—why Sartre entitled his first novel *Nausea* and why the works of existentialists are filled with terms like "fear and trembling," "anguish," "dread," "despair," "forlornness," etc. Suppose you agree with Sartre that things exist without any intrinsic meaning or purpose. Many people feel that, unless things have an inherent or intrinsic purpose, they have no purpose at all. There need to be "absolutes." The implicit reasoning behind this is as follows: if things have no intrinsic purpose, if they have only the purpose or value we freely confer on them (or "imbue" them with), then we could just as well *change our minds* and give them another contrary purpose or value. Thus, since their value is not "part" of them, so to speak, they "really" have no value at all. This is disturbing—even frightening. Most of us don't want our values to be arbitrary. In that case, it would seem, today helping others so that they flourish and are happy is "good," but tomorrow, torturing them might be. This is why the realization of our complete freedom to make such choices can lead to feelings of disorientation. Sartre liked to compare it with the feeling of *vertigo*: I feel vertigo, he thought, because I realize that I *can* hurl myself over a precipice (regardless of whether I *want* to). Nothing is stopping me. Similarly, we *can* (even if we don't now *want* to) decide that torturing people for fun is "good." If value is really *our choice*, what's to stop us? The realization of such absolute freedom can be frightening, disorienting—indeed, sickening. Thus, just as one can become sick from vertigo, one can become sick (nauseous) from the realization of the contingency of value, the realization of one's freedom.

Let us pause to address the question of faith. One might think that God is what is needed to save the day. Sartre and Camus (the existentialist writers Joss Whedon found relevant to his intellectual awakening as a teenager devoid of religious faith) belong to a nontheistic branch of existentialism, but there are theistic existentialists, too.[9] Dostoevsky said, "Without God, anything is possible." Nietzsche talked about the "death of God" as a metaphor for the loss of certainty and absolute value. Does all of this talk of "anguish," "despair" and "nausea" simply result from a lack of faith in God? To this, an existentialist of Sartre's sort might reply that the puzzle does *not* dissolve if we let *God* be the being that confers

---

[9] There are many varieties of existentialism. As I have already noted, there are both theistic and nontheistic existentialists. For obvious reasons (Whedon mentions them explicitly as influences), I concentrate in this essay on nontheistic existentialism of the sort espoused by Sartre and Camus. Those interested in other forms of existentialism can find a good introduction in Walter Kaufmann's *Existentialism from Dostoevsky to Sartre*.

value.[10] To show this, I will put a Sartrean twist on an old dilemma. In his dialogue *Euthyphro*, Plato was concerned with what makes something "pious" (for our purposes, *good*). The famous dilemma he posed was this: Do the gods desire things because they're good, or are they good because the gods desire them? Can the will of the gods (or, as we in our culture would say, God) be what *makes* something good? Well, if things are good or bad *solely because* of the gods' (or God's) will, then there is nothing about the things *themselves* that makes them good or bad. For example, if rape is evil *only* because it is God's will that no one rapes—that is, if God's will is completely free and undetermined by any features *intrinsic* to rape—then God *could have* decided otherwise, i.e., that rape is good. If God's choice is free and undetermined, there is no necessity or reason for it. Most people, faced with the Euthyphro dilemma, respond as follows: Since it is *not* arbitrary whether rape is good or bad, the evilness of rape cannot be based solely on God's will. Therefore, God wants us not to rape because rape is evil, not the other way around. But if so, the question with which we started still has no answer: what *makes* rape evil, since God's will cannot be what makes it so? The problem the Euthyphro dilemma poses for us is not that *we humans* are too finite or flawed to give things value; it is that value, if it is not arbitrary, cannot result solely from the free choice of *any* valuing being—whether God or man.

The problem, then, is very deep. Existentialists such as Sartre claim that value is based on free choice. But apparently, if it is based *solely* on free choice, value must be arbitrary. This seems unacceptable to many people, because value, if anything, *cannot be arbitrary*. It cannot be a matter of a coin toss, so to speak, if rape or torturing people for fun is good or evil.[11] Thus, existentialism has seemed to some to imply *nihilism*—the view that *nothing* is really of value.[12]

Hopefully by now you can feel Early's pain. But perhaps pain is not the only response to absurdity. We don't have to descend into alienation or

---

[10] Certainly, this is true insofar as Sartre is concerned with our *subjective* experience or consciousness. If God determines meaning, each of us still has to decide what that is, e.g., by freely adopting a certain religion or thesis regarding God's will. Nothing forces us to make one choice rather than another. Thus, essentially we have the same problem of choice of values *whether God exists or not*. Camus makes much this point in *The Myth of Sisyphus*: "I don't know whether this world has a meaning that transcends it. But I know that I do not know that meaning and it is impossible for me just now to know it. What can a meaning outside my condition mean to me?" (51).

[11] The response we have to Early's threat to rape Kaylee if she doesn't cooperate, and to his seemingly sadistic willingness to actually do it if need be, is to regard him as a monster. But we would also regard as monstrous those who do not think of his threat as monstrous.

[12] Further analysis of Sartre's thesis that freedom is the basis of value can be found in David Detmer's *Freedom as a Value*.

lassitude (like *Nausea*'s Roquentin) or a sadistic will to power (like Early in "Objects in Space"). For some existentialists have written of a *joy* that can accompany the realization that "objects in space" have no meaning in and of themselves, but only the meaning that we confer on them. Recall the quote with which I began this essay, from Camus' *The Myth of Sisyphus*: "Happiness and the absurd are two sons of the same earth." Camus is saying, essentially, that happiness can be found in the recognition and acceptance of the absurdity of one's condition. Even if one's activities seem pointless (Sisyphus is condemned by the gods to push a large stone to the top of a hill, only to watch it roll to the bottom again, on and on, eternally), one can choose to embrace one's life in all its absurdity for what it is and as one's own, and thus *transcend* the absurdity.

Thus, we, like River, can accept things as bare objects (hence, "absurd") and *choose* to imbue them with whatever value (meaning, function) brings joy, not despair. From our subjective standpoint (and that is all we have), *conferred value feels just like value.* If I love my son, and feel absolute joy seeing him smile, it does not lessen the joy if I contemplate that I have after all *chosen* to love him. Yes, I *could* choose otherwise, but I *won't* and don't *want to.* And maybe, like River, we can even find joy and wonder in contemplating those objects (like guns) that *can* be (but *need not* be, if we so choose) instruments of death.

In his commentary, Whedon states that River's ability to experience the gun as she does (by seeing it as a branch) shows her goodness and kindness. To some, this may seem to evade the deeper question, since it apparently takes what is "good" and "kind" for granted.[13] One would not want simply to say, "Since we are free, we can always choose the good," if what is "good" is ultimately *constituted* by our free choices. That would not be helpful, just as "Do the right thing" is empty advice if one does not *already* know what the "right thing" is. As Early notes, he has his "code," too—the "code" of the bounty hunter. (Yes, bounty hunters have "codes" and "ethics," and so do mafioso.) But, apparently, Early's "code" allows him to threaten rape and murder, and to fulfill that threat, with some relish, if his aims as a bounty hunter are thwarted. If you are choosing what "code" to follow for yourself—the beneficent one of River, or

---

[13] Nietzsche argues in *On the Genealogy of Morals* that kindness, meekness, humility, etc., only become "virtues" within a moral system born under social conditions in which people were subject to others. This, he says, is true of our Judeo-Christian morality. By contrast, Greco-Roman morality, which emerged from a society of conquerors, regards valor, strength and even cruelty (under certain conditions) as part of goodness and virtue. (Recall the Colloseum and its games.) Nietzsche envisions a new kind of person, an *Übermensch* (Over-man), who consciously creates his own values and thus lives "beyond good and evil." (See *Basic Writings of Nietzsche*.)

the malevolent one of Early—what deeper "code" can guide you? For a nonarbitrary choice—one with a reason—can only be based on some *prior* system of values.

Since this essay is near its end, I will leave it to you, dear reader, to ponder the puzzles that stem from the idea of value being constituted by free choices. Instead, let us close by considering the final scene of the episode, in which Early floats in space, helpless, awaiting his own suffocation—he, soon to be a mere "object in space," flotsam, space junk. "Well," he says, "here I am." Joss Whedon says in his commentary that he does not intend to give answers to the questions about meaning he raises. That is because he is sympathetic to the idea that everything *is* "absurd." We are all just objects floating in space, awaiting our end.

But our response to that is *our choice*.

SOURCES

Camus, Albert. *The Myth of Sisyphus and Other Essays.* New York: Vintage International, 1955.

Detmer, David. *Freedom as a Value: A Critique of the Ethical Theory of Jean-Paul Sartre.* La Salle, IL: Open Court, 1986.

Kaufmann, Walter. *Existentialism from Dostoevsky to Sartre.* New York: New American Library, 1975.

Nietzsche, Friedrich. *Basic Writings of Nietzsche.* Trans. and ed. Walter Kaufmann. New York: The Modern Library, 1992.

Sartre, Jean-Paul. *Nausea.* Trans. Lloyd Alexander. New York: New Directions, 1964.

Whedon, Joss. Commentary on "Objects in Space," Disc 4 of *Firefly: The Complete Series.* Twentieth Century Fox DVD, 2003.

Lyle Zynda received his PhD in philosophy from Princeton University in 1995. After spending a year teaching at Caltech, he took up his current position in the philosophy department at Indiana University South Bend (IUSB), where he is now associate professor. Dr. Zynda specializes in philosophy of science, philosophy of mind, cognitive science, epistemology, metaphysics and logic. He has published articles in internationally renowned journals such as Synthese, Philosophy of Science *and* Philosophical Studies. *He also periodically teaches a course at IUSB called "Philosophy, Science and Science Fiction."*

This is an insightful look at the Zoe-Wash marriage, reminding me of how effortlessly I think of these two as real people, forgetting their from-the-brow-of-Joss birth story.

If the show had survived, I like to think that I would have had the chance to write more for these two. I had already, in fact, begun a subtle lobbying campaign with that end in mind. And maybe hope isn't lost. If Animated Buffy ever becomes a reality, I may have a chance to revisit characters from that world. Perhaps something similar needs to happen in the Fireflyverse. What do you say?

More Than a Marriage of Convenience

MICHELLE SAGARA WEST

CONSIDER WASH.

Sort of sounds like a command from your mother when she isn't being particularly garrulous. Or a verb. Or a name you might give someone because you're young and you think funny names for children *are* funny.

But for those of us who were heavily indoctrinated in all things *Firefly*, Wash is the name of one of television's most interesting men. Why? Well, consider the actor who plays him. Alan Tudyk, it can be argued—although not safely in my hearing—is not the most attractive of men; he's neither tall nor classically good-looking, has a slightly funny nose and an extremely flexible face, if his expressions are anything to go by. He's even worn a fake mustache for the cause. Oh, and a really horrible shirt. He's handled invisible gear shifts. He's made up functions for a nonfunctioning console.

But though Alan Tudyk is at the heart of the character he plays, it's the character himself that's of interest. Of great interest. Back to the why, now.

My answer is this. First: he's a geek. No, really. Look at the set of dinosaurs that he keeps for those long hauls in space when he has nothing else to do. Second, he's got in ample supply those characteristics that so often accompany healthy geekdom: a sense of humor; a ready wit; an ability to be, in many ways, the open or sensible mind—in his empathy for Simon's situation, and in his attempt to place murder (of Simon) somewhere on the unacceptable end of what are already questionably legal assignments. Third, his relationship with his wife.

Now, consider Zoe.

Zoe does not suffer from the slings and arrows of unfortunate parental malice. Her name isn't so much a command as she is, and if she's always ready for action, she's not a verb. She is, as has been pointed out elsewhere in this book, what Wash refers to as "a warrior woman." The thing that surprises is the weight both of those words have in this remarkable show: she is *both* a woman *and* a warrior, a soldier without compare. Since she knows who she is, rather than who she's supposed to be, she's capable of actually having a sane relationship and even of acknowledging its importance.

She knows how to take care of herself. But then again, so does Jayne, and he'd make no one an ideal wife. Or a husband. Zoe knows how to restore or keep order, but arguably, so does Mal, the man to whom she owes her career sense of loyalty and the only man who can give her orders.

We now have two thoughts to hold, so hold them both: Wash and Zoe.

In what is perhaps the finest of the episodes that aired, "Out of Gas"— I'll go out on a limb and say the best, period (with the safe knowledge that Joss Whedon agrees with me)—we're offered a glimpse of Wash and Zoe's past.

Zoe's first words of significance involving the man she would eventually marry? "He bothers me." When asked why, she said, "I don't know. Something about him just...bothers me."

The rest was left to our imagination, something that Joss has always excelled at—although he's rarely left so much that's gentle and worthwhile to our imagination, going instead where the darkness drives him. With humor, of course.

Wash and Zoe. Typical first meeting, in some ways; romance is always an old story. Girl meets boy. Girl and boy dislike each other instantly. Stuff happens. Girl and boy realize they're *in love*. Girl and boy are parted for some time, and then eventually, something happens that throws them together—their distance serving as the act that makes them worthy of each other, go figure.

Except that in *this* relationship, the antagonism is all one-sided—*he* bothers *her*. It's not clear that Wash even *notices* Zoe when he's first asked to take on the job of piloting the Firefly. And that? That's geek all over. I can imagine—because, you know, it's a free country—that when *she* decided it was time, he kind of looked stunned and woke up. Who wouldn't? Zoe is the most attractive and compelling woman on television these days. Or she was. But I promised that I wouldn't write four thousand words composed entirely of "FOX Sucks." I'm just saying.

If Wash were just a hapless idiot, the whole dynamic of the marriage would just...suck. It wouldn't work at all. Zoe isn't a girl, and she's not an alpha female mother; her role on the ship, in fact, is emphatically *not* that of a mother. That's Inara's role, front and center. Zoe's not looking to mother Wash, and if Wash weren't competent at what he does—which, in this case, is literally save their lives on a regular basis with his incredible ability behind the controls of *Serenity*—I can't imagine she'd've looked twice at him. Once she'd decided he was worth a first look, that is.

But she clearly decided she wanted that second look, and he clearly decided to pay attention, because they're in each other's pockets for much of the show. They're in the same small, dank room; they're often physically in contact—but it's not a contact that screams Hot Sex, although they have that as well. (That seems to be the only force television networks accept as a reason for two people to get together: the need to have hot sex.)

So what is it about Zoe and Wash that *works?* What is it about Joss Whedon's insistence—against the express wishes of the people producing the show—that the marriage not be stricken from the show entirely, and the angst of early romance slotted into its place instead? What about *this* couple made them so clearly a good, solid match for each other?

Why did Joss, in fact, insist on having them at all?

Because he wanted this show to be about real people, in real situations. Adults, struggling with life.

Okay, you can stop holding those thoughts now, because we've come to the part of the rant where they're useful. Wash and Zoe.

The marriage of Wash and Zoe is an *adult* marriage. It's not the *Buffy* idea of marriage, where youth and hope can't quite overcome fact and incompatibility. This marriage fits the context of the show itself: adults in a grim situation, making their way in the world. Adults *do* marry. It happens frequently. Once married, you'll notice, they don't agonize about it constantly—and angst of this particular kind wouldn't suit Wash or

Zoe's characters well—because it's a choice they've made, aware of who the other person is, and it's founded on respect. On communication. And on a great deal of affection and consideration.

People sometimes think that respect is one of those "mother" words: it's nice enough, but it's not about the *passion*. Well, okay. It's also not about the sex. It's about the clear understanding of, and appreciation for, who the other person is. Contrast Wash and Zoe with Mal and Inara, and you can see how the missing ingredients work against the latter couple in their dance around each other. They don't know how to tell each other the truth, even if it's painful; Wash and Zoe do. Mal can't respect Inara's chosen career. Wash and Zoe don't have that problem. Mal has no clue how to be affectionate with anyone but Kaylee—who he's clearly not attracted to; Zoe can be. And she offers Wash a joyful, playful affection.

Wash's poem about Zoe and the subsequent pillow in the face are acts of affection. Affection good. But if it were only affection that was shown, this would be a superficial marriage, and a far less real one.

Wash is comfortable, dedicated, slightly goofy; his sense of humor, his sense of humanity and his boyish playfulness are things that Zoe lacks—and I think she needs them. We all do.

Zoe is a killer, a soldier, a dead shot. But she's strong and she doesn't waver, and these are things that Wash lacks in a world where they're necessary.

They fill a need for each other that isn't based on need alone, and because they're entirely different people, they express it in different ways. In "Out of Gas" Mal gave Wash an order. Wash told Mal to blow off, and Mal made it clear that it wasn't a request. This, while Zoe lay in a state close to death. In a similar position, Zoe would have obeyed. Wash knew this, and didn't care; he wasn't trying to *be* Zoe; he was trying to live up to what they have together.

In "Bushwhacked" there was plenty of the dichotomy that is Wash and Zoe on-screen, and it was my favorite part of the episode. Zoe was stiff-lipped, silent, guarding her own in privacy and certainly unwilling to share the important things with an unfriendly stranger in a position of authority. But Wash? Hell, he loves Zoe. He wants the 'verse to know it. Certainly he let the uncomfortable squirming interrogator know it, and in detail, and without being aware of just how much he was giving away. Because he does have a lot to give—another thing she needs.

I have to admit that "Out of Gas" was the first episode of *Firefly* I watched. And because the ensemble was so damn convincing, it was definitely not the last; I watched them all, and with a television hunger that I rarely feel. It was damn good to see a strong couple whose lives and duties are separate—whose togetherness doesn't depend on the Big Cling. And I wanted more of it.

So I did what most *Firefly* fans have done: I went to the Web and spent hours browsing different sites. I came across one description of *Firefly* that irritated me immensely because it referred to the "troubled marriage" of Wash and Zoe. My first thought? *Is this person married, or has he spent much time around people who are?* Except with more swearing.

Buffy was about high school. *Angel* was an abortive attempt to go adult. *Firefly* was about adults. And adults in long-term relationships argue; it's one of the ways in which we communicate. Sometimes, there's heat.

In "Our Mrs. Reynolds" Zoe comes up with the famous, "You know that sex we were going to have? Ever?" line in her irritation. I didn't interpret that as blackmail, or as a real threat—it was a very definitive statement of annoyance and irritation. But annoyance and irritation were gone by the time Saffron was—because the wiles that worked with Mal, and would certainly have worked with Jayne, did not work with Wash. Saffron realized they wouldn't. And Zoe realized that they hadn't.

What did we realize? What should we have known, if we didn't? That what Wash and Zoe have, simple impulsive attraction can't break. The attraction was there—it just wasn't the only thing that mattered. Because in committed relationships, attraction to other people is always going to exist; it's just not the driving force that seems to consume so many angst-ridden relationships offered up as "real" to prime-time viewers. Commitment isn't an accident. It's not an act of fate. It's a vow; it's a focus; it's a purpose.

In "War Stories," when Wash is feeling insecure—as we all do from time to time—I *loved* the interaction between him and Zoe. I loved that Mal was out of it, and left out of it, while they talked over, across and behind him; they were dealing with their issues in the open, and if he was one of them, he was almost beside the point. And knew it.

Zoe's choice to let Wash accompany Mal was stupid. Why? Because Zoe's the expert; Zoe's the competent soldier. But it was my kind of stupid, because it was *real*. She was upset at Wash, she was angry at his lack of confidence, and she reacted emotionally. It was not her finest moment, but sometimes you can't put work before family. It certainly was not Wash's finest moment either.

Does this mean "troubled marriage"? Not in my books. It means *real* marriage, that constant state of negotiation between two people who themselves aren't perfect.

A troubled marriage is indicated best by the eye-rolling lack of respect between two people. It's the subtle put-downs that pass as humor. It's the passive aggression that doesn't allow for real conversation or resolvable conflict. This is not what they were doing. They treated each other seriously, let the anger show; they offered each other this much respect.

Wash was jealous. Not because he thought Zoe preferred Mal, but because there was a part of her life he didn't share. This, too, happens in real life.

But as in real life, and in any relationship based on respect and good faith, it's not a showstopper. (That would be FOX. Ahem.) Wash went with Mal. They were caught by Niska, who has a tiny problem in the laid-back department (and in the being alive department—because, why is he? Okay, that was a digression). Niska had them both imprisoned, because he had decided to practice the philosophy of torture for his own edification. This would not, in the minds of many, be the ideal time for a man to argue with the captain of his wife.

But Wash and Mal did get into that argument, when everything else was looking pretty grim. "What would Zoe be doing?" Wash asked in desperation. Mal answered: "Talking less." And certainly *not* panicking. When Niska started torturing, Mal started talking. But not to Niska; he talked to Wash. He talked about Zoe. He talked about Zoe ignoring his order *not* to marry Wash. And he kept on talking about this, as the torture went on. Why? (And why are there idiots who thought this was supposed to be a real conversation as opposed to something that saved sanity and stopped a man from breaking?) Because Mal knows that Zoe is Wash's focus, the center of his stable universe, the thing that matters at heart.

Insecurity and jealousy adorn that heart, but they aren't the whole of it.

When Zoe came to buy them free, she chose Wash. Without a thought. But even that was not unalloyed; she chose Wash because Wash isn't a soldier; because she knew it was a miracle that he hadn't already broken. Mal is a soldier, and she trusted Mal to survive.

He did. They all did. And Wash and Zoe were happy again by the end of the show, even if Mal did insist on tweaking Wash. Having had a glimpse of Zoe's life, Wash was more than content to live his own.

Does this mean they're in the clear? No. Because—as I said above—marriage of any stable flavor is a constant rebalancing of priorities that requires a constant communication. In "Heart of Gold" Zoe brought up what was obviously a well-trod argument: she wanted a child. And Wash didn't want to bring one into uncertainty and possible death. Zoe pointed out that they're *never* going to be in a perfect position to have a child, because a perfect position just doesn't exist in this 'verse.

Some people were surprised that it was Zoe who wanted children and Wash who was hesitant—but I don't understand why. I think those people have a view of Zoe as one thing and one thing alone—but Zoe is a woman, as feminine as it suits context, and has always been willing to take the big risks. What's a bigger risk in the life she leads, with the job she loves and the role she's chosen, than a child? It's in her personality to take that risk. Wash is risk-averse. He knows what he can be responsible for, and he's not certain he can do this. It's not that he doesn't want children; he's just more afraid of what it might mean.

And we're never going to know how it all plays out.

Joss was brave here: having children—lack of children, lack of desire on one partner's side—is possibly the most real threat to marriage that exists. And he let it play out, on the screen, showing vulnerability on both sides.

But in creating this couple, he's been brave on many fronts. Wash and Zoe's relationship is honest. It's not the Ozzy and Harriet example of a "good marriage"; it's not the soap equivalent, where everything is filmed through Vaseline lenses and people are *perfect*, until they're suddenly not *in love*. In love and love are not the same, and Joss is drawing that line. By testing commitment, by showing real people in tough situations, by offering both their joy and their anger, he's highlighting imperfections. He's stating, clearly, that there *are no perfect people*. Without perfect people, there is no such thing as perfect love. Instead, there are flawed, imperfect people—and in Wash and Zoe, the flaws mesh, rather than clash.

Successful marriage is a wedding—in a less than literal sense—of the flaws and needs and strengths of imperfect people. And in gracing us with Zoe and Wash, in fighting for their on-screen existence, in insisting on the marriage as vital to the show itself, he gave us something as close to the perfect depiction of a television marriage as I've yet seen.

Michelle Sagara West doesn't watch much television these days because she's still in mourning for Firefly. *That said, she watches the DVDs on a semiregular basis, and has traumatized other new viewers by forgetting to mention that the series was cancelled when she loans the set out. She can talk about* Firefly *for hours on end. And sometimes, she talks to the right people (see, editor). She is also a novelist, who has eight published novels as Michelle West and four novels originally published as Michelle Sagara, which will be reprinted by BenBella Books, one every six months, starting in September 2005.*

This essay made me stop and think about Zoe more vigorously than I had ever consciously done before. It made me realize again that I had rarely thought of her as a character at all before, as a creation of Joss Whedon, even though I actually saw him create her. Zoe—and Wash— were to me the realest of real people. I think this essay goes a long way toward explaining the origin of that feeling. When a character is given a full life and a full range of emotions by a genius writer, and a full set of tools for expressing those emotions, in the form of a superb actor, you end up with the most convincing of illusions.

"Thanks for the reenactment, sir." Zoe: Updating the Woman Warrior

TANYA HUFF

WHAT IS IT ABOUT ZOE that makes her the first truly believable warrior woman on television? Television, and genre television especially, has given us a host of female characters who were more than ready to belt out a chorus of Helen Reddy's "I am woman, hear me roar!" But the roar was always a lot more believable than the woman. Just what is it that makes Zoe different than Xena or Buffy or the Relic Hunter or—going back a bit—Wonder Woman?

Superficially, there are no obvious differences. Zoe, like the others, is a beautiful woman who doesn't hesitate to plunge into battle with both fists and weapons. She has no sword or supernatural destiny or magic bracelets, but she's a part of almost every action sequence from "Serenity" to "Objects in Space." Look a little closer, though, and you'll see that the warrior isn't all of who Zoe is. The fight doesn't define her every action on the screen, and that gives her a believability other women warriors can only dream of.

Most importantly, Zoe hasn't fallen victim to the fate of most strong women on television, who are invariably hyper-feminized into male fantasies—fantasies that don't challenge the worldview of that all-important nineteen-to-thirty male demographic. Yes, the woman warrior has a sword or a gun or kung fu action, but she's also wearing enough makeup to star in a Vegas review and, as if that wasn't enough, micro-miniskirts, high-heeled boots and push-up breast plates...which is not to say that firm support isn't important while kicking ass, just that cleavage shouldn't be a fighter's first weapon. Look at poor Gabrielle over in the *Xena*verse. The tougher she got, the less she wore.

Zoe keeps her clothes on to fight. She dresses—and undresses—like an adult. If she takes her clothes off, it's because she's in bed with her husband (who is also unclothed), not because she's about to charge into battle. In fact, in a practical move seldom made by television characters male *or* female, she *adds* a bulletproof vest when it seems likely the sale of the protein bars to Patience in "Serenity" will go south. Yes, her pants are tight. So are Mal's. The difference? Mal's are sexualized with Kaylee's "Captain Tightpants" comment in "Shindig." Zoe's never are. It's also interesting that when there's a dress to be worn, as in the ambush that begins "Our Mrs. Reynolds," it's Mal who puts it on, not Zoe.

This is not to say that Zoe has been neutered, the other way in which strong female characters have been made less threatening—although usually this is a reaction to brains, not brawn. Dana Scully of *The X-Files* would be a prime example of neutering; so would Velma on *Scooby Doo*. (To give Joss Whedon and Mutant Enemy credit, Fred—*Angel's* Velma—was shown to have a variety of healthy appetites.) Zoe is in full command of her considerable sexuality. She's not only personally aware of it but aware that others are too, and that's fine by her.

In "Jaynestown," she grinned at Jayne's "Hell, I'll pinch ya" response to her teasing comment, "Is that Jayne? Is it really him? Pinch me, Wash, I must be dreaming," and she laughingly swatted his hand away. No matter how little she's personally attracted to Jayne, his interest is neither unexpected nor a threat. In "Shindig," she declared, "If I'm gonna wear a dress, I want something with some slink." Wash's reaction had a wonderful, visceral honesty: "You want a slinky dress? I can buy you a slinky dress. Captain, can I have money for a slinky dress?" Zoe knows the effect she'd have in slink and Wash's response was the default response for anyone with a functioning libido. So was Jayne's "I'll chip in." It was not so much Zoe's matter-of-fact, "I could hurt you," as it is Jayne's silent, "Yeah, that's true," that lifted the exchange above the ordinary television presentation of a beautiful woman. Not to mention that the entire exchange was a rare acknowledgment that women warriors are still women and appreciate a change of wardrobe now and then.

A little later in "Shindig," when the crew was sitting around the cargo bay trying to figure out how to jump Badger's people and Jayne says, "Zoe could get naked," Wash's "Nope" had the feel of *same old, same old* about it—an ordinary reaction to a familiar scenario.

The characters on the show aren't blind and the audience isn't blind and no one was pretending any different—Zoe is a gorgeous, sexually aware adult woman. Deal with it.

The emphasis here is on the word "adult": in that initial list of woman warriors, one of those things was not like the others. Buffy wasn't a woman. She might have been considered an adult when the show ended—and I'm of two minds about how much she was actually allowed to leave her teens and teenage problems behind—but for most of the series she was a girl. One heck of a tough girl dealing with some major issues, granted, but still not a woman. Having been through these difficult years ourselves, those of us looking for a woman warrior we could truly relate to sympathized with Buffy's problems, but many of us—especially women in my age group—spent a fair bit of time toward the end sighing and murmuring, "Honey, grow up."

Zoe isn't looking for a boyfriend; she has a husband. She's not trying to figure out her place in the world; she knows where she stands: on *Serenity,* beside Mal. We're given all this during the credits. When we're told that some of the crew are fighters during the voice-over that was deemed necessary on network—although thankfully lost on the DVDs—we're shown Zoe with Mal and Jayne, guns drawn. Zoe's images under the actual credits begin with her standing next to Mal, gun drawn; then we see her in the war carrying a big gun, and then protecting *Serenity* and her crew. Finally, after all these shots of the warrior, we are shown the woman, leaning back in Wash's arms: laughing, happy, content. That search for definition that's so much a part of Buffy—of every teenager, let alone the Slayer—is not Zoe's problem. This is not to say she doesn't have problems, just that finding herself isn't one of them.

For women on television, men are always a problem.

Zoe is carrying on a relationship with two separate men—her husband Wash and her captain Malcolm Reynolds—and that traditionally results in hijinks and conflict out there in television land.

Mal is fully aware of just how attractive Zoe is, but their relationship has nothing to do with that whole hormonally charged man/woman dynamic. Zoe is Mal's strong right arm, his anchor. He knows she'll be standing there beside him no matter what slightly dubious plan he comes up with, and no matter what her expressed opinion of that plan may be. During the bar fight that opened "The Train Job," there was no conversation about what they were going to do, but Mal knew Zoe would be there to back him up. "I just wanted you to face me," he explained with a smile to the Alliance supporter who had just insulted him, "so she could get behind you." But it's not only Zoe's physical backing Mal needs; he needs her input. In "Trash," after Saffron laid out her plan for breaking in to steal the Lassiter, he frowned and said, "Zoe, you ain't said a word. Time to weigh in." It was perfectly clear that no decision would be made until after Zoe had her say. She has, in point of fact, become the sergeant to his captain.

Small military digression: Zoe was very likely also a sergeant during the war. There's no other explanation for the way she responds in "The Message" with, "Private," to Tracey's "Hey, Zoe." Corporals just generally don't take that tone, even master corporals. But there *are* a number of levels to the rank of sergeant, and Mal is definitely the senior NCO. Mind you, privates don't call sergeants by their first—and apparently only—name, so it's possible she was just one remarkably tough corporal.

Zoe's relationship with Mal also helps to set her apart from the standard television woman. They're friends and comrades; two gorgeous, sensual, ostensibly heterosexual people with absolutely nothing sexual happening between them. Zoe is the only person Mal trusts and he in turn is the one authority she acknowledges. They share a history that no one else on the crew can touch—no matter how much they try, no matter how much they care. Mal and Zoe's backstory, their shared history, permeates even the smallest things: the way they eat fruit, cutting it into small pieces because of what happened when they were cut off at New Kasmir and the Alliance threw them apples loaded with small grenades. It's like Saffron says to Mal in "Trash," explaining why she didn't shoot when she got the drop on him: "You and Monty fought in the war together, right? Yeah, I smelled that. The war buddy bond is tough to crack."

That the strength of Zoe's bond with Mal causes some friction between herself and her husband—who has his own interesting concepts of authority which seem to only occasionally include the captain—is perfectly understandable to the viewer. (I hesitate to say to the mature viewer, but honestly, you have to get relationships to get Zoe and Wash. Not everyone gets them at first.) Wash knows his wishes will come second should they contradict the captain's orders and he doesn't like it. He pokes at this all the time, right from the first scene Wash and Zoe share in "Serenity."

WASH: What if we just tell him?
ZOE: He's the captain, Wash.
WASH: Right, I'm just the husband.

This brings us, of course, to "War Stories." In spite of overt plot points, Niska and the maintaining of reputations and the largest number of scenes that include extended bloody violence in any of the thirteen episodes, "War Stories" was actually about Mal's relationship to Zoe, her relationship to Wash and, to a lesser extent, Wash's relationship to Mal. The episode was an in-your-face examination of multiple levels of twisted subtext that perfectly illustrated the self-awareness that made *Firefly* such tremendous television.

Because Zoe loves Wash, she lied to him about the captain's reaction to his plan, in order that he not be hurt by the rejection. Wash understandably objected to the lie. He was having his face rubbed in the closeness between Zoe and Mal and he just couldn't take it anymore—which was one of the reasons he blackmailed the two of them into allowing him to take Zoe's place on the shuttle. The other reason? He was afraid his wife—who he sees as a warrior woman—sees him as weak. He didn't fight in the war. He quite clearly doesn't like to hear war stories. Mal and Zoe share this strength; but Wash also has strength, and he needed Zoe to acknowledge it. That neither the show nor Zoe had ever ignored his actual strengths—his flying skills, which have gotten them out of any number of tight situations—isn't the point. He needed to prove he was strong like they were strong.

When Zoe came to Niska for "her men," there were a number of ways to read her choice. The wife's choice: if I have to choose between my captain's life and my husband's, I choose my husband. The soldier's choice: rescue the weaker man now; the stronger has a better chance of surviving until I get back with the big guns. The command choice: I save the people I'm responsible for first. The second-in-command choice: take him, not me, says the commander; I'll go down with the ship. Every choice meant rescuing Wash and leaving Mal behind. Take a good look at Mal's face during this scene. Wash might have been unsure, but Mal knew exactly who Zoe was going to choose. And Zoe knew Mal knew it. There was no reason for her to hesitate because there was never any question of who she'd chose.

Did it kill her to walk away and leave Mal there? Yes. Could she have done it any other way? No.

When Mal and Wash were together they talked about Zoe. When Zoe and Wash were together, they talked about Mal. When all three of them were finally together in the common room at the end of the episode, they turned all that subtext into text, acknowledged the television elephant in the room (the potential for Mal and Zoe to be attracted to each other) and dealt with it. Mal isn't attracted to Zoe. Zoe isn't attracted to Mal. With it there in front of his face, Wash had to acknowledge that. Jayne got an eyeful and acted like a heavily armed Greek chorus: "Now something about that is just downright unsettling."

And it was. Fans look for subtext, and the only way to keep them from assuming there are relationship vibes between any two overtly attractive, heterosexual characters—especially two sharing the kind of history that Mal and Zoe carry—is to come right out and say there isn't. We, the fans, needed to be convinced the same way Wash did. Zoe and Mal are friends; to have it any other way would be...unsettling.

Because Zoe loves her husband. He turns her on—witness her response to the adrenaline-rush end that came with escaping the Reavers at the end of "Serenity." ("Sir, I'd like you to take the helm, please. I need this man to tear all my clothes off.") She, in turn, excites him, and he was quite enthusiastically clear about that when being interviewed by the Alliance in "Bushwhacked." ("The legs. Oh yeah, I definitely have to say it was her legs. You can put that down. Her legs...and right where her legs meet her back. Actually, that whole area.") He supports what she does although he worries about her going into danger. She supports what he does—any time Wash is doing some tricky flying, Zoe's right there behind his chair, often with her hand resting on his shoulder. They talk about the things married couples talk about: spending time together away from work, sleeping, having children. The words husband and wife were frequently and affectionately used. It's incredibly unusal to be given a television relationship that involves mutual respect and attraction and is allowed to have a few rocky patches without degenerating into an excuse to have two characters snip at each other. A line like "Have you been drinking, husband?" on any other show would have degenerated into a nag, nag, nag byplay, but here, on *Firefly*, it's a nothing more than a somewhat archaic request for information.

How rare is it for a television warrior of any gender to even *have* a long-term relationship? Relationships invariably become prologues, there only for the payoff of cheap and easy angst as either the relationship—or non-warrior in it—dies. Relationships that last are complex, and television, for the most part, doesn't do complex well, preferring instead the primary colors of "You killed the one I love; I have nothing left but the fight." Writers and producers seem to think that relationships make a warrior weak without, apparently, ever considering how they can also make a warrior strong. A good part of Zoe's strength, of why she can keep on fighting, comes from her relationship with Wash—comes from knowing she has him to come back to.

There were words said, back when *Firefly* was on the air—and rumor has it that some of those words were said by the fine people at FOX—that Wash and Zoe's relationship wasn't obvious enough. That makes me wonder what relationship they were watching because, besides the overt interaction, besides Wash's emotional reaction to Zoe's injury in "Out of Gas," these two touch all the time. Not once, but twice, Zoe tucks a napkin into the front of Wash's shirt. You don't get more obvious than that.

And yet, in spite of the fact she's all woman, Zoe is also clearly one of the boys, not one of the girls. When she said, in "Bushwhacked," "Jayne, you'll scare the women," she was being perfectly serious—as funny a line as it is to the viewer. Inara and Kaylee were standing together; Zoe obviously wasn't a part of "the women." This us-and-them attitude was made clear right from "Serenity," when she was standing in the cockpit with Jayne and Mal and Wash, laughing about the trick Mal had just played on Simon.

Zoe doesn't only share their sense of humor—although hers is by far the driest on the ship—she fights like one of the boys, too. No round, feminine weapons. No fancy high kicks. No magic lasso. She's got a shotgun and a sidearm, and a strong right cross. Do they toss in a female villain so Zoe has someone to catfight? No. Zoe fights the same bad guys the boys do. With a little less bulk, she may fight smarter, but she fights. When Mal needs muscle, he takes Zoe and Jayne.

Firefly may have a small tendency to turn Zoe into a superwoman. She can fight. She can love. She can be the voice of reason. She can be the voice of passion. She can sum up complex lines of dialogue in a few pragmatic words ("So, not running now?"). She can be wise ("First rule of battle, little one, don't ever let them know where you are."). She can crack wise ("'Course there are other schools of thought."). She can follow. She can lead. She can even, heaven help us, bring home the bacon and fry it up in a pan ("Mmm, wife soup. I must've done good."). Thank God she's also opinionated, violent, jealous, sarcastic, suspicious and not always right. Not to mention somewhat ethically challenged. Her problem in "Serenity" with dumping Simon on the feds was that the feds wouldn't let them walk, and her objection to Jayne's suggestion that they kill Dobson was that killing a fed is stupid. Not wrong: stupid.

Three-dimensional people, that's what it's all about. Because three-dimensional people equals three-dimensional women. Make one of those women a warrior and you've got Zoe: a complex, adult married woman, fully clothed, with a strong right cross, a sense of humor, an awareness of her own sexuality and a big gun. Can a television-watching, postmodern, feminist sf geek ask for anything more?

Tanya Huff lives and writes in rural Ontario, Canada, with her partner Fiona Patton, seven cats and an unintentional Chihuahua. Her twentieth book, Smoke and Shadows—*an urban fantasy in which the cancellation of* Firefly *is cited as evidence that we live in a world where anything can happen—was out in hardcover in the spring of 2004 and will be out in paperback in the spring of 2005. Book two,* Smoke and Mirrors, *will be out in hardcover in July 2005.*

Inara was the Firefly *character that I felt I understood the least well, despite her prominence in my episode "Shindig." She had a quietness and a gentle amusement that are among the hardest qualities to convey in writing. One ends up pushing too hard, writing too much, then having to go back and, with brutal pen, remove half of it. In the end, few words are written in dialogue, many in the stage directions, and the script is handed to the actress with the unspoken wish that she "run with it." You could capture Zoe in a cool aside, Kaylee in an exclamation, but Inara lived in the pauses.*

The pre-romance between Inara and Mal had that wonderful trembling-in-suspension quality of the best television relationships. It was unable to move forward, not because of artificial barriers, but because someone would have had to change something in their nature in order for it to be allowed to move forward. They are dancers caught in gelatin. Only not so sticky.

At any rate, that's what I know about Inara. Joy Davidson knows a lot more, and it's good stuff.

Whores and Goddesses: The Archetypal Domain of Inara Serra

JOY DAVIDSON

JOSS WHEDON SEEMS BLESSED with a gift for bringing subversive feminine archetypes to life. First he gave us Buffy, Darla and Jasmine. Later, he offered up *Firefly*'s Zoe, the fearless warrior, and Inara Serra, the exotically graceful Companion. While I am in awe of Zoe's fierce power, it's Inara who stirs me—perhaps because she *is* me, at least, in some ways.

It is barely a stretch to suggest that Inara and I are descendants of the same ancient erotic healing tradition. I am a highly educated psychologist and sex therapist; she is a scrupulously trained courtesan and—I would argue—sex therapist. My professional work demands that I draw upon my knowledge, my instincts and my heart, while remaining always at arm's length of my clients. Inara's profession draws upon those resources, too, while allowing for more intimate contact. But despite this distinction, the same impetus often lies at the center of our work: to elicit our clients' trust and truth, to bring their dreams to light, and out of the relationships we foster, to embolden their truest desires.

The ancient tradition I share with women like Inara has captured my imagination as fully as any fictional universe ever has, and I suspect that it has afflicted Joss Whedon, too. For in creating the character of Inara Serra, he has opened a portal to a sweeping saga filled with all the goddesses, priestesses, whores and healers of human history. No small feat, that. But then, he is the guy who turned a petite valley girl into the kick-ass savior of the world.

Whedon has been quoted as suggesting that Inara's character was fashioned after the Renaissance courtesan and the Japanese geisha. But, in point of fact, Inara is a descendent of far earlier incarnations of the carnal femme. I have no way of knowing whether Whedon took to the mythology texts in constructing her character or whether Inara sprang from deep within his collective unconscious like Athena from the head of Zeus. Either way, Inara's overt sexuality and inherent vulnerability imbue her with archetypal richness. She is easily the primordial goddess, the holy whore, the besmirched harlot and the compassionate healer. Every data stream we see, all we know of her, propels us through a psychic wormhole and toward a collision course with the cultural artifacts of Earth's checkered past.

As much as Inara reflects the past, she is equally a contemporary *Everywoman*, or, more accurately, *Everywhore*: liberalism's enterprising dream-girl, radical-feminism's oppressed victim, the conservative right's sinful temptress…and, let's not forget, popular culture's love-struck, intimacy-phobic, "I-gotta-be-free" girl, too. Inara successfully straddles the juiciest memes of ancient history, the present day and an alarmingly possible future.

A HIERARCHY OF WHORES

During Inara's first meeting with Capt. Malcolm Reynolds, she was all business and boundaries, brashly demanding a discount on his asking price for the shuttle in exchange for bringing the legitimacy of her profession to

Serenity. Suspicious of her motives for traversing the outlying planets, Mal asked what she was running from. Inara denied running at all.

"If it's Alliance trouble you got," said Mal, "you might want to consider another ship. Some on board here fought for the Independents."

"The Alliance has no quarrel with me. In fact, I supported Unification." Inara couldn't have chosen a worse rejoinder.

"Didja?" said Mal. "Well, I don't suppose you're the only whore that did."

"Oh—one further addendum," she tossed in, all businesslike. "That's the last time you get to call me a whore."

"Never again," Mal promised, lying. Thus, the chemistry of their relationship was firmly established, and the interminable jousting commenced.

Mal's reluctance to dignify Inara's professional status reflected far more than his hatred of the Alliance; his reticence was packed with thousands of years of emotional dynamite. To fully comprehend the distinction between "Companion" and common "whore," we need to time-travel back more than twenty thousand years to a world that archeologists, anthropologists and historians have constructed from fragments of physical evidence, and peruse a controversial slice of idyllic ancient history that may or may not have existed quite as it is described by those who tell the tale.

WHEN GOD WAS A HELL-OF-A-WOMAN

Once upon a time, well before the advent of recorded history, there existed a world that revolved around women. Women were honored as the givers of life, the embodiments of the Great Goddess, Queen of Heaven, and they were the sole tenders of her temples. Culture, religion and sexuality were entwined and inseparable, for they emanated from the same source: the Goddess herself. Priestesses led their tribes in ritual celebrations of Eros through ecstatic union with the divinely feminine life force. Freedom and equality reigned for many thousands of years.

Then a terrible transformation ensued. Beginning around 3000 B.C.E., hordes of invaders from distant lands began plundering this utopian, matriarchal society, wresting power from women's hands. The ravagers imposed their male warrior gods upon their conquests, slowly subsuming the Goddess under their dominion. At first she was relegated to a position of shared or secondary authority. She became the mother of the god, as Isis is the mother of Horus. She became the wife of the god: Hera to Zeus and Isis to Osiris. She became the daughter of the god, like Athena, born of Zeus. Eventually, however, she was erased altogether.

During this period of religious transition, the people of larger Mesopotamia—an area that corresponds roughly to modern Iraq, eastern Syria and southeastern Turkey—began to make records of their own lives and the oral histories of previous generations. From these records come the earliest references to sacred prostitution, the predecessor of what we know today as the sex trade. In ancient times, however, people didn't merely trade in sex; rather, they shared union with the Goddess through her fleshly embodiment, the temple priestess.

The goddesses of this period, though worshipped in multiple locales under a variety of names, were all related to Kali Ma, the Hindu "triple goddess" of creation, preservation and destruction. As the source of birth, existence and death, Kali's world was an eternal living flux, a dark and liquid chaos from which all life arose and disappeared again in endless cycles. The subordinate gods, which Kali bore and destroyed, addressed her as "the Original of all manifestations." "Thou alone remainest as One ineffable and inconceivable," they pronounced.

As mother and creator, Kali emanated *karuna*, meaning "the treasure house of compassion." Karuna was the quality of mother-love directly experienced in infancy and later amplified to embrace all forms of love: tenderness, sensual pleasure, eroticism. Tantric sages called karuna the essence of religion—that is, the essence of the Goddess, for the Goddess was religion itself, and karuna flowed into the world through the Goddess' agents on Earth, women. The Goddess' sacred whores were thought to be specially anointed teachers of karuna.

The term karuna may be at the root of modern Italian's *carogna*, or "whore." Pagan Rome gave the Great Goddess the title of Mater Cara— mother beloved—for she combined all the qualities of sexuality, motherhood, spousal intimacy, friendship, generosity and mercy, or *caritas*,[1] which the Christian church later purged of sexual implications and called "charity."

The goddesses Ishtar and Innana were also Kali in her Sumerian and Akkadian guises. The essence of karuna was associated with the Great

---

[1] "Caritas" should be familiar to fans of *Angel* as the name of the karaoke club that offered safe haven to demons. In "Lullaby," Caritas was destroyed. In an alleyway outside the demolished nightclub, Darla used a shard of wood from Caritas' rubble to stake herself, releasing the child she carried in her belly from its prison. In this, her first act of love—of *karuna*—Darla created a new life as she destroyed her own—representing the eternal cycle of the Goddess' work.

Mother no matter how she was addressed, and with all women as her earthly representatives.

In ancient Babylon, beneath the ziggurat peaks of the temples of Ishtar,[2] her priestesses lay with men in exchange for monetary offerings. To enter the body of the priestess was to come as close as a male could ever dream to the source of divine power and comfort. Through congress with her, the warrior was cleansed of the ravages of war, the transgressor purified. By sharing karuna, a man received far more than carnal delight; he received blessing.

Scholars have suggested that such deep respect for the sacred feminine was a serious threat to the priests of later monotheistic religious sects who sought to position themselves between the people and the sacred source. To do so they had to remove women from the path to power, and that meant not only eradicating the Goddess herself, but also locking the door that led directly from the feminine body and its pleasures to the divine. The priests achieved this end by turning truth upon its head and reducing female sexuality to a source of sin and shame—a vicious undertaking to which we in the twenty-first century (and those in the twenty-sixth-century Whedonverse) are still held hostage.

The shrines of Ishtar were schools of exquisite refinement and artistic culture, as well as centers of knowledge about sexuality and fertility rituals. Temple priestesses and maidens learned skills that could heal male sexual problems—making them the predecessors of today's sex therapists. But, despite Babylonian reverence for the priestesses of Ishtar, the status of women in that country had been severely weakened by the grip of patriarchy. Babylonian laws offered neither equality nor protection to women. Men were the lawmakers and women were subordinate. Fathers decided whether daughters should marry or serve in the temple. Occasionally, married women of the upper classes served in the temples before taking their marital vows, a vocation that in no way diminished their marriage prospects. In fact, priestesses hailing from aristocratic families enjoyed more personal freedom than married women or the poorer temple maidens. They could own property, including slaves, and retain their own possessions. However, not all women who engaged in sexual service were so fortunate. Sacred whores who worked beyond the temple walls were more vulnerable to the foibles of their drunken

---

[2] She was also known to Sumerians as Innana, to the Phoenicians and Egyptians as Astarte, to the Greeks as Aphrodite and to the Romans as Venus. In the Old Testament, she was labeled Ashtoreth, meaning "shameful thing."

or violent patrons, and those who were unaffiliated with the temple suffered the harshest of lives, for they lacked protection, property and respectability.

In patriarchal ancient Greece, the worship of the goddess Aphrodite continued to benefit from the services of the holy whore, but the goddess herself was demoted from her former incarnation as the great, life-and-death-giving deity to the lesser goddess of beauty and love. Plato later wrote of severing her further into two facets: Urania, who ruled platonic love, and Aphrodite Pandemos, or Aphrodite of the Commoners. In this weakened form she was also known as Aphrodite Porne—the titillator—and the term *porne* came to designate the prostitute. It was Porne who was worshiped in the famous temples of Corinth, where the practice of sacramental sexuality eventually deteriorated into expensive prostitution. However, prostitutes continued to serve as priestesses during festivals where great processions were held in conjunction with prayers, sacrifices and feasts, commemorating a time when invading armies were repelled by the priestess' invocations to the goddess Aphrodite.

Among the porne, the highest echelon was occupied by the hetaera, literally "companion." The hetaera was renowned for her refinement, wit, intelligence and artistry. These were the only Grecian women permitted to attend symposia or take part in intellectual discourse. Some were known to be among Plato's inner circle, but most were slaves, owned by brothel-keepers or purchased by enamored patrons, much like any other form of property. At the indulgence of their owners, they might eventually be given their freedom, or they might become beloved concubines and treated as secondary wives—at least until their beauty and usefulness faded.

Class distinctions among strata of prostitutes continued to appear throughout history in the Near East and the Orient, as well as in Europe. Some further examples:

In fourteenth- and fifteenth-century Germany, women in the houses of pleasure were known as "traveling women," and were generally orphans, poor and widowed women or daughters of the pariahs of society: gravediggers and hangmen. These unfortunate girls were unable to marry, but they could use their bodies to earn a living as they moved from town to town. If they were successful and chose to settle down, they could reside under the protection of a well-organized tradeswomen's guild. The women of the town would elect a Brothel Queen as overseer who was sworn in by the town council. Guildswomen enjoyed certain privileges within the community; they were not shunned and they incurred the protection of the law. Those who did not belong to the guild were run out of town.

In Renaissance Italy, well-bred young women were often forced into the life of courtesans out of financial necessity when their families were no longer able to afford proper dowries or an aging parent fell upon hard times and needed assistance. What was a young woman to do in a world where "working girl" meant only one thing? Like the hetaera, a courtesan could become the mistress of a rich and powerful benefactor. Unfortunately, most courtesans died young or in poverty.

In the *Firefly* episode "Shindig," Inara's client Atherton Wing hoped to convince her to remain with him on Persephone as his personal Companion.

"I'm trying to give you something, you know. A life. If you want it," he told her.

In making his offer, Atherton failed to consider that Inara already had "a life," or that to the extent that freedom and self-sufficiency were of value to her, offering to make her his "private property" was asking her to accept less privilege than she already possessed, not gifting her with more. Apparently, Atherton had little interest in proposing she become his wife. Like wealthy benefactors centuries before him, he adhered to the threadbare tradition of turning courtesans into mistresses.

In Japan of 1618, the birth of the Yoshiwara pleasure district produced a lineage of courtesans that would one day evolve into the geisha. This "floating world" catered to the men of Edo (an early designation for Tokyo) for 300 years until prostitution was outlawed and the district was shut down in 1957.

The Yoshiwara also became a thriving cultural center for art and Kabuki. Artists created intensely sexual and erotic imagery known as *shunga*—the forerunner of today's controversial *hentai*. Westerners would have categorized shunga as pornography, but, in Japan, shunga was enjoyed without the slightest embarrassment or shame, perhaps owing to the underlying Shinto belief system that supported Japanese metaphysical life. Devoid of moralistic dogma beyond its veneration for the mysteries of nature, Shinto perceived sexuality as an appetite to be satisfied like any other, within proprieties of time, place and circumstance.

Among the celebrated courtesans of the floating world, the *Tayuu* of the early days were exceptional women, unrivaled in beauty and talent. A Tayuu lived in pampered luxury while being schooled in the scrupulous standards of behavior required of her. Tayuu were allowed the privilege of rejecting or accepting any suitors, much like Companions, and were appointed two child attendants whom they mentored and trained in the customs of the floating world.

In later years the Tayuu gave way to a class of courtesans known as *Oiran*. Oiran were peerless in the art of handling men, skilled at suggestive repartee, cultured and exquisitely attired. They dealt with men of all social backgrounds and were adept at contending with the complex etiquettes that accompanied each rank. A prospective suitor would meet at least three times with an Oiran before he could hope to win her favors. To do so he had to be prepared to spend vast amounts of money, display impeccable grooming and come equipped with a reputation as a skilled lover. A man with little savoir faire would have to seek company on the side streets, where a less refined and choosy lady could be found.

The Companion of the *Firefly*verse more closely resembled the Tayuu and the Oiran in status and rigors of training than the geisha, their successors, who today are not prostitutes at all, but represent a dwindling breed of social hostesses.

One key difference between a Companion like Inara and a Japanese courtesan of the Yoshiwara was the level of respect each could expect from clients. Inara, by frequenting primitive border planets, could not expect her clients to maintain consistently high regard for her status and position beyond the most rudimentary manners required to secure her services. At any turn she might find herself surprised by a client's demeanor.

In "Jaynestown," Inara accepted as a client a young man whose controlling father had engaged her to help dispose of his virginity. When Fess arrived at the shuttle to meet Inara, his father inappropriately, but predictably, accompanied him. Inara tried to explain to daddy that he was not meant to be present in the place of union, but the man cut her off mid-sentence and, gesturing to the tea service set before them, barked, "What's this…?" Inara again tried explaining the Companion greeting ceremony, a tradition with hundreds of years of history, but once more he interrupted her rudely, blustering that his son was not yet a man and that he had brought her to their moon to bed the boy, not to have a tea party!

Inara had no choice but to take the befuddled man by the arm and steer him toward the door; under no circumstances was he permitted in her "consecrated place of union." This was her temple, and it was not to be dishonored, whether out of ignorance or deliberation.

Once he was gone, Inara told Fess that Companions choose their clients very carefully, and that she would not have come to their territory had it been to meet with his father.

"You're different than him. The more you accept that, the stronger you'll become." She kissed him tenderly, sharing the karuna that was as much her inheritance as the genteel tea ceremony.

Later, lying in bed, Fess whispered that he thought he'd feel different after sex. "Aren't I supposed to be a man now?"

"A man is just a boy who is old enough to ask that question," Inara told him. "Our time together is a ritual, a symbol. It means something to your father. But it doesn't make you a man. You do that yourself."

Inara's kind and skilled response illustrated the delicate balance of qualities she brought to her encounters. Like the sacred prostitutes of old, erotic pleasure was only a fraction of the services she rendered. Teacher, healer and wisewoman were equally valued skills—at least by some.

A WOMAN'S WORTH

In "Shindig," Atherton Wing seemed to have difficulty understanding the limits of the liberties he was entitled to take with Inara. But the conflict that erupted between Mal and Atherton reflected a deeper and more enduring struggle over the question of a woman's worth.

At the grand ball on Persephone, Atherton hinted of his disdain for women of Inara's profession by implying that other men were gazing at Inara solely because "all of them wish you were in their bed."

At this, Inara blanched. "Oh, she blushes," he taunted. Then, seeing her displeasure, he recovered his manners. "Not many in your line of work do that. You...you are a singular woman, and I find...I find I admire you more and more."

Inara seemed touched by Atherton's endearment, though she probably should have been disgusted. His flattery was a transparently saccharin attempt to disguise his contempt for those who lacked the temerity to be embarrassed when reminded that their value was hidden between their legs.

Only moments later, Atherton flaunted his possession of Inara by manhandling her in front of Mal. Seeing that Atherton's grip on her arm had left white marks, he politely drew her onto the dance floor. No sooner was she in his arms than he lapsed into sarcasm:

"Is this the hardest part, would you say, or does that come later?"

"You have no call to try to make me ashamed of my job. What I do is legal...and how is that *smuggling* coming?"

Inara had leapt just as easily into her part in their adagio. Like bickering teenage siblings, Mal and Inara were well matched at substitut-ing antagonism for affection. Of course, Inara refused to let Mal snatch the moral high ground, for in pursuit of his own dubious freedom, she knew that he, too, was selling himself to the highest bidder.

"My work's illegal, but it's honest," Mal insisted. "While this...the *lie* of it...that man parading you on his arm as if he actually won you, as if he loves you, and everyone going along with it. How can that not bother you?"

Inara's capacity for artifice certainly bothered Mal. "He treats you like an ornament. Other men look at you and discuss if you're worth the cost." Mal bristled with intolerance for the kind of relationship that catered to the indulgences of a man like Atherton—the kind of man who, not so coincidentally, had supported and benefited from Alliance transgressions.

Just as Mal and Inara finally stopped squabbling and began to enjoy the dance, Atherton decided he'd seen enough of their two-step. He marched over to them and roughly hauled Inara off the dance floor.

"Watch yourself there. No need for any hands-on," Mal burst out.

"Excuse me. She's not here with you, Captain. She's mine."

"Yours? She don't belong to nobody." Mal was incensed.

"Money changed hands. Makes her mine tonight. And no matter how you dress her up, she's still—"

Mal's fist landed hard on Atherton's jaw before he could complete the contentious sentence. Although Mal was known to brandish similar language, permitting the "W" word to spill from Atherton's lips was un-thinkable. Mal might have deplored Inara's choice of profession, but he respected *her*, a fact that distinguished him from Atherton. So did the set of simple, yet powerful ideals that drove Mal's actions in relation to Inara, as well as the rest of the world: *People don't belong to other people; they don't belong to conglomerates and collectives. Every man and woman is an inherently free creature, and she should be entitled to make her own choices, for better or worse.*

The universe, however, did not always operate in sync with Mal's philosophy.

Aboard *Serenity*, Mal had created a safe zone where freedom, loyalty, equality and accountability held sway even as the ship hurtled between a motley collection of primitive border territories. On those planets, Earth's oldest traditions had seeded themselves within nascent societies, and they bloomed with the customs and beliefs of bygone eras. From one culture to the next, human interrelationships and power dynamics sprouted in inconsistent and often mysterious patterns. A woman might be burnt as a witch on one moon and on another given to a stranger as a hospitality gift. Mal understood that on Atherton's home sphere, a woman like Inara served as a rich man's trinket, a luxury status symbol that could be bought at whim—no more, no less. This infuriated Mal, for, despite his flippancy with Inara, he honored women as warriors and comrades. But her capitulation to the caprices of men—especially men of a certain class—provoked a congested fury in Mal. Companion or whore, ruby or glass, it was all the same to him if she allowed herself to be reduced to a shiny bauble, crafted for display and contracted to sparkle, when he knew her to be so much more.

By the same token, Mal's stern reproach to his "new wife" in "Our Mrs. Reynolds" further illuminated his thinking:

"Got no use for a woman who won't stand up for herself. . . . You don't wait to be told when to breathe, you don't take orders from anyone. . . . Be like a woman is, not some petrified child. There's more than seventy Earths spinnin' around the galaxy and the meek have inherited not a one."

And when Jayne suggested trading one "Callahan full-bore autolock with customized trigger" named Vera for one soft-spoken, full-breasted customized wife named Saffron, Mal read him chapter and verse: "She's not to be bought. Nor bartered, nor borrowed or lent. She's a human woman; doesn't know a damn thing about the world and needs our protection."

Even more surely than his impassioned rhetoric, Mal's longstanding relationship with his first officer Zoe demonstrated his admiration for women who take no guff. Like Inara, Zoe also carried the energy of certain powerful ancient figures: Athena, the Greek warrior goddess, Kali in her preserver and destroyer aspects, and Ishtar-Innana who, in her undiluted form as a Sumerian and Akkadian deity, presided over the chaos of war. The Sumerians referred to war as "the dance of Innana," and the Akkadians called the battlefield "Ishtar's playground." In this commanding guise she was both the Whore Goddess and the War Goddess, uniting the energies of lust and combat, of life and death.

Mal seemed to rely upon and trust the woman warrior—but only so long as her combative energies were split off from her more classically feminine attributes. He didn't know what to make of an Aphrodite-identified woman like Inara, so split off from her fierceness, short of protecting or resisting her. Perhaps after standing shoulder to shoulder with strong women in battle, after witnessing their flesh torn away by enemy fire, Mal wasn't too keen on being party to the buying and sell-

ing of charms for the amusement of Alliance sympathizers. Nevertheless, when Mal punched out Atherton over the "W" epithet, he usurped
Inara's right to contend with her escort's churlish behavior on her own
terms. By using his fist to speak *for* Inara rather than trust that she could
and would speak for herself, he proved himself as guilty as Atherton of
reducing Inara to an alluring but insubstantial ornament.

Together, Inara and Zoe contained woman's most ardent archetypal
aspects: beauty, seductiveness, compassion, eroticism, wisdom, brav-
ery, strength and fierceness. All the essences of the triple goddess were
present, but artificially separated from one another, for, initially, only
Inara appeared to display karuna and only Zoe embodied the destroyer.
But if we look more closely at their development throughout the *Firefly*
series, we see that with the passage of time, both women grew more
complete. As the last episodes of the season unfolded, each began filling
out where, earlier, she had seemed thin. Zoe grew more sexual, playful,
maternal. And Inara took up arms.

A LONELY GODDESS

Inara was Companion to many, but who was Companion to Inara?

Inara's professionalism decreed that she measure closeness in cau-
tious metrics. She tasted lust, inhaled intimacy's fragrance, but the elaborate rituals and thoughtful protocols of her work ensured against the
itch of messy attachments.

Inara's nomadic life aboard *Serenity* spared her from extended contact with anyone on the planets who might pose a complication of the
heart. And aboard *Serenity*, her consummate self-discipline enabled her
to hold the line she'd drawn her first day aboard ship, remaining sup-
portively engaged but never intimately involved with captain or crew.
The very configuration of her private space held her apart from the rest.
Soft lighting and opulent, jewel-toned fabrics conferred a lush sensual-
ity upon the interior of her womblike shuttle. Like Inara herself it was
connected to the ship, yet *sans umbilicus*. Just a catwalk and a psychic
moat away, *Serenity's* vast, neutral spaces proclaimed a starkly contrasting communal spirit.

Inara made efforts to enforce strict etiquette for anyone—especially
anyone with a captain's rank—wishing to cross her threshold; but Mal,
like a persistent child hell-bent on testing limits, preferred teetering at
the edge of her boundaries or obstinately penetrating them. And despite

Inara's palpable attraction to him, she relied on those castle walls as protection, along with insult and sarcasm as her standard armor.

We know very little about Inara's history. We know she entered Companion training as a child and that she was precocious, focused, perhaps in line for the lauded position of House Priestess. We don't know why she cut herself adrift in a boundless galaxy—maybe a lifetime of formality and ritual had become suffocating, or a tragedy befell her—or a scandal, and she was forced to leave. We know nothing about her prior relationships. She might have been a virgin—that is, a woman who belonged to no one, a woman unto herself, who had been guarding her heart with the ferocity of a mama lion, shielding it from infiltration by the damning mysteries of her own emotional depths.

In "War Stories" Inara's loneliness was laid bare when she encountered a certain client whose presence on *Serenity* magnetized the crew, especially Jayne ("I'll be in my bunk!"). Having run the gauntlet of crew members' gazes, a highly placed female Alliance member known only as "the Councilor" was being entertained in Inara's temple.

Inara dribbled oil over her back and gently massaged her, murmuring, "You have such beautiful skin...."

The Councilor interrupted, turning on her side to meet Inara's eyes:

"There's no need for the show, Inara. I just need to relax with someone who's making no demands on me."

Inara seemed to weigh her response carefully. "Most of my clientele is male, do you know that?" she said softly.

The Councilor didn't. "If I choose a woman, she tends to be extraordinary in some way. And the fact is, I occasionally have the exact same need you do. One cannot always be one's self in the company of men."

"Never, actually," said the Councilor.

"So...no show. Let's just enjoy ourselves."

In this rare moment of vulnerability, we glimpsed a shadow of Inara's isolation and sensed her yearning for a taste of the karuna she gave so freely. With the Councilor—another powerful woman with her own secrets to keep—Inara was able to shed pretenses and, we can only hope, revel in the splendor of shared intimacy.

Seeing Inara with the Councilor, we're reminded of the time Mal accused her of living a lie during their turn on the dance floor in "Shindig." Back then, we hadn't yet seen quite enough of Inara to know how she felt about "the show." In just a few moments with the Councilor, we saw that she understood her choices had a price.

In "Heart of Gold" we discovered that it was a steep one.

HEART OF GOLD

Inara received a distress call from Nandi, a former Companion who was running a bordello on an outlying moon. Rance Burgess, a filthy-rich, misogynist bully, claimed that one of her girls was carrying his child, and when he threatened to "take what's mine" if the DNA sample he brutally extracted from her proved his paternity, Nandi sought Inara's help. When Mal offered to lend a hand, Inara assured him he and the crew would be paid.

"You keep your money. Won't be needing no payment," he said.

"You will be paid," said Inara. "I feel it's important we keep ours strictly a business arrangement."

Inara didn't see his stung expression. No doubt his feelings for her were growing, and this time her effort to keep him at arm's length drew blood.

Once the crew arrived at the Heart of Gold and Mal had a chance to size up Burgess, he realized they were dealing with the worst sort of villain: "a monster that thinks he's right with God." Their only recourse was to cut and run, taking Nandi and the girls with them. But Mal hadn't counted on Nandi's steely resolve:

"Captain Reynolds...it took me years to cut this piece of territory out of other men's hands, to build this business up from nothing. It's who I am. And it's my home. I'm not going anywhere."

Mal tried to protest, but Nandi was unmoved: "Rance Burgess is just a man....And I won't let any man take what's mine. I doubt you'd do different in my position."

Eyes locked on each other, admiration flickered. Mal broke the silence: "Well, lady, I must say—you're my kinda stupid."

Their understanding solidified later, as they made preparations to do battle with Burgess and his men, and spoke fondly of Inara.

"She's like you, more than a little," said Nandi.

"And how exactly is that?"

"She hates complications."

"They do crop up though, don't they?" said Mal.

Deeper into the night, with more than a few shots of rice wine under their belts, complications grew nicely between Nandi and Mal, as they made love with a raw and tender passion.

Just steps away from Nandi's room, Inara was coaching pregnant Petaline, whose labor had begun to build in intensity. And down in the town square, Rance Burgess stood before a crowd of men, with one of

Nandi's girls perched at his side. She'd been feeding him information about activity at the Heart of Gold.

Burgess wrapped one arm around her as he addressed the men:

"Now Chari here, she understands a whore's place, don't she? But Nandi, and those others, they spit on our town. They've no respect for the sanctity of fatherhood, for decency or family. They got *my child* held hostage to their decadent ways and *that* I will not abide!"

Applause welled up from the mob of townsmen. Burgess continued his oratory: "We will show them what power is! We will show them what their position in this town is! Let us all remember, right here and now, what a woman is to a man!"

He turned to Chari, no longer smiling.

"Get on your knees," he ordered.

Startled, she looked out at all the men watching. But Burgess was insistent, and she dropped to her knees.

With Chari, Burgess reenacted the first holy holocaust: the annihilation of the divine feminine by the malevolent power-mad invaders. At first, the feminine principle embodied by Chari was merely debased, reduced to a service whore. Later, the Goddess would be sacrificed.

The next morning, Inara bumped into Mal as he was leaving Nandi's bedroom. He fell all over himself making excuses for his presence there, but Inara pooh-poohed his discomfort, playing her hand with familiar, flippant disregard.

"So you're okay? Well, yeah, why wouldn't you be?" Mal stammered.

"I wouldn't say I'm entirely okay," Inara retorted. "I'm a little appalled at her taste."

She walked off smiling, leaving Mal speechless. But back in Petaline's room, Inara slumped to the floor and, huddling in the corner, sobbed her heart out.

Things began to move quickly: Inara coached Petaline through the delivery of her baby, but no sooner had the infant come into the world than Burgess materialized behind Inara, laser pistol in hand, to steal the child away.

In the hallway Nandi stepped in front of him: "Ain't leaving here with it."

"This is my blood, woman."

From behind him, a slender arm appeared, with a curved razor in hand. It was Inara, holding the blade steady under Burgess' chin, its point drawing a trickle of blood from the side of his throat.

"No. *This* is your blood." Deadly earnest, she demanded he hand off the baby to one of the girls. "Or I'll spill more blood than you can spare."

Burgess gave the baby to one of the young women...and then, in one quick motion, he elbowed Inara so hard in the stomach that she staggered backward. He fired his laser from the hip. The beam seared straight through Nandi's chest and she crumpled to the floor. As Burgess raced away, Inara and Mal's eyes met in mutual horror.

The wheel of life—the cycle of creation and destruction—had spun full circle.

And it would spin again.

Symbolically, the events at Heart of Gold recapitulated the smiting of the Goddess so many millennia ago. But this time, in this small corner of the galaxy, patriarchy's power would flare only briefly before being decisively snuffed out.

Mal took off after Burgess and returned to the bordello dragging the captured and bound offender back to the house, along with most of his men. Even tied up and hobbled, Burgess' arrogance knew no limits: "PETALINE! YOU BRING MY BOY OUT! RIGHT NOW! YOU HEAR ME? I WANT TO SEE MY SON!"

Petaline appeared in the doorway holding the baby against her breast with one arm. All eyes were upon her as she approached Burgess, wobbling on his knees in the dirt where Mal had shoved him. The new mother goddess was preparing to dispatch the once-threatening patriarch.

"Rance...this is Jonah," Petaline said, all syrupy, glancing between Burgess and the baby.

"Jonah, say hello to your daddy."

Petaline raised her free arm. In her hand she held a pistol. She pointed the barrel straight at Burgess' head. His eyes clouded over, disbelief dawning.

Petaline fired.

Burgess toppled facedown in the dust.

"Say goodbye to your daddy, Jonah," Petaline said.

Much later, back on *Serenity*, Mal and Inara met on the catwalk leading to her shuttle. Both knew it was "truthsome" time.

"I learned something from Nandi," Inara told Mal. "Not just from what happened, but from her. The family she made, the strength of her love for them. That's what kept them together. When you live with that kind of strength, you get tied to it. You can't break away. And you never want to."

She was really speaking of Mal, of the family he had created from scrap, the loyalties he had nurtured, the gravity of the love from which she'd struggled to float free.

"There's something that I...that I should have done a long while ago. And I'm sorry...for both of us...that it took me this long." She paused for breath and then said, "I'm leaving." Inara's face began to crumble, tears welling up. Quickly, she turned away and set off across the catwalk. Mal didn't follow.

Inara had only one more significant encounter with Mal in the final episode before the series' premature cancellation. Here, Mal reached out to tenderly stroke Inara's bruised lip, but she shied away, then fled—even though it seemed as though every tiny, twitchy muscle fiber in her body strained toward his touch. Would attachment damn her so utterly, or was she protecting Mal with her valiant restraint?

Perhaps the upcoming film, *Serenity*, will answer these lingering questions. Yet, even without resolution to the story's romantic mystery, by giving us *Firefly*, Joss Whedon has given us a meticulously crafted, fully realized vision. He has given us a tale that urges us to reconsider our prejudices and knee-jerk assumptions about sin, sensation and social institutions. He has given us compellingly flawed characters that wear our own familiar defenses with a deliciously subversive swagger. And, best of all, he has given us that far-flung future in which all the paradoxes and peculiarities of our terrible human history are brought to bear, making even the end of the Earth seem like just another crinkled page in destiny's journal.

Joy Davidson, PhD., is a certified sex therapist and licensed marriage and family therapist, with a doctorate in clinical psychology. A veteran writer, with dozens of national magazine articles to her credit, she has also been the relationships and sexuality columnist for Playgirl *magazine,* Men's Fitness *magazine and MSN's* Underwire. *She is the author of* Fearless Sex: Overcome Your Romantic Obsessions and Get the Sex Life You Deserve *(Fairwinds, 2004) and* The Soap Opera Syndrome: The Drive for Drama and Excitement in Women's Lives. *She also cocreated the award-winning video series,* Playboy's Secrets of Making Love to the Same Person Forever, *Volumes I and II. She has also written for two other Smart Pop books:* Five Seasons of Angel *and* What Would Sipowicz Do?

Permit me to quibble. Taylor, in an aside, points to the tendency of secondary female characters on Buffy *to serve as damsels in need of saving. I rush to point out this was only because it couldn't always be Xander. Someone had to damsel! Quibble over, the main point of the essay is clearly valid. Yes, the men of any Jossverse have a tendency to be substantially doofier than the women.*

My view on this is that television tends to need to tell stories clearly and quickly. Iconic characters are a tremendous help in doing so. That means that there won't soon be a shortage of instantly digestible television men-of-action and the women who nag them. Let us now celebrate the characters that give us something a little different.

The Captain May Wear the Tight Pants, but It's the Gals Who Make *Serenity* Soar

ROBERT B. TAYLOR

IT'S ABOUT HALFWAY THROUGH *FIREFLY*'S SIXTH EPISODE, titled "Our Mrs. Reynolds," that Jerry Lee "Wash" Warren, pilot and resident man-child of the starship *Serenity*, admits that his warrior wife Zoe could kill him "with her pinky."

The viewer believes him without question. After all, the first time we saw Wash in the series pilot, he was at *Serenity*'s helm, busy playing with his dolls. Well, okay, they were dinosaur dolls, so perhaps technically they qualify as action figures. ("This is a fertile land and we will thrive," said one toy dinosaur to the other in Wash's cute two-dino play.) Still, it wasn't the most manly of introductions.

By contrast, when the viewer was first introduced to Zoe, she was in the midst of battle, ducking down into a bunker while explosions rocked the land around her. This, the scene told us, is a hard woman. Loving, sexy as hell, occasionally a smart-ass...but with nerves of steel and a wicked glare that can bring lesser men to their knees. Especially men who play with dinosaur toys and just happen to be married to her.

And Zoe's not the only woman in the *Firefly* universe who can easily have her way with the men around her. In the very same episode where Wash confided how quickly his wife could dispose of him, the beautiful imposter Saffron (the "Mrs. Reynolds" of the title) used her wits and sexuality to render essentially every male *Serenity* crew member useless. Her diabolical plan was only disrupted once Inara, who possesses a fair amount of brains and beauty herself, exposed Saffron as a murderous traitor up to no gorram good.

Thank the heavens for Inara, who also saved the crew's hides at the end of "Trash." And while it could be argued that the crew succeeded thanks to Mal's planned use of *Serenity*'s resident Companion as a fail-safe, it's no surprise that Inara was the one chosen to save the day should all else come crashing down.

Of the nine people that call the hull and hallways of *Serenity* home, four of them consistently stand out as being exceptional. They are the women of *Firefly*—Zoe, Inara, Kaylee and lastly, that mystery in human form that drives the show, River Tam—and they are, at times, incredibly strong, extraordinarily passionate, intelligent beyond their years and, perhaps most importantly, comfortable in their own skin. Many times, they are all of these at once.

The women of *Firefly* are powerful and profound. And, as the viewer learned very quickly, they could probably steer *Serenity*'s course just fine by themselves. The *Firefly* universe is our universe, pushed ahead hundreds of years into the future. And in that time, it seems the women have evolved at a much higher rate than their male counterparts. In *Firefly* creator Joss Whedon's version of the future, women are seen as equal with men on the battlefield. Zoe is a respected soldier, and the fact that she ends up remaining at Mal's side after the civil war ends is as much a testament to Mal's reliance on her as it is her loyalty to her old sergeant.

Conversely, women are also free to revel in their own sexuality, something that remains taboo in many parts of the world even today. Not so in the *Firefly*verse, where prostitutes are treated like high-ranking nobles and respected for their vast knowledge learned while studying to become a Guild-sanctioned Companion. Whedon has created a reality where sex is not something to be outlawed or looked down upon, and beauty not a trait to be taken lightly.

As for the men of *Firefly*, it appears they haven't evolved quite as far as their opposite-gender counterparts. The guys of *Serenity* still fall into the same old traps that we men always do. They shoot before they think (see: Jayne, in pretty much any episode). And it sure didn't take long at all for Saffron to gain the upper hand on her "husband": she fluttered a few eyelashes, showed a bit of skin and had Mal at her mercy. Of course, Mal admitted in that very episode that he hadn't gotten laid in quite a while, so he was a particularly easy mark.

(Side note: What kind of rugged sci-fi ship captain doesn't get any play with the opposite sex? Inara is a well-respected prostitute who fornicates with only the highest class of clients. Kaylee was busy getting naked with a fellow mechanic the first time she set foot on *Serenity*. Wash and Zoe spend countless hours in the bedroom—and you just know Zoe is the boss in there, as well. These women are not bashful about fulfilling their carnal needs. Meanwhile, Simon is painfully awkward when trying to woo an obviously willing Kaylee. And what about the poor captain? Joss and his writers must have wondered the same thing, so they finally rectified the situation and got Mal some lovin' in the next-to-last episode filmed...which, incidentally, never aired.)

Mal's lack of female companionship and his inability to express how he feels to Inara doesn't necessarily mean that he's not a fine captain. But when it comes down to it, if squared off against the women of *Serenity*, the men would almost certainly lose, perhaps falling victim to the ladies' brawn. Poor River did turn out to be a fabulous shot, didn't she? And let's not forget: in "Shindig" Inara had to teach Mal how to swordfight. This deserves repeating: Inara, a prostitute, had to instruct Mal, a respected war veteran, on how to properly wage battle with a sharp metal stick.

More likely, though, the women would outwit the fellas. In "Heart of Gold" an old acquaintance of Inara's said the men of *Serenity* should triumph in a battle against a wicked landowner "if they've got guns or brains at all."

"Well," replied Inara. "They've got guns."

The heroes of the science fiction genre have been, to this point, almost universally men. Sure, you get your occasional *Alien* sequel with Ellen Ripley once again fighting off hordes of outer-space nasties, but mostly, galaxy-saving has been a job for—as Jayne Cobb would say—someone with "man parts."

Look no further than *Star Wars*, the science fiction universe that continues to set the standard, even as those pesky prequels continue to underwhelm. Who is it that finally brings the Empire to its knees? A bunch of men with names like Luke, Han and Lando. Sure, Princess Leia possesses an awful lot of spunk, but even she essentially serves as the damsel in distress throughout the original trilogy, held captive first in the Death Star and later in Jabba's Palace. And, turning our attention to the prequels, we are presented with Queen Amidala, a mere cipher of a character whose defining characteristic seems to be awful taste in men.

In the *Star Trek* universe, women were originally used mostly as objects of sexual longing—another notch on James T. Kirk's bedpost. It took three *Trek* spin-offs before a woman got to captain her own ship, and even then, Capt. Kathryn Janeway's buttoned-up stuffiness always made her a somewhat androgynous character.

When Whedon decided to bring his own space western to the small screen, the concept of a sexy, strong and willful heroine was not new to him. For seven seasons, vampire slayer Buffy Summers—Whedon's most enduring creation—served as the very definition of the empowered young woman. In Buffy, Whedon created a new sci-fi/fantasy archetype that has since been copied ad nauseum. (Look no further than the myriad of post-*Buffy* TV shows that featured a female lead who is young, beautiful and could kick your sorry ass—*Dark Angel* and *Alias*, to name just two.)

But, while Joss applied his girl-power formula to Buffy herself, the show's other female characters—Willow, Cordelia, etc.—were repeatedly used as damsels in distress, helpless and in need of Buffy to save them, especially in the early seasons. As the show progressed, Willow eventually grew into an engaging female role model, but a new damsel took her place, Buffy's sister Dawn, who fit that role so well that it led to the now-famous Buffy quip, "So, Dawn's in trouble. Must be Tuesday." Even today, Buffy is regarded as the very definition of the powerful female figure, but the fact that the other women in the *Buffy* cast often fell into the same old sci-fi/fantasy clichés is usually overlooked.

That's not the case with *Firefly*, where Whedon has created not just one but an entire shipful of female role models, each talented in her own ways, and none prone to needing rescued. In fact, the only time the women of *Firefly* ever end up helpless is when they are gravely wounded, shot in the gut as Kaylee was in the pilot or hurt in an explosion like Zoe in "Out of Gas" (an injury suffered while saving Kaylee . . . another typically heroic gesture from *Serenity*'s second in command, while the men stood around slack-jawed).

Serenity's alpha females are depicted as being superior to the males in job skills that are universally reserved for those with a Y chromosome. Is there any doubt Zoe is the finest soldier we've so far seen in the *Firefly*verse? And although Mal's first choice for ship mechanic was a strong young lad, he, of course, quickly showed total ineptitude while at work. Enter Kaylee, who has forgotten more about used spaceship engine parts than Han Solo and Chewbacca ever knew.

Then, there is River, who, in early episodes of the show, only served two purposes—(1) to stand as the show's MacGuffin, a plot device that gave the dreaded Alliance (and other assorted baddies) a reason to stay hot on *Serenity*'s trail, and (2) to exhibit some token Joss Whedon weirdness that tingled the spine and brought the viewer further into the story. ("Two by two, hands of blue.") River was introduced to the viewer as fragile, helpless and naked, with only her big brother to protect her. She was prone to psychotic fits and incoherent ramblings. Hardly a character who could be classified as strong or exceptional.

Slowly, that began to change, and River evolved right in front of our eyes. A hidden power rose up from the inside—a force that was perhaps symbolic of all the headway women have made in *Firefly*'s version of the future. We realize that her outbursts aren't fits of craziness but instead attacks against the men who did her wrong. (She slashed at Jayne in the kitchen not because she's insane, but because of the Blue Sun logo that adorned his shirt.) By the time River picked up that gun and efficiently disposed of three male guards in "War Stories"—with her eyes closed, no less—we realized that this character wasn't a MacGuffin at all. She was the primary focus of the show.

In that episode, River became the flesh embodiment of the time-honored phrase, "Hell hath no fury like a woman scorned." She's a girl done wrong, who just happens to be both incredibly brilliant and awfully dangerous, an action hero perhaps only a few steps away from a full-fledged mission of revenge. (You know all the damage Uma Thurman does as The Bride in Quentin Tarantino's *Kill Bill* saga? Well, River's just as tough, twice as smart and psychic to boot. Just think of the hurt she could bring down on those pesky "hands of blue" guys!) Standing in her way is only going to prove futile, as the bounty hunter Jubal Early learned in "Objects in Space."

Much like Saffron before him, Early was able to get the jump on most of the crew, and again, it's one of *Serenity*'s resident girls who is able to turn the odds back in our heroes' favor. There is so much unknown about River Tam, especially when it comes to the things she's capable of. So, when River's voice echoed off *Serenity*'s metal walls, insisting that she and the ship were now one—a merged being—it was not all that surprising that Jubal almost started to believe it. And possibly some of the crew. And, heck, maybe us folks watching, too.

Of course, River didn't magically merge with the ship. She just out-witted Jubal, an outcome that is not surprising. After all, there must be some reason why it was River who the Alliance/Blue Sun malefactors abducted for their nefarious schemes. They coveted her vast intelligence for sure. Who knows what other talents of hers they tried to harness? By the time the screen faded to black at the end of "Objects in Space," River may very well have been the smartest, the strongest and the most intimidating crew member of a certain Firefly-class vessel.

The impressive standing and noble spirit of the female of the species is on display not only on *Serenity*, but also in every nook, cranny and terraformed planet in the *Firefly* universe. When a no-good moon baron threatened a brothel of mostly female prostitutes in "Heart of Gold," the bordello's madam, a headstrong ex-Companion named Nandi, said bluntly, "Rance Burgess is just a man, and I won't let any man take what's mine."

Having abandoned the Guild long ago, Nandi was not a well-respect-ed Companion like her old friend Inara. But she was a thriving busi-nesswoman who built her establishment from the ground up on that dusty moon, and when Mal recommended that Nandi and all of her workers board *Serenity* and flee from their current predicament, Nandi bravely refused. The evil Burgess was defeated, although it cost Nandi her life. Inara's former colleague died a hero to her people.

(Perhaps, in comparison, we should consider the less-than-noble death of Mal and Zoe's old war buddy, Tracey. Tracey participated in a shady organ-smuggling operation, asked Mal for help, turned against the crew, took Kaylee hostage and died a traitor. Tracey was a guy, which should probably go without saying. Jeez, Joss, can't the men of *Firefly* ever catch a break?)

Meanwhile, check out the show's tenth installment—"War Stories." When Inara informed Mal that she was bringing a client who was an "important political figure" onto *Serenity*, Mal assumed the client would be a man. So did the viewer since, in today's society, politics is still a male-dominated arena. There was much puzzled astonishment when Inara's client turned out to be a gorgeous blonde woman wearing a breathtaking silver and blue dress.

"Huh," commented a slack-jawed Mal.

"Oh, my!" offered Book.

Jayne promptly announced, "I'll be in my bunk," and bolted for some privacy.

Actually, it's a little surprising that the concept of sex between two women shocked the crew, considering the enhanced status of most females in the *Firefly* universe. Who wouldn't want to get naked with one? As for the concept of sex between a man and himself...well, as Jayne demonstrates so aptly, we men are doomed to suffer our never-ending weaknesses. And if you're going to serve alongside the superior women of *Serenity*, succumbing to even one flaw just isn't going to cut it if you expect to compare favorably.

Jubal Early wouldn't agree with that assessment. "Man is stronger by far than woman," he remarked during his failed attempt to commandeer *Serenity*.

Yeah right, buddy.

Not in *this* 'verse.

Remote control in hand, Robert B. Taylor monitors the TV landscape from his couch in Pittsburgh, Pennsylvania. His findings are diligently reported in his column, "Taylor on TV," which runs weekly in The Herald, *the newspaper of record for Rock Hill, South Carolina. In addition to tracking quality television, Taylor (call him Bob when you see him on the street) also works as a freelance news writer and editor. And if he wasn't repeatedly distracted by his shiny* Firefly *and* Buffy the Vampire Slayer *DVDs, he might find the time to complete one of his unfinished screenplays or novels. Give him a shout at bobtaylor52@yahoo.com.*

Holder's essay interests me, because it addresses an aspect of the cre-ator-audience relationship that I hadn't much thought about before. She talks about the hope that a viewer brings to a new show from an established voice, like Joss'. It's the same thing that happens when you buy the next book from a favorite author, anticipating a new love. And it's the real reason that successful television creators are given so much money to create their next show. The network isn't just gambling that this person has the keys to creating hits, it's also assured that many of the fans of the established show will ride waves of hope to the next creation.

Hope, by definition, is double-edged. It reflects a faith in the creative vision of a single person, which must be deeply gratifying to that per-son, but it also sets up expectations that are certain to be disappointed in some people.

Firefly *represents an interesting phenomenon, the celebrated fail-ure. It disappointed some fans as it unfolded, and disappointed the rest when it folded. But the fact that we're all still talking about it—that must count for something too.*

I Want Your Sex: Gender and Power in Joss Whedon's Dystopian Future World

NANCY HOLDER

WORKING ON TIE-IN MATERIAL for other planets in the Whedonverse has left me acutely aware that no work of popular culture is a spheroid unto it-self. At the 2004 Slayage conference in Nashville, the phrase most com-monly repeated by the academics who presented nearly 200 papers on *Buffy the Vampire Slayer* was Joss' famous statement, "Bring your own subtext." We all do it; we can't avoid it. We watch TV through the lens of our own worldview, and no discussion of any aspect of *Firefly* is free of it.

I bring to this essay an interest in the portrayal of women as equals (or superiors!) in popular culture. As I began to watch *Firefly*, I looked for a subtext that might support the theory—and the wishful hope of a mother of a daughter—that the creator of the quintessential kick-ass heroine Buffy the Vampire Slayer also endowed his female *Firefly* characters with a similar high-end power quotient.

Alas, my cup runneth under—but I can't specifically blame Joss for this. I can blame the western genre in general, and I will, and I can blame Joss for his decision to make a western in the first place.

And I will.

First, some history on Joss as feminist hero.

Buffy the Vampire Slayer broke ground when it first aired in 1997: it was an action-hero show starring a young girl who was stronger and braver than any boy around. It paved the way for other grrl-power shows including *Alias* and *La Femme Nikita*, and has been the subject of innumerable essays and several books. Even my own *BtVS* novels and guides to the show are listed under the header Feminism/Gender Issues on a Web site for science fiction fans.

Spun off from *BtVS* was *Angel*, a show about a male vampire originally introduced as a love interest for Buffy. Forced to leave Buffy, Angel moved to Los Angeles, a place so rough-and-tumble that the first person Angel saved wanted to move back to cowboy country—Missoula, Montana.

By virtue of his vampirism (and, one may argue, masculinity), Angel was the most physically powerful character on his show. Angel could usually outperform female vampires such as Darla and Drusilla—i.e., beat them up in a fair fight. When Spike, another male vampire, also moved from *BtVS* to *Angel*, part of the fun was the pissing contest that resulted from two super-strong guys competing with each other. Women characters served as important support staff: Fred, the scientific genius, and Cordelia, the seer and moral compass. Both women took up arms, but were never in the same fight club as their male counterparts. However, the notion of the always-female Slayer as Angel's physically powerful equal—whether it be Buffy, Faith, or the crazy Slayer, Dana—was upheld.

Significantly, at least for me, Fred turned into the god-king Ilyria, who was the physically strongest and most magical of all the characters, even after Angel and company diminished her powers in order to save her life. This is the sort of thing Joss did for girlkind, and did so well, on *BtVS*. How wonderful to see his feministic bent duplicated on *Angel*.

But let's hit rewind: *Buffy* remained, of the two shows, the one that was, as Buffy herself says, "All about power." Buffy got her supermojo because she was the Slayer. She figured out later how to distribute this power among many other proto-Slayers, all female, but it was her decision to make herself one among many—a community, a civilization—rather than face the (unbeatable) monsters alone.

But what was perhaps more interesting than this *Wonder Woman* redux was the fact that *BtVS* redefined *male* power. Quoting Gail Berman, president of FOX Entertainment and the woman who brought *Buffy* to the small screen, "We'll have more Buffys when we have more Xanders."[1] Berman points out that Xander willingly subordinated himself to a powerful female—who had rejected him sexually, by the by—and, of all the Scoobs, consistently acted as her most loyal lieutenant. He was the Zoe, if you will, to her Mal. But more on *Firefly's* denizens in a moment.

Buffy was about power, and many posit that *Angel* was about redemption. Then comes the third jewel in the Whedon TV crown: *Firefly*. And what's that about? It's got a gun-totin' gal in a pair of breeches named Zoe and a ship's engineer in pigtails named Little Kaylee. Also, a beautiful woman who owns and runs the Best Little Whore Shuttle in the 'Verse. Was this yet more evidence of strong Jossian women characters wielding yet more power?

Alas, no. Because *Firefly* is not about something new. It's all about the past. Of the three faces of Joss, *Firefly* is the most reactionary and traditional, a show in which Joss went backward regarding the empowerment of women. Before I am accused of Joss-bashing (never; I would offer myself to the Reavers first), let me explain why I think *Firefly* could do nothing more than it did—which wasn't all that much—to push the portrayal of female power.

The first reason why this was not *Buffy in Space* is that in the case of *Firefly*, the medium is intrinsically part of the message.

Buffy and *Angel* may both be described as horror or dark fantasy shows, *Angel* with at least an original intent to add a *soupçon* of the noir detective genre. But *Firefly* is a western. A science fiction western, to be sure; as such, it is the descendant of two western TV series with science fiction elements: *The Wild Wild West* and *The Adventures of Bris-*

[1] See full discussion and interview in *Buffy the Vampire Slayer: The Watcher's Guide, Volume 1*, by Christopher Golden and Nancy Holder (Simon and Schuster, 1998).

co County, Jr. These were steampunk shows, where nineteenth-century good guys employed scientific marvels ahead of their time to further the cause of justice on the actual Western frontier. All the main characters on both shows were men, although the sassy and bold dance hall performer Dixie Cousins would occasionally pop up to bedevil Brisco on *Brisco County, Jr.*

The surfeit of male characters in *WWW and BCJ* is not surprising, specifically because they're westerns. In his essay on the western genre, popular culture essayist Ken Sanes posits that westerns are inherently macho, about "battling forces larger than oneself." The western hero is a "knight with honor in a savage land" (to quote the theme song from *Have Gun Will Travel);* he is like a force of nature himself, free of the burdens of civilization—a wife, kids, a job, getting along with other folks. He is a loner, the good guy at the end of the street in the show-down, the handsome stranger who gallops in off the plains to give the more civilized folks a hand, then rides back out...alone.

As Sanes says:

> The theme of Westerns...is about the conflict of man against wild, masculine, nature, and of good men against wild men. In other words, it's about the bridling of masculine desire. In the battle with nature, the men capture and break horses and cattle, in a conflict of control and strength versus wild power.... They subdue and destroy "wild" Indians.... In addition, the good men stand up to, subdue, and kill wild men with unbridled desires, who get drunk, rob, threaten, make noise, steal and kill by nature.[2]

Rather than bringing civilization, these men make it possible for others to create and maintain civilization. Riding the range, these lone-wolf heroes visit the outposts of civilization, which Sanes enumerates: "space stations, ranches, towns or forts...exist[ing] in a sea of dangerous nature that can close in any time."

Welcome to the 'Verse, and the Outer Rim.

The Golden Age of TV westerns—the decades of the fifties and sixties—existed in an age prior to the celebration of female virility. Back in the fifties and sixties, women served as humanity's ladies auxiliary. The menfolk did the meaningful work, while their women supported them

---

[2] See "Westerns: The Founding of Civilization as the Bridling of Masculine Desire" by Ken Sanes. http://www.transparencynow.com/west.htm

emotionally (and nurtured their children). Title IX, legislating equality for females in sports programs in educational institutions that received federal aid, was not passed until 1972. Physically active and/or aggressive women were as unusual in most cultures prior to that time as they were on TV.

The westerns of the fifties and sixties featured male main characters battling the hostile forces of Sanes' West: Marshal Dillon, Bat Masterson, Paladin, The Virginian, Ben Cartwright of *Bonanza* and a host of others, who were usually either bachelors or, very frequently, widowers. They were the heroes, strapping on their phallic symbols (their guns) to subdue an overabundance of wildness. They were not civilizers per se, although they might dwell in a civilized outpost—the Ponderosa, or Dodge City. In all cases, they rode in where others feared to tread.

There were, however, strong women in a few of these shows, paving the way for such a possibility on our show, *Firefly*. There were assistant cowgirls—one was Penny, the plucky niece on *Sky King* (1951 to 1952 and 1955). Sporting "pigtails and pistols," Gail Davis starred on *The Annie Oakley Show* (1953 to 1956). And of course, the inimitable Dale Evans costarred in *The Roy Rogers and Dale Evans Show*, and starred in many western feature films. A French-Kids!-WB co-venture cartoon series with a very brief (three episodes) U.S. run was *The Legend of Calamity Jane*. And there was a 1984 TV movie starring Elizabeth Montgomery titled *Belle Starr,* about the famous outlaw.

A strong single woman appeared in *Gunsmoke* (which ran from 1955 to 1975): Miss Kitty Russell ran the Long Branch Saloon, and she was a platonic friend of the hero, Marshal Matt Dillon. However, as has been pointed out on the IMDB site for *Gunsmoke*, Marshal Dillon often saved her from great danger.[3] And Sanes offers up the idea that saloons were a sort of neutral zone, where wildness could both be exhibited and then repressed—in drunken brawls, the gunning down of cardsharks and the bedding of women.

On *Big Valley* (1965 to 1969), Victoria Barkley was a wealthy widow and the family matriarch, whose grown sons followed her orders. But she owned an outpost of civilization—a vast "spread," which she had not wrested from wildness. Her husband had. She only inherited the spoils of his victory.

Neither of these women were tamers of wildness. They were not marshals, wagon train leaders or pioneers. Their roles revolved around as-

---

[3] http://us.imdb.com/title/tt0047736/

sisting with civilization. While they wielded power, it was not a power of equality—they weren't equally good at subduing the hostile elements of the West as men. Theirs was a power of parity—within their sphere of influence, they had as much power as a man did in his.

This sensibility emerged more fully on *Dr. Quinn, Medicine Woman.* "Mike" Quinn was a doctor from the East who sought to improve the lot of marginalized folks. She had no interest in gunning down outlaws or establishing order (that was left to Joe Lando, her hunky noble-savage-style boyfriend and eventual husband). She was the ultimate feminine influence on the badlands of wildness, civilizing the (formerly) Wild West with newfangled notions of justice and equality.

These women characters operated in either the historical West, or in the contemporary world of their day, from the nineteenth century to the 1950s—arguably a man's world. *Firefly* was set in the twenty-sixth century—where, one might argue, Joss could have made it anybody's world. But I suggest that he couldn't. If he had, *Firefly* could not have been a western.

At every opportunity, Joss sought to inform his audience that a western was what they were watching. From the twangy scores to the costumes to the jangly g-droppin' dialect of the main characters, Joss cast *Firefly* firmly in the West-that-was. He made it exotic sf by blending seemingly anachronistic historical western elements with Chinese/Asian details, a precedent set in the western fantasy TV series, *Kung Fu*, which ran from 1972 to 1975.

No on-screen explanation was given for this western look, although a viewer could fill in the blanks that this was a postapocalyptic, *Road Warrior*-style artifact of traditions carried away from "Earth-that-was." The amalgam of western and Chinese was explained on the DVD commentary by Joss, who said he wanted to hint that America and China had been the last of the great Earth superpowers before Earth went away.

The shooting script for the Chinese shadow puppet show in "Heart of Gold" reveals that the people of Earth abandoned the barren, polluted planet, which eventually disintegrated after severe volcanic activity. Thus, humanity left the former reaches of civilization to carve out a new world in the harsh landscape of the frontier—welcome to *How the West Was Won: The Next Generation.*

So, I argue, for *Firefly* to retain its integrity as a western, it had to conform to the basic requirements of western-ness. It required a male lead. Even more specifically, the fact that Mal was on the losing side of the great war against the Alliance harkened back to the western trope of the battle-weary post-Civil War veteran cast adrift, as in shows like *The Rebel* (1959 to 1961), *The Outcasts* (1968 to 1969) and *Bronco* (1958 to 1962).

Following this disaffected-veteran tradition, Mal purchased a wagon (*Serenity*), and at the beginning of the series, his only purpose in life was to "keep flying"—i.e., to stay on the move. The people he attracted were equally rootless. Kaylee, Wash and Jayne signed on because Mal offered them adventure and employment; Inara figured she could increase business. Zoe owed him her life and would have followed him wherever he went. Simon and River were fugitives. Book was a shepherd whose real mission remained unknown. This dysfunctional little wagon train began to learn how to function together, because in whatever form he works, Joss is interested in family (viz., his commentary on the *Firefly* DVD set).

Even though he operated within the constraints of the western, Joss did manage to push the power-gender envelope—just not as far as would have been possible had he decided to work in a less reactionary genre.

But let's get down to it: where exactly are the gender issues the same-old, same-old, and where are they something shiny and new?

A female writer friend of mine had this to share in an e-mail: "This is a series in which power is very largely defined as physical power, which is mostly employed (and possessed) by male characters."

She's right.

Let's start with Zoe, who holds a position of authority as Mal's second in command. Go, Feminist Joss! She is loyal unto death because Mal saved her life during the Battle of Serenity Valley (in scenes in which not a single other female soldier was to be seen). Until the arrival and development of River, Zoe was the most physically powerful woman on the ship. She shoots and brawls; she's got Mal's back in a bar fight. She wears pants and she says "ain't."

At the end of the day, she returns to her husband Wash's side. Yes, the same Wash that Feminist Joss casts as the pilot who is often left behind, childishly playing with dinosaurs and taking messages for the folks doing the more active, dangerous jobs. He's a little bit like the ladies auxiliary of humanity.

The same Wash who says, "People don't get me and Zoe."

Ker-plunk. There's the end of Zoe's machisma, and the crash and burn of Joss' strafing run on stereotypical male-female power issues.

What is it that people don't get? That Zoe is a warrior and he is not? That he's a little goofy, warm and fuzzy and she, not so much (until her man wows her in bed)? In the Earth-that-is, we Americans currently have female soldiers fighting (and dying) in a war; one may assume that among them, some have (male) spouses and significant others who are not soldiers. Is that what Wash thinks people don't get?

Come back with me now about twenty years, to an ad that ran on TV wherein some handsome guys and some foxy chicks were engaged in a tug of war. All the guys pulled on one end of the rope; all the gals pulled on the other. And the girls won! The first time I saw it, a woman in the room raised a fist and said, "Right on!" as if some amazing moral victory had just been achieved. "The chicks beat the strong guys!"

I said to her (rather impatiently, as I recall), "It would be 'right on' if the outcome of the contest had ever been in doubt." In other words, if either the guys or the girls could have won and we would all still want to purchase whatever product the ad was pushing, lost to me now in the eons of time. The image that has stayed with me is the pride of a fellow woman consumer, happy to claim victory even in a fixed competition.

I was recently reminded of the pandering of the media to the *appearance* of strong female characters when I took my daughter to see *The Princess Diaries 2*. I admit to some sensitization on the subject of the princess' characterization because I had read an online discussion concerning the notion that women with power in Hollywood now had daughters to raise, and were publicly stating that they were interested in making movies that empowered their girls—while still being able to make money in order to feed, clothe and educate them by producing movies people actually wanted to see.

Sitting beside my eight-year-old in the darkened theater, I watched her trying to make sense of the main plot point: the princess is being forced to get married as a prerequisite to assuming the throne. She must be married *because* the kingdom will then have a male ruler by proxy. It is carefully explained during the course of the film that if she had been a prince, there would have been no such requirement. The young princess eventually refuses, insisting that she is every bit as fit as any guy to rule her people.

I doubt it had ever occurred to my little girl that her ability to do something had ever been in question because of her gender. I think the film confused her, and then made her doubt herself. Under the pretext of presenting a feminist point of view, *Princess Diaries 2* actually undermined her sense of entitlement and empowerment.

This may be a naïve view on my part, but my point is, Joss would have never made such a misstep with Buffy. He took care of this "you girl people are so very equal" nonsense very fast in *BtVS*. In the first ten seconds of the first episode, in fact, when the predatory boy who snuck a hottie into the school for illicit smoochies got his throat ripped out by said hottie, who turned out to be a vampire. This scene was the equivalent of Joss saying, "Okay, these are the clichés, and they're so over." And thereby made television history.

However, with the decision to make a western, Joss had to use clichés to stay congruent with his chosen genre.

So, Zoe is like unto the princess, except that she does have to get married to rule her kingdom. Look at "War Stories," in which Mal learned that Wash was jealous of his relationship with Zoe. He taunted the insecure husband to keep him from shattering under torture, and to his credit, Wash was aware of Mal's ploy. But at the end of the episode, Mal brought the subject out in the open, mockingly announcing that the jig was up and that he and Zoe must at last consummate their reckless passion. Zoe's response is to tell him, "Take me, sir. Take me hard." Thus she continued to cast herself as his second—and as a submissive sexual partner—safely reassuring Wash that she was his.

His, because *Mal* had *already* reassured Wash that Zoe belonged to Wash. Though the superior male in the hierarchy of their community, Mal had relinquished any *droit du seigneur* he may have had over Zoe, underscored by his bonding with Wash as comrade-in-arms during their torture. And Zoe, by behaving only as the object of Mal's desire, made it possible for Mal to give her back to her husband.

To elaborate: If Zoe had said, "Damn, sir, I'm ready to hop in the sack with you," she would have been revealing an autonomous desire for the very extramarital affair Wash fears. She would be *acting* sexual instead of *reacting* sexually. But by positioning herself solely as the vessel of her leader's desire, she can "safely" mock any sexual interest she may actually have in him. She said, "Take me, sir. Take me hard." She did *not* say, "I'm gonna take you, sir. I'm gonna take you hard."

Because she was presented as submissive, she is "excused" from responsibility for any perception that she belongs to anyone but Wash. And belonging to him connotes inequality to him.

The relationship between Wash and Zoe suggests that *Firefly* operates in an even more traditional sexual universe than our own, that *Firefly* is cleaving to a historical-western universe where a rootin', tootin' female is an unusual but tolerated anomaly: an Annie Oakley, a Calamity Jane. But she *is* an anomaly. This is not the case (*The Princess Diaries 2* notwithstanding) in the early years of the twenty-first century.

What about Patience? Does it follow that this woman who owns "half a moon" is an anomaly? She's shot Mal; she's got her mean, desperado-looking boys, and she's tough. In my survey of western TV series before *Firefly*, there is no one like her, unless one gives her the home-court advantage for having power because of her wealth, as Victoria Barkley did. But Patience indicated that she achieved her status on her own, unlike Victoria, who inherited hers.

It's noteworthy that Patience (unlike Victoria, played by glamorous Barbara Stanwyck) clearly takes no pains with her appearance, and could be argued to look "mannish." Sanes refers to lone women who defend their homesteads with a rifle and a sneer as "masculinized women." Such women have to confront wildness in more traditional masculine ways: with guns and brute force. They are generally not pretty.

As with Dixie on *Brisco County, Jr.*, the rule on *Firefly* seems to be that women can and do still accrue power through sexual attractiveness. The best example of this is Inara, a courtesan, whose beauty and sensual dress open doors for her wherever she goes.

This power comes at a steep price, however, for Inara is part of the *demimonde* of mistresses and other women who are not as respectable as "good girls." In "Shindig," when the catty women at the ball humiliated Kaylee, all it took to bring them down was a few digs (from a man) about their ringleader's sexual looseness. Inara's escort, Atherton Wing, thought he was complimenting her—or was he counting coup?—when he told her that half the men in the room wished she were their dancing companion, and all of them wished she were in their beds—indicating that she was fine for whoring, but only marginally fine for a social gathering. He felt entitled to belittle her, and it would have been bad for business for her to protest. Yet the status quo of their universe is such that his behavior, while perhaps boorish, is congruent with societal expectations.

His treatment of Inara provoked Mal to punch him out, which triggered a duel of honor between the two men. Mal explained to Inara that his own habit of calling her a whore is different from Atherton's, because it is a sort of socially conscious protest about what she does with her considerable gifts as a human being. To him, she is not a whore; she is a woman who is pursuing the profession of whoring. Her profession places her in a degrading situation in their society, and that's what bothers him . . . or so he says.

Kaylee is framed as an Annie Oakley/Calamity Jane tomboy (a form of masculinization), who yearns to be a prettified girly-girl on occasion. She was wounded when Mal made fun of her desire to own a beautiful (?) party dress. Heck, she's just Little Kaylee, the pigtailed cowgirl, who had puppy sex with the moronic first engineer of *Serenity* and has no idea how to move from mild flirtation to a real romance with Simon. It follows, then, that Mal would also angrily defend her from Jayne's crude sexual jokes at the dinner table—an act that, however nobly intended, is actually quite patronizing.

The threat of rape is a repeated theme, from "Our Mrs. Reynolds" to "Objects in Space." In "Our Mrs. Reynolds," when the bandits threatened to force Farmer Jayne's wife to have sex with them, Jayne suggested they reconsider...because his gal was so ugly. As the faux woman about to be raped, Mal's immediate (supposedly humorous) response was to feign hurt feelings at being deemed "unworthy" of the potential rapist's attention because "she" was not attractive.

In the world of *Firefly*, the power of sexuality—of gender—appears to lie with definitions of women as perceived by men...but also as women perceive themselves in their relationships with men. There was a telling moment when Inara brought a feminine client (the Councilor) aboard *Serenity*. Alone to savor pleasure together, Inara and her client agreed that they would lay aside expectations to perform or be "on" since they are two women, and all that show is for the benefit of men.

Men must be reacted *to*, and women still comply. It is men, not women, who need the ego-stroking assurance that their sexual partners are having a great time. Inara and her female client chuckled over this notion and agreed to abandon it while they were together. But implicit was the idea that both of them are used to being "on" when they are dealing with men. That this boosting of the male ego is not only useful, but required.

Imagine Faith giving lip service (sorry) to the male ego in bed or anywhere else. And yet a woman as powerful as the Councilor—who travels with her own security guards—accepts it as a necessary evil of current cultural mores.

The reinforcement of traditional sex roles was also played out in "Our Mrs. Reynolds." Saffron's abject subservience toward Mal was viewed as shocking by the rest of the crew, but again, as my friend writes to me:

> In viewing "Our Mrs. Reynolds," several things struck me. The first and most obvious is that while the regular characters are appalled, they are appalled in the way that present-day people react to forced prostitution— it is horrifying but a concept we know of, if only as a hateful crime. The reaction is not, "Okay, if you were waiting in the maiden house, where were the men waiting?" Wash's analogy of weirdness is not, "Remember

that planet we visited where three fourteen-year-old boys all wanted Kay-lee to allow them to please her?" but rather, juggling geese.

Mal equated succumbing to Saffron's sexual invitations as a loss of power, with which he is preoccupied. A tightly wound control freak (also sorry; well, no), he is most ill at ease with what he cannot control—Inara's profession, the shepherd's faith, a universe that let him down. When he misread Inara's readiness to confess her love for him, he assumed she was going to tell him that she allowed Saffron to overpower her with a kiss, as he was overpowered. This repeats the western trope of the wily, sexy woman, like saloon gal Dixie Cousins, who can get the better of men by appealing to their baser natures—and only if she is physically attrac-tive—*in a male-defined way*. Women may find each other beautiful, but power is to be found when a man deems a woman beautiful.

And to be lost when a man does not—see above re: rape. Accord-ing to male values (as seen through the eyes of Jayne and Mal, who are surely not otherwise men who share any values) it is more valuable to been seen as beautiful enough to be raped than to be seen as ugly enough to be spared.

In the unaired episode "Heart of Gold," the inequality between the sexes was underscored when Inara asked Mal to protect a brothel owned by a Companion-school dropout—to protect "the girls" from the evil land baron who was the expectant father of a pregnant prostitute's un-born baby. The villain bullied and belittled the women, who were saved only when Mal's crew brought in their big guns...so to speak.

Which brings us to the fourth feminine presence on *Serenity*—River. After River's special psy-gifts were activated, it turned out that she was the strongest person on the ship—the Ilyria. She can sharpshoot with the best of them and single-handedly take out the bad guys. And yet, River is not in command of herself (at least not at the point the series ended). She is more like a loaded gun, looking for someone to aim her.

Like her ancestor Ophelia in *Hamlet*, River is part of a grand tradition of whacked-out, fragile and tragic women whom men (usually) seek to save. A long search finds no male counterpart on TV, although I would argue that on *BtVS*, when Spike was chipped, and later insane, he was briefly characterized in the same way. He viewed himself as having been emasculated—"neutered"—and he eventually recaptured his masculin-ity in an over-the-top attempt to rape Buffy (although one may alter-nately argue that his need to dominate her stemmed from his realization that he was the weaker one in the relationship).

River is fey, whereas Spike at his most insane remained a brooding, Byronic hero, searing his own flesh with a crucifix…and still sexually alluring, as he spent large sections of ensuing episodes naked to the waist. River's insanity is idealized, romanticized—in the first shot of her in the series, she was naked and in a fetal position, like a baby. Mal assumed she was Simon's sex slave and rushed to defend her, and his fury was chivalrous and heroic in a traditional masculine way.

Once she joined the crew, however, River was sexless; she has no sexual interest in any of the men, nor they in her. Her most meaningful conversations with men were with her brother, or with Book, who is celibate.

To recapitulate, as *Firefly* stands it is a futuristic western, and it follows that a liberal amount of traditional gender-coding was necessary to remain faithful to the genre. My friend says it this way:

> This [our discussion] is starting to remind me of the scene from *Yes, Prime Minister*…where the new Prime Minister is getting advice on what he should wear and what sort of background he should have for his speech. If he's going to be saying something new and daring, go with a very conservative suit and surroundings; if it's going to be the same old rhetoric, break out the paisley.

Joss couldn't redefine the western genre and still position his show as a western-science fiction hybrid. So in some measure, Joss needed to adhere to the Code of the West: pretty little gals and big strong men; villains, heroes and damsels in distress.

However, I also argue that Joss did tweak sexual identities here and there. He would not be my captain if he did not. As I've already stated, the fifties and sixties western series often featured no women at all in their casts. *Firefly* is very nearly fifty-fifty male and female characters, and the female characters are not simply present as window dressing or "corsages"—something you wear to the prom, but do not actually need (even to go to the prom, much less for life in general). While Inara wears beautiful, sexy outfits, the other women do not. Zoe could easily have been cast as a male role, as could Kaylee. In traditional western TV shows, they both would have been male.

And despite Inara's attraction to Mal, Zoe's love for Wash and Kaylee's interest in the doctor, none of them defines her primary goal in life as attracting a man. Inara decided to leave the ship when she realized her feelings for Mal were getting in the way of her career. Zoe didn't like

Wash when she first met him, and continued to act as Mal's first officer despite the fact that Wash was jealous of their relationship. Kaylee not only left her boyfriend, the clueless first engineer, but took his job. She's not hoping that Simon will marry her so she can stop working and make strawberry pie and calico dresses. And Simon is not praying for a good husband for River, to take over the care of his trying little sister.

It may be that the female characters are reworkings of the Miss Kitty/ Victoria Barkley position in the traditional western power hierarchy: the strong woman who stands alone. Neither Miss Kitty nor Victoria Barkley behaves as if "find a husband" is at the top of her to-do list. But Miss Kitty lives in the same vaguely wild *demimonde* as Inara, and Victoria Barkley has already been found highly attractive by the male sex as the trophy wife of a land baron.

But it is the absence of any discussion about finding husbands for these gals on *Serenity*—in other words, the acceptance of single women living as single women, rather than as nonsexual beings in a holding pattern— that reveals Joss' innate feminism. My captain thereby deftly avoids the elephant crapping all over the living room of *The Princess Diaries 2*.

So, the scoreboard: *BtVS* was about grrl power; *Angel* was about Buffy's boyfriend. *Firefly* was about the West. For it to work as a western, it couldn't be about grrl power. And while the gender-power subtext of *Firefly* may be rooted in past and current inequalities, Joss has, once again, pushed things forward. There are capable women serving alongside men, fighting the good fight and protecting the weak. Which, in the final analysis, puts this show closer to the envelope-pushing *Dr. Quinn* than to the more traditional lone-gunman-cowboy trope, and may be why I didn't hate him after I watched it.

Still, *Dr. Quinn* worked. It took the tropes of the western and tweaked them—but in one way only: by casting a civilizing female in the central role, rather than using the more traditional lone hero of westerns gone by. *Dr. Quinn* was more the cousin of *Little House on the Prairie* than it was the daughter of *Johnny Yuma*. *Buffy* and *Angel* were the sassy grandchildren of *Dracula*, *BtVS* by way of Hong Kong chop-socky cinema and Angel via *film noir*.

But here's the deal: I'm sure no one forced Joss to set his next show in what is arguably the least flexible of all the genres—the western, which celebrates the way things used to be. His own choice precluded the empowerment of women as a main theme. One can ask, does the creator of Buffy have an ongoing obligation to emblazon the eternal flame of grrl power?

No, of course not. Joss is an artist, and he's free to explore whatever material he chooses. But I, the mother of a young girl who only recently learned that some people think princesses are only good for marrying princes, cannot help my disappointment that on *Firefly*, it really is cooler to be a boy.

Sincere thanks to Robert E. Vardeman (writing as Jake Logan and Karl Lassiter) for his extensive knowledge of the western genre.

Nancy Holder is a four-time Bram Stoker Award-winning author, and was nominated a fifth time for one of her Buffy novels. She also received a special award from Amazon.com for The Angel Chronicles, Volume 1. *She has written or cowritten over three dozen projects in the* BtVS *and* Angel *universes.* Buffy the Vampire Slayer: The Watcher's Guide, Volume 1, *coauthored with Christopher Golden, appeared on the* L.A. Times *best-seller list and was described in* Entertainment Weekly *and the* Wall Street Journal *as "superb." She lives in San Diego with her eight-year-old daughter, Belle, a daunting karate student and key soccer defender, who, as of this writing, is eagerly awaiting her first softball season.*

With total honesty, I must say that Mr. Wright made me angry with the following essay. But I've taken a fortifying walk and punched a sofa and I feel a little better now. The essay is one man's opinion, well-said and well-reasoned, and I am left with a measure of respect for someone who takes a position so out of the line of usual Whedonverse criticism—this is indeed a brave man. I suggest that you take on this essay yourselves, gentle readers, and see what you think. In fact, one of the central points, that iconic figures from different genres may simply not mix in a satisfying way, is quite possibly true.

I will add this.

Wright implies, in several places, that Joss Whedon may not have approached his shows with a feminist agenda. That some choices might have been an expedient nod to what Wright condescendingly calls "delicate modern sensibilities." On this point I am qualified to speak. Damn right Joss approached his shows, all of them, with the absolute soul-deep belief that women have no need of or interest in being protected. Joss is a feminist. Long may he wave.

Just Shove Him in the Engine, or The Role of Chivalry in *Firefly*

JOHN C. WRIGHT

1. THEORY FROM AN UNWISE HEAD

A head wiser than mine is needed to explain why Joss Whedon's *Firefly* failed to please a wide audience. Personally, I thought the show was rich with character, strong on action, well acted and tightly plotted, with special effects dazzling to the eye and dialogue sparkling to the ear.

And yet, even so, I saw even loyal fans of Whedon's other monumental works, *Buffy* and *Angel*, recoil from *Firefly* as from a bad smell. hi Sharon !

I will make no attempt to plumb this enigma, except, perhaps, in one small particular. My theory here is that Joss Whedon could have over-come (at least some of) the natural awkwardness involved in straddling two genres by treating the elements of both genres respectfully. I submit that partly because of the nature of science fiction he could not, and partly because of the nature of modern sensibilities he did not, treat one element of the western properly in *Firefly*: the element of chivalry.

Chivalrous behavior receives no honorable treatment in modern entertainment. Chivalry is a concept unpopular with delicate modern sensibilities; it is a concept by its nature alien to the genre of science fiction. On the other hand, showing men of honor who abide by a Code of the West is a natural and graceful element of the western. The Code is typically American, rugged and unrefined but recognizably chivalrous: frontier chivalry, so to speak.

2. THE DANGERS OF CROSSBREEDING

Joss Whedon's *Firefly* was a magnificent failure. It was magnificent be-cause it was daring, witty and well-written; it was a failure because the audience (or, rather, the advertisers and producers whose business it is to estimate what will please that audience) neglected it. No matter how highly we few, we happy few, esteemed the show, we were too few for it to continue.

That *Firefly* was witty and well-written needs no testimony aside from itself. Biting wit flew up from the dialogue like sparks from an anvil. That it was daring is proved merely by naming the show's genre: *Firefly* is a science fiction western, a space opera horse opera. A hybrid of this kind had never been done on television before. Even in novels, such experimental crossbreeds are rare.

Innovative daring has its peculiar risks. Every act of storytelling relies on an assumed set of protocols between the storyteller and the audience; it is an unspoken contract. If the storyteller violates the assumptions and expectations of the audience, woe to him, for the audience feels not merely disappointed, but cheated. An innovator is one who changes the protocol. If the audience rejects the change, its reaction will range from confusion (if the audience is generous) to contempt (if not).

The protocols for each genre differ. A romance where no one falls in love would cheat the expectations of its audience, but so would a romance in which the heroine wins the hero by means of a love potion or a hypnotic ray. A detective story in which no one commits or solves a crime would violate the protocols of a whodunit, but so would a detective story in which the hero is told the murderer's name in a dream, by a ghost, instead of using deductions from clues.

The specific risk of combining two genres, as in a sf western, is that certain protocols are incompatible with each other. One such incompatible protocol is the treatment of chivalry.

3. IT CAN BE DONE

It must be said, however, that Joss Whedon has a history of marrying distinct genres with distinct protocols and achieving distinct success. *Buffy the Vampire Slayer* married the protocols of the angst-ridden teen romance, dwelling on the turmoil of high school life, with the supernatural dread of the horror story, perhaps with a dash of teen detective novel and chop-socky action thrown in for good measure: Dracula meets Kung-fu Nancy Drew at Sweet Valley High. Our heroine both was allowed to anguish over whether her boyfriend was cheating on her and over whether her boyfriend would be eaten by a vampiress. She had to win his heart, as in a teen romance, and to save his soul, as in a Weird Tale. *Buffy* also abided by certain protocols of the superhero genre: the heroine leads a double life; her civilian life jars against her secret duties as a world-saving crusader.

The humor inherent in this miscegenation of genres is shown even in the title of the show: the Vampire Slayer here was not as some grim-yet-stalwart biker in mirrored shades brandishing a katana, but a ditzy valley girl in heels, named, of course, Buffy. The title would have lost zing had it been *Jane the Vampire Slayer*, or even *Lucretia the Vampire Slayer*.

Along the same lines, *Angel* was a marriage of the horror genre with the film noir genre. The hero here, the brooding Angel of Angel Investigations, was a gumshoe. He walked the lonely and dirty backstreets of Tinsel Town, heartless Hollywood, where a Thousand Dreams Come to Die. The criminals preyed on the seamy acquisitive side of human nature, and even the good guys had feet of clay. These are all protocols of the film noir genre. The twist here is that the gangsters are vampires and the crooked mouthpieces are demons and the shifty informer is a psychic from another dimension.

But the marriage of futuristic science fiction and old-timer western may be innately harder than either of these things.

4. CHIVALRY DEFINED

Chivalry is a concept unique to the Christian era. It is the notion that those who are terrifying and ferocious in battle should be honorable even with their foes as well as courteous, mild and humble toward those they protect: women and children and old men. Galahad was famous, after all, not merely for his ferocity in bloody fray, but also his gentleness in court.

The contrast between the invulnerable Superman and mild-mannered Clark Kent is the contrast of perfect chivalry. It is not a coincidence that Superman's three pals are the fair Lois Lane, the young Jimmy Olsen and the gray-haired Perry White: a woman, a youth, an old man. Had Superman's secret identity been a wealthy playboy rather than a naïve reporter from a hayseed town in Kansas, the choice would not have been as chivalrous, for the element of meekness would be absent.

We of the modern West tend, through familiarity, to see chivalry as a common attribute of heroism. We are used to soldiers who come home from war and don civilian garb again and settle down as shopkeepers and used car salesmen: lions in combat turning into lambs at home. We never notice the humbleness involved in reducing war-heroes to garage mechanics. In the pagan world, greatness had no such bipolarity. Achilles was as proud and wrathful toward Agamemnon as he was toward Hector. That Ulysses was dressed as a beggar in his own homeland where he was rightfully king was a sign of his humiliation, not his humility. Many the hero of ancient tale is as rough and proud toward his underlings as he is toward the foe.

When heroes are not chivalrous, they are usually one or the other: meek toward the enemy or fierce toward those they are supposed to protect. Captain Jean-Luc Picard of *Star Trek: The Next Generation* might be regarded as too meek. When Picard is shown resisting Cardassian torture or Borg absorption, his virtue is that of a victim who endures stoically: the heroism of a martyr rather than of a victorious soldier. The audience at no point is asked to step back and admire the military glory or bold generalship of Captain Picard.

Mad Max of *The Road Warrior* is the opposite. When Max pushes a mute and brain-damaged child over broken glass out onto the hood of a speeding truck during combat to recover the shotgun shells needed to

kill the enemy, we are meant to admire his tough-mindedness, his ferocity, not his gentle protectiveness toward the weak.

A chivalrous soldier also treats prisoners of war with the same combination of sternness and honor, without being either too meek or too
savage. Again, the two examples given above are instructive. In the meek
Star Trek universe, Klingon prisoners are not even stripped of their gear
and are allowed, while in the brig, to build functioning weapons out
of components their captors leave with them. Picard is not cashiered
over this or any other incident betraying the lax military standards of
Starfleet. Discipline is as alien to their universe as money.

In the savage *Mad Max* universe, on the other hand, Max chains up
a relatively harmless prisoner hand and foot, and leaves him them to
wrestle with the guard dog over who gets the cold and leftover dog food
at the bottom of the can.

We are meant to be charmed with the enlightenment of the gentle
Star Trek future just as we are meant to be horrified by the cruelty of the
barbaric *Mad Max* future.

5. THE PROTOCOLS OF UTOPIA AND APOCALYPSE

These two examples hint at why science fiction tends not to be a literature of chivalry: the future tends either to be too utopian to need so war-
like a trait as chivalry, or tends to be too dystopian to be able to afford
so unwarlike a trait as chivalry.

In high-tech futures, women and children—Tasha Yar or Wesley
Crusher, for example—can be shown possessing the intellectual skills
or the phaser marksmanship needed to defeat the foe. Brute strength or
high-hearted courage is not required. In utopia, the era will surely be
too enlightened and egalitarian to have men protect women and children.

In low-tech futures, the shocking nature of the barbarism after the
fall of civilization is often portrayed by showing a casual attitude toward the lives of women and children. After the apocalypse, even the
she-wolves and cubs must fight alongside the wolves for the scraps of
survival. Children are taken into combat because there is no home, no
safe place to leave them.

An argument can be made that both futures are unrealistic.

If the postapocalyptic society were as underpopulated and desperate
as the society of the primitive tribesman or Bronze-Age farmer, it would

adopt the survival strategies of the tribesman, and for the same reasons. Any tribe exposing young women to the rigors of hunt or battle rather than motherhood would be outnumbered in a generation or two by tribes less liberal with their daughters' lives. Hence, the fertile young women would not be sent out on the tanker truck as part of a suicidal fighting squad when the roaming bands of postapocalyptic thugs come raiding.

In the same vein, it might be argued that while Tasha Yar can pull a phaser trigger as well as Worf the Klingon, soldiers (even soldiers of the future) have other tasks, such as carrying fallen comrades or killing a foe hand-to-hand, that, on average, a man can do better than a woman of equal training, merely because of his physical frame. If the psychological differences between the sexes are natural, they will not change with time, and if cultural, they might or might not, depending.

A cultural change required for the future wars of a society more egalitarian than our own would be, for example, that the young men will be trained to face combat without a masculine warrior mystique, without a sense of that mysterious thing called masculine honor, and trained to regard exposing young women to the rigors of war—death, wounds, maiming, capture, torture, rape and so on—as a neutral matter. Whether the psychology of war makes this possible or not, future societies, even fairly egalitarian ones, may well recoil in disgust at the idea of teaching their young men such callous indifference toward their young women.

Such arguments about realism, however, are pointless. Whatever one's opinion on the matter, utopian science fiction will continue to show children and women as heroes and heroines, needing no protection, as long as the current society of the readership does not accept that as a norm to be taken for granted; likewise, apocalyptic science fiction will continue to show women and children as barbarically fierce and tough, as long as the current society would be shocked or saddened by that portrayal. Science fiction is about what changes, not about what stays the same.

A future society with the same arrangements, assumptions and institutions governing the man-woman relation or the parent-child relation would not interest readers. For example, the institution of incestuous polygamy as portrayed in Robert Heinlein's *The Moon Is a Harsh Mistress* is interesting speculation, whether it is bad anthropology or not. Part of the interest of the book is not merely the rebellion of the moon colony, but also the quaint and curious customs of the natives. You would not listen to a sailor spin a yarn about some distant land whose exotic folk have customs all just the same as ours, nor to a similar yarn about some distant future. In contrast, the love affair between Clarissa MacDougal and the Gray Lensman Kimball Kinnison is as chaste and Victorian as that between Dejah Thoris and John Carter, Warlord of Mars. The exotic nature of the marriage customs of Tellus or Barsoom form no element of the interest the reader has in these tales, because the customs are not exotic: both couples marry in chaste monogamy and bear (or hatch) their children in wedlock.

Because the underlying assumptions of chivalry are unchanging ones as far as our society is concerned, chivalry makes ill fodder for feeding science fiction, for a sense of wonder thrives on novelty.

The western is a different sort of beast.

6. THE CODE OF THE WEST

Unlike science fiction, the western genre expects a certain amount of chivalry in the heroes: this can be a rough-and-ready, homespun sort of frontier chivalry, but it must be present.

The hero in *High Noon* has to walk into the street to face four gunmen alone as the whole cowardly town turns its back on him, rather than take his new bride Grace Kelly and flee to the hills, because, well, sometimes a man's gotta do what a man's gotta do, and there ain't no two ways about it.

Again, it is an unrefined sort of chivalry: the sheriff does not meet with pistols at dawn, there are no seconds in tall black hats handing out silver-chased dueling pistols and none of the other trappings of a mortal duel between aristocrats. The unvarnished essentials are still the same: men who are willing to kill and die for abstractions like honor and justice, and to defend the weak (women, children, old men). The cowboy is supposed to kill cattle rustlers and Apache with his trusty six-shooter or bowie knife, but be mild and good-mannered around the schoolmarm and her spunky kid brother and the old preacher.

There is a particular subgenre of western that might be called the unchivalrous western, the exception that tests the rule. A show like *Maverick* stars a gambling womanizer who is a coward; a film like *Unforgiven* drains all the glamour and romance from the gunfighter by showing what a terrifying thing it is to kill a man, or to be the type of man who can kill without being terrified.

These variations on the theme were fascinating precisely because the surrounding environment of the genre forms a backdrop for the contrast.

Against other backdrops, the effect would be absent. Had Bart Maverick been a gambler in Edwardian Paris or modern Las Vegas, his womanizing and cowardice would not have been a particularly interesting element of the plot, because, unlike the Old West, these are not environments harsh enough to call for chastity or physical courage. Likewise, had William Munny (*Unforgiven*) been a cutthroat on a pirate ship, his inhuman cold-heartedness would not seem so shocking. We expect to find chivalry and human feeling among cowboys, but not among pirates.

The exception proves the rule: the Code of the West is in the marrow of the western.

7. THE CODE OF THE SKY

In this writer's judgment, *Firefly* was simply unsatisfactory in its treatment of this crucial western element.

A look at the cast of characters will tell us why this is. Of the menfolk aboard *Serenity*, none were suited for acts of chivalry except, perhaps, the captain.

The pilot, Wash Warren, was seen more often with a dinosaur toy in his fist than a gun. Indeed, the main plot point about this character was that his wife, Zoe (played by the gorgeous Gina Torres) was a veteran soldier, and that he was not. That plot point would have been overshadowed had Wash been seen performing acts of derring-do. Had he been seen protecting his wife from danger, the whole point of making him a "male war bride" would have been lost.

What of the other men? Dr. Simon Tam is highly protective of his sister and willing to take risks (as in the episode "Ariel") to save innocent lives with his doctoring skill. A man can be brave without being chivalrous in the specific way I have defined it here: fearsome in battle and meek at home. A noncombatant like a doctor does not and cannot be expected to display this quality.

Shepherd Book may have had a violent past, but he was a noncombatant on two counts: his age and his religion. Note that the religion of the "shepherds" is nowhere specifically defined. Only ax-murderers are allowed to be portrayed as Christian these days; delicate modern sensibilities find only Eastern mysticism inoffensive. But since the character is in the role of the preacher-man, and his dress and comportment are basically Christian (he is a missionary from Southdown Abbey), we can assume his office forbade acts of violence.

Jayne Cobb was, of course, a thug. Our delight in this character was that he was immoral in an innocent, almost childlike way. In the pilot episode "Serenity," we see Jayne joining the crew during a stickup because the captain bribes him; and in the episode "Ariel," he betrays the crew because of a bigger bribe and reaffirms his loyalty (or rather, his self-interest) only when Captain Mal has him in a cycling airlock with no suit. Had Jayne ever been seen acting with honor and chivalry, it would have negated the whole point of the character. The whole humor of the episode "Jaynestown" is that Jayne is no sort of hero.

The thing to notice here is that any of these characters could have been translated into western archetypes with relatively little change: the steamboat pilot, the sawbones, the preacher, the roughneck.

None of the womenfolk, however, belong in a western. The women aboard include the engineer, the first mate, the doctor's sister and the high-class courtesan.

The engineer is Kaylee Frye, whose personality is so sunny and winning that she seems almost an elfin sprite. She is the typical heroine of what I above called utopian science fiction: her role as the ship's mechanic requires no brute strength. Mechanical problems aboard ship are solved by brains and gumption.

The first mate, Zoe Warren, is a heroine of apocalyptic science fiction. The whole point of having a gorgeous woman in the sidekick and combat-buddy role (a role traditionally assumed by a man) is to make the point that things in the future will not be as they are now and might actually be a lot rougher than they are now.

The doctor's sister, River Tam, is a noncombatant on three counts: woman, child and lunatic. In addition, she is hunted by vicious government agents and has been subject to torture and cruel medical experimentation on her brain. A character more well-suited to bring out a protective desire in a man cannot be imagined. And yet, even here, there are hints that she does not need protecting. In the episode "Objects in Space," she nicely outwits the bounty hunter seeking her; in the episode "Ariel," she is able to shoot several guards with superhuman accuracy and speed. There are hints that she can sense the Blue-handed Men seeking her from a distance. If she is psychic, or a supergenius, she has uniquely science fictional attributes with which to defend herself.

The courtesan Inara Serra (played by the staggeringly beautiful Morena Baccarin) ironically holds a high rather than low place in the exotic society of the future. In the episode "The Train Job," Inara is sent out to talk to the local lawmen as the only "respectable" person aboard. Obviously preachers, engineers and doctors do not qualify. When the local lawmen are awed, the point is that things in the future will not be as they are now, and things may even be the reverse of what we have now.

As science fiction premises go, having courtesans be respectable is not particularly outrageous. The British of two centuries ago, who regarded actors and actresses as vagabonds and harlots, would be surprised to see a culture, like ours, that adores the acting professions; our surprise would be no different from that of the British to see a culture that respected whores. Of course, part of this idea is merely meant to be ironic: we smirk to see a cop afraid of a hooker rather than vice versa.

Now, it might be argued that Inara is a western character: the saloon girl with the heart of gold is a respected stock character of the western. On the other hand, whenever Captain Mal gets protective of her, the plot always shows this to be foolishness on his part. In the episode "Shindig" his sword-duel to protect her honor (whatever the honor of a harlot might consist of) is played for laughs, as Mal is incompetent at swordfighting. Inara greets the attempt with disdain rather than pleasure. Girls in the Old West might have admired their menfolk for protecting them; the women of outer space resent it.

Nor is this theme restricted to Inara. In the episode "Our Mrs. Reynolds," a young, stammering, painfully shy and innocent Saffron is introduced as accidentally married to Mal. His protectiveness and chivalry are exploited as a weakness, as the girl turns out to be some sort of highly competent superspy working for the enemy and playing Mal for the fool.

Nor is this theme restricted to Captain Mal. In the episode "War Stories," in which the pilot Wash argues with his wife and insists on going on a dangerous mission in her place, nothing is made of the fact that this act saves her from kidnap and torture: the portrayal makes Wash's behavior seem merely petulant rather than heroic, as if there is something wrong with a husband trying to safeguard his own wife. (One wonders what the marriage oaths of the shepherd religion contain.)

8. CAPTAIN MALCOLM

The Code of Space differs from the Code of the West in several important respects. Captain Mal spares no pains to protect his ship and his crew, as a good captain should, and he is willing to protect his passengers, even when they are more trouble than they are worth. However, the women, old men and children of science fiction are fully able to fend for themselves.

In fact, there seems to be no evidence at all of a "code" guiding Captain Mal's actions. When, in the episode "The Train Job," he agrees to steal some cargo for the unsavory Niska, his sentiment (rather than any fixed moral principle) does not allow him to carry through with the job when he discovers the cargo is medical supplies. Certainly there is an emotional difference between stealing medicine and stealing money from someone who might want to buy things (things like medicine, perhaps); but there is no difference in principle. Captain Mal is noble enough not to have a thief's code of honor, which otherwise requires him to carry through with the bargains he has made, savory or not.

9. JUST SHOVE HIM IN THE ENGINE

The other pillar of chivalry, aside from protecting the weak, is dealing honorably with the enemy. In "The Train Job," Captain Mal has captured Crow, Niska's henchman. Crow is on his knees, bound, and answers Mal's request that they be let out of their contract with Niska with a bloodthirsty threat. "Keep the money. Use it to buy a funeral. It doesn't matter where you go, or how far you fly. I will hunt you down, and the last thing you see will be my blade."

Without any further ado, Mal kicks Crow into the engine, where he dies a swift and ghastly death, chopped to red splatter in an instant by the rotors.

Now, I approve of this scene. I like it. It shows that Mal is hardcore. When someone threatens him, he takes the threat seriously. Captain Mal Reynolds treats problems with a brutality we would not see even from John Crichton, much less Jean-Luc Picard or John Sheridan: no pussyfooting around. It is almost refreshing.

That said, the scene was also unrealistic.

I am not saying (though perhaps I should) that the scene was unrealistic because a real captain would have shot the man in the gut and let him slowly bleed to death, screaming like a stuck pig, rather than risking foreign object damage from bone fragments in the engines of his beloved ship. No, we can excuse a messy and spectacular death on the grounds of the dramatic value, or even on the (rather dark and nasty) humor value.

But the scene was unrealistic because a real crook, even a hardened one, would pause to contemplate that killing a crime boss' right-hand man obligates that crime boss to hunt him down and kill him, preferably by torture. Any boss that fails to do so telegraphs that he cannot protect his men; and a crime boss that cannot protect his men cannot remain a crime boss. It is, in fact, the demands of a code of honor that compels the crime boss (in this case, Mr. Niska) to seek out Captain Mal for death-by-torture in the episode "War Stories." It would be impossible for such a code not to exist, and impossible that a wrong-side-of-the-law type like Captain Mal would be unaware of it.

The reality of war is what makes men treat captured enemies with a certain level of military courtesy. Only a zealot or a barbarian is so confident, or so ignorant, as not to believe one of his own will stand in the same spot his current prisoner stands in, or so bloody-minded not to care. The same logic applies to those who live outside the law.

Likewise, in the real Old West, the reality of frontier life put women, children and old men in a protected class. They were not expendable. The women and children were the promise of the future, and the old men were the wisdom and experience of the past. Young men, who were expendable, protected the others. In order to protect them, the young men had to be gentle to them at home and fearsome to their enemies on the battlefield, or, in a word, chivalrous.

10. COULDA, WOULDA, SHOULDA

Joss Whedon did not add, and may not have wanted to add, an element of chivalry into his space western. Portraying woman characters according to the protocols of the western might well alienate a large segment of his audience. Delicate modern sensibilities do not approve of anything as rough and manly as westerns, in which responsible adult men protect women and children. Westerns are not, after all, all that popular these days.

It also must be said that *Buffy* and *Angel* are innately in harmony with modern sensibilities. *Buffy* portrays a young girl as a deadly fighter possessed of strength and guts and fortitude greater than a grown man: whether the writer's intent or not, this concept cannot help but please the feminist. *Angel*, quite simply, has the villain of centuries of horror fable, a vampire, as the good guy, but one who (unlike the similar hero-vampire of *Forever Night*) is not entirely good. Again, whether this is the writer's intent or not, any sympathetic portrayal of a hated outcast cannot help but please the modern individualist, as it cannot help but condemn race-prejudice, if only metaphorically. This may be why these two shows were more popular than *Firefly*. Captain Mal is something of a cold character, and a tough veteran is simply not as sympathetic as a blonde valley girl or a tormented, soulful vampire.

The advantage of setting his western in space was that Joss Whedon could realistically give his characters and society modern, morally relativistic and egalitarian values, while keeping only so much western flavor as suited the story.

Making his space western more like a western might have made it even less popular. Even hinting that young women should not serve as cannon fodder on the bloody field of war on an equal footing with men could cause some modern thinkers to faint like overheated Victorian matrons: for good or ill, the public is delighted with radical egalitarianism, and disgusted by chivalry.

John C. Wright is a retired attorney, newspaperman and newspaper editor who was only once on the lam and forced to hide from the police, who did not admire his newspaper. He presently works (successfully) as a writer in Virginia, where he lives in fairy-tale-like happiness with his wife, the authoress L. Jagi Lamplighter, and their three children: Orville, Wilbur and Just Wright. His publications include The Golden Age, The Phoenix Exultant, The Gold Transcendence, Last Guardians of Everness *and the forthcoming* Mists of Everness, *all from Tor. Visit his Web site at http://home.clara.net/andywrobertson/nightlastofallsuns.html.*

This comedic comparison of the worlds of Firefly *and* Enterprise *is especially interesting to me as someone who has had a foot in both Whedonia and Trekland. Early in my career, I wrote a freelance episode of* Star Trek: Deep Space Nine, *and even before that I sharpened my skills pitching (and occasionally selling) at* Star Trek: The Next Generation. *I loved every minute.*

I have a tremendous affection for Trek, *going all the way back to the Kirk-Spock-McCoy triumvirate. And I continue to think that there is something important to say within a hopeful version of a human future. Spock, Data, Odo . . . the way they puzzle over humanity makes us see ourselves with alien eyes, and makes us wish we were better. There must be a place for a show that celebrates the noble, questing part of the human spirit, that tells well-crafted stories about good-hearted explorers and the worlds they encounter without thought of profit, conquest or conversion. And then there's life.*

One of Conrad's observations is about the three-dimensional aspect of Wash's flying skills. The same may be said about Firefly *in general. It was distinctly three-dimensional. We tried hard to make the characters, as well as the ship, feel "lived-in." Mal exhibits real heroism when he does the right thing despite his human nature, not because of it. That's the brand of hope that* Firefly *sells, and it is potent stuff.*

Mirror/Mirror: A Parody

ROXANNE LONGSTREET CONRAD

SO THERE I WAS, SHELVING MY DVDs (which with 6,432,278 can take quite a while, believe me) and a good friend of mine mentioned that I ought to leave space for *Enterprise*,[1] which I thought was funny, as like all good archivists I keep things in alphabetical order.

"Can't do that," I said. "That would put it next to *Firefly*. My God, what if there was cross-contamination?"

---

[1] You know, the one they *don't* call *Star Trek: Enterprise*. I can't figure if they're trying to disassociate the show from the franchise, or if Gene Roddenberry's estate filed a restraining order to keep the whole thing at least fifty feet away from even such Xeroxed but relatively successful attempts as *ST: Voyager* and *ST: DS-9*.

It might have been the cold medication, but I had this weird psycho did-I-take-the-yellow-pill-or-the-blue-one moment in which I magically saw the brilliant characters of *Firefly* encountering a positronic-based anomalous nanite singularity with reversed polarity, and being magically swapped out with their approximate equivalents on *Enterprise*.

And once I'd started thinking about it, well, it was really hard to stop. It all began to make a weird kind of sense, really. It's like the two shows are evil twins, one light and one dark. You know, that whole "Mirror, Mirror" thing, which the original *Trek* did so well.

I felt compelled to share. Sorry.

Welcome to the show—er, shows—as they might have been, if only some malign intelligence were in charge.[2]

INT. *SERENITY*, DAY.

> MAL, ZOE, WASH, KAYLEE and JAYNE are snarking at each other on the bridge, which is (as usual) littered with crap, broken parts and plastic dinosaurs. In short, it looks like an actual place someone might work and carry on a life, if they weren't all that good at housekeeping. Because they are so caught up in the fast, brilliant dialogue they're exchanging, they don't notice anything's wrong until the ship JOLTS, throwing Zoe unexpectedly into the strong arms of Captain Mal, who fails to grope her as nearly any other man (including Shepherd Book) would do. Wash nevertheless gets tetchy over his WOMAN getting TOUCHED. Jayne offers to WIPE MAL'S COOTIES OFF HER. Mal sends them both *I'd-kill-you-but-I-might-need-you-someday* looks. Sooner or later, Zoe loses patience with the macho posturing and asks what the hell they hit, at which point everyone recollects that they did, in fact, hit something.
>
> When they try to take a look, nothing works; Kaylee and Wash wiggle around banging wrenches and getting dirty and finally bring up the viewscreen, which is small and kinda clunky and sometimes doesn't work too damn well, and we view A GENERIC SPECIAL EFFECT.[3]

> ### WASH
>
> Wow. That looks really slick, but kind of uninspired. What is it?

---

[2] If you think either Joss Whedon or Berman & Braga fit this description, feel free to jump on the fan-wank train.

[3] Oh, come on, you know the one. Swirly swishy thingie, with cool glow effects. *Star Trek* holds the patent on 'em.

MAL

Money swirling down a drain. If you'd be so kind as to get us the hell away from it....

But before Wash can, they're inexorably sucked into the wormhole/ black hole/swirly Day-Glo EFFECT, and everything goes to credits and crappy music sung by Diane Warren.

INT. *ENTERPRISE*, DAY.

CAPTAIN ARCHER sits in his chair, looking steely-jawed and perfectly groomed. In fact, everyone on the *Enterprise* bridge looks perfectly groomed. A speck of dirt wouldn't be caught dead on the impeccable surfaces. In fact, it's so shiny that it's likely no one on the *Enterprise* actually has fingerprints, or if they did, would be so rude as to leave them on the furniture.

Some dialogue is exchanged. Untouchable sex-kitten T'POL expresses her disdain for humans. CHIEF ENGINEER CHARLES "TRIP" TUCKER III[4] attempts some witty repartee. ENSIGN TRAVIS MAYWEATHER stares blankly at the slickly designed console, which is very pretty even though technically the *Enterprise NX-01* should be clunkier and more primitive, as it was a first attempt, than the *NCC-1701*, which came later and was state-of-the-art. ENSIGN HOSHI SATO sits without too many lines, trying to determine how many currently-raging intergalactic wars her inadequate translation skills are responsible for. LIEUTENANT MALCOLM REED, pretending to know something about weapons and tactics, mostly wonders why the hell he's not dead yet.

Mayweather reports something unusual on sensors. Nobody gets too excited. T'Pol declares it is "fascinating" or "intriguing" or "something I have never seen before," which leads us once again to believe that the Vulcans really don't get out much. They put it up on the glossy plasma-screen viewer, which of course works perfectly, as everything does on the *Enterprise* until the plot calls for it to malfunction, and all give lip service to how unusual it is. T'Pol offers a technobabble explanation for its formation ("Likely this is the result of oscillation overthruster waves counteracting the annihilating particles of the subspace distortion, resulting in that strange mauve color.") and recommends they go around it. Archer vacillates. While he's taking a poll on

---

[4] Dear God, there were two before him.

what to do about the Unusual Phenomenon, the ship is sucked in, and much to their shock, the crew of the *Enterprise* hears a rough, twangy, unusual theme song being played instead of their usual syrupy lyrics. To no one's great surprise, Hoshi faints.

INT. *ENTERPRISE* BRIDGE, DAY.

There is a FLASH OF LIGHT, and MAL, ZOE, WASH, JAYNE and KAY-LEE appear. Mal bounds out of the Captain's Barcalounger™, blurting out an elaborate Chinese curse, which no one watching understands but would nevertheless be interesting and cool if you found someone who spoke Mandarin and could translate it for you.[5] Zoe and Jayne *instantly* draw their pistols and start checking corners for hostiles. Wash sits, stunned, in the pilot's chair.

> WASH
>
> Ooh, look at all the pretty lights!
> (reaches for the controls)

> MAL
>
> Don't touch ANYTHING!

Kaylee, equally enchanted, runs around the bridge gleefully fondling the hyper-machined sets and looking as if she's found true love. Mal grabs her by the back of the coveralls and slings her into the first available comfort chair.

> MAL
>
> ZOE!

> ZOE
>
> (imperturbable)
> Yes sir?

> MAL
>
> Where the hell is *Serenity*?

> ZOE
>
> Don't know, sir. Want me to go ask nicely and find out?

---

[5] Like, for instance, "Meh, tah mah duh hwoon dahn."Or, for those of you without access to the Internet, "Mother-humping son of a bitch!"

MAL

No.

ZOE

(surprised)
No, sir?

MAL

I don't want you to ask nicely.

Just about that time, some pre-Federation red shirts[6] pelt onto the bridge. They would no doubt demand to know what these ruffians have done with Captain Archer, only Jayne semi-accidentally BLOWS HOLES in the first fella out the door, so the rest duck and scatter.

JAYNE

Oops.

MAL

Ta ma duh! [7] Jayne, that just wasn't very damn friendly.

JAYNE

Sneakin' up on a man after he's been bushwhacked into the IKEA-verse? Bastards ruttin' well deserved it.

Mal and Zoe exchange a look.

ZOE

He's got a point, sir.

INT. *ENTERPRISE* SICK BAY, DAY.

SIMON, RIVER, INARA and SHEPHERD BOOK have been deposited in sickbay, where where DR. PHLOX[8] confronts them with waspish bad humor. Surprisingly, they all get along. River is especially fascinated by his head-bumpiness. When Dr. Phlox explains that he's an

---

[6] Oh, come on, I don't care what color you dress 'em up in, they'll always be red shirts to me.

[7] "Please, perform a sexual act upon me until I go blind." (Hey, Mal? Be careful. We're fans, you know.)

[8] Phlox is far too cool to be stuck on *Enterprise*. I say we give him plastic surgery and take him back to *Serenity*. He'd fit right in.

alien, Shepherd Book patiently corrects him, saying there are no such things as aliens. Phlox considers this for a few minutes and allows that he is, in fact, just a guy underneath all that bumpy-forehead business. They all settle down for a good game of lab bowling, and Phlox arm wrestles Simon for the position of Head Doctor.

INT. *SERENITY* BRIDGE, DAY.

The *Enterprise* crew is in disarray, wandering around the narrow, cluttered bridge, bumping into each other, looking in vain for comfy seating arrangements. The computer is patiently announcing a failure of life support in Mandarin (or possibly also in Cantonese).[9] Hoshi, deprived of her props, panics and is unable to translate an Earth language. Archer orders a complete survey of the ship. Trip, attempting to comply, *trips* over a pile of grimy tools stacked there *very carefully* by Kaylee (everyone *else* knows where she leaves her stuff!) and knocks himself unconscious, which is really just as well for everyone.

T'Pol stands motionless on the bridge, refusing to touch anything. She is catatonic from the smell,[10] but thankfully she looks very, very good.

Reed frantically punches buttons on *Serenity*'s console.

Mayweather, fed up with all this, slithers under the console and starts patching things together. The screen flickers to life and reveals A REAVER SHIP bearing down on them with frightening speed.

ARCHER

I suppose we'd better try some diplomacy. A long speech will probably do the trick.

They all look at him.

ARCHER

No?

REED

I'll shoot you myself, sir.

---

[9] "Jeo-shung yong-jur goo-jang. Jien-cha yong-chi gong yin." Just in case you were interested.

[10] Just think about what's been on that ship. Cows. Dead bodies. Crappy burned dinners. JAYNE. Even regular humans might flinch, much less Vulcans.

INT. *ENTERPRISE*, DAY.

> The crew of *Serenity* hijack the ship, interview the crew for suspicious signs of two-dimensionality and end up abandoning pretty much everybody on the nearest habitable planet. Kaylee soups up the engines more thoroughly (though much more unreliably) than any bumpy-forehead, Day-Glo, time-traveling, nanite-infested alien presence has in three dang years. And they begin a quarrelsome, uneven journey through the universe in which the ship constantly fails and is repaired, parts are required and cannot be magically fabricated out of someone's butt, and actual peril ensues. Jayne discovers they have guns built right in. Look out, Nellie. Talk about your final frontiers....

You get the picture. In short, I think that *Serenity's* crew—who are tough, adaptable, self-sufficient and hold to somewhat flexible ideas of right, wrong and iffy—would rampage through the *Enterprise* universe kicking ass, taking names and issuing T-shirts to prove it.[11] The crew of *Enterprise*, well.... They'd better grow some spines, right quick. Because their futures no longer involve aliens who can't shoot straight, magic science or gadgets to help them cope with the stress of being smarter than everyone else.

Why do I think this would be true? Well, I've put a lot of thought into it, while I was under the influence of cold medication (that's my story, okay?), and here are the top five reasons why each of the *Firefly* characters will succeed in their chosen new goonyverse, whereas the *Enterprise* characters will become, ah, Reaver-food. Or possibly dinner entertainment.

CAPTAIN MALCOLM REYNOLDS, now commanding *Enterprise*

1. Can intimidate *anyone* with a stare, a little smile and the power of his incredibly tight pants.
2. Shoots first.
3. Will never use the phrase, in the ultimate critical moment of a fight, while holding an opponent at gunpoint, "You're not worth it." If his enemy wasn't worth it, he wouldn't damn well be doing it, would he? *Blam.* And a cap in your ass too for even thinking it.
4. Did I mention the tight pants?
5. If you've seen "Trash," you'll know.[12]

---

[11] Mine says, I KICKED A KLINGON'S ASS AND ALL I GOT WAS A T-SHIRT AND A BOWL OF SQUIRMING EELS, BUT I *LIKE* CHINESE FOOD. I got Mal to sign it "Captain Tightpants."

[12] Stark naked and still winning. I *love* this man.

ULTIMATE OUTCOME: In ten years, he'd own the most kick-ass mercenary fleet in the history of the universe. In twenty, he'd own the universe. The Ferengi would be paying *him*. Forget about Archer; they'd be asking, "Kirk *who?*"

ZOE, now second in command of *Enterprise*
1. She's the nicest former soldier on the ship.
2. Remember who her competition is.
3. Even *aliens* have to stop and admire her before they shoot, she's so beautiful.
4. Diplomacy? She once bargained for the lives of her horribly tortured captain and husband without a tremor of reaction . . . and accepted her captain's severed ear as "change" without blinking.[13]
5. She's not afraid to lose. She's lost before. That gives her all the edge she needs.

ULTIMATE OUTCOME: She loves Wash. She'll never leave Mal.[14] She'll go on to be second in command of the most kick-ass mercenary fleet in the history of the universe, and *Universe Weekly*'s cover model of the decade.

JAYNE, now weapons/security officer of *Enterprise*
1. He's survived the wrath of Mal Reynolds. Who's gonna even TRY to kill him?
2. He gets along great with the Klingons. They have a lot in common.
3. His physical presence alone ensures that no one, but no one, will draw a gun during a business meeting. Except Mal. Or Zoe, if Mal asks.[15]
4. A whole new universe in which nobody knows who he is? Talk about a great business opportunity. . . .
5. Has an up-close-and-personal relationship with his gun in a way that the previous occupant of the weapons officer chair can't even imagine. Or would want to.

---

[13] Her performance in that scene alone was enough to make cults form around her. Why no one has pointed out that she's a goddess in disguise . . . . Oh wait! *Angel* did, when Gina Torres became the (evil) goddess Jasmine. Hmmmm. . . .

[14] What about "Take me, sir. Take me now!" did you not understand?

[15] And she'd shoot him in the back, too. Fair fights? On *Firefly*? Only if we have superior numbers.

ULTIMATE OUTCOME: Alas, poor Jayne. Nobody could ever take him in a straight fight, but he gets fired by Mal for perverting the vast computing capability of the ship to download Romulan porn. He then spends his money on whores and booze, and ends up knifed in the back in a bar fight. But hell, who's really surprised?

KAYLEE, now chief engineer of *Enterprise*
1. If it moves, she can fix it. That includes electrons.
2. Once she fixes it, it mostly stays fixed. Except when it doesn't. Entropy exists, after all. But she's adaptable, and real, real cute.
3. If she doesn't know it, she'll learn it. To her delight, this opens up a huge universe of possibilities, because she's *exotic* for a change.[16]
4. She can make any ship and any crew feel like a family.
5. Since nobody else in this universe seems to know a darn thing about fashion, she and Inara are bound to be popular as makeover artists.

ULTIMATE OUTCOME: She designs *Enterprise NCC-1701* as a doodle on a cocktail napkin. Ends up teaching the Vulcans a thing or two about having fun at social occasions. Generally charms the pants—literally—off the half of the universe that Inara doesn't get around to.

WASH, navigator on *Enterprise*
1. He can outfly a Reaver. Nothing on this side of the wormhole will present much of a challenge.
2. He understands the idea of *three-dimensional space*. This will consistently baffle the Zindi, who are accustomed to Archer's two-dimensional flat attack patterns.
3. When captured by the Zindi for nefarious torture, he'll be able to look them in the eye and say, with perfect confidence, "Do your worst; I survived Niska." He won't even need Zoe to rescue him. There is no alien in the *Enterprise* universe as scary as the *regular people* in his.
4. The very idea of Wash in any kind of a uniform is ridiculous. Bless him.[17]
5. Toys. He's familiar with them. It gives him that fighting edge.

---

[16] That's part of what makes Kaylee such a delight. She's a regular girl. Got a gift for machines, but she doesn't regard herself as special or exceptional or even pretty. Contrast that to the women of *Enterprise*, who are (a) pretty or (b) special or (c) all of the above. All the damn time.

[17] Unless it's a mismatched Hawaiian shirt uniform. Which, hey, who wouldn't join up for that?

ULTIMATE OUTCOME: Wash and Zoe fight, love and stay together, raise a passel of kids, and dear God, they're happy. There
are no stupid rules about banning kids from the ship. Mal's their
godfather, dammit. There's a playpen on the bridge. End of discussion.

INARA, Companion on *Enterprise*
1. Talk about the diplomatic corps! She and Zoe together could set
   up an empire, if they wanted. They settle for making the universe
   safe for Mal Reynolds.
2. Nobody in the pre-Federation universe ever uses the term
   "whore."[18]
3. Wide-open market for teaching about the fine arts of the bed-
   chamber and the honorable history of the geisha, demimondaine
   and courtesan. Just market it as "body-centered feng shui."
4. Instead of using an empath on future ships, why not Companions? Beats the heck out of holodecks.
5. The downside: Klingons may prove a challenge even to Inara's
   grace and poise.

ULTIMATE OUTCOME: After years of flirtation and fencing, Mal
and Inara finally settle into a comfortable, but never boring, relationship. She becomes immensely rich and is received on any
world, anywhere, with the greatest of respect (not to mention an-
ticipation). Girl power!

SIMON TAM, assistant ship's doctor on *Enterprise*
1. Smart. Very, very, very smart. (But not *quite* smarter than Phlox.)
2. Possible criminal mastermind. He planned the *Serenity* crew's
   most lucrative haul yet.
3. He's so well-groomed he might be mistaken for an *Enterprise* crew
   member, except for his sense of humor.
4. His moodiness will serve him well with Dr. Phlox, who loves a
   cheer-up challenge as much as Kaylee.[19]
5. If he survived the culture clash from the central planets to *Serenity*, he'll survive this.

---

[18] And if they do, it's not around Mal Reynolds. He's the only one who gets to call her that.

[19] Come to think of it, having Phlox and Kaylee on the same ship might violate some basic law of nature....

ULTIMATE OUTCOME: Simon (resentfully) works as Phlox's assistant until Mal "acquires" his second ship, the *Drunken Vulcan*, and Simon assumes his rightful place as Doc-in-charge. He is, unfortunately, responsible for creating the idea of a holographic doctor. Luckily this plan is lost to history, as Jayne spills home-brewed bathtub whiskey on the cocktail napkin containing the holodoc plan instead of on Kaylee's advanced warp drive design.

RIVER TAM, crazy person at large on *Enterprise*
1. There is no "blue hand group" after her *here*.[20]
2. Crazy? Yeah, but she shoots straight. Even without looking.
3. She makes way more sense to the alien races than Hoshi ever did.
4. Survivor? Hell, she went across space naked in a freezer. Not to mention had her amygdala stripped. Ouch. Like Wash, she's got nothing to fear from the Zindi.
5. *Enterprise* medicine can get her all straightened out with a simple oil rubdown and orange lights. Heck, it works for T'Pol. . . .[21]

ULTIMATE OUTCOME: River gets her head straight and becomes Mal's under-captain, helming the *Drunken Vulcan*. This gives her the chance to meet a newer and more interesting class of villains, one of which, to her brother's chagrin, she marries. He's better than a Reaver. But not that much.

SHEPHERD BOOK, chaplain on *Enterprise*
1. Most sky pilots don't shoot quite so well as Book.
2. Most of them don't bench press enough weight to impress Jayne, either.[22]
3. He has a Mysterious Past, which may entail dark government secrets.
4. Despite the fact he has a problem with killing, he's still scary enough to kick the crap out of most aliens *Enterprise* tangles with. (Those he can't scare, he can convert.)
5. Biggest survival trait: religious, but not preachy. Commands respect.

---

[20] However, she mistakenly hears of the still-touring "Blue Man Group" on Vega 19, and blows the crap out of some sapphire-painted performance artists. Later, there's that ugly business with the Andorians. . . .

[21] Also, apparently, for a large audience of teenage boys.

[22] Was it just me, or was the shepherd buff enough to have come out of prison instead of the monastery? Unless they have a 24-Hour Fitness next door to the chapel. . . .

ULTIMATE OUTCOME: On discovering the P.C. nondenomina-
tional religious vagueness of the *Enterprise* universe, Book goes
about setting up his own religious retreat/dude ranch along with
a Vulcan cousin of T'Pol. Meditation Tuesdays and Thursdays,
hunting and fishing on Mondays, Wednesdays and Fridays. Hot
tubs. Clothing optional. We're all God's children here.

The summary:

From *Serenity*	From *Enterprise*
Captain Reynolds: • Lusts after Inara • Deadly when crossed • Would kill for his crew	Captain Archer: • Doesn't lust. Occasionally gets wistful. • Indecisive when crossed • Might die for his crew, if pushed
Zoe: • Tall • Gorgeous • Unhesitatingly violent when required	T'Pol: • Tall • Gorgeous • Unhesitatingly nonviolent, must be talked into so much as a nerve pinch
Wash: • Lusts after his wife. A lot. • Plays with toys • Hell of a pilot	Mayweather: • See Archer, above • Too mature (and boring) to play with toys • Only an adequate pilot, possibly because of the lack of playtime
Jayne: • Deadly when crossed • Deadly when in a bad mood • Basically an untrustworthy bastard, but one who you want pointed *at your enemy* • Also, deadly	Reed: • Honorable • British • See Archer, above
Kaylee: • Brilliant with machines • Naturally ebullient • Earthy and sexual	Trip: • Has to have a staff to take care of things • Naturally morose • *Wishes* he were earthy and sexual, or failing that, wishes he could go into Pon Farr

Simon:	Phlox:
• VERY smart • Snappy dresser • Potential criminal mastermind	• Equally as smart • Crappy dresser, but then, he's an alien, so it's okay • Could be a great criminal mastermind, if it was posed as good, clean fun
River: • Crazy • Deadly • Kinda cute!	Hoshi: • Whiny • Ineffective • Kinda not
Inara: • Even more drop-dead gorgeous than Zoe • Smarter than Mal • Capable of killing you *and* making you like it	*Enterprise* is too P.C. to have a hooker onboard
Book: • Spiritual • Hell of a good shot • Not afraid to fight the good (or bad, or ugly) fight	*Enterprise* is too P.C. to have a chaplain, as well

Firefly gave us something special.

Not tired Xeroxed copies of ramrod-butted, predictable heroes, but something more interesting and rich: real people, with real pasts and traumas, priorities and selfish interests. Not since *Blake's 7* have we seen a crew so dysfunctional, or so deliciously effective.

Want proof? Kaylee got her job as mechanic (*Serenity* doesn't have anything so exalted as "engineer") while boffing the greasy git who had the job before her. Zoe survived the horrors of a war few want to remember. Inara lives in a rich, complicated tapestry of sex, deception and heartbreak. Jayne's a blunt instrument without many redeeming qualities—who nevertheless makes us love him. River's fragility and bursts of violence are both equally terrifying. Simon's trembling devotion to her breaks the heart, not to mention the nerves of Standards & Practices, what with all the subtext. Book embodies all the layers of a man come late to his faith, with (hinted) experience of evil few can match.

And Mal. Captain Mal Reynolds, with his smooth face and lightless eyes, polite manners and ruthless sense of right and wrong.

Mal harkens back to an old and favorite hero of mine: Paladin, in *Have Gun Will Travel*. A man of impeccable ethics, not-so-strict morals, flexible loyalties and inflexible honor. A man for whom ladies were saints (even while he enjoyed them as sinners). A man without a home except the one he made for himself.

Mal, River reminded us once, is Latin for *bad*. Bad to the bone, and good to have on your side.

I'm going to wave my magic wand now and put these guys back on *Serenity* where they belong. They're too good for *Enterprise*, and frankly, I'd hate to leave *Serenity* in the hands of the E! crew. Book me passage on that Firefly, right next door to River and Simon. I'll pack my six-gun and a Cantonese-Mandarin-English dictionary, and look forward to eating at that warm, inviting dining room table with the crew. Becoming part of the family.

Hope you'll join me.

Somebody's got to watch Jayne.[23]

Roxanne's novels include Stormriders, The Undead, Red Angel, Cold Kiss, Slow Burn *(as Roxanne Longstreet),* Copper Moon, Bridge of Shadows *and* Exile, Texas *(as Roxanne Conrad). Her most recent work (as Rachel Caine) is the Weather Warden series, which includes* Ill Wind, Heat Stroke *and* Chill Factor, *with three more to come in 2005 and 2006. Her new Silhouette Bombshell series arrives in August with* Red Letter Days: Devil's Bargain. *She also recently published (as Julie Fortune) an official Stargate SG-1 novel,* Sacrifice Moon, *and coedited the BenBella anthology* Stepping Through The Stargate: Science, Archaeology and the Military in *Stargate SG-1*.

Her short fiction has been featured in numerous magazines and anthologies. She confesses to an unnatural love of television, and if there's a science fiction or fantasy show in the last twenty years she hasn't seen, she'll eat her Betamax tapes. Visit her Web sites at www.artistsin-residence.com/rlc and www.rachelcaine.com.

---

[23] Speaking of that... I'll be in my bunk.

If you don't know the name David Gerrold, then you should. He wrote the "Trouble with Tribbles" episode of Star Trek. *This is the episode of television that I most often cite as the template for my own work. To take a show and twist it, generating humor without denigrating the world and its characters takes a light touch that I greatly admire. Here Gerrold presents a far-ranging look at some of the thornier problems that come with meaningful analysis of any television show, and at* Firefly *in particular.*

Firefly, I think, is a show that challenges us to ask the kinds of questions that Gerrold tackles here, to make us consider the wider world in which it is set and to speculate about directions the show would have taken had it survived.

Star Truck

DAVID GERROLD

OKAY, I ADMIT IT. I couldn't resist the obvious pun. I have no shame.

Now let's talk about *Firefly*.

There was a moment near the end of the pilot—the episode is called "Serenity"—that told you exactly what kind of a show this was going to be. An Alliance agent has grabbed River Tam. They're in the cargo bay. He's holding her hostage with a gun to her head. "Don't anybody move!" Everybody is frozen. Malcolm and Zoe come striding up the ramp. Mal's posture is one of annoyance; he and Zoe have just had a bad business meeting. As the bad guy opens his mouth to shout an order, Mal—still walking—doesn't even hesitate: he just raises his gun and puts a single bullet right between the bad guy's eyes. "Get rid of him, let's get out of here."

The message is clear: I have neither the time nor the patience for this bullshit.

Unfortunately, the geniuses at FOX Television Network chose not to air the pilot episode first. Fortunately, its replacement, "The Train Job," had another one of *those* moments. Very bad guy Niska has hired Mal and crew to rob a train. It turns out that the stolen cargo is medicine, much needed by the desperate locals. Mal and crew decide to return the medicine and give Niska back his deposit. Niska's thugs show up and demonstrate why they—and Niska—are very, very bad guys. But Mal is no dummy; his crew gets the drop on Niska's goons. Cut to: head goon on his knees on the cargo ramp, hands tied behind his back, with Mal leaning down into his face, holding a wad of bills. "Here's Niska's money back. Tell him the deal is off. Tell him that we're even." The thug says, "Keep your money, I'm not delivering that message to Niska. The last thing you see will be my ugly face." Mal says, "I thought so," and kicks the goon firmly in the chest. The goon tumbles backward down the ramp and gets sucked immediately into one of the ship's engines. (Not good for the engine, even worse for the goon.)

Cut to: second goon, on his knees, hands tied behind his back, on the cargo ramp, with Mal leaning down into his face, holding the same wad of bills. He starts to give the same speech. "Here's Niska's money—" This is the smart goon. He says, "Yes! Yes! I got the message! I'll tell Niska!"

What was the point of these two scenes?

Simple. Malcolm Reynolds is *not* James T. Kirk. He is not Jean-Luc Picard. He is not another Starfleet wussy. Malcolm Reynolds is a whole other class of human being.

Brutal? Well, yes—but it's not enough to *say* that a character is brutal; you have to demonstrate it. What you demonstrate tells the audience everything.

It's about subtext.

What's subtext? Subtext is all the stuff you *don't* say. It's the stuff you *show*. Subtext is demonstration. The two scenes described above demonstrate more about Malcolm Reynolds' character than any number of revealing monologues, confessions, flashbacks and commentaries from others. This is not a man to cross.

In subsequent episodes, we started to see the same kind of defining moments for the other characters. In "Out Of Gas" we learned that Kaylee's relationship with starship engines borders on the carnal—she was having sex with the ship's engineer in the engine room and, when caught in the act, patiently explained how to fix a recalcitrant widget. In that same episode, Jayne Cobb's recruitment showed exactly where his values lie—a warm bed, higher wages and a modicum of respect will buy his loyalty. We also learned a little bit about Wash and Zoe's backstory as well: he was a goofy flyboy in a Hawaiian shirt; something about him just didn't sit right with her. It's an interesting beginning to the most devoted relationship onboard. And—just as important—we also got another small piece of Mal's relationship with *Serenity*. He didn't buy the big yellow spacecraft; he bought the Firefly instead. Love at first sight? Or something else.

But the process of demonstration isn't limited solely to the physical characters. Demonstration is also a key part of world-building.

A couple of examples from *Star Wars* should suffice. Early in the first picture (*Episode IV: A New Hope*) we see R2-D2 and C-3PO walking across the desert. In the background, sprawled across the sand are the huge bones of some massive creature—possibly a sandworm? It doesn't matter. Neither of the characters comments on it or even acknowledges its existence. In fact, it's irrelevant to the scene. The picture would work just as well without it—but by its presence, it sends a very clear message to the audience: no, we are *not* on Earth. It also says that this planet has life on it—not just the creature who conveniently left its bones on the sand dune, but all the creatures it feeds upon as well. (It isn't until *Episode VI* that we actually see one of these things in action—well, the front end anyway; it's that big mouth in the sand.)

Another example takes place aboard the Death Star. Han and Luke, dressed as Imperial stormtroopers with Chewbacca in handcuffs, are heading down to rescue Princess Leia. When they disembark from the elevators, we see a silver protocol droid walking past. Unlike C-3PO, however, this droid has a non-humanoid head. It looks insectoid. What does the existence of this droid this tell us? Simply this: if C-3PO is humanoid so that he can perform protocol tasks for human beings, then this unidentified droid is insectoid so that he can provide protocol services for an unseen insectoid race. Greedo's species, perhaps? Or something else? We don't know. It's never explained. But the existence of the specialized droid tells us that it has a function somewhere. It's not just scenery; it's world-building. It's a detail in the background that tells us something about the world our heroes operate in.

Coming back to *Firefly* now, we can see some of the same attention to detail, some of the same thoughtfulness in world-building.

First, however, we have to acknowledge that the budget for one episode of a television series is nowhere near the same scale as a feature film's can be. The average feature film will spend anywhere from fifteen million to a hundred million dollars for one hour of finished product. The average television series will spend somewhere between one and two million dollars for forty-four minutes of story; there just isn't the same level of available resources. Television producers have to recognize their limitations and work within them, substituting ingenuity for money and spectacle. *Firefly* demonstrates that effective storytelling is not a function of budget size.

On the one hand, we can look at the details shown in any given episode and say, "Oh, look, they've raided the costume shop, they've gone to the prop warehouse, they're using the back lot"—but that's a simplistic dismissal. The details in the background of these episodes are not accidental. They are selected—they are *chosen* from available resources—to create the *feeling* of another culture.

We are told, in dialogue, across several episodes, that the Alliance is terraforming frontier worlds and dropping colonists with the barest means of subsistence. This means that most of the settlements we see on outlying worlds will be ramshackle frontier towns, crude and shabby. Not all, of course (this is, after all, a future society with advanced technology), but the creation of a new settlement is still going to be an expensive effort. It's not impossible for an unfeeling authority to skimp—it doesn't make a lot of sense, unless the prevailing culture places a higher priority on money and resources than it does on human life, but it's not impossible.

But let's dig a little deeper. The Alliance is terraforming useful worlds—it's not always clear if these worlds are planets or moons, and it's certainly not clear how the terraforming is being accomplished—but however the process is performed, it is probably not a process that takes a few thousand years, or even a few hundred. In this universe, terraforming seems to take a much shorter time. Twenty years? Fifty? It's not clear. Never mind. The end result is that almost all terraformed worlds look like the FOX back lot in the Malibu hills. (Where they shot *M*A*S*H*.)

In truth, terraforming of any kind is likely to be a violent process—violent to the planet. And the result will not be an Earthlike world. It might be livable, but it won't be Earthlike. Why? *Because there are no Earthlike planets. There are only lazy writers.*

Allow me to elucidate.

Earth is an extraordinary world—to call our homeworld "unique" is insufficient. Life exists on this planet only as the result of a cosmic lottery of impossible events. To even be capable of holding life, a star must first form in a zone of livability. Too close to the center of the galaxy and the radiation will be too intense for life as we know it. Halfway out the spiral arm is about right. And the star has to be the right size—too small and it burns out too soon; too big and planetary formation is affected.

The star has to be at the right place in the stellar sequence and give off a useful spectrum of light; then it has to have planets within its own zone of livability. For a planet to be life-bearing, it has to have certain necessary conditions—it has to be the right size; it can't be a gas giant and it can't be a monster, or the radiation will be too intense. If a planet is to have life as we know it, then it has to have an abundance of carbon, hydrogen, oxygen and nitrogen. It has to have temperate zones so that there is available water.

And…it has to have a moon.

Why? Because a moon exerts its own gravitational effect on a world. A moon steadies a planet's rotation. Without a moon, a planet wobbles on its axis—the planet can end up with one pole pointed directly at the sun. Such an inclination makes life impossible. So a moon is essential.

Astronomers now believe that Earth's moon was formed when a Mars-sized object collided with Earth—collided at just the *right* angle to tear out a large chunk of material and put it into just the *right* orbit. This cosmic impact removed the lighter crust of the planet, leaving the heavier metals more available. The iron core of our world creates a magnetic field, which protects us from cosmic radiation.

Still with me? Earth's steady rotation, its stable orbit, the planet's distance from the sun, the availability of water and oxygen, the widespread temperate zones, the results of all the foregoing all make life nearly inevitable—but the conditions to create this particular zone of livability were not. We are the winners of a galactic lottery, a lottery so impossible that it's unlikely that we will encounter any other winners. (Unlikely, not impossible.) The only rational explanation is that the universe is so large that somewhere, sometime, some planet has to win that particular lotto. Possibly even more than one planet.

So it's not impossible that the Alliance would find suitable worlds to terraform. What is unlikely is that they would be Earthlike—even after terraforming. They would be nearer to the parent star or farther out, which would affect the amount of light available. The star would not have the same visible spectrum as Sol, which means that colors would appear different and some plants might not grow as well. They would have different inclinations, either more or less severe. The composition of the atmosphere would be different, with either more or less oxygen. Likely there would be an increased presence of other elements, like sulfur or methane. Most noticeably, the gravity would not be 100 percent Earth-normal. It would be greater or lesser.

Difference in gravity is so profound that at this point in human history, most of us have no awareness just how important it is. Plants grow differently under different gravity. Animals grow differently. Bone structure is affected. Muscle strength is affected. Walking is affected because center of gravity is different. On lighter worlds, lighter materials would be needed to build structures. On heavier worlds, construction would have to be sturdier. There is no one-size-fits-all for colonies. Even a slight increase in gravity creates an enormous fuel penalty for launching ships into orbit.

But somehow, the Alliance has developed a method for terraforming that produces Earthlike worlds.

We can accept this blindly, or we can operate from a different assumption—that *Serenity* doesn't go to planets outside of its own zone of operability.

To be fair, this is a "refrigerator door" question. What's a refrigerator door question? That's where you go to the movies, you have a great time, you go out for pie and coffee afterward and sit and chat; it's a wonderful evening. Eventually you end up at home, you kick off your shoes, you empty your bladder, you turn on the news, you decide to see if there's any ice cream left, and while you're standing there in front of the refrigerator, one hand still on the handle, you suddenly realize, "Hey! Wait a minute! If E.T. could fly at the end of the picture to get away from the guys chasing him, then why didn't he fly at the beginning of the picture?" And you stand there, frozen in thought while the popsicles get soft.

Eventually, you decide one of two things: either you got conned by the filmmaker, or the reason E.T. didn't fly away at the beginning of the picture is because he didn't have a bicycle.

With *Firefly*, we have the same choice—to question or to accept the filmmaker's vision. On the one hand, we can argue that the producers simply chose not to address this aspect of the universe they've built, that the stories they have to tell are more important than answering the questions that only the astronomers will be asking—and this would be a fair justification. Television is not about science lessons. (Unless you're watching *NOVA* on PBS.)

On the other hand, we can argue that the Alliance has limited its operations to its own "zone of livability"—only to those worlds where it has duplicated Earthlike conditions. We can accept this as a possibility (unlikely, but still a possibility) with sufficiently advanced technology. We can accept it and move on.

But there's also a third way to look at this, consistent with both horns of the above dilemma: television is a "contrived" reality. The trick is not to let the contrivance show.

The average movie or television show doesn't attempt to recreate reality—it simulates it. It moves you rapidly through a series of incidents and locations to give you a sense of events. In that regard, a movie or a television show is just a different kind of amusement park ride, only instead of sitting in a boat and riding past dancing dioramas of pirates or bears or horrible little dolls singing a perniciously infectious song, you sit on your couch and watch brightly colored images of dancing pirates, animated bears and horrible little children. Just as a ride gives you a vicarious adventure, so does a television show; the primary difference is that you don't have to wait in line for forty-five minutes.

Just as rides have their own vocabulary of storytelling, so does television, and that vocabulary has a specific rhythm. Every fourteen minutes (at least), the story is interrupted so someone can remind the audience they smell bad. During the fourteen minutes of story, the job is to keep the audience tuned in so that they stick around for the reminder that they smell bad.

So television is mostly about those things that will keep the guy in the chair from reaching for the remote; they're about flashy cars and big guns, guys punching other guys, sexually available women with big breasts, fast car chases with lots of screeching tires, suitcases full of money, blood and gore and eviscerated bodies, ticking clocks, lots of computer screens and things blowing up—lots of things blowing up. The bigger the better. Hurricanes, tornadoes, volcanoes and earthquakes are good too. Not to mention an occasional nuclear weapon, asteroid or alien spaceship.

American television almost never tackles the existential questions: *Who are we? Why are we here? Where are we going? What are we creating? What does it mean to be a human being?* When you start asking those kinds of questions, audiences stop worrying about whether or not they smell bad. So television isn't going to acknowledge that those questions exist—or if it does, it will tiptoe around the edges and pretend that the questions are easy enough to resolve in forty-four minutes, just in time for the inevitable hygiene reminder.

Nevertheless, it is possible to rise above the limitations of the vocabulary, and more than a few shows have done so; it is not coincidental that many of them have been science fiction (*The Twilight Zone, Star Trek: The Original Series, Babylon 5*). The underlying core of science fiction is the existential question: *what does it mean to be a human being?* Only science fiction approaches this question not from the inside, but from the outside—way outside.

Firefly is a unique show. It's not quite science fiction, but it uses the science fiction vocabulary. In truth, it's the Old West transposed to the future, to interstellar space—thus providing the storytellers with the opportunity to tell stories that span both mythic realms.

The characters are soldiers of fortune, mercenaries, merchants and occasionally thieves. They approach their situation with skepticism, cynicism and street-level integrity. They are honest on the local level— they treat people with respect—but they have no problems ripping off authority because institutions are faceless and impersonal, often cruel and thoughtless.

But nobody has to tell us this. We see it demonstrated repeatedly, in every episode.

We also see the bits and pieces, the edges, the details, of the societies they move through. Some of these societies are wealthy, some are barely eking out a living; some are superstitious, some are resigned to the dispassionate brutality of fate. In "Shindig" we visit a society that has an antebellum flavor—it's a Jack Vance novel directed by John Ford. Here we learn that sweet fresh fruit is a delicacy.

In any story, food is the most profound way to connect an audience to a character. (Human beings pay very close attention to the two primal urges: food and sex—with food generally outranking sex because there are more ways to do food than there are to do sex.) (You've got your eyebrow raised? Consider this: you can go without sex a lot longer than you can go without food. I rest my case.)

In the pilot episode, "Serenity," Mal and crew had a valuable cargo to sell to Patience, the woman who ran a nearby colony. It turned out that those copper-colored bars in the sealed cases were actually slabs of high-quality protein. One Hershey-sized bar was enough to feed a family of four for a month—or longer if you didn't like your kids.

In the same episode we saw the crew sitting around the table in the galley—several were using forks, but Mal and Zoe were using chopsticks. This wasn't accidental. It was one of those sly, subtle details that tells you something about these people and where they came from. We might not have known what it meant yet, but it was one more little way of distinguishing the characters. Simon and River were using forks. Perhaps this was the director's way of suggesting that people of wealth could afford real silverware but the common people, the poor people, could not. Mal and Zoe were identified with the rugged settlers of the frontier, not the privileged class.

The subtextual message of food is a common theme in film and television shows—because it is food that most demonstrates the quality of life of the characters. Food is not just something for the characters to play with while they talk about the plot; it's one more way for the filmmakers to tell you something else about the universe these folks live in. Kaylee's love of strawberries demonstrates that fresh fruits and vegetables are hard to come by aboard a spaceship. Nor can you expect to find healthy produce when you visit a subsistence-level colony barely eking out its own survival in the muck and mud. This is why processed food-bars are so valuable on the frontier—they guarantee survival. And this is also why the characters aboard *Serenity* respond so enthusiastically to good cooking: a luxurious meal says that you've risen above bare survival, that you are operating at a level of success.

The series engages in other world-building tricks, some subtle and some not-so. Clothing, for instance, is used to suggest a cultural tossed salad. In the crowded streets, we see a variety of costumes: everything from an Arab burnoose to a modern business suit. In one bar, a waitress was dressed in a traditional Japanese kimono. Inara often wears clothing that resembles an Indian sari. In "Shindig" we saw nineteenth-century military uniforms and crinoline dresses. But Malcolm Reynolds always wears boots and a vest—it's all-purpose garb, suggesting that he's a cowboy.

But we don't see space suits and we don't see perfectly tailored Day-Glo uniforms. Not on the streets. We only see space suits when someone has to go EVA. And we only see uniforms aboard the Alliance starships, nowhere else.

What this says is that a multitude of different cultures have colonized the frontier, each one bringing its own special flavors: food, clothes, religious beliefs. There are also occasional throwaway references to "Earth-that-was" suggesting that the Earth that *is* might not be such a great place anymore.

None of these questions is specifically answered. The possibilities are simply suggested; the viewer's imagination has to fill in the blanks. This is great storytelling. It drags you into the world and gives you the opportunity to look into the nooks and crannies, peek around the corners, lift up the carpet and see what dirt has been swept underneath. The details in the scenery add layers of depth to the story; they give you things to think about.

Occasionally, however, there are details that aren't consistent—aspects that don't quite stand up to rigorous questioning. Here are some of my unanswered questions about the *Firefly* universe:

If this is a future with faster-than-light travel, then why does *Serenity* have old-fashioned jet turbine engines? Well, they *look* like jet turbines, they sound like jet turbines and they suck in air and bad guys like jet turbines—except they don't blow up like jet turbines, so maybe they're not really jet turbines, they just look like it. But if they're not jet turbines, then why do they look and act like jet turbines? (Probably because E.T. didn't have a bicycle, okay?) Just what are they? Let's call them spindizzies and move on to the next.

Consider this one: if this is a future that has advanced weaponry—like the force-blasters of the Alliance and the sonic nosebleeders of the Men With Blue Hands—then why is everyone else using old-fashioned rifles and six-shooters? It seems to me to be a very bad idea to risk shooting a projectile weapon inside a pressurized hull—yet, almost every episode, somebody is pulling a gun on somebody, with that familiar gun-cocking sound that says, "I mean business."

Here, on Earth, today, there has already been significant research in weapons that accelerate thousands of tiny magnetized grains to shred a target; railguns can fire projectiles faster than bullets; even particle-beam weapons have been demonstrated in the lab. Why not guns that shoot needles? Or phased lasers? (No, wait—that's been done.) Or guns that shoot bolts of electricity or even sonic blasts? There are safer weapons to use aboard a starship and better weapons to use on a planetary surface. Is the use of contemporary weaponry in this series a lapse of vision—or is it a deliberate choice to make a point? Perhaps old-fashioned projectile weapons are the easiest and cheapest to manufacture. (And gunpowder can be produced with charcoal and urine.) So, maybe....

Maybe we're making an assumption that these are bullet-firing weapons. Maybe they're not. And maybe, like the jet turbine engines, however they work, the look-and-feel of this technology is also a deliberate choice, specifically made to evoke the Old-West flavor of the series. The more recognizable technology we see, the more we identify with the circumstances of the worlds portrayed...?

We could argue that this is a science-fantasy adventure series—that it's not about scientific or technological accuracy, it's about storytelling—and yes, that would be correct too. But even a fantasy has to have its own internal logic, and it has to stay consistent with that logic. The viewer will suspend disbelief; he will not suspend common sense. Anytime a producer makes a hasty decision, dances too close to the edge, there's a risk that some of the viewers will hesitate, will stop and scratch their heads, and say, "Huh? What'd they do that for?" You can get away with that once, even twice, but you can't make a habit of it.

Fortunately, *Firefly* works hard to create a consistent context for its stories, and if you accept the occasional anachronistic flavor of the show, you can have a lot of fun with it. The real attraction here, as in any successful series, lies in discovering the inner natures of the characters and watching them work out their relationships.

We pretty much know the backstory for Mal and Zoe, and Simon and River. Mal and Zoe are former soldiers who fought against the Alliance. Simon has rescued River from an experimental Alliance research facility and the two of them are running from the law. Those are the key plot points for the overriding story arc; those are the engines that drive the series.

We also have a few small bits and pieces of backstory for Jayne, Kaylee, Book and Inara. We know that Inara secretly loves Mal—well, that's about as big a secret as the hole in a doughnut; never mind. We know that Kaylee has a crush on Simon. And we know that Jayne's integrity is negotiable; his loyalty to Mal and the others is questionable.

The character we know the least about is Book, the shepherd.

Every other character aboard *Serenity* has a specific job aboard the ship. Wash is the pilot/navigator; he delivers the crew to each adventure. Jayne and Zoe are the enforcers, the necessary muscle for dangerous jobs. Kaylee is the engineer; she keeps the ship running. Inara is the "ambassador"—okay, she's a Companion, a courtesan, a high-priced prostitute; she opens doors for Malcolm Reynolds. Simon is the doctor; he sews the crew up after every misadventure—and River is aboard because she is Simon's sister. River is also a telepathic, precognitive witch, but so far that skill hasn't really been applied to any specific problem solving.

So what does Book do?

Book is a shepherd, a preacher, a priest, a shaman, a monk—he's a man of God. Hello? What's wrong with this picture? Why is he aboard *Serenity*? What job is he performing? Is he the cook? The librarian? The upstairs maid?

What's wrong with this picture is that Mal doesn't believe in God. At least, he says he doesn't. In fact, he's noticeably rude to anyone who brings the subject up. So why does he allow Book to remain onboard, using up food and oxygen, requiring the expenditure of additional fuel and life support resources? Book doesn't have any money to pay for his passage, or not much—that's established in the pilot episode—so how is he paying his way?

Here's a hint: look at the teaser to "Serenity." Look carefully. Mal and Zoe were fighting for the Independents, desperately trying to hold their position in the face of a massive enemy assault. Just before going into action, Mal pulled out a cross and kissed it. We never see him do that again. Shortly after that moment, the Independents surrendered the position...and apparently, soon after that, they lost the war. What was not shown, what remained unstated, was that somewhere along the way, Malcolm Reynolds also lost his faith.

That's why Book is aboard. Ostensibly, he's a chaplain; ostensibly, he's a voice of reason and compassion. But that's only the surface appearance. It's my suspicion that he's actually aboard the starship to challenge Mal's cynicism, resignation and unexpressed internal despair. I suspect that even Mal doesn't yet realize why he has accepted Book as part of his crew; Book's faith is a challenge.

For the sake of discussion, let's assume an alternate reality where *Firefly* doesn't get cancelled and stays on the air for several years, giving us new episodes, new adventures and new discoveries about the characters. Mal's confrontation with his own loss of faith would be inevitable; it's hardwired into the series' structure, and Book the shepherd would be the agent of that confrontation—because deep down inside, Malcolm Reynolds wants to be challenged. He *wants* to be dragged—kicking and screaming, if necessary—back into his own idealism, his commitment to a future that works for everyone, with no one and nothing left out.

How do we know this? Well, first, because despite Mal's insistence that he is not a nice man, his behavior continually indicates otherwise. His brusque lack of manners is a deliberate way of concealing how much he actually cares about the people around him. He is willing to risk his life and his ship to save a member of his family.

There's another reason too, a much more cynical reason: this is part of the basic television formula. Gruff heroes always have tender hearts; the gruffness is how they hide it. It's the John Wayne formula. Big boys don't cry. They can feel, but they can't show it—except by being rude. (That's a strange transaction, isn't it?) But that's how you know they care, because they're rude. (So, I guess that means everyone who's rude in the world really cares, right? What's wrong with *this* picture? Never mind. It's television, Jake. It's television.)

In truth, we know very little about Malcolm Reynolds and how he got this way. We can make some guesses, but the producers haven't given us many details. There's some sense that he came from a poor family, that he was once imbued with faith and idealism and that the military was a great career for him. The show has given us indicators that he is now a soldier of fortune, a mercenary, an opportunist and, once in a while, even a dreamer.

Something happened in the war—we don't know what it was—but it wasn't just that the Independents lost the war. It wasn't just their betrayal at the battle portrayed in "Serenity"'s teaser. It was something else. Something more. At some point, something happened, where Mal discovered that the leaders of the Independent movement were no longer worthy of his trust and commitment.

In all likelihood, we will never find out what that event was. If the series were to return, and if it were to run for several years, that would be a fruitful line of inquiry for future episodes to explore. Malcolm Reynolds is a vividly drawn character—he is decisive, he is ruthless when he has to be, he has integrity, he is a giver and he even has a sly, dry sense of humor. All of this together makes him admirable and even likable. There is no question that he will inspire loyalty among those who serve with him. (Even Jayne Cobb must eventually come to a recognition that he will be better off serving Malcolm Reynolds than betraying him.)

Ultimately, this is the reason for in-depth world-building: to provide a grand stage on which the characters will perform. The more believable the world, the more believable the characters—the bigger the problems, the more heroic the opportunities. The greater the opportunities, the more interesting and exciting the characters have to become. When they bite off big problems, they have to grow the jaws to chew them. That's the success of this series. These characters live hard, play hard and bring it all to life.

David Gerrold is the author of numerous television episodes including the legendary "Trouble With Tribbles" episode of Star Trek. *He has also written for* Land of the Lost, Babylon 5, The Twilight Zone, Sliders *and other series. He has published forty-three books, including two on television production. He taught screenwriting at Pepperdine University for two decades. He has won the Hugo, the Nebula and the Locus awards. A movie based on his autobiographical novel,* The Martian Child, *is now in production.*

I was always curious about how our little Mandarin surprises would be received. A phenomenon that I myself noted with alarm on the set was that on the first take, the actor would perform a pretty accurate recreation of what he had just heard on his translation tape. But by take seven or eight, the tones and phonemes had usually migrated a bit. And the writer on set is not generally going to want to request a ninth or tenth take to try to fix the problem. I had some concern that we were going to be broadcasting gibberish so gibbery as to be insulting. And perhaps, sometimes, we did. But Sullivan has plumbed the source material and does a lovely analysis of what we intended to say.

Chinese Words
in the 'Verse

KEVIN M. SULLIVAN

JOE WHEDON (STAY WITH ME HERE) graduated from college in 1987, moved to Los Angeles and "changed his name from Joe to Joss, the Chinese word for 'luck.'"[1] A dozen years later, a 1999 episode of his television series *Buffy the Vampire Slayer* ("Wild at Heart," 4–6) had Oz the werewolf in a T-shirt with the Chinese characters for *dabian* (tragic incident).[2] Then he cheated on his girlfriend. A 2000 episode ("Fool for Love," 5–7) had a flashback to a Chinese vampire slayer, who spoke a line of Chinese. Do you see a pattern emerging here? No? Well, I'll make one up then. The seeds were already in place for his 2002 series *Firefly*. Whedon went from a Chinese person speaking Chinese in China to a future melting pot where, in his own words, "everyone speaks Chinese; there's Chinese writing everywhere. And it's just sort of been incorporated into American culture."[3]

---

[1] Havens, 2003, p. 17.

[2] I concede that the characters could also be representing Japanese *taihen* ("serious," "terrible").

[3] Quoted in Havens, 2003, p. 135.

Whedon has given two reasons for including Chinese in *Firefly*. First, he wanted to show what would happen if America and China joined into a hyperpower. His "Anglo-Sino Alliance is in fact sort of America and China as two major planets in the Core. The Central Planets are Sihnon, which is basically China, and Londinium, which is basically America."[4] Second, he wanted to have a world where "the person with no education, who, you know, was the last person you'd expect, speaks Chinese off the bat. And it just gives it a lovely kind of lived-in texture."[5]

So what is this world, or 'verse, like? We heard a multilingual jumble of chatter and chanting at the Eavesdown Docks on Persephone ("Serenity, Part 1"), but the only non-English, non-Chinese line in the series was from Niska ("War Stories"), and it was barely audible. Our psychotic ear-refunder, according the shooting script, told his torturer in Czech: "They have enough for a slice."

But otherwise we heard people speaking English with a little Chinese thrown in, often exclamations to themselves (*wo de ma he ta de fengkuang de waisheng dou*,[6] "holy mother of god [sic] and all her wacky Nephews [sic]," "Our Mrs. Reynolds"), a set phrase or tag question (*xiexie*, "thank you," "Shindig"; *dong ma?*, "understand?," "The Train Job" and elsewhere) or words thrown into an English sentence (*yuben de*, "stupid," to describe the "Shindig" duel). The only Chinese conversation was a single exchange in "Our Mrs. Reynolds" when Kaylee said, "You don't deserve her, you fink" (*Ni bu gouge, ni hunqiu*), and Mal responded with "Mind your own business" (*Guan ni ziji de shi*).

We never got the opportunity to see a Chinese-dominated planet during the series, but they must have existed. After all, Inara's Sihnon is Whedon's main Chinese planet. We did see one Chinese-looking person speaking Chinese: the shadow-puppet theater narrator in "Heart of Gold" (played by Jim Lau; Lau is a Chinese family name). In the same episode we also heard a native-English-speaking Asian, Emma the prostitute (played by Doan Ly, a Vietnamese name). Perhaps if *Firefly* had lasted longer we would have seen more Asians in the foreground speaking English and Chinese.

A non-Chinese person speaking Chinese was such a fact of life that no one in *Firefly* remarked on it. The only time any character acknowl-

---

[4] Whedon, 2002. The American planet is spelled "Londinum" in the "Serenity, Part 1" script, but there, as with Whedon here, the word sounded like "Londinium."

[5] "Here's How It Was: The Making of *Firefly*," 2003.

[6] See the back of the book for a glossary of the Chinese, with Chinese tones indicated.

edged speaking Chinese was in "Trash" when Inara called Mal a "petty thief," then tried to backpedal by saying that she actually meant "*suoxi*" ("petty," in the sense of "trivial"). Mal replied, "That's Chinese for 'petty.'" Even less-cultured folks like Mal aren't duped by Chinese usage (or by feminine wiles).

Speaking of culture and registered Companions, there was at least one cultural difference in the way different characters used Chinese. Wash used *laotian, bu* ("oh, god [sic], no," "Safe"), Jayne used *Yesu, tama de* ("Hay-soose [Spanish *Jesús*]-mother-of-jumped-up—," "Jaynestown"), and even Mal used *wo de tian, a* ("dear god [sic] in heaven," "Bushwhacked"), despite being angry at God about losing the war. However, Inara used *renci de Fozu* ("merciful buddha [sic]," "Our Mrs. Reynolds") and former Companion Nandi used *zhen mei naixing de Fozu* ("extraordinarily impatient Buddha," "Heart of Gold"). Companions seemed to have more Asian culture in their Asian language.

While we never heard anything as extraordinary as Nandi's "extraordinarily impatient Buddha" in English, Chinese didn't completely substitute for ordinary English expressions. Jayne used *dong ma?* ("understand?") with Simon in "The Train Job" and *understand?* with Simon, Mal, Kaylee and Wash in "Jaynestown." Mal used *bizui* ("shut up") twice in "Serenity, Part 1" and *Nimen dou bizui!* ("Everybody shut the hell up!") once in "Serenity, Part 2," but he also said "Shut up!" in "War Stories." Inara summoned one knocker into her shuttle with *Qingjin* ("Come in," [actually, "Please come in"]) in "Serenity, Part 1" and another with "Come in," in "Our Mrs. Reynolds." Simon never called River "Sister" or "Sis," but he frequently called her "River" instead of *meimei* ("little sister," used by Simon only three times: "Safe," "Ariel," "War Stories"). Not even swearing had to be in Chinese. When Wash was angry with Mal about Zoe in "Out of Gas," he used *qu ni de* ("screw you"). When he was angry with Mal about Zoe in "War Stories," he said, "Screw you!"

I've read speculation online that the Chinese in *Firefly* was mostly swearing and that a primary reason for using Chinese was to get past the network television censors. But even being generous with what qualifies as swearing, I'd put the Chinese swearing at only about 45 percent of the Chinese expressions (forty-four out of ninety-seven expressions). If you include repeats of expressions, the proportion of swearing drops to 43 percent (fifty-four out of 126). I'm all manner of generous, so rather tame utterances like *laotian, bu* ("oh, god, no"), *renci de Fozu* ("merciful buddha [sic]") and *wenguo pi* ("smelled a fart") are counted in that 45

percent. I even threw in *Nimen dou bizui!* (literally, "All of you shut up!")
because the writer's original English was "Everybody shut the hell up!"

The show also didn't need Chinese to get past the censors. English
cussing made it to the airwaves, too. The above "Screw you!" and "bastard" (not *hundan*) from Wash in "War Stories" got on the air during
American television's family hour. So did Mal's, River's and Simon's utterances of "son of a bitch" ("The Train Job," "Safe" and "Jaynestown,"
respectively). There were also all those uses of *gorram/gorramn*, apparently substituting for *Goddamn*. Moreover, *rutting/ruttin'* (as in a male
deer that's looking to mate) and the more obvious *humped* were used for
the F-word.

Some of the Chinese swearing and non-swearing was less than authentic because they were translations of non-Chinese-speaking writers' playful English. For comparison, here are some of the authentic
words and phrases: *bizui* ("shut up"), the casual tag question *dong ma?*
("understand?"), *feiwu* ("junk"), *goushi* ([piece of] "crap"), *wo de ma*
("mother of god [sic]," but more "my God"), *xiexie* ("thank you") and
Zhen daomei! ("Just our luck!" or just "What bad luck!").

On the not-so-much side of authenticity were expressions like *Bizui, nin hen butitie de nansheng!* ("Shut up, you inconsiderate schoolboys!"—at least when hurled at Jayne and Wash in "Objects in Space"),
daxiang baozhashi de laduzi ("the explosive diarrhea of an elephant"),
fangzong fengkuang de jie ("a knot of self-indulgent lunacy"), *gen
houzi bi diushi* ("engage in a feces-hurling contest with a monkey"),
taikong suoyou de xingqiu saijin wo de pigu ("all the planets in space
flushed into my butt"), all but the first three words of *wo de ma he ta
de fengkuang de waisheng dou* ("holy mother of god and all her wacky
Nephews") and *zhen mei naixing de Fozu* ("extraordinarily impatient
Buddha").

Whether authentic or not, the Chinese in *Firefly* was mostly Mandarin, the variety[7] of Chinese that's native to northern and southwestern
China and is the basis for the national standard language. Joss Whedon
said that he had wanted to use Cantonese (the less official-sounding variety used in parts of southeastern China, including Hong Kong, and in
many overseas communities), but he was stuck with Mandarin because
he "didn't check the translations to find out they're Mandarin" until sev-

---

[7] There is a linguistic-political debate about whether Chinese is one language with mutually unin-
telligible dialects or is a language family like the Romance languages (Spanish, French, etc.), but
that distinction isn't important for our purposes.

eral months into taping.[8] The Chinese translator for the pilot used Mandarin, and the series translator, Jenny Lynn, just continued its use.[9]

But a little Cantonese got in anyway. Mal ordered Cantonese *Ng-Ka-Pei* (*nggaapei*, a medicinal-herb wine) in "The Train Job," not the Mandarin form *wujiapi*. In addition, *Serenity*'s alerts in "Out of Gas" were in both Cantonese (*Gausaang haitung guzoeng. Gimcaa jeonghei gungjing.*) and English ("Life support failure. Check oxygen levels at once."). Unfortunately for all the fans who speculated, the use of Cantonese for those alerts had no significance. The Chinese line was supposed to be Mandarin, but the voice actress who did the postproduction voice-over used Cantonese instead. The Chinese translator pointed out the problem, joined the Screen Actors Guild and did future voice-overs herself.[10] Unfortunately, unlike the Cantonese line, these were very faint (and not in the scripts).

While the Chinese was almost all Mandarin, not all pronunciations were standard (Beijing form). The American-Taiwanese translator would try to check the standard pronunciations in the one business day per episode she usually had for translating. But at times she'd "opt to stick with the Taiwanese pronunciation because it was easier for the non-Chinese speaker to say."[11] For example, the translator used *sagua* for *shagua* ("idiots," "Trash") for that reason; it was also "a shout out to Amy Tan and her cartoon Chinese-Siamese cat [*Sagwa the Chinese Siamese Cat*, on American public television]."[12] In addition, *shi* became the Taiwan form *si* in *goushi* ([piece of] "crap," "Shindig" and "Ariel") and in other words because, the translator said, "it sounds a little less 'refined' than the Beijing way to say it. And since we are talking 'crap,' I decided to keep it less refined."[13]

"Sh" might not seem difficult for English speakers to say, but it's not the same sound as the English "sh." For this "sh," in Standard (Beijing) Mandarin, you have to pull the tip of your tongue back slightly as you say it, as with the American "r." The "sh" sound of *xiexie* ("thank you," "Shindig") is different. For this one, you need to put your tongue tip near your upper gum ridge and touch the roof of your mouth with the top of your tongue (just behind the tip) as you say it. English "sh" is

---

[8] Whedon, 2002.

[9] Lynn, 2004a.

[10] Ibid.

[11] Ibid.

[12] Ibid.

[13] Ibid.

in between the two Mandarin "sh" sounds[14] and what the crew usually used for both. There are other tricky sounds as well.

Given the difficulty of many Mandarin sounds for foreign speakers, it's not surprising that the crew didn't sound like Mandarin native speakers. This was even more noticeable with Chinese tones. First, what are tones? Tones are spoken pitch patterns, or intonation. English and other languages have pitch patterns as well, but they're used at the sentence level. For example, if you say, "Don't do that," *don't* has a level or slight falling pitch. If your listener clarifies with "Did you say 'don't'?" *don't* has a rising pitch for the yes-no question. But in Chinese, each syllable has a pitch pattern that distinguishes it from similar-sounding syllables. If English had such tones, it might go like this: Remember what Inara said in "The Train Job" about Mal barging into her shuttle? What if a falling *don't* meant "don't," but a rising *don't* really did mean it was "manly and impulsive" to enter uninvited? They'd be different words, and Mal might have had an excuse for barging in (not that he needed one).

To take an example from the show's Chinese, River is Simon's *meimei* ("little sister") with a high, falling tone on the first syllable and a neutral tone on the second. If it were two high, falling tones, Simon could be calling this genius "stupid" (written with different Chinese characters). That didn't happen, but neither Simon nor other users of *meimei* started out at a high pitch. Another frequently used expression was *dong ma?* It means "understand?" with a low-dipping tone on *dong* and a neutral tone on the question marker *ma*. But it could mean "[You] frostbitten?" with a high, falling tone on the *dong* (written with a different Chinese character). The crew and Womack the Fed probably could have used that after visiting Tracey's ice planet in "The Message." While Womack (who used *dong ma?* in that episode), along with Jayne and Mal (who used it in other episodes), didn't use the high, falling tone of "frostbitten," they also didn't dip low enough into their vocal ranges for "understand."

But we shouldn't be too hard on the cast. To help them learn these difficult Chinese lines, they were given only simplified phonetic spellings and audiotapes made by the translator. The translator wasn't able to be on set, so "aside from a non-Chinese-speaking script supervisor, there was no one to correct them on tones or pronunciation."[15]

Let's now turn to writing. As with speaking, there was a mixture of English and Chinese and not much else. However, Jayne's jacket patch at

---

[14] Norman, 1988, p. 140.

[15] Lynn, 2004a.

the beginning of "The Train Job" read *Polizei* ("police" in German), and a banner at the setup for Durran Haymer's party ("Trash") was in Japanese. The banner revealed that Haymer's Japanese flower arranging and artificial flowers (*ikebana to zouka*) came from the Taguchi-ya Ikebana Store.[16] Perhaps future episodes would have shown more languages.

The Chinese writing in the background provided a Chinese flavor even when everyone was speaking English, especially in the Persephone street scene in "Shindig." The crew discussed fluffy and slinky dresses in English with the words *youmei* ("elegant") and *jiangjiu de fuzhuang* ("stylish clothing") on the store windows in front of them and *youlanche* ("tour bus") on the bus behind them. Meanwhile, Jayne was wearing a T-shirt that said *yong* ("soldier," more commonly "brave"; also worn in "The Train Job," "Ariel" and "War Stories").

Jayne's "Shindig" shirt meaning was revealed by *Firefly* costume designer Shawna Trpcic, who tried "to stump everybody"[17] with Jayne's Chinese T-shirts. Let's get unstumped on his other shirts. As you might expect, the shirt with "Blue Sun" ("Bushwhacked," "Ariel") said "blue sun" in Chinese characters (*qingri*). The shirt with "28" ("Safe," "Out of Gas," "War Stories") said *zhandou de xiaojingling* ("the fighting/militant, elves"), and the shirt from "Heart of Gold" said *wanmei mao* ("perfect cat"). The shirt that this Hero of Canton wore in "Jaynestown" had a pistol image and said *wannao* ("troublemaker," or "rascal"). That contrast sums up the episode nicely. Lastly, the shirt he wore in "Trash" read *dairuomuji* ("dumb as a wooden chicken," or "paralyzed by fear"). The writing was most visible when he was paralyzed by drugs on Simon's operating table and fearful of what Simon was going to do to him for getting "stupid" and betraying the Tams. Coincidence?

Many fans noticed that the Chinese characters for "Blue Sun" changed from the *qingri* on Jayne's T-shirt (and on the background signs in "Serenity, Part 1" and River's cracker boxes in "Shindig"). On space station advertisements in "The Message" and in an image on the official series Web site, they were *lanri*. The Chinese translator for the series changed the art department's choice after she saw Jayne's T-shirt design and "ran it by a few people, who agreed with [her] that even though *qing1se4* is blue, you wouldn't use that particular word for 'blue' to modify the word 'sun.'"[18]

---

[16] Taguchi is a common Japanese family name; *-ya* is a Japanese suffix for store names.

[17] "Audio Commentary for 'Shindig' Episode," 2003.

[18] Lynn, 2004a. *Qing1se4* is the color blue or green (*se* is "color"). Numbers in the word denote tones (see the glossary at the back of the book for more on tones). *Lan* means "blue" or "indigo plant"; *ri* means "sun" or "day."

A more obvious error was that some Chinese characters were written backward. The *dian* of *wei dian* ("Danger Electricity") on the trash bin in "Trash" was backward even though it's the same *wei dian* frequently visible on the white duct outside *Serenity*'s cargo bay.[19] *Jing* ("police") on the sheriff's shoulder patches ("The Train Job") and *yisui* ("fragile") on Tracey's crate stickers ("The Message") were backward as well. *Yisui* was also written forward on postmaster Amnon's uniform in that episode, but "fragile" seemed out of place there.

As for anyone actively reading any of this Chinese, we only saw it in "Safe." Simon's father, in flashback, and an Asian shopkeeper both read Chinese newspapers. While in that same shop, Simon picked up a decorative plate and, according to the shooting script, "(reads the Chinese) 'Jiangyin,[20] Prairie Paradise.'" In addition, Inara could probably read the Chinese calligraphy she was writing ("Bushwhacked"), but she wrote only basic words: "*nian, yue, ri; chun, xia; nian*" ("year, month, day; spring, summer; year"). We can assume, though, that everyone was able to read at least simple Chinese because "danger" (*wei*) was written without any English on *Serenity*'s white duct, the hatch that led topside and at least one crate in the cargo bay during "Ariel." The sign in "Safe" ("Management Not Responsible for Ball Failure," *Ruguo taiqiu huaile, na me guanli jiu bu fuze de*) probably didn't need to be bilingual, except for the audience.

Many in that *Firefly* audience love the use of Chinese. Despite Joss Whedon's statement that the only words translated into Chinese were those used when "we didn't need to know what they meant,"[21] many fans wanted to know. After only a few episodes had aired, fans in online communities were begging for weekly translations, and Mandarin-speaking fans would try to provide them. Translation debates sometimes followed. The translator thinks this enthusiasm is "a testament to the kind of fans we had for the show, people who had an interest in digging deeper to learn something new."[22]

Fans have continued to use Chinese in *Firefly* message board posts,

---

[19] This *dian* is also one of the few traditional characters (unsimplified, as still used in Taiwan and Hong Kong but not Mainland China) seen in the show. *Wei* has only one form.

[20] Jiangyin is also a city in China's Jiangsu Province. The name means "river," or "Yangtze river," plus "[shady] south bank of a river." It is indeed located on the south bank of the Yangtze River, halfway between Shanghai and Nanjing ("Introduction," *Jiangyinshi Renmin Zhengfu Wang* [Jiangyin City People's Government Net]).

[21] "Here's How It Was: The Making of *Firefly*," 2003.

[22] Lynn, 2004a.

such as *dong ma?* ("understand?") and *xiexie* ("thank you"), and they used a passel of Chinese swear words when the show was cancelled. *Firefly* insiders have also used Chinese on the official series forums. Soon after the show was unofficially cancelled, Morena Baccarin ("Inara") posted a message to fans and closed with "Shei-shei"[23] (*xiexie*, Kaylee's "thank you" from "Shindig"). Kelly Wheeler (producer's assistant and blogger on the official series Web site), posting in a thread about signs of *Firefly* fanhood, included, "Oh, and do I think of my little sister as 'mei-mei'? Darn right."[24] When a fan reported she was moving to China to teach English, Adam Baldwin ("Jayne") replied, "Ding Hao! [very good] What an adventure!"[25] This last expression wasn't even used in *Firefly*.

Fans also use Chinese from *Firefly* and other Chinese expressions in fan art, fan fiction, song parodies (filk) and role-playing games. Fan meet-ups (shindigs) sometimes have decorations with Chinese writing. Fans even use Chinese in daily life with the uninitiated, including getting away with swearing at work or in front of children.

In short, the *Firefly* fandom of Browncoats mirrors the *Firefly*verse, a Chinese-influenced universe ultimately in existence thanks to Joss ("Luck") Whedon. As mentioned above, Browncoats like to dig deeper. If you dig deeper into the word *joss*, you'll find that the meaning "luck" comes from the base meaning "Chinese idol" (representing a deity). So whether you want to think how lucky you are to have *Firefly* and Joss' other creations or want to jump on the "Joss is a god" bandwagon, you're safe. *Dong ma?*

SOURCES

BOOKS

DeFrancis, John, ed. *ABC Chinese English Comprehensive Dictionary.* Honolulu: University of Hawaii Press, 2003.

Havens, Candace. *Joss Whedon: The Genius Behind Buffy.* Dallas: BenBella Books, 2003.

Norman, Jerry. *Chinese.* Cambridge: Cambridge University Press, 1988.

---

[23] Baccarin, 2002.

[24] Wheeler, 2003.

[25] Baldwin, 2003.

WEB SITES

Baccarin, Morena. "Never say Goodbye, from Morena" thread, Official *Firefly* series message boards, December 19, 2002, forums. prospero.com/foxfirefly/messages/?msg=3859.1.

Baldwin, Adam. "I'M GOING TO CHINA, BABY!" thread, Official *Firefly* series message boards, March 30, 2003, forums.prospero. com/foxfirefly/messages/?msg=7239.19.

Chineselanguage.org. "Chinese Character Dictionary," *Chinese languages,* chineselanguage.org/CCDICT/index.html.

Chinese University Press. *Lin Yutang's Chinese-English Dictionary of Modern Usage,* humanum.arts.cuhk.edu.hk/Lexis/Lindict.

Harbaugh, Rick. *Zhongwen.com: Chinese Characters and Culture,* zhongwen.com/.

"Introduction," *Jiangyinshi Renmin Zhengfu Wang* [Jiangyin City People's Government Net], www.jiangyin.gov.cn/jiangYinGov/chinese/introduce/introduce.aspx?categoryNum=01&title=introduction [in Mandarin].

TigerNT. *Chinese-English Online Dictionary,* www.tigernt.com/cedict. shtml [from the database of Erik Peterson].

Whedon, Joss. "Joss and Tim Interviews 11/13/02: Joss Whedon," *FOX Broadcasting Company: Firefly,* November 13, 2002, www.fox-tv.com/firefly/features.htm. [Also available at: "firefly is" (Media: Video: Joss Whedon video #01), *FOX Home Entertainment: Firefly,* www.foxhome.com/firefly/main.html.]

Wheeler, Kelly. "You know your [sic] a firefly fan when...." thread, Official *Firefly* series message boards, February 21, 2003, forums. prospero.com/foxfirefly/messages/?msg=6461.38.

OTHER

"Audio Commentary for 'Shindig' Episode," *Firefly: The Complete Series,* DVD (Twentieth Century Fox Home Entertainment, 2003).

"Here's How It Was: The Making of *Firefly,*" *Firefly: The Complete Series,* DVD (Twentieth Century Fox Home Entertainment, 2003).

Lynn, Jenny. E-mail interview with author, November 11, 2004 [2004a].

————. E-mail interview with author, November 15, 2004 [2004b].

Kevin M. Sullivan is a writer and a teacher (MA, English: Teaching English to Speakers of Other Languages). He's taught English in the United States and English, linguistics and humor studies in Japan. He's also presented and published English-teaching research, paraphrased and indexed idioms for a vocabulary textbook (Impact Words + Phrases, Longman Asia, 1997) and written humor pieces. English alone couldn't satisfy his language passion, so he's been seeing seven others on the side, including Mandarin. A few languages took out restraining orders, but they've worked things out.

I am rarely consciously aware of a musical score. I suppose this means that it works on me as it should, emotionally. Although I do find it a little troubling that I sometimes cannot hear a score even when it is pointed out to me....I can't tell one piece of the music from another, guess at what it's meant to convey or even suggest what instrument might be making the sound. But when I read a description like what follows here, I realize that there's an entire level of something very like storytelling that I am missing. Goltz makes me want to listen.

Listening to *Firefly*

JENNIFER GOLTZ

I WATCH *FIREFLY* FOR THE CHARACTERS, the dialogue and the world Joss Whedon has created. To tell the truth, I watch it all the time. I have made devotees of my sister, my brother and several students, and though it pains me to lend my copy out, I do it. When I first saw the show, I didn't pay particular attention to the musical score, even though my musical training might seem to bias me in that direction. I simply don't watch television or film for the music. Certainly the Indian vocal melody at the beginning of "Heart of Gold" caught my ear; I still love the combination of world musics in *Firefly* and the richness that comes from blending different cultural sounds. But as I continued to watch, what fascinated me most about the soundtrack was how it helped to tell the story.

In the special features on the DVD, the composer, Greg Edmonson, said that he wrote from the emotion of the moment, not from the character. I have my doubts about how true his statement is; from my vantage point, he seemed to write from both emotion and character. The more I watch, the clearer it becomes that Edmonson has developed a specialized collection of musical symbolism for the series, most of which was introduced during the first episode. Whether or not it was what he and Joss intended, this is what I hear and how I think about the music for *Firefly*, and it has opened up aspects of the story in ways nothing else has.

The main musical signature of the show—which I'll call *Serenity*—recalls the theme song. *Serenity* played nearly every time they returned to the ship, trudging into the cargo bay. We heard it whenever they were getting ready to engage in clandestine dealings, or when they were doing crime, and we heard it just as often when life was just going on normally. When they flew off after an adventure turned out all right, we heard slide guitar, a little strumming, sometimes a fiddle: it was the sound of their home, the sound of everything being right with the world. And the fiddle and guitar are portable instruments, perfect for the lifestyle of the crew; the music they make calls up tunes played out in the open, by people who were hundreds of miles away just yesterday. *Serenity* conjures the nomadic lifestyle the crew leads and underlines the western aspect of the show.

Serenity got punched up in the first episode in two different ways. When the "tourists" were in the cargo bay getting their things, as Mal and Zoe discussed the stolen cargo, the *Serenity* signature turned sort of goofy and bluesy. There was a bounce in the music, a twang that was echoed in the Fed's clumsiness. Joss mentioned this scene in the special features interview: reveling in this comparatively unimportant stage business is something a regular action show could never do. Later in the episode, *Serenity* turned majestic during the gallop to the ship. Yes, our heroes prevailed in the gunfight, as their signature guitar/fiddle music told us, but here it sounded like a classic western movie. If it weren't such a suspenseful moment, with the Reavers closing in, it would be pretty funny.

It's true that some of the signatures communicate emotion. We heard the first one of these at the end of the battle scene in Serenity Valley, as the ships left Mal and the rest of the soldiers behind. The ambient noise of the scene faded out and *Sad Violin* took over. The solo violin sounded lonely, playing a desolate melody in a minor key. The same signature returned later in the episode when Mal confronted Simon with the news that Kaylee was dead. Setting up the joke, *Sad Violin* played as we saw Simon running down to the infirmary in slow-motion fragments; the signature stopped abruptly when we saw Kaylee was alive. But the instance of *Sad Violin* that may be the most emblematic came at the very end of "The Message." This is the passage Edmonson discussed in his special features interview: he was concerned that it was too beautiful for a TV show. The heart-wrenching theme played as the crew mourned Tracey's death at his gravesite. As the last scene of the last episode the actors shot, it was especially powerful—a musical farewell to *Firefly*.

The other emotional signature is the sound of impending danger: I call it *Peril*. Since the crew is so frequently threatened, *Peril* comes up a lot. When the Alliance found them scavenging in the first episode, we heard it: a low pulse, like a heartbeat, with deep chimes and low strings. *Peril* is ominous in a nonspecific way, with hollow tones that, on some level, bring to mind how alone the crew is. The same music came up as Mal, Zoe and Jayne entered Badger's den, and in countless other scenes over the series. Even when the crew doesn't realize they're in danger, we know: when the Fed got free (after mercilessly thwacking Book in the head), he first went for the cortex, then a couple of guns; meanwhile, *Peril* underlined the scene. Watch any episode and you'll know *Peril* right away.

Unlike *Sad Violin*, *Peril* is heard in conjunction with other signatures which communicate characters, such as *Alliance*. Whenever we saw a hulking Alliance vessel, we heard French horns—cited in the interviews as reminiscent of *Star Trek*. The horns are shorthand for enormous, bureaucratic, antiseptic spaceships. *Alliance* was often layered with *Peril*: together, we were given the sense that the Alliance was threatening our heroes. Of course, the Alliance did not constitute the only danger. *Reavers* got their own music, a crash of industrial metal percussion beating out a relentless rhythm. The metal evoked nightmarish inhumanity, usually growing out of the low metal chimes and pulse of *Peril*.

Niska received his own signature as well, a middle-range reed instrument playing melodies ornamented in an Eastern European or Middle Eastern style over a low drone. We learned about his character in part through his musical signature, just as we did with the other character signatures: *Niska* evokes the Russian/Arabic/Jewish bad guy, friendly at first but terrifying and exacting if crossed. Jubal Early had a signature too, but I'll get to that later.

Simon and River were accompanied by a piano played sparsely, like a young pianist experimenting with harmonies on the keyboard, with a high violin drone in the background. We first heard *Simon/River*, overlaid with *Peril*, in the first episode, when Simon was trying to get Mal to run from the Alliance. We heard it alone during Simon's long speech and when he and River were safe in her room at the end of the episode. I find their music deeply emotional, evoking a sense of memory. In the same way that the portable instruments of *Serenity* conjure the sense of being on the run, the *Simon/River* signature is played by an instrument that can't be moved; with the sound of the piano comes the image of the distant house and family they both long for.

Notably, Book didn't seem to have any music of his own, and he remains the character most determinedly difficult to unravel. Aside from "The Hero of Canton," neither did Jayne—although I would interpret this as confirmation that, with Jayne, what you see is all you get. Zoe, Wash, Kaylee and Mal shared *Serenity*; this was just another way we understood their connection to each other and to the ship. Inara seemed to get special music only when she was in her shuttle, and most elaborately when she was giving herself a sponge bath, brushing Kaylee's hair or entertaining a female client. The *Serenity* guitar became delicate and melodic, fingerpicking a line that sounded both Spanish and American. It turned *Serenity* gorgeous and rich, like her clothing, like the inside of her shuttle and like her nurturing attention.

In later episodes, the potential relationship between Inara and Mal began to receive more attention. Soon, their feelings got a musical signature, too. *Inara/Mal* is piano-based, similar to *Simon/River* but more tuneful and songlike. The two signatures weren't easily confused—*Inara/Mal* was full of warmth and immediacy, while *Simon/River* felt disconnected and somehow focused on the past. We heard *Inara/Mal* at the end of "Our Mrs. Reynolds," when Mal confronted Inara. We knew she was about to admit her feelings for him because of this music; it shifted to *Serenity* when Mal misunderstood, assuming Saffron had seduced her. *Inara/Mal* played an important role in "Heart of Gold" as well. Inara's old friend Nandi sensed the two had feelings for each other, and with *Inara/Mal* in the background she alluded to their mutual affection, citing that both of them hate complications. Later, after Inara saw Mal leaving Nandi's room the next morning, *Inara/Mal* played beneath Inara's weeping. But I'm also intrigued that *Inara/Mal* accompanied Mal's sex scene with Nandi. It seems too easy to interpret in this juxtaposition that Mal was thinking about Inara; perhaps what we were hearing was a more abstract longing for love, or feeling of intimacy, from both Mal and Nandi.

A more complete musical piece always accompanied Tracey's recording in "The Message." It too featured piano, but in this case I think the strongest interpretive connection here was between the piano and the idea of home. Tracey's story—which began as a lie but came true by the episode's end—was entirely concerned with getting home. As the crew mourned at the gravesite, under a final hearing of Tracey's recording, his piano music played a few moments before *Sad Violin*, accompanied by other orchestral instruments, joined in to deepen the emotional effect.

The musical signatures in *Firefly* were established surprisingly quickly, for the most part within the first episode, and I believe that even if viewers weren't consciously aware of their correlation to emotions and characters, the signatures enhanced the narrative. This was one reason that we thought Simon was a bad guy in the beginning of the first episode. He didn't get his *Simon/River* music until he told their story; earlier in the episode, *Peril* played under his shots, leading us to think he would endanger the crew.

I had just started to focus my attention on these signatures when I watched "Objects in Space" again. The music was hugely important in this episode: as I watched it, I let the music tell me the story, and it changed my thinking about the characters and the show.

Jubal Early had tracked River down and planned to take her away. He had a distinctive musical signature: a low reed instrument (a bassoon or bass clarinet) played in a narrow range, seething and alive. High above it, a violin whined a high drone. His music—I'm calling it *Jubal Early*—sounded ominous and frightening; there was no question that he was bad. As he listened to the crew from outside the ship, his music projected the inevitable trouble he brought.

River listened from within; this point in the episode was where I first noticed that *Simon/River* has a very similar high violin. This could certainly have meant that Jubal Early was still there, listening and searching for her, even when we didn't see him. But as the episode progressed, the music for River was clearly differentiated from *Jubal Early* through editing and long pauses in the musical soundtrack, and the high violin continued to be present in both signatures. The crew proposed that River might be a reader, or even an assassin, in their discussion around the table. Later in the episode, we understood that Jubal was a reader and a bounty hunter. The dialogue suggested to us that River and Jubal have something in common; the music, in my opinion, confirmed it.

This got me thinking about "Bushwhacked." As the crew explored the derelict ship, we heard *Simon/River*, although River was still back on *Serenity*. So maybe the piano is a more general signature, communicating the abstract concept of family and love: there were families on the ship, and perhaps that was all the music was meant to imply. But if what I'm getting from "Objects in Space" is true and River is a reader, then maybe *Simon/River* was telling us that River read/felt these ghosts. We saw shots of the things these families left behind, but what we heard in the soundtrack was River's "presence" on the ship as she psychically experienced their terror.

Getting back to "Objects in Space," tracking the musical signatures can show the power dynamic between characters. When Early found Simon and they began to talk, there was no music. They spoke past each other: Simon asked if Early was "Alliance" but Early misheard him, responding that he didn't think of himself as "a lion." The tension of the situation was amplified by this quirk in the dialogue, the fact that they couldn't understand each other. Slowly, as Early brought out the gun—to demonstrate the connection between function and meaning—*Jubal Early* came in under the scene. Understanding this music as purely emotional, it certainly communicates the ominous undertone. But when I thought of this music as symbolic of Early himself, the sense I got from this point in the scene was that Early was in control: his music dominated the scene, giving Simon no choice but to do what Early told him to do.

Of course, River seems to have custody of *Simon/River* for this episode. The episode was really about her, and her music needed to stay with her. If *Simon/River* had begun to play under this scene between Simon and Early, what would it have meant? Perhaps we would have felt that River knew about their conversation, or that she was lurking around the corner, or perhaps we would have felt Simon's love for her sister. I think I would have sensed that Simon had the upper hand, or at least had a chance—and that would have undermined the tension of the plot.

There is plenty of music on the show I haven't mentioned: the theme song that sticks to you like peanut butter; the somewhat out-of-place chamber music playing during "Shindig"; Jayne's hilarious song (and his even more hilarious Easter egg performance of it); the drumming under the action sequences; the Irish-fiddle-meets-Chinese-instruments down at the Persephone docks. While I love it all—especially that theme song—none of that music participated in the complicated storytelling the way that the signatures I'm thinking about did.

There is also the promise of music for the film. I haven't quite worked out how the overblown pan flute fits in. It showed up, often having to do with River, all over the series. But sometimes it had nothing to do with her. It may just have been a color Edmonson used to set off *Peril*; it seemed to pop up when *Peril* was around. Or it might have had a more specific purpose that I don't understand yet. There's also the question of the two men with "hands of blue." At the very end of "The Train Job," when we first see them, *Peril* was juxtaposed with a big metallic gong. There is something going on there, as we know, and I'm expecting to find out more through the musical score as well as the script when the film comes out.

In every episode, the musical score intensified my experience of this intelligent, remarkable show. Using and combining all these signatures, Greg Edmonson brought out aspects of *Firefly*'s story and characters that were never explicitly revealed in the other elements of the series. When I give my attention to it, which gets easier the more I open myself up to it, the music deepens the characterizations, adds layers of meaning and points toward answers to questions in the story.

Jennifer Goltz teaches voice and music theory at Scripps College in Claremont, California. She specializes in performing new music, and writes about music of the turn of the last century and the relationship between performance and analysis. She can be heard on Cold Water, Dry Stone: The Music of Evan Chambers *(Albany Records, 2001) and* American Grab-Bag: Songs by Logan Skelton *(Centaur Records, forthcoming). In her spare time, she sings with the Ann Arbor-based klezmer band* Into the Freylakh, *with which she has released two CDs:* Into the Freylakh *and* The Shape of Klez to Come.

This is a rare opportunity for a viewer (or a writer, for that matter), to get fresh recollections from an actor on a recently completed body of work. Jewel gives us real reactions to scenes as she remembers them during the actual shooting, and also manages to put them in the context of the episodes as a whole. It's a difficult feat to see a show with objectivity after you've had a part in it, and she does a tremendous job.

As the author of "Shindig," though, I must say that I was under the impression that I had coined the term "Cap'n Tightpants," and that it was subsequently adopted for general use. Or perhaps the tight pants were simply one of those things in the Zeitgeist.

Kaylee Speaks:
Jewel Staite on *Firefly*

JEWEL STAITE

I'VE JUST WATCHED MY *FIREFLY* BOX SET for about the twentieth time. I was going to try to write about one specific thing, hopefully something really intelligent, but I couldn't decide. Should I write about one particular episode? One particular relationship? Or even one particular character? Is there one thing that sticks out the most, to me, that would make a great essay for this book?

The truth of the matter is there are about a hundred things I could write about. There are so many beautiful moments that I love to watch over and over again, and there are so many lines delivered that make me laugh hysterically or cry hysterically, which I can do both of at once, if provoked. So I'm going to write about them all. I'm going to give you my top five favorite moments from each episode (and a couple of off-camera moments as well).

I apologize in advance if I gush uncontrollably. I love this cast like family, and I respect all of them immensely. I believe these people were born to play these roles, and I think their individual brilliance shines through more than once in each episode. I also love Joss. Without Joss, none of these memories would exist. He is our true captain.

That said, I will begin with our pilot episode.

"SERENITY":

1. This is such a small moment, I know, but I love it all the same: When Inara is in her shuttle, and she radios *Serenity* to see what our coordinates are, Wash says, "We missed you out here." She looks away and sort of smiles, and she says, "Me, too." I love Inara's moments of vulnerability. Morena plays that so beautifully. Her eyes are always slightly secretive. What is Inara hiding? What is her past? Why *did* she leave Sihnon? (Well, I kind of know, but I'm not telling.)

2. The scene where Kaylee has just been shot, and Inara, Simon and Mal are bending over her. I love this moment because right here, Nathan split his pants right up the back. We didn't know each other REALLY well at that point, "Serenity" being our first episode, so it was a nice icebreaker. As he bent over, we heard this really loud "Rrrrrrriiiip!" and he blushed and said, "I think I just split my pants!" I think that's how the term "Captain Tightpants" was born, actually, and then the term was later inserted into "Shindig."

3. Jayne watching Kaylee get operated on. It's such an interesting, unexpected thing for Jayne to be doing. Would he do the same for any other character? I'm a firm believer that Kaylee is the only one on the ship that Jayne trusts. People love to argue that point with me, but I really do believe that. I don't think Kaylee would ever turn on anyone, and Jayne must pick up on that. I think he truly wants her to live.

4. The scene where Simon and River reunite, when she jumps out of her box. Sean and Summer have such great chemistry. They're sitting so close their foreheads are almost touching, and Simon is practically clinging to her. His dedication to his sister is one of the most admirable things about his character. This scene makes me cry.

5. Mal shooting Dobson. It's very unexpected. And it shows in a nutshell what Mal really thinks of the Alliance. And it's kinda funny.

"THE TRAIN JOB":

1. Jayne's reaction to the drunk in the bar, at the beginning of the episode, as the drunk says, "Today is an auspicious day!" Jayne looks around skeptically and says, "Suspicious? What day is it?" And then later, almost in the background, "What month is it?"

2. In this same scene, I love Mal telling off the drunk. "And I'm thinking you weren't burdened with an overabundance of schooling, so why don't we just ignore each other till we both go away?" I love the flashes of Mal's vocabulary every once in a while. He's not an uneducated man.

3. The scene between Mal and Inara in her shuttle, after Kaylee has left. There is some heavy-duty flirting going on here, and I think a struggle for power as well. Mal and Inara are both very confident people and relatively self-assured. She matches his quick wit, too. He asks her, "So, are you servicing crew now?" and she snaps back, "Only in your lonely, pathetic dreams." I like the comedy coming from Mal, and I like how at ease they appear to be with each other.

4. Mal and Zoe's conversation once they're on the train about whether or not to carry through with the job. I love Zoe's sarcasm. "Sir, I think you have a problem with your brain being missing."

5. My favorite part of this episode is near the end, when Zoe and Mal are returning the goods. The sheriff meets them there, and seeing that they've made the right decision, he makes a comment about how in some situations a man has a choice. And Mal responds with, "I don't believe he does." I love, love, LOVE Mal in this moment. Underneath everything, he has this wonderful conscience.

"BUSHWHACKED":

1. The ball game at the beginning of the episode is a nice moment because you get to see how the crew interacts with each other in their downtime. They're actually having fun and playing around with each other. Some of this was cut out in the final edit, because of time constraints, I'm sure, but it's still a cool scene. And I love River watching the game with that quizzical expression on her face, "doing the math," so to speak.

2. When all of the crew is assembled on the bridge, studying the floating ship. The camera travels past everyone and out into the corridor to River, who is sort of smiling. She whispers, "Ghosts."

3. I absolutely love the music in this episode, particularly the music playing when Mal and Zoe are searching for the goods/survivors. The music is almost sighing here, especially when the camera passes over the doll lying in the trunk. Very creepy.

4. The interrogation scenes. These are hilarious, and say so much about each character. The only little bit I wasn't too thrilled with was my interrogation scene with all of my technobabble. And no,

I'm not one of those actresses who hates everything she does and can't stand to watch herself and blah, blah, blah. I can appreciate some things because I worked hard on them. But this speech was thrown at me literally the night before, and then the scene itself was shot at midnight or something like it, so I was delirious with exhaustion and hardly knew my lines. Aside from that, Zoe's interrogation is great, especially her "Fought with him sometimes, too," about her husband. And I loved all of Alan's stuff. Most of it was improvisation. Tim Minear, our director of that episode, just kept the camera rolling while Alan went on and on. We were keeling over laughing. Alan is so hilarious. Oh, and one other thing I want to mention: does anyone else notice how Commander Harkin is different with Book? I honestly don't know much more about that than anyone else does, but I noticed a dynamic that changed there. Thought I'd point it out.

5. The very last bit of this episode, when the ship is being blown apart. The slow-mo, the music, everything about it is sad and final.

"SHINDIG":

1. Mal's obvious jealousy whenever Inara has a client, and specifically in this episode, when she's decided to meet with Atherton. It's more than jealousy, of course. He cares about her. He doesn't want her to have to do this line of work. He doesn't realize that she actually enjoys it, and enjoys her status as a Companion. He seems to be always trying to convince her she's better than that. Inara sees it simply as disrespect for her profession, and for her character as well. Respect is everything to these two. They both want to be respected by the other, and they're both under the impression they're not.

2. The scene in town, where everyone is looking at the models in the windows. Zoe makes a comment about wanting slink in her dress, and Jayne says something relatively disgusting. Still laughing, Zoe says, "I could hurt you." It's small and easy to miss, but Gina's delivery is hilarious. I also love how Jayne is guffawing off-camera at Mal's insult to Kaylee. This shows Jayne's total lack of sensitivity. And as the scene continues, Badger's "invitation" for a sit-down, and Mal's retort with, "I'd prefer a bit of a piss off." There are lots of great moments in this scene.

3. I love how Mal hardly reacts when Kaylee calls him "Cap'n Tightpants." I love any time Kaylee gets to offend or tease Mal.

4. Mal's defense of Inara. It's interesting how he has no problem calling her a whore, but as soon as someone else insinuates it, he takes that as the moment to come to her defense and perhaps impress her a little bit. And I love the line, "Turns out this IS my kinda party!"

5. I have to say something about River's Badger impression. Summer is great at accents, among about a million other things. But I remember the first time we heard it, which was during the rehearsal for that scene, and how everyone's mouths fell open.

"SAFE":

1. River cursing at the beginning of the episode. It's a different side to her than we've seen before. She's becoming more confident.

2. Zoe comforting Book after he's been shot. She says how they don't make Simon rush for "the little stuff."

3. Mal's decision to go to the Alliance for medical help. Mal's devotion to his crew is very evident here, but so is his devotion to Inara. She basically talks him into it. He knows she's right, but he also knows he's going to experience a world of trouble in going to the Alliance, too. He makes the sacrifice.

4. I love the scene between Simon and River in the "sick room" once they've been kidnapped. She says, "You gave up everything to find me, and you found me broken. It's hard for you." It breaks my heart when she says this.

5. Jayne's delivery of the line, "Hey, Doctor. Glad you're back now. On the ship." This is of course right after he's dumped all the stuff he stole from Simon back in his room. I don't know why, but it always strikes me as hilarious.

"OUR MRS. REYNOLDS":

1. Near the beginning of the episode, when the crew is getting drunk in the town. Saffron puts the garland on Mal's head, and he grins at Jayne and points, mouthing, "My hat!" It's so rare that everyone's happy. I love those moments.

2. When Mal murmurs, "Is it Christmas?" after Simon revives him from the "good-night kiss."

3. Jayne saying, "That's why I never kiss 'em on the mouth." Probably one of my all-time favorite *Firefly* lines.

4. I love the kiss Mal gives Kaylee on the forehead when she feels like she hasn't done a good job. He is always very quick to comfort Kaylee.

5. The scene at the end where Mal confronts Inara. He starts by complimenting her, calling her graceful, and then he basically accuses her of lying about falling. I love how Inara stutters a "Wh-whaddaya mean?" and her reaction when she realizes that he thinks she kissed Saffron instead of him. She doesn't even try to argue it.

"JAYNESTOWN":
1. River fixing Book's Bible. I love her incredulity at Noah's Ark, and how she won't give the ripped pages back. And I love Book letting her have them back.
2. Wash drunk. Alan plays one of the funniest drunks I have ever seen. Playing drunk is really difficult, because you're usually trying too hard to be drunk, which is the wrong way to go. Most drunks try to act sober. Anyway, Alan does it brilliantly. I can't tell you how many times I've rewound this part of the episode to watch over and over again.
3. There's a really small moment when Mal, Zoe and Kaylee are getting on the mule, and Zoe says, "Is it really Jayne Cobb? Pinch me, I must be dreamin'!" And Jayne says, "Hell, I'll pinch ya." Zoe sort of reaches out and swats him away, and the two of them share a little laugh. I'm pretty sure some of those actions were improvised (my memory being foggy because it was so hot and muggy that day), but it's a brilliant little moment.
4. After one of the mudders has been shot, Jayne yells at the people assembled in the square. He says, "There ain't people like that. There's just people like me." That delivery couldn't have been more perfect.
5. River's "Just keep walkin', preacher-man." Genius.

"OUT OF GAS":
1. There are so many beautiful things about this episode, it's hard to choose just five. I love the shots of the ship, silent, unmoving, empty. I love the music playing over these shots, too. All the music in this episode is heartbreaking.
2. I LOVE the scene where Mal pushes Wash up against the wall in the infirmary, and how calm Mal's face is, how he's looking Wash straight in the eye. This scene could have played out like a power struggle, but it's more than that. Wash knows he has to get up to the bridge. He knows Mal is right. And I love Mal's regret in having to be violent with Wash. You can see it in his face.

3. During Mal's speech about how he wants to send off the rest of the crew in the shuttles, he's almost absently patting a pipe above his head. It's a bittersweet, really beautiful moment. He has such a love affair with this ship.

4. "Everybody dies alone." My eyes well up when Nathan delivers this line.

5. I love the end of the episode, when Wash is giving Mal a blood transfusion and the whole crew is gathered around him. Mal has no defenses up here. He's almost childlike in his wooziness, and I love how he makes everyone promise to be there when he wakes up. It's a very human moment for Mal.

"ARIEL":

1. River's violent outburst toward Jayne. Where is this coming from? Is she foreseeing something? It's so abrupt, and so extreme.

2. I love the "learning of the hospital lingo" montage with Jayne, Zoe, Mal and Simon. A lot of it seems improvised (I didn't get to be there). I love Simon taking stuff out of Jayne's hands like the teacher that he is.

3. In the hospital on Ariel, when Zoe zaps the doctor in the bank and says simply, "Clear." Gina is so good at being deadpan.

4. One of the creepiest moments in the whole series (I think) is when River looks up to the ceiling and says, "Doesn't matter. They're here. . . ." when the men with the blue hands arrive. It's terrifying.

5. The scene at the end, between Jayne and Mal. Mal is so furious here. I really do believe that he might kill Jayne for this. And I love Jayne's moment of honesty: "Don't tell them what I did." It makes me forgive him.

"WAR STORIES":

1. The scene in the shuttle between Mal, Zoe and Wash. It's always interesting to see more of the dynamic between these three characters, and even more interesting to see Zoe back down from Wash in this scene.

2. This whole episode basically revolves around Nathan and Alan. They are so great together in this. Offscreen, they're really close friends, and I think it shows here. And at this point, I think we all had a really good grasp of who our characters were. I love the scene when they're blindfolded, screaming at each other. I wonder

if some of those things would have been said if the blindfolds were off and they were looking each other in the eye.

3. I really like how Zoe doesn't flinch when Niska gives her back the "refund" of Mal's ear. And I also love how she doesn't hesitate in choosing which man she wants.

4. River shooting the three men with her eyes closed. It's no mystery that she's a genius, but something like this isn't just smarts. She has skills we don't know about yet.

5. The moment where Mal almost has the advantage on Niska's henchman, and Jayne's about to shoot. Zoe says, "This is something the captain has to do for himself." Mal goes, "No, it isn't!" And Zoe says, "Oh!" and the henchman is riddled with holes. I love the little bits of comedy that sneak themselves into dramatic moments like that.

"TRASH":

1. The scene between Mal and Saffron once Monty has flown away. Christina Hendricks, the woman who played Saffron, was absolutely brilliant (and really sweet in person too, nothing like her character), and she and Nathan had true chemistry. I love when he's frisking her, and she says, "You missed a spot." Mal retorts with, "You can't miss a place you've never been."

2. The scene between Jayne, River and Simon in the bunk-room. Specifically the line, "Jayne is a girl's name," delivered by River. I adore this line.

▸ 3. The special effects of Bellerophon. They're beautiful and really well done.

4. Everyone's reactions to Mal being naked: Inara's amusement, Zoe and Wash about to burst into hysterical laughter and Kaylee's indifference. I love how happy Mal is, too.

5. Another scene with Simon, River and Jayne, when Jayne's paralyzed. "Anybody there?" River pops in. "Anybody else?" And of course: "Also? I can kill you with my brain." How true, how true.

"HEART OF GOLD":

1. The scene where Mal's explaining the job, and Jayne's saying he's not going to do it without up-front payment. Mal says, "They're whores," and immediately Jayne responds, "I'm in."

2. Zoe explaining the "3-point, 4-hour watch" and Wash chiming in,

"3-point, 4-hour…should do it," without having any idea what she's really talking about.

3. I love Book reassuring the girls that no one's going to die. He's so sure that everyone will come out safe. He has such confidence in Mal and the crew.

4. River watching Petaline giving birth and peering at her stomach. "Who do you think is in there?"

5. The last part of the episode, when Mal and Inara are having a discussion up on the catwalk. For a moment there, you really think what Inara's talking about, the thing she should have done long ago, is a kiss, or a confession. I love Mal's expression when she says she's leaving.

"OBJECTS IN SPACE":

1. River exploring the ship at the beginning of the episode. Her "vision" of Book as he says, "I don't give half a hump if you're innocent or not. Where does that put you?" gives me the creeps. And I love the moment when Inara says, "I'm a big girl, just tell me," juxtaposed with Mal's "None of it means a damn thing." What does Inara need to be told? I love Summer's movements throughout all of this. She seems to move as if off-balance, but still really graceful. The music and the sounds around her are interesting, too. The sound of the waves after she leaves Mal and Inara, and when she's picking up the stick, a river running and birds chirping. I like this glimpse into her mind, where reality is seriously altered.

2. During Kaylee's speech to the crew, I love how River is listening underneath them, balanced on the railings of the catwalk. She looks so comfortable in such an awkward position. She always seems to appear kind of weightless in her movements and with her body.

3. The scene between Early and Simon where Simon asks him if he's Alliance. Early says, "Am I a lion?" It's such a strange moment. Early is very powerful and very much in control, but yet unsure of himself. Not careful. I think Simon senses this and loses some of his fear of him.

4. Early's close-up when River is telling him what she knows of his past. Richard Brooks, who played Early, was such a wonderful man. Really kind, really sweet. But he's so believable in this character. It's his insanity that makes him frightening. The cuts to him

laughing, making faces, just sends the wrong kind of shivers up my spine. It's really disturbing.

5. River's speech about wanting to be Early's bounty, and everyone's reactions to it. I always cry during this.

"THE MESSAGE":

1. Simon screwing up with Kaylee, yet again. I love Sean's big grin, how Simon really thinks he's on the right path here. He just has no clue how to deal with women at all. I also kept screwing up my Chinese here. I don't think I ever said the same thing twice. They ended up having to cut away from it in the end because I was basically speaking jibberish.

2. The long scene at the beginning (with a commercial cut in the middle of it) where the postman gives us Tracey's body. This scene took two whole days to shoot, and by the end of it, we all had the giggles pretty bad. Morena and I were busy shoving each other from behind without warning to see how many times we could make each other fall. Pretty much everything short of breathing was making us laugh. We had everyone going by the end of it all. That was the last day of filming for a few of us.

3. The scene where we're all listening to the recording of Tracey and standing over his casket in a circle. This is another off-camera moment, but one of my favorites. Nathan decided it would be hilarious to sort of follow the camera around as it moved from one of our faces to the other in the circle, so the camera would pass by him several times. One minute he was beside Alan, the next, beside Ron, and the next leaning on Gina's shoulder, and at the end when the camera pans down to Tracey, he's cuddling him in the casket. Again, we were all kind of tired and delirious, so this was probably a lot funnier to us than to anyone else, but we were literally crying with laughter during this.

4. Wash's reaction to "Mal's dead army buddy" walking onto the bridge. This is true Alan Tudyk humor. Go big or go home, right? I love this moment.

5. The last scene, where the crew of *Serenity* is delivering the body of Tracey to his family. This wasn't exactly a ball to shoot, because it was in the studio, and so the snow wasn't real. I don't know what they used, but it tasted like a mixture of snow and paper, and it got up your nose and in your mouth and it was just gross. But the actual scene turned out beautifully. The music, the lighting, the

reactions, everything came together so well. To me, this was the "end" of *Firefly*. We knew we were cancelled here, and we were all genuinely heartbroken. It's a beautiful scene, but very hard for me to watch.

Thank you for letting me share my "Top Five" with you. It's hard for me to remember anything negative that went along with the filming of this show. It was such an enormous relief to be able to join the cast again for *Serenity*, because we truly fell in love with these characters. It's hard to let go of something you believe in so much. The *Serenity* set was filled with a lot of relief, and a lot of laughter, of course, and a lot of happy tears. There is a sense that this is still not over. It's hard to put a finger on what's so special about this project and about this group of people, but it's just one of those things you have to trust in, and relish. I am very, very proud.

Jewel Staite has been in the film and television industry since the age of five, when she began modeling for Sears in exchange for clothing. Aside from playing Kaywinnit Lee "Kaylee" Frye in Firefly *and* Serenity, *Jewel's recent roles have included Teddy Blue in* Cheaters *and guest parts on* Wonderfalls *and* Dead Like Me.

Jenny Lynn has been one of the hardest-working members of the Firefly *universe, contributing far more than the translations cited here. Let us applaud her fine work.*

Unofficial Glossary of *Firefly* Chinese

CREATED BY KEVIN M. SULLIVAN

THE CHINESE PRONUNCIATIONS and English in quotation marks ("") come from retyped Internet postings of the *Firefly* shooting scripts; some typos may have crept in. Words not in quotation marks are less certain. Words followed by an asterisk (*) are from the recollections of the *Firefly* Chinese translator, Jenny Lynn.[1] Asterisked English is not necessarily precisely what was submitted to her for translation. While Ms. Lynn kindly filled in some gaps, she has not verified the accuracy of this unofficial glossary as a whole.

After the script Chinese pronunciation, in square brackets ([]), are the words in China's official alphabetic spelling (*hanyu pinyin*) and Chinese characters. Both traditional and simplified characters are given when there is a difference. When the English meaning needs clarification, one follows in square brackets.

Mandarin Chinese Tones:
 1 high, flat; *2* high, rising; *3* low, dipping [shifts to 2nd tone before another 3rd-tone syllable]; *4* high, falling; *5* neutral [used with many grammatical words and ends of compound words]

---

[1] Lynn, 2004a, 2004b.

SERENITY, PART 1

MAL: *Ta ma duh!* [*Ta1ma1 de5!* 他媽的 · 他妈的] ~
"Fuck me blind!"

MAL: *BEE-jway.* [*Bi4zui3.* 閉嘴 · 闭嘴] ~ "Shut up."

KAYLEE: *Shr ah.* [*Shi4a5.* 是啊] ~ "Affirmative."

WASH: *Ai ya! Hwai leh!* [*Ai1ya1! Huai4le5!*
哎呀！壞了！· 哎呀 ！坏了！] ~ "Shit on my head!"

MAL, again: *BEE-jway.* [*Bi4zui3.* 閉嘴 · 闭嘴] ~ "Shut up."

WASH: *Jun ta ma yao ming. Joo-ee.* [*Zhen1 ta1ma1 yao4ming4.
Zhu4yi4.* 真他媽要命。注意。· 真他妈要命。注意。] ~ "Watch
your back." [This is pretty damned dangerous. Pay attention.]

INARA: *Ching jin.* [*Qing3jin4.* 請進。· 请进。] ~ "Come in."

MAL: *Nee ta ma duh tyen-shia suo-yo duh run doh gai si.* [*Ni3 ta1ma1
de5 tian1xia4 suo3you3 de5 ren2 dou1 gai1si3.*
你他媽的天下所有的人都該死。· 你他妈的天下所有的人都该
死。] ~ "Fuck everyone in the universe to death."

INARA: *mei-mei* [*mei4mei5*妹妹] ~ "little sister"

SERENITY, PART 2

MAL: *Nee mun doh BEE-jway!* [*Ni3men5 dou1 bi4zui3!*
你們都閉嘴！· 你们都闭嘴！] ~ "Everybody shut the hell up!"

WASH: *kwong-juh duh* [*kuang2zhe3 de5* 狂者的] ~ "nuts" [crazy]

MAL: *shiao mei-mei* [*xiao3mei4mei4* 小妹妹] ~ "little sister"
[*Xiao3* means "little," and *mei4mei5* means "younger sister."
Xiao3mei4mei4 means "younger sister"/"your own youngest
sister"/"young girl," and the final *mei4* doesn't change to *mei5.*]

JAYNE: *Hwoon dahn!* [*Hun2dan4!* 混蛋] ~ Bastard!

ZOE: *Ai ya, wo mun wan leh.* [*Ai1ya1, wo3men5 wan2le5.*
哎呀，我們完了。· 哎呀，我们完了。] ~ "We're in big trouble."

SIMON, deleted scene: *Shuh muh?* [*Shen2me5?* 什麼· 什么] ~ "I'm
sorry?"

THE TRAIN JOB

MAL: *Ching zie lie ee bay Ng Ka Pei?* [*Qing3 zai4lai2 yi4bei1
ng5gaa1pei4?* 請再來一杯五加皮？· 请再来一杯五加皮？]

~ "Can I have one more glass of Ng-Ka-Pei [a medicinal-herb wine], please?"

  Mandarin pronunciation of drink: *wu3jia1pi2*; Cantonese Tones: *1* high, flat (or falling); *2* high, rising; *3* mid. flat; *4* low, falling; *5* low rising; *6* low, flat

MAL: *Oh, juh jen sh guh kwai luh duh jean-jan....[O1, zhe4 zhen1 shi4 ge5 kuai4le4 de5 jin4zhan3...* 噢，這真是個快樂的進展.... • 噢，这真是个快乐的进展...] ~ "Oh, this is a happy development...."

KAYLEE: *Kuh-ooh duh lao bao-jurn....[Ke3wu4 de5 lao3 bao4jun1....* 可惡的老暴君 • 可恶的老暴君....] ~ "Horrible old tyrant...."

KAYLEE: *jen duh sh tyen tsai [zhen1 de5 shi4 tian1cai2* 真的是天才] ~ "an absolute genius"

JAYNE: *dong ma? [dong3 ma5?* 懂嗎 • 懂吗] ~ "understand?"

JAYNE: *go tsao de [gou3 cao4 de5* 狗操的] ~ dog-humping [dog-humped]

BUSHWHACKED

JAYNE: "*Wuh de ma.*" [*Wo3 de5 ma1.* 我的媽 • 我的妈] ~ "Mother of god [*sic*]." [literally, My ma!]

MAL: "*Jen dao mei!*" [*Zhen1 dao3mei2!* 真倒霉] ~ "Just our luck!"

WASH: "*tyen shiao duh*" [*tian1 xiao3de2* 天曉得 • 天晓得] ~ name of all that's sacred [from "The Message" script; God knows what]

WASH: "*Tzao gao.*" [*Zao1gao1* 糟糕] ~ "Crap." [Damn!]

MAL: "*Wuh de tyen, ah.*" [*Wo3 de5 tian1, a5.* 我的天啊] ~ "Dear god [*sic*] in heaven."

JAYNE: "*Hwoon dahn.*" [*Hun2dan4* 混蛋] ~ "Jerk."

SHINDIG

WRIGHT THE SLAVER, x2: "*Way!*" [*Wei4!*喂！] ~"Hey!"

ATHERTON: "*bao bay*" [*bao3bei4* 寶貝 • 宝贝] ~ "sweetheart"

BADGER: "*wun gwo pee*" [*wen2guo1 pi4*聞過屁 • 闻过屁] ~ "smelled a fart"

BADGER: "*pee-goo*" [*pi4gu5* 屁股] ~ "bottom" [butt]

INARA: "*Lao pung yo, nee can chi lai hun yo jing shen.*" [*Lao3peng2you5, ni3 kan4 qi5lai5 hen3 you3 jing1shen2.* 老朋友，

你看起來很有精神。· 老朋友，你看起来很有精神。] ~ "You're looking wonderful, old friend."

ATHERTON, x3: "*gos se*" [*gou3shi3* 狗屎] ~ "crap" [dog crap]

INARA: "*gos se*" [*gou3shi3* 狗屎] ~ "crap" [dog crap]

KAYLEE: "*Sheh-sheh*" [*Xie4xie5* 謝謝· 谢谢] ~ "Thank you"

KAYLEE: "*Shah muh?*" [*Shen2me5?* 什麼· 什么] ~ "What?"

KAYLEE: "*Tsai boo shr.*" [*Cai2 bu2 shi4.* 纔不是· 才不是] ~ "No way."

MAL: "*yu bun duh*" [*yu2ben4 de5* 愚笨的] ~ "stupid"

SAFE

YOUNG SIMON: *Jien tah-duh guay!* [*Jian4 ta1 de5 gui3!* 見他的鬼！· 见他的鬼！] ~ Like hell! [literally, see his ghost]

GABRIEL TAM: *Nah mei guan-shee.* [*Na4 mei2 guan1xi5.* 那沒關係。· 那没关系。] ~ In that case, never mind.

GABRIEL TAM: *tyen shiao duh* [*tian1 xiao3de2* 天曉得· 天晓得] ~ God knows what

YOUNG SIMON: *dah bien-hwa* [*da4 bian4hua4* 大變化· 大变化] ~ big change

RIVER: *Liou coe shway duh biao-tze huh hoe-tze duh bun ur-tze.* [*Liu2 kou3shui3 de5 biao3zi5 he2 hou2zi5 de5 ben4 er2zi5.* 流口水的婊子和猴子的笨兒子。· 流口水的婊子和猴子的笨儿子。] ~ Stupid son of a drooling whore and a monkey

SIMON: *niou-fun* [*niu2fen4* 牛糞· 牛粪] ~ "cow poop"

KAYLEE: *swai* [*shuai4* 帥· 帅] ~ "cute" [handsome]

SIMON: *luh-suh* [*le4se4* 垃圾] ~ "garbage"

SIMON: *pyen juh duh jiou cha wen* [*pian1zhi2 de5 jiu1cha2yuan2** 偏執的糾察員· 偏执的纠察员] ~ stubborn disciplinarian*

KAYLEE, x2: *luh-suh* [*le4se4* 垃圾] ~ "garbage"

MAL: *Fei hua.* [*Fei4hua4.* 廢話· 废话] ~ "Nonsense."

MAL: *Ma shong!* [*Ma3shang4!* 馬上· 马上] ~ "Now!" [right away]

WASH: *Lao-tyen, boo.* [*Lao3tian1, bu4.* 老天，不] ~ "Oh, god [sic], no."

MAL: *jing-tzang mei yong-duh* [*jing1chang2 mei2yong4 de5* 經常沒用的· 经常没用的] ~ "consistently useless"

SIMON: *Mei-mei* [*Mei4mei5* 妹妹] ~ Little sister

GABRIEL TAM: *choo fay wuh suh leh* [*chu2fei1 wo3 si3 le5** 除非我死了] ~ over my dead body* [literally, [not] unless I die*]

PATRON: *nyen ching-duh* [*nian2qing1 de5* 年輕的· 年轻的] ~ "young one"

OUR MRS. REYNOLDS

SIMON: *Dahng rahn.* [*Dang1ran2* 當然·当然] ~ "Of course."

KAYLEE: *Nee boo go-guh, nee hwoon-chiou.* [*Ni3 bu2 gou4ge2, ni3 hun2qiu2.** 你不夠格你**混球**.·你不够格你**混球**.] ~ "You don't deserve her, you fink." [You're not good enough, you bastard.*]

MAL: *Gwon nee tze-jee duh shr.* [*Guan3 ni3 zi4ji3 de5 shi4.* 管你自己的事.] ~ "Mind your own business."

MAL: *Da-shiong bao-jah-shr duh la-doo-tze* [*Da4xiang4 bao4zha4shi4 de5 la1du4zi5** 大象爆炸式的拉肚了] ~ "The explosive diarrhea of an elephant"

MAL: *hwoon dahn* [*hun2dan4* 混蛋] ~ "bastard"

WASH: *Wuh duh ma huh ta duh fung-kwong duh wai-shung doh* [*Wo3 de5 ma1 he2 ta1 de5 feng1kuang2 de5 wai4sheng5 dou1* 我的媽和她的瘋狂的外甥都·我的妈和她的疯狂的外甥都] ~ "Holy mother of god [sic] and all her wacky Nephews [sic]"

INARA: *Run-tse duh FWO-tzoo....* [*Ren2ci2 de5 Fo2zu3....* 仁慈的佛祖....] ~ "Merciful buddha [sic] ...."

ZOE: *jien hwo* [*jian4huo4* 賤貨·贱货] ~ "cheap floozy"

WASH: *jing-tsai* [*jing1cai3* 精彩] ~ "brilliant" [splendid]

WASH: *Dung ee-miao.* [*Deng3 yi4miao3.* 等一秒.] ~ "Hold on a second."

WASH: *Ai ya!* [*Ai1ya1!* 哎呀] ~ "Damn!"

SIMON, deleted scene: "*mei-mei*" [*mei4mei5* 妹妹] ~ little sister

JAYNESTOWN

WASH: "*Je shr shuh muh lan dong shi!?*" [*Zhe4 shi4 shen2me5 lan4 dong1xi5!?* 這是什麼爛東西！？·这是什么烂東西！？] ~ "What is this garbage!?"

JAYNE: "*Yeh-soo, ta ma duh....*" [*Ye1su1, ta1ma1 de5....* 耶穌，他媽的....·耶稣，他妈的....] ~ "Hay-soose [Spanish *Jesús*]-mother-of-jumped-up—" [Jesús, damned—]

BARTENDER: "*shiong mao niao*" [*xiong2mao1 niao4* 熊貓尿·熊猫尿] ~ "panda urine"

JAYNE, offscreen: *guh jun duh hwoon dahn!* [*ge5 zhen1 de5 hun2dan4!* 個真的混蛋!·个真的混蛋!] ~ a real bastard!

ZOE: "*Hoo-tsuh.*" [*Hu2che3.* 胡扯] ~ "Shut up." ["as in 'get out'"] [nonsense]

WASH: *"Gao yang jong duh goo yang."* [*Gao1yang2 zhong1 de5 gu1yang2.* 羔羊中的孤羊] ~ "Motherless goats of all motherless goats." [Orphan goats among young goats.]

OUT OF GAS

ZOE: *"fei-oo"* [*fei4wu4* 廢物・废物] ~ "junk"

MAL: *"fei-oo"* [*fei4wu4* 廢物・废物] ~ "junk"

WASH: *"Chur ni-duh."* [*Qu4 ni3 de5.* 去你的。] ~ "Screw you."

JAYNE: *"guay"* [*gui3* 鬼] ~ "hell" [ghost, demon]

VOICE OF SERENITY, x2: *"Jeo-shung yong-jur goo-jang. Jien-cha yong-chi gong yin* [*sic*]*."* [Cantonese: *Gau3saang1 hai6tung2 gu3zoeng3. Gim2caa4 jeong5hei3 gung1*[3]*jing1*[3]. 救生系統故障。檢查氧氣供應。・救生系统故障。检查氧气供应。] ~ "Life support failure. Check oxygen levels at once."
    Mandarin pronunciation: *Jiu4sheng1 xi4tong3 gu4zhang4. Jian3cha2 yang3qi4 gong1ying4.* ["*Yong-jur*" is *yong4ju4*/Cantonese *jung6geoi6* appliance 用具.]

Cantonese Tones: *1* high, flat (or falling); *2* high, rising; *3* mid, flat; *4* low, falling; *5* low, rising; *6* low, flat[2]

MAL: *"suo-yo duh doh shr-dang"* [*suo3you3 de5 dou1 shi4dang4* 所有的都適當・所有的都适当] ~ "all that's proper"

MAL: *"Dong3 ma?"* [*Dong3 ma5?* 懂嗎・懂吗] ~ "Understand?"

VOICE OF SERENITY, again, x2: *"Jeo-shung yong-jur goo-jang. Jien-cha yong-chi gong yin* [*sic*]*."*

PIRATE CAPTAIN: *"go se"* [*gou3shi3* 狗屎] ~ "crap" [dog crap]

VOICE OF SERENITY, again, x4: *"Jeo-shung yong-jur goo-jang. Jien-cha yong-chi gong yin* [*sic*]*."*

ARIEL

MAL: *"Ching-wah TSAO duh liou mahng"* [*qing1wa1 cao4 de5 liu2mang2* 青蛙操的流氓] ~ "frog-humping sonofabitch" [frog-humped hoodlum]

AGENT MCGINISS: *Nee hao?* [*Ni3 hao3?* 你好？] ~ Hello?

---

[2] Thanks to a *Firefly* fan for the second word in the Cantonese and Mandarin versions.

JAYNE: "*Shee-niou*" [*Xi1 niu2* 吸牛] ~ "Cow sucking"
SIMON: "*mei mei*" [*mei4mei5* 妹妹] ~ little sister

WAR STORIES

WASH: *Tai-kong suo-yo duh shing-chiou sai-jin wuh duh pee-goo*
[*Tai4kong1 suo3you3 de5 xing1qiu2 sai1jin4 wo3 de5 pi4gu5* 太空
所有的星球塞盡我的屁股・太空所有的星球塞尽我的屁股] ~
"All the planets in space flushed into my butt"
SIMON: "*Mei-mei*" [*Mei4mei5* 妹妹] ~ Little sister
MAL: *fahng-tzong fung-kwong duh jeh* [*fang4zong4 feng1kuang2 de5 jie2*
放縱瘋狂的結・放纵疯狂的结] ~ "a knot of self-indulgent lunacy"
MAL: *niou-se* [*niu2shi3* 牛屎] ~ "cow dung"
MAL: *Tzao-gao!* [*Zao1gao1!* 糟糕] ~ "Damn it!"
MAL: *Tah mah duh hwoon dahn.* [*Ta1ma1 de5 hun2dan4.* 他媽的混蛋
・他・妈的混蛋] ~ "Mother-humping son of a bitch."
BOOK: *Huh choo-shung tza-jiao duh tzang-huo!* [*He1 chu4sheng5
za2jiao1 de5 zang1huo4!* 喝畜生雜交的髒貨！・喝畜生杂交的脏
货！] ~ "Filthy fornicators of livestock!"

TRASH

SAFFRON: "*BUN tyen-shung duh ee-DWAY-RO.*" [*Ben4 tian1sheng1
de5 yi4dui1 rou4.* 笨天生的一堆肉] ~ Stupid inbred stack of meat.*
SAFFRON: "*HOE-tze duh PEE-goo!*" [*hou2zi5 de5 pi4gu5!* 猴子的屁
股] ~ monkey's butt!
MAL: "*EE-chee shung-hoo-shee.*" [*Yi4qi3 shen1 hu1xi1.* 一起深呼吸]
~ Let's take a deep breath.
INARA: "*Suo-SHEE?*" [*Suo3xi4?* 瑣細？・琐细？] ~ "petty" [trivial]
INARA: "*Nee mun DOH shr sagwa.*" [*Ni3men5 dou1 shi4 sha3gua1.*
你們都是傻瓜・你们都是傻瓜] ~ "Idiots. All of you."
SIMON: "*BOO hway-HUN duh PUO-foo*" [*bu4 hui4hen4 de5 po1fu4*
不悔恨的潑婦・不悔恨的泼妇] ~ "remorseless harridan"
MAL: "*Shun-SHENG duh gao-WAHN.*" [*Shen2sheng4 de5 gao1wan2.* 神
聖的睪丸・神圣的睪丸] ~ "Holy testicle Tuesday." [Holy testicle.]
SAFFRON: "*Wahg-ba* [sic] *DAN duh biao-tze.*" [*Wang2ba5dan4 de5
biao3zi5.* 王八蛋的婊子] ~ Whores of SOBs.
KAYLEE: "*Tah-shr SUO-yo DEE-yure duh biao-tze duh MAH!*" [*Ta1

shi4 suo3you3 di4yu4 de5 biao3zi5 de5 ma1!* 她是所有地獄的婊子的媽!· 所有地獄的婊子的妈!] ~ "whores in hell!" [She's the mother of all the whores in hell!*]

THE MESSAGE

KAYLEE, offscreen: "*Nee GAO-soo NA niou, TA yo shwong mei-moo?*" [*Ni3 gao4su5 na4 niu2 ta1 you3 shuang1 mei3mu4?* 你告訴那牛牠有雙美目？· 你告诉那牛它有双美目？] ~ "Why don't you tell the cow about its beautiful eyes?"

WOMACK: "*Dong ma?*" [*Dong3 ma5?* 懂嗎· 懂吗] ~ "understand?"

MAL: "*TYEN shiao-duh*" [*tian1 xiao3de2* 天曉得· 天晓得] ~ "name of all that's sacred" [God knows what]

KAYLEE: *shiong-tsan sha-sho* [*xiong1can2 sha1shou3* 兇殘殺手· 凶残杀手] ~ ass-kicking killer* [ruthless killer]

WASH: "*Wuo duh MA*" [*Wo3 de5 ma1* 我的媽· 我的妈] ~ "Mother-of-Jesus" [literally, My ma!]

HEART OF GOLD

INARA: "*gun HOE-tze bee DIO-se*" [*gen2 hou2zi5 bi3 diu1shi3* 跟猴子比丟屎] ~ "engage in a feces-hurling contest with a monkey"

NANDI: "*TZOO-foo nee, mei-mei.*" [*Zhu4fu2 ni3, mei4mei5.* 祝福你妹妹] ~ "Blessing on you, dear sister."

NANDI: "*Mei Mei*" [*Mei4mei5* 妹妹] ~ Little Sister

PUPPET THEATER NARRATOR: ... *way tzwo-juh man-tzai ur choo.* [... *wei4 zuo4zhe5 man3zai4 er2 qu4* .... 為做著滿載而去。· ...为做着满载而去。] ~ "Swollen of her, they left." [literally, ... for the sake of making fully loaded and left][3]

JAYNE, offscreen: "*dong MA?*" [*dong3 ma5?* 懂嗎· 懂吗] ~ "you understand?"

NANDI: "*jen mei NAI-shing duh FWO-tzoo*" [*Zhen1 mei2 nai4xing4 de5 Fo2zu3* 真沒耐性的佛祖· 真没耐性的佛祖] ~ "Extraordinarily impatient Buddha"

NANDI: "*Wang bao [sic] DAHN—*" [*Wang2ba5dan4—* 王八蛋—] ~ "dirty bastard sons-of—" [SOBs—]

---

[3] Thanks to Patrick Zein for this entry.

WASH: *"niao SE duh DOO-gway"* [*niao3 shi1 de5 du3gui3* 尿濕的賭
鬼・尿湿的赌鬼] ~ "piss-soaked pikers" [urine-soaked habitual
gamblers]

OBJECTS IN SPACE

JAYNE: *"FAY-FAY duh PEE-yen"* [*fei4fei4 de5 pi4yan3*狒狒的屁眼] ~
"a babboon's [*sic*] ass-crack"
INARA: *"BEE-jway, neen hen BOO-TEE-TYEH duh NAN-shung!"*
[*Bi4zui3, nin2 hen3 bu4ti3tie1 de5 nan2sheng1!* 閉嘴，您很不體
貼的男生！・闭嘴，您很不体贴的男生！] ~ "Shut up, you inconsiderate schoolboys!"
INARA: *shiong-mung duh kwong-run* [*xiong1meng3 de5 kuang2ren2*
兇猛的狂人・凶猛的狂人] ~ "violent lunatic"

Written Chinese Mentioned in Sullivan's
"Chinese Words in the 'Verse"

On Persephone ("Shindig")
    you1mei3 优美[traditional: 優美] ~ elegant
    jiang3jiu5 de5 fu2zhuang1 讲究的服装 [traditional: 講究的服裝] ~
      stylish clothing
    you2lan3che1 游览车[traditional: 遊覽車] ~ tour bus

Jayne's T-shirts
    *yong3*勇~ soldier ("The Train Job," "Shindig," "Ariel," "War Sto-
      ries")
    qing1 ri4 青日[early form of: 青] ~ "Blue Sun" ("Bushwhacked,"
      "Ariel" and elsewhere in "Serenity, Part 1" and "Shindig")
    zhan4dou4 de5 xiao3jing1ling2 战斗的小精灵 [traditional: 戰鬥的
      小精靈] ~ the fighting, or militant, elves ("Safe," "Out of Gas,"
      "War Stories")
    wan2mei3 mao1 完美猫 [traditional: 完美貓] ~ perfect cat ("Heart
      of Gold")
    wan2nao4 玩闹 [traditional: 玩鬧] ~ troublemaker, rascal
      ("Jaynestown")
    dai1ruo4mu4 ji1 呆若木鸡 [traditional: 呆若木雞] ~ dumb as a
      wooden chicken, paralyzed by fear ("Trash")

Other

lan2 ri4 蓝日 [traditional: 藍日] ~ "Blue Sun" ("The Message")

wei1 dian4 危电 [simplified: 危 电] ~ Danger Electricity (most episodes)

jing3 警 ~ police ("The Train Job")

yi4sui4 易碎 ~ fragile ("The Message")

nian2, yue4, ri4; chun1, xia4; nian2 年 月 日 · 春 夏 · 年 ~ year,
month, day; spring, summer; year ("Bushwhacked")

wei1 危 ~ danger (without dian4: "Ariel," "Trash," "Objects in Space")

Ru2guo3 tai2qiu2 huai4le5, na4 me5 guan3li3 jiu4 bu4 fu4ze2 de5.
如果台球坏了，那么管理就不负责的. [traditional: 如果台球壞
了，那麼管理就不負責的.] ~ "Management Not Responsible for
Ball Failure" ("Shindig")

SOURCES

Books

DeFrancis, John, ed. *ABC Chinese-English Comprehensive Dictionary.*
Honolulu: University of Hawaii Press, 2003.

Web sites

Chineselanguage.org. "Chinese Character Dictionary," *Chinese languages,* chineselanguage.org/CCDICT/index.html.

Chinese University Press. *Lin Yutang's Chinese-English Dictionary of
Modern Usage,* humanum.arts.cuhk.edu.hk/Lexis/Lindict.

Harbaugh, Rick. *Zhongwen.com: Chinese Characters and Culture,*
zhongwen.com/.

TigerNT. *Chinese-English Online Dictionary,* www.tigernt.com/cedict.
shtml [from the database of Erik Peterson].

Other

Lynn, Jenny. E-mail interview with author, November 11, 2004
[2004a].

———. E-mail interview with author, November 15, 2004 [2004b].